Douglas's life is in danger, and only Laural knows.

Fearful and dazed, Laural slipped from her alcove and made her way from the great hall into the courtyard near the stables. She stopped by the place Douglas had so recently held her. She thought of his body lifeless and bleeding, a traitor to the king, and for naught. He would lose his life to Lord Cambraige.

If only she knew how to reach Black Hawk, but he was gone. Gone to protect the king against Douglas. And Douglas, he must be told of Lord Cambraige's duplicity, but how? *Oh, Black Hawk, I need you now.*

He trusted her, yet in the end she had failed him; failed to uncover this most devious plot; failed him as she had failed her father. The thought startled her. Did she truly believe she was at fault for her father's death?

Laural looked at her hands, wet with sweat. "Nay!" she said aloud straightening her shoulders. "I must not fail, again. I do love him. I must not fail. I must do something. I will do something! But what?"

A look of mulish stubbornness set on Laural's usually sweet face. Tucking her bliaut into her wide belt, Laural ran toward the stables, yelling for a stableboy to saddle her horse.

CAROLYN R. SCHEIDIES makes her home in Nebraska with her husband Keith and their two children. Carolyn is active in her church's puppet ministry as well as the pro-life movement. She writes inspirational romance because "what better way to help someone know God's love than through the eyes of characters who live it."

Books by Carolyn R. Scheidies

HEARTSONG PRESENTS
HP94—To Be Strong
HP160—To Keep Faith
HP176—Where There Is Hope

Black Hawk's Feather

Carolyn R. Scheidies

Heartsong Presents

To Stephen Reginald and Rebecca Germany
for giving me a chance. Thanks!
1 Thessalonians 5:13a

A note from the Author:
I love to hear from my readers! You may write to me at
the following address: **Carolyn R. Scheidies**
Author Relations
P.O. Box 719
Uhrichsville, OH 44683

ISBN 1-57748-047-3

BLACK HAWK'S FEATHER

All of the characters and events in this book are fictitious. Any
resemblance to actual persons, living or dead, or to actual
events is purely coincidental.

Cover illustration by Brian Bowman.

PRINTED IN THE U.S.A.

prologue

I will lift up mine eyes unto the hill,
from whence cometh my help. Psalm 121:1

❧

Tension rippled through the earl's gaunt shoulders as he reigned in his restless destrier. Snorting, the thick-muscled warhorse slashed his long, well-groomed tail against the flies buzzing about his round flanks.

The Earl of Comfrey eased up on the reins once more, aware his golden chestnut's unease was due to his own tension. "What say you?" he asked, his eyes on the tall, well-formed knight who rode so easily beside him. "I shall not rest easy until I know Leelah is properly looked after. I don't worry about myself, but my daughter. . ."

At the bluff overlooking Comfrey's lands, the dark knight pulled up his huge bay gelding with an ease and command that drew the older man's admiration. As far as the eye could see, trees spread out before them, disappearing into a dense mist rising off the icy blue lake which curled about the base of the far hill.

"It is worth fighting for, Comfrey."

Both knew they spoke of more than the vista stretched out before them.

"You comprehend the problem?"

The knight surveyed the older nobleman whose gray cape fluttered in the breeze. Though dressed in sturdy tunic and leggings, the earl in no way resembled the peasant whose clothing he wore with such grace. Lord Comfrey's dress contrasted sharply with the knight's gold-edged black tunic, and in the deep forests and secret glades of the Welsh countryside, the knight felt out of place.

"His Majesty be well pleased with thee, Comfrey. He knows thee as an honest marcher lord. You hold the borderlands by his leave and his blessing."

"I would not forswear my sword oath to King Edward." Comfrey's blue eyes narrowed.

"Many others have." The knight shrugged the soft wool cape from his broad shoulders revealing his well-muscled torso. He gazed down over Comfrey's fief, a gift of gratitude from King Edward I. Like his father Henry, Edward continued efforts to subdue the Celtic people and force the freedom-loving people to submit to him as overlord.

While the dark knight did not wholeheartedly agree with the king's methods, he had sworn a sword oath and would do as his king and friend bid him. Glancing toward the shorter nobleman, the knight was startled at the deep sadness in the man's eyes.

"It should never have happened." Comfrey said quietly.

Turning from Comfrey, the knight stared into the valley. Silently he waited for Comfrey to continue.

"If only David had not raised that revolt in '82." Contempt dripped from the earl's lips. "Traitor to his own people as well as to the king."

He continued with a sigh. "Despite capturing Hawarden Castle, his revolt would have failed right then had he not convinced his cousin Llewelyn to join him."

"Edward could not forgive such treachery," said the knight. "He had pardoned them once. Their unprovoked attack could not be overlooked."

"Aye, but the Celts love their freedom. Who can blame them? They ask nothing more than to be left alone to govern their own affairs. Why must they submit to a foreign overlord?"

Indolently, the knight smiled at Comfrey's vehemence. "So speaks thine own Welsh heart." He sobered. "'Tis prudent not to speak so openly."

"Mayhap." Comfrey studied the commanding knight beside him. "I choose my words and my company carefully. I hold my land from Edward, but I shall not deny my heritage. I am the King's own true liege man, though my mother's blood burns within me."

He sighed from the depths of his being. "I realize, as most of my Celtic countrymen do not, that the English side of me will one day win this battle to unite England and Wales—even Scotland. I see how effectively King Edward is codifying our laws to bring about true justice and fairness before the law even for the lowliest serf.

"'Tis a good thing Edward does. Henry may have been a saint, building Westminster Abby, but his leadership, at best, was ineffectual. 'Tis time we assert ourselves as a unified and independent free nation."

The knight's large destrier shook its massive head and shuffled back a pace from the cliff. "You speak with the voice of a prophet," the knight said. "You lecture of nations when most men of rank refuse to see beyond their own fiefs, their own petty castle walls. Even your women are captive to whomever holds the land. Does not Lord Cambraige lay claim to your fief by some ancient Celtic title?"

"He is greedy for my land, land he would lief claim but for the king's support. Still he seeks what all Celts seek—freedom. The English too seek freedom from their Norman overlords." Wiping his hand across his brow, the earl murmured, "God's will be done."

Breaking from a low bush, a rabbit momentarily startled the horses. The two men quickly calmed their mounts. The knight continued solemnly, "You speak high treason,

Comfrey. I hate to think what would happen to your lovely daughter should your views regarding freedom become common knowledge. Beware the French king hear not of your prophecy, seeing as how he is convinced King Edward holds the English crown solely by his leave alone. I wonder you trust one such as myself who holds French lands."

"Like most other lords," Comfrey grimaced, then added, "Our sovereign holds a different opinion. One day, my friend, we shall be free and independent Englishmen. We shall speak with the English tongue, not that of the French king. And who better to bring about this change than our own King Edward? I fear not the French king, but those much closer to home."

"Aye," said his companion. "His Majesty will do what he can to lend you support. He is a great and a good man."

"In stature as well as heart," agreed Comfrey. "Even the lowliest peasant falls to his knees in homage. But even our king is not God. He cannot be everywhere at once."

"Since coming to the throne, Edward has done his best to consolidate his holdings. War seems to invigorate, rather than drain him."

Comfrey surveyed the man who towered over him. "Is his hair still thick? Does he still decry his nickname? I had hoped, once, to take my Leelah—Laural—to court. As things stand, it is impossible to leave Comfrey unguarded for so long a time."

Chuckling, the knight said, "Always His Majesty despises the name 'Long Shanks,' and his hair is still thick, though it has changed color over the years. He is ever loyal to those who agree with him, but he finds it difficult to accept anyone who disagrees. Still he is a fair man and usually a reasonable one. Lady Laural would be safe under his protection. It might behoove you to make the acquaintance of the queen. It would not do your daughter harm and might well augur well for her future."

"Mayhap, but I trust you more. I know Edward is a just man, except where the Celts are concerned," broke in Comfrey, "but the blood of Celtic warriors runs in Leelah's veins. His Majesty's anger burns yet at what he perceives as treachery on the part of the Welsh men of rank and power."

Without speaking, their thoughts turned to the king's response to the treachery of David and his cousin Llewelyn, a response untempered by compassion. The heads of both graced the tower of London until there remained but empty skulls. The dark knight shuddered at the memory.

Though he shirked not his duty, he took no part in the cruelties carried out on David. Comfrey interrupted his thoughts.

"Henry hemmed in the Celts with his lords, but now these barons are crazy with greed and brook no interference in their affairs, even from King Edward—despite their oaths of allegiance. They do as they will to their Celtic subjects, laying a heavy burden on the people. It be no wonder that the people seek their freedom."

"Far different it be on your lands, friend."

"Aye," Comfrey gazed down over his beloved land. "This too has its dangers. My own blood kin brand me as a traitor to our people and seek my life, while the other borderland lords intrigue to deprive me of both my rights as a freeborn Englishman and my lands. I see no end to it."

Sensing the tension in his master, Comfrey's destrier snorted and threw up his head. Lord Comfrey settled him quickly. "I see little future for me. I have no son, but my daughter. . ." He struggled with his emotions. "She is all I have. Her welfare is my highest concern. She must marry well. If she is to survive she must marry, and soon."

"Have no fear, my friend." The dark knight lay a large hand on the man's shoulder. "Her welfare is now mine. You may rest easy. It will be as we agreed."

The two men exchanged a look of total understanding.

one

My help cometh from the Lord,
which made heaven and earth. Psalm 121:2

Lady Laural Comfrey pushed back the strands of her luxurious molasses-colored hair that kept escaping the two long plaits which swung to her hips. Moon silver sparkled through the rich tones of her hair from some distant Viking ancestor. Her unusual hair made her impatient, not realizing how it framed her fragile elfin beauty.

At the moment, her heart-shaped face was anxious and her usually smiling lips turned down in a frown.

"Papa, I wish you would stay home this forenoon. Please grant me this one favor. Don't go out hunting with Lord Cambraige and his men. The steward wishes to speak with you and. . ." She grasped the rough cloth of his tunic.

Lord Comfrey searched his daughter's apprehensive eyes. "I do not wish to argue, daughter, but I must needs meet with Cambraige. Mayhap we can settle our differences amicably." He patted the delicately embroidered, rich white silk bliaut she wore over her chemise. The soft blue contrasted sharply with the dark blue of her eyes which had taken on shades of gray in her concern.

"My men will also join us, Leelah." His long gentle fingers, more suited to a man of letters than of war, touched her soft cheek.

His pet name for her softened her expression. "How can you trust Lord Cambraige? He is a devious and deceitful man who is greedy for your lands."

11

"'Tis the complete truth of the matter, Leelah. All the more reason to disorder his plans. I am not without influence."

Around them the servants and pages bustled about the huge great hall, cleaning up after the breaking of the fast. In the cool of the morn, the fires raging in the mammoth fireplaces at either end of the long room cast but paltry heat and less light.

On mats and benches around the room, men-at-arms, attended by their squires, conversed or played chess or other games. At times arguments erupted which were quelled by a single look from Lord Comfrey.

Laural might well have continued her entreaty, but for the nail-studded door which swung open with a deep groan. Crisp morning breeze swept in lifting the edges of Laural's gown. Along with the breeze came the ponderous Lord Cambraige.

His hard boots clanked ominously against the stone floor, and Laural wondered if she shivered more from the cold air or from the chill in Cambraige's dark eyes.

"Father, please don't go," Laural entreated one last time.

"Comfrey, 'tis time to depart. My horses and men wait impatiently while you dally with the womanish fears of your daughter." Lord Cambraige's eyes moved swiftly but thoroughly over her slight form, bringing a blush to her pale cheeks.

Comfrey's face darkened at Cambraige's barely veiled contempt. "You shall be civil toward Lady Laural, Lord Cambraige. She is a highborn lady, not one of your scullery wenches to be bowed by the import of your rank."

Lord Cambraige bowed stiffly. "I forget myself, Comfrey. Then again, as the English King's man you forget your obligations to your own countryman."

"I forget nothing, Cambraige. Let us be gone. Our quarrel is not for the ears of a lady."

"Or other fools," grumbled Cambraige, glaring at the earl's knights.

"Godspeed, Father."

In an unexpected show of sentiment, Comfrey kissed his daughter's cheek. "My dear, fear not. My life is in the hands of God." Momentarily his eyes darkened and he lowered his voice. "Should something untoward happen, I have made provisions for you, Leelah. Do not be afraid, God will never leave His own without the comfort of His presence." With those cryptic words, he followed Cambraige out the door.

Late that afternoon, Laural sat in the women's bower, diligently laboring over the tapestry on her lap. Her lips moved in prayer as uneasiness settled within. Her concentration broken, she stifled a cry of frustration as she picked out her last row of tiny delicate stitches.

Sitting near the high narrow window, she gazed out over the courtyard below, her thoughts pushing away the giggles and quiet conversation of the few other women in the bower with her.

There were not many women, these wives of her father's knights, and she did not feel fully comfortable with any of them. Without the presence of her mother, other lords did not send their daughters to the castle to learn to be wives, and her father had refused to send her away after her accident.

For a moment Laural stared at her hands, at the flexed fingers which refused to straighten. Behind her she sensed more than heard the sudden uncomfortable silence, the eyes staring at her unsightly hands. How she hated her hands, hated the stares and shudders they brought forth.

Anger burned inside, an anger she tried to quell. "God

forgive me," she whispered. "I—"

The thought remained unformed as a horseman galloped into the courtyard and flung himself from his horse. Even from a distance, Laural's heart quickened at the look on the man's face.

Flinging the tapestry from her, Laural leaped to her feet, but before she could make her way to the door, it smashed open and the burly knight of uncommon height burst into the room. Blood flowed down his cheek, and his eyes held terror which communicated itself quickly to her attendants, who proceeded to screech in horror.

"Enough!" commanded Laural keeping her own composure with difficulty. She gasped as the knight dropped to his knees in front of her.

"My lady. You must needs come away with me straightway."

"Destrun, my father?"

"He is dead, my lady, and I must take you safely to the king."

"What happened? Where is Father?"

"Come, we must go straightaway. There is no time to lose."

Without another word of argument or complaint, Laural nodded. Immediately Destrun took her arm and hurried her from the room. At the twisting stairs, he apologized briefly. "My lady, we must hurry." With that he swung her into his strong arms and strode with her down the stairs into the great hall.

There Lord Cambraige awaited, a deadly smile on his lips. "And where art thou headed, my lady?"

Destrun carefully set her down before facing Lord Cambraige. "At my master's leave, I take her to King Edward. She is under his protection now."

"Faugh!" The lord's heavily gloved hand connected with Destrun's face.

"Stop that!" commanded Laural, her eyes blazing. "I must needs know of my father."

"Your Welsh countrymen swept down upon us in a surprise raid, my lady," said Lord Cambraige, his tone dripping with sarcasm.

She steeled herself to meet his contemptuous gaze. "He is dead. You are certain."

"He is even now being brought back on a litter. After the funeral, you shall accompany me back to my castle."

Laural straightened. "I think not, my lord. Father would have me go to the king. My father's men with Destrun will escort me—"

"Your father's men-at-arms are also dead, my lady."

Suspicion glimmered in her eyes. "How convenient for you."

The blow came so swiftly, Laural had no time to dodge. Stumbling backward, Laural's leg buckled, and she landed on the floor in front of Lord Cambraige. Grabbing her hair, he forced her to look into his face.

His actions only inflamed her. "Let me go. You have no right to touch me." Raising her hand she would have levered herself to her feet, but at the touch of her hand Lord Cambraige shuddered and moved back.

"Keep those claws off my person."

Laural's face flamed. Her eyes chilled. "Then give me leave and I shall depart for the king's court." She permitted Destrun to assist her to her feet.

"You'll do nothing of the sort, my lady. As of now, I claim you and your father's lands for myself. I am the rightful overlord."

Anger mingled with horror. "You would then wed the

daughter of Lord Comfrey for his lands?"

"Wed? What foolish nonsense. You have a disordered mind, my lady, to think any man would wed the likes of a feeble wench like yourself."

"The land is mine. It will belong to he who weds me." Laural managed to control the trembling which began in the region of her heart and was spreading quickly to her knees.

"Ah, but with you as my ward, I hold it all. There is nothing you can do."

Destrun stepped forward. "Lord Cambraige, her father—"

"Faugh! What care I for the favor of a dead man?" He touched the sheathed sword at his side. "Unless you desist, you shall lie at your lady's feet."

"Then die, I shall."

Laural stepped between the men, her hand on Destrun's arm.

"You are no good to me dead, Destrun," she murmured and felt the knight relax his hold on his sword. Under her breath she added, "Ride. Ride to the king with the news."

"Lady Laural," cried a page. "They're bringing the master home."

Heedless of Lord Cambraige, Laural hurried out of the hall to meet the litter borne by several of Lord Cambraige's men. At the sight of her father's bloodied body, Laural's head began to swim. "Papa. Oh, Papa, no. No!" she cried.

As darkness clouded her vision, all she could hear was Lord Cambraige's heinous laugh.

Destrun caught her as she fell.

two

He will not suffer thy foot to be moved:
he that keepeth thee will not slumber. Psalm 121:3

❧

King Edward I paced the floor of the great hall in long quick strides. His boots clanked loudly on the planked floor and his sheathed sword swung at his side in time to his pacing. The tall, lanky monarch halted before the huge fireplace at the far wall which yawned its scorching heat into the chilly room. Smoke and grease stains from the continual fires in the huge hearths begrimed the vaulted ceiling overhead. Tapestries hanging on the walls to provide some insulation from the chill air fluttered softly as he passed.

Pivoting he glared at the broad-shouldered young lord standing at attention before the hearth in his long rich tunic. "Faith! I shall not stand for this. What say you? Would you force me to move now in force? And for what?"

The Norman lord kept his rugged face in an enigmatic mask, and the king continued his tirade. "On what proof? As far as we know, Lord Comfrey met his death in a surprise raid. I doubt if you would find proof to the contrary. If it was a raid, the mountains now shield the perpetrators. Strange that none of Comfrey's men returned, save one."

What passed as a grimace flashed across the Norman lord's features, then disappeared before the king could name the emotion evoked. "Destrun heard the shouts and the fighting," the lord observed, "but he was too late to know the truth of the matter. Whatever his suspicions, his lips are sealed for the safety of his mistress."

17

"Lord Cambraige lays claim to Comfrey," Edward said, his face suffused with rage.

"And Lady Laural," the rugged lord reminded him.

"And Lady Laural. Dost thou think he will take her to his bed?" Pacing back and forth, the king missed the lord's look of dismay.

With difficulty the young lord hid his fury. "If he has, he will die."

King Edward stopped once more to survey the lord's tightly controlled features. "Lord Comfrey was a friend of your father's."

"And mine. He saved my life more than once."

"You would save the life of his daughter and the land for your king."

"I swore to Lord Comfrey."

"What would you have me do, invade the borderland for the sole purpose of snatching the chit from the hand of Lord Cambraige who swears fealty? My men-at-arms will not be placed in jeopardy for the likes of a Celtic wench."

Anger flashed momentarily. "Lord Comfrey was the king's true liege man. Is not his daughter worth thy protection? As for Lord Cambraige, he is overeager to please Your Majesty, but only when thou art in his domain or he in yours. Puts me in mind of David."

Edward paused and growled, "It is not like in the old days when breaking an oath of fealty was more dishonorable than death. If your wench is like her Celtic countryman. . ." Edward shook his great head as though banishing thoughts of the tortures meted out at his command. "I will not countenance such treachery in any man." He turned sharply, "Nor in any wench." The king's mien hardened.

Ready to parlay in honor, Edward refused to deal with those he suspected of rebellion or dishonorable conduct. At such times, the just king faded into the fury of the monarch who would not be mocked.

"Lady Comfrey is her father's daughter," said the lord, standing firm against the king's anger. "Does the king himself countenance the death of his trusted vassal, the kidnaping of his daughter who rightly claimed the king's protection?"

Running long fingers through his uncertain shade of hair, King Edward groaned. "Long I suffer the willfulness of Cambraige who believes his cause just, but I have reason to believe as you. There have been rumors. Mayhap he is over-eager for his own head to join those of his traitorous countrymen on the Tower of London."

"Nay," responded the Norman lord. "He is a deep player is Cambraige. It is not a simple thing to outface him."

For all he was a soldier and a loyal subject of his monarch, he was unable to shake off the sight of David's body lying forgotten in the streets. After being dragged by horses, hanged, drawn, and quartered, there was little left to behead. If the enraged King wished to send a message of warning to his Welsh subjects, he had succeeded. . .but at what price?

The small dark Welsh were fighters time out of mind. Long they held their country from invasion. True, David had played the king false, but Llewelyn had believed he was the rightful ruler of his country. Would not any man so fight for his people, his land, his freedom?

What had it all accomplished? Rebellion still lurked beneath the benign facade of the wealthier noblemen. What of Laural? Anger burned within him at the very thought of Lord Cambraige. If only he might have the king's leave to go to her.

Without a flicker of an eye, his heart lifted in silent prayer.

Keep her safe, Lord God. Show me how I might help her. Protect her, Lord God, protect her.

Then the question came full-blown and he posed it to his monarch. "Do you not wish to know the complete truth of the matter?"

Though he highly valued the advice of his friends, the king did not care to be backed into a corner. "What say you?" he snapped. "Believe you then Lord Cambraige in truth has Comfrey's blood on his hands?"

"'Tis well-known Lord Cambraige fixes his affection on Comfrey's title and his estates and hungers for the power of a marcher baron. He is also, you may recall, of Celtic extraction, however distant. Aye, I believe his profession of loyalty to be mere sham. He be not your loyal liege man, Sire."

"Faith!" expostulated the king. "You name my fears." He swung about, almost stamping the floor. "Treachery. The crown despises dishonorable men who pander for their own gain. How does a forsworn knight connive behind the back of his rightful lord instead of meeting him face to face on the field of battle? By faith, I weary of intrigue. Where is the clean victory of battle? Enemies meeting face to face in honor?"

Closing his eyes, King Edward sighed deeply. "I had hoped for a respite. The queen needs me." He opened his eyes, and the Norman lord marveled at their piercing quality. "I have need of thee again, good friend. I need someone to discover the truth of the matter from inside Lord Cambraige's own walls." For a moment he remained silent, studying the man before him.

A slight smile touched his lips. "I do not like intrigue, but it suits you well. Only you can find the truth we need. Only then shall I move."

The tall lord nodded, his eyes gleaming with repressed humor. "I have charity for the work, Sire. I am not wont to tend court for such long a time."

A scratch sounded at the door, and a servant girl entered at the king's impatient command. "Why is it that you seek my favor?"

Trembling the woman bowed low. "Your Majesty. 'Tis her ladyship. L. . .lady Ramona. She seeks audience."

Impatience faded from the king's face, replaced by a sly glance toward the young lord. "Tell her ladyship she might speak with his lordship later."

Still trembling, the maid hurriedly made her obeisance and left the chamber with all-to-evident relief. The king smiled, "'Tis not her royal guardian which has drawn the attention of my ward."

The lord took a deep breath. Words did not come to his lips. What was there to say that Edward would accept?

If truth be fully told, he tired greatly of the affected attentions of the not-so-shy court women who fawned over him. He, a lord with estates in both England and France who called no man overlord but the king himself, was a prime target for the altar. Forgoing marriage, many women would have been satisfied to be asked to his bed or have him in theirs.

He managed to fend them off, his courtly manners at times sorely tried. As the king preferred battle to treachery, the lord preferred battle to the inner workings of court life. Even at twenty and seven, he felt old and desired only to take a wife and settle down to raise strong healthy sons to follow in his wake.

Wife? His thoughts turned unwillingly to the king's ward, Ramona, widow of the Count Trudou. A brazen young widow, Ramona made good use of her feline green eyes, lush red hair, and her sensuous body to tempt him.

As the serpent must have tempted Eve in that first garden paradise, he thought with distaste.

Her indiscreet behavior troubled him. She made no secret that she wished his seal ring to grace her slender finger. Lately the king seemed more inclined to listen to her.

"She needs a firm hand," Edward had told him not two days past. "She must have a husband not only strong enough to keep her in check, but also to hold her lands from those who would see me dishonored. A high-spirited filly, she is," he'd said, then smiled.

The Norman lord had held his peace. It would not do to petition the king too early. He knew what Edward would tell him: "Lady Ramona is a high born lady, above the ken of the Celtic wench."

No it had not been the time. Was it now too late to speak? If only he could tell the woman begone, but Ramona was the king's ward, and Edward held her in more affection than she deserved. The king spoke of treachery but saw it not in the bosom of the women of his own court. He trusted them overmuch. The lord did not. As a bachelor, he was well versed in the simpering ways of certain court women and of their schemes.

With relief he would leave the court. He had grown restless attending the king in leisure when Laural was in need of him.

"You shall leave on the morrow then?" asked Edward.

"Nay, sire. The night is not mine enemy." The corners of his lips turned up in the slightest of smiles. "I shall learn the complete truth. If there is treachery planned, you shall learn of it straightaway."

"Take care not to overset your king. I care not to see your head swing for a traitor. . .if traitor he is. I leave you to that and your Celtic miss. If she be true, bring her to me once the truth is laid bare."

The lord bowed at the king's concession. "Fear not, Sire. Lady Laural may bide under Lord Cambraige's hand, but she will not pledge her loyalty to the king's enemy."

Edward put his hand on his friend's shoulder. "Then go, friend. Go where I cannot. Be my eyes, my ears, and bring me word again."

"And you?"

"I must needs attend my queen for soon she shall be delivered of another child." Edward's face brightened momentarily, his eyes tender with love for his wife, the woman he had married when she was but an infanta of ten. A faithful husband himself, he was not loathe to wish for others the same state of wedded bliss.

The lord made no disguise of his admiration for the man as well as the king. "God bless you with a healthy male issue, Sire."

"Aye." The king's face clouded at the somber thought of the frailty of his heir, Prince Alfonso. So many of his children, and there had been many, had died in infancy. "May the Lord attend your way as well. May He reward you with the information we need."

As the king paused dramatically, the lord waited for dismissal, only to be pulled to attention by the king's next words. "I have long thought to reward your faithful service to the crown as my father rewarded your father. Should your mission prove successful, I might well favor you with the hand of the lovely Ramona. 'Tis time the wench remarried, and her lands would be ample reward."

Quickly the lord took his leave, lowering his eyes to hide his dismay from the smiling monarch.

three

From the barren round room in the tower, Laural peered down over the courtyard, deadly quiet except for the harsh laughter of Cambraige's men, the snort of their horses, and the distant clang, clang of hammer on metal from the smith.

She missed the usual routine of the day, the children running back and forth, women hurrying about their chores. She missed the laughter most of all.

Silence bore heavily on her grief-stricken heart. Comfrey and all it stood for was no more. In the distance one lone bird warbled its song, but it brought no more than a twitch to Laural's bruised lips. She touched them now, fingering the slash in her cheek from the corner of her lip to her chin where Lord Cambraige's mail glove had caught and torn her soft white skin.

The throbbing of the untended wound was nothing compared to the pain in her chest threatening to crush her in its intensity.

Leaning her head against the thick cold stone outer wall, Laural closed her eyes. *Lord, why? Why did You let this happen? Father loved and trusted You. He taught me to do the same.*

She paused, her heart overflowing with questions vying for expression, yet she hesitated. *Is it wrong to ask why? Lord Jesus, I know You are real. I know You are more than a formality. I know You are there, somewhere, but where were*

You when Father was murdered?

Clenching her fist she banged it against the rough stone, then pulled it back with a half groan, half yelp as a jagged edge sliced into her wrist. Her father had taken much pride in the lovely castle, newly built but twenty years past. He had had the white stone quarried and sent block by block to the land given him by the king himself. From those stones he had built a place not only of strength, but also of beauty and comfort. But strong as it was, it could not keep out either evil deeds or evil men.

"Lord Jesus," Laural breathed, "even You were not exempt from the evil of Your day." As the blood dripped from the shallow wound, she thought of the picture of Jesus in the chapel.

"Look Leelah," her father had told her. "See that blood dripping down from his wounds? That blood is what covers our sins. See His eyes, the love in them? Despite what they did to Him, He loved and forgave. Leelah, He has not changed. Jesus died for you and me. He died to take away our sin."

Leelah had stared up at her father·with ten-year-old wonder. "The holy church does that, doesn't it?"

"No, daughter. The priest can only help us see Jesus. Only Jesus can save us. Only Jesus can forgive our sins and make us right with Him."

"This seems so strange Father. Can this be true? Why don't others believe this way?"

"Many do, Leelah. From priest to peasant, many know the truth. God doesn't live in the church. He lives in the hearts and lives of everyone who asks Him to live within."

In awe Laural had asked, "Would Jesus really want to live in me?"

"Do you want Him to? Do you always want to be able to

pray to Him anytime, day or night?"

"You mean, I don't have to pray only in the chapel? You mean Jesus will really talk to me!"

"Yes, all you need do is ask, and He'll speak to your heart." Lord Comfrey had wrapped an arm about his daughter's thin shoulders. "Once I was able to read a copy of the Scriptures, Leelah. I didn't know whether or not I'd ever get another chance, so I memorized a few verses which became very important to me."

"What were they, Father?" Laural's eyes grew even wider and her respect for her father deepened. What a wonder, to have ready access to God's Holy Word!

"One went something like this. Umm. Let me put it in a way you'll comprehend." Rubbing his chin, he thought on it a moment before continuing. "This comes from the third chapter of the book of John. 'God so loved the world, that He gave His only Son Jesus, that whosoever believes on Him would not die but have everlasting life.' Whosoever means you or me, anyone who trusts in Jesus."

He repeated the verse until Laural knew it by heart. "I do believe, Father. I do."

Laural shook her head to clear the memories of her childhood. She still believed, but she certainly didn't understand. She stared down at her hands. "Jesus, why? First we lost Mother. Then I had that dreadful accident. Now F. . .father. What am I to do?"

She gazed unseeing out of the narrow arched window into the bright blue sky. The sun shown down and a slight breeze ruffled the trees. It all looked so peaceful, yet the waving of Lord Cambraige's standard instead of her father's flag gave lie to serenity of the scene.

Nonetheless, in the quiet of her heart she heard the still small voice. "I am here. Do not be afraid."

In the days which followed, Laural clung to that promise.

Banished from her well-appointed bedchamber to the tower room, Laural chafed at the restrictions placed upon her. What need had she of the brawny guard at the door who glowered at her as though his posting was entirely her fault? Did Lord Cambraige think she would raise an army against him? The man must be crazed to think such a thing when her father's guards lay buried beside him. Laural shuddered.

The one time she had been allowed out of her cell was for her father's funeral. The event had been carefully orchestrated by Lord Cambraige. Solicitously he stood beside her, apparently to support her in her time of grief. However Laural recognized the promise of retribution in the grip on her arm and in the warning in his eyes should she say or do anything to defy his wishes. Though outwardly she kept her composure, inside the questions tumbled over themselves.

Why? Why did Lord Cambraige fear her? Unless. . .unless there was something havey-cavey about the situation. With the questions, her suspicions multiplied.

As Laural sat through the long service, she had escaped her grief by thinking of the songs and stories of her Celtic people. Their poets, strumming on their harps, sang of the time King Arthur would one day rise again to lead them to greatness.

She remembered the deeds of her own childhood legend, Black Hawk. She hugged to herself every chivalrous tale of the knight who righted wrongs, who championed justice to an often oppressed people. What spoke to her even more than his compassion for the vanquished or his assistance to damsels in distress was his concern for the lowliest serf. Black Hawk was her ideal—a man of integrity, if he truly existed. In a world torn by pain and strife and change, he remained the one constant in her life.

Like her father before her, Laural cared about the lives and well-being of those who so willingly served her family. The Welsh were a high-strung, courageous and honorable people who valued the fairness of her father. True it was not unknown for the small dark Welsh on their sturdy mountain ponies to harry the countryside or to retaliate for English forays into their almost impassable passageways above the white-topped Snowdon. But what treachery to swoop down through the mountain passes known only to them and mur-der her father while leaving Lord Cambraige alive. *If it was their treachery?*

Surreptitiously Laural had watched Lord Cambraige, his large frame making him appear slow although he could move swiftly when aroused. The particular glint in his eyes at viewing the long, drawn out funeral ceremonies had given her pause. The moment came for her to kiss the lips of her father, lips now cold in death. Inside she shuddered. This lifeless shell was not her father. Gone the warmth of his presence, the light in his eyes, the smile on his lips.

No, all that was her father lived not in this body laid out before her. For a moment tears blurred her vision. At Lord Cambraige's sardonic gaze, she blinked them back. Delib-erately she envisioned her father striding down the streets of heaven and the Lord's smile of welcome.

"Good-bye, Father," she murmured.

Steeling herself, she bent to brush the cool dry lips. Though she kept herself under strict control, inside she shrank from this custom.

Fleetingly she wondered why many of the customs of the time, which others took for granted, made her recoil. Over time she had learned to control the outward manifestations of her feelings, but they never changed. It had been discon-certing to glance up and find Lord Cambraige watching her with a knowing look in his eyes.

"Lord, please help me through this," she whispered, fighting the darkness hovering near. How blessed it would have been to sink into its oblivion, but not now. Now she must be strong for her people.

That evening Lord Cambraige had commanded her presence beside him at the dais overlooking the great hall as troubadours played and sang. Fleetingly Laural thought they had not the natural poetic bent of her people.

Roasted venison, mutton stewed in imported spices, and tender pigeons graced the table along with a soup of onions, leeks, crab apples, minced meat, and beans. Thick slices of bread filled the bottom of the bowl, sopping up the soup poured over it.

The tantalizing odors only served to nauseate Laural, who wished for nothing more than to be allowed to retire. "My lord," she began, "I am fatigued. With your permission, I would take my leave."

A taunting smile touched Lord Cambraige's lips. Under the cover of the raucous irreverent laughter of his men-at-arms, he held a tidbit from his trencher to her lips. "I think not my lady Laural. It behooves you to stay and make us merry. "

When she refused to open her lips, he growled, picked up the trencher, and threw it to the dogs grappling for the crumbs and bones thrown to them. The lord's scarred tan mongrel snapped up the meaty treat. When the late earl's sleek gray animal grabbed for a morsel, Lord Cambraige's boot connected with the dog's ribs, sending him flying. Yelping in pain, the dog growled before slinking off into the corner.

"You didn't need to do that," Laural said, then sounded her own yelp as Lord Cambraige backhanded her. She tasted blood. Furious, Laural waited not for permission. Without leave she rose to her feet and hurried from the hall.

The next morning a serving maid carried a tray to her room and Laural broke fast with cider and a hard biscuit. "Will you bring up my gown? Surely it is time for chapel, and I must dress straightaway."

The sturdy maid, who had been part of the castle staff since before Laural's birth, shook her head. "Mass has already been said by Lord Cambraige's own priest and his lordship has called the tenants to pay their death duties."

"What!" exclaimed Laural. "Mazda, you must help me dress. Hurry."

Not long thereafter, Laural stood in her thin chemise as Mazda pulled a midnight blue tunic over her head and laced up the sleeves. Around her waist Laural clasped a thick belt encrusted with diamonds and rubies. For the first time, she allowed Mazda to pulled her hair up under a simple wimple held in place by a stiff cap. If she was going to outface Lord Cambraige, at least she would do it looking her best.

For a long moment she stared out the window at the sky. Rain had fallen earlier in the night, and gray clouds skidded across the clearing sky. "Lord," she prayed. "Help me. I have to discover the truth of this matter. Give me favor in his eyes to protect my people."

She paused. Her people? Lord Cambraige claimed otherwise. How soon before he claimed not only the castle, but the title as well. What about Destrun? From Mazda, Laural had pieced together Destrun's escape. Using the confusion ensuing from her faint as well as the press of wives and relatives of those slain, the knight had swung aboard his destrier and raced across the open courtyard to the east gate.

Laural guessed her friend had managed to race past the guard and over the drawbridge before Cambraige could have the portcullis lowered. Though Lord Cambraige belatedly commanded a party to follow and apprehend him, Destrun had managed to elude his pursuers. Lord Cambraige blamed Laural, as though her response to seeing the body of her father had been but a ruse.

Her head still ached from the yank on her hair which had snapped her neck. The rage on Lord Cambraige's face had brought an unexpected smile of relief to her face. "I take it Destrun got away." Silently she'd added, *He is alone Lord. Take him safely to the king.*

If only she might do the same, but she remained a prisoner in her own home. "Lord, help me," she said again.

Taking a deep breath, she glided toward the door. "Guard," she called. "Guard."

Chains clanked, a bolt groaned, and the heavy door moaned as the rather dull-witted sentry opened the door with a decided frown on his fleshy jowls. "My lady. How may I serve you?"

She heard the irony in his voice and nodded. "I wish to speak with his lordship."

She gave no hint of her own trepidation as she marched toward the door. Confused by her boldness, the guard moved aside. "I don't think—"

Sarcasm clipped her words. "Think you I can harm his lordship? Come along if you will. Guard your master from the Celtic wench."

He flushed at her gibe. With a hand on the sword at his side, he followed her down the narrow winding stairs to the great hall where she found Lord Cambraige hunched over the long refectory table. On his left sat a supercilious priest with an arrogant greedy look, so different from the humble man of God who had been as much a friend as a priest to Laural and her father.

At Lord Cambraige's side, the steward periodically wrote

in the large account book open in front of him. In front of
the table a line of retainers, farmers, tenants, and freemen
waited their turn to pay the death duty. It was her father
who had died, their lord. It should have been Lord Cambraige
who paid.

James, the steward, glanced up and met her gaze. Anger
vied with frustration in his eyes. Did she also read a plea? In
front of the table a peasant bowed and mumbled a question.
Lord Cambraige boomed out, "Your mare, my man."

The priest whined, "And for the church, your second best
horse."

"But I have only one, my lord, and aye need 'im ta plow."

"He speaks the truth, my lord," James spoke up. He received a cuff for his efforts.

Waiting on the sidelines, Laural paused, watching and
listening as the new lord and his priest greedily extracted
enormous amounts. Her father had treated the people with
respect. Could she make Lord Cambraige do likewise?

Her stomach quivering, Laural boldly approached the
table. One after another, the peasants expressed their sympathy at her loss. A few brushed moisture from their eyes.
The outpouring of love melted Laural's heart. Tears formed
in her eyes. She had to help her father's vassals.

At the table, Lord Cambraige regarded her with a mixture of speculation and animosity. "Why are you not in your
room? Get you gone wench."

The growl rising from the gathered villeins startled him.
Laural followed his gaze and his realization that most of his
men at that time of day were either in the courtyard, out
hunting, or guarding the battlements. In the great hall,
Comfrey's people far outnumbered Lord Cambraige's men-
at-arms.

His moment of uncertainty gave Laural the courage to speak.

"My lord Cambraige. These are honest, hard-working people who will give you good service if you deal with them justly, but they are needed in the fields. Can this not be put off until the need for their animals is not so great? Surely you realize the better equipped they are, the better they work Comfrey's fields as well as their own."

Muttering, Lord Cambraige conferred with the priest. James nodded ever so slightly toward her. Laural waited, praying. Behind her the men grew silent. Laural tensed, her hands clasped together so tightly she feared she'd have to pry them apart. Each moment that passed was an eternity.

Suddenly Cambraige curtly dismissed the peasants. "You shall remember this largess from your new master." As he got to his feet, the peasants streamed from the hall quickly, fearing, and with good reason, that Cambraige might change his mind.

"Thank you, my lord," Laural told the bulky Cambraige.

He merely glared. "I will extract every pence at a future time. And next time, I'll see to it you are not around to plead their cause."

Laural licked her dry lips. "Not be around?"

His snort of laughter sent shivers through her. "Have I not informed her ladyship? We shall be removing to Cambraige Castle straightway. You will join us there."

"This is where I belong. I wish to stay here."

"And have your knight ride in with reinforcements to free you from my protection? I think not." His smile did not reach his eyes. "Without their mistress in residence, Comfrey's peasants shall lose all will to defy me. If they do not, trust me, I am not loath to use whip or sword to bring about total obedience. Remember that Lady Laural. I am not loath to use the lash on a horse, or a serf, or a wench who will not bow to my will."

Shocked, James spoke out before Laural could silence him. "You would not—"

Lifting up the slight, balding steward, Lord Cambraige threw him against the wall. James's head connected with a crash. Anguished, Laural watched the light fade from his eyes as he slid limply to the floor.

Lord Cambraige grabbed her arm. "Let the servants see to him."

"What if he is dead?"

The man shrugged. "What if he is?"

Goaded beyond recall, Laural raised her hand to slap Lord Cambraige. Since her hands did not open completely, her nails raked his face. "How dare you! You monstrous fiend. Have you no compassion?"

With a roar, Cambraige grabbed her wrist and wrenched her arm behind her back. Horrified, Laural watched blood bead up and trickle from the scratches. For a heartbeat the two stared at one another. Uttering an oath which made Laural blanch, Lord Cambraige ogled her person with a salaciousness which sickened her.

"I like my women feisty," he spat out, "but not crippled. Don't you ever, I repeat, ever touch me with those claws again." Lifting her as though she weighed nothing, he flung her next to the steward, who was beginning to groan.

As she fell, Laural knew she had made a deadly enemy.

four

The Lord is thy keeper. Psalm 121:5

Few would have recognized the legendary Black Hawk prowling about the white stone castle at Comfrey.

Dressed in a dull brown knee-length tunic over a pair of coarse braises made from thick homespun cloth, he looked like a peasant. The sheepskin over his tunic that was belted at the waist was tattered, and only cloths wrapped about his feet kept them from the cold rough ground. Around his head hung what appeared to be a filthy bandage, and his face sported several days' untended growth of hair. The villagers and farmers shook their heads at the desperate plight of the poor man—obviously a fellow given to strange humours.

The earl had ever made certain his people had food and clothes enough. The land itself was laid out in the newer three-field system. Two sections would soon be planted while the third lay fallow for the year. Already the farmers stood behind their ploughs, making straight furrows down and back, down and back with the cattle the new lord would have taken from them.

Women in long homespun skirts and their children tended the individual plots allotted for their personal use. Busy at their tasks, they spared little time considering the peasant who wandered about, apparently without wit or purpose. Other women knelt by the edge of the lake pounding their handmade garments clean with wooden paddles made by their husbands.

The peasant ambled along the lane, sidling off into the

forest, ever keeping the castle walls in sight. He eyed the guards moving back and forth on the battlements and keeping watch on the bridge.

Comfrey would not be an easy castle to take in siege—if it should come to that. The moat flowed wide and deep from the cold lake waters and would be difficult to cross. The castle walls were high and thick and nearly impossible to breech given the impossibility of reaching the walls over the moat. Fleetingly he wondered if Cambraige had left his men with the longbow made infamous by the Celtic warriors. A good bowman could let fly five shafts in the time it took for a crossbowman to fire one shot.

He hated the thought of a long drawn-out siege which would devastate the prosperous farms and villages around the castle. He'd seen the result before, land scorched and blackened for miles. Peasants dying from starvation while the defenders of the castle held off their attackers.

Comfrey could well hold off an army for who knew how long. Not only did the castle have the usual provision of salted and smoked rations, but also fresh water with a well right inside the keep. Further, Comfrey raised vegetables within the walls of castle itself. It had been well planned to keep out the enemy, yet it 'twas the enemy who lurked within.

Fleetingly Black Hawk considered what the king would think of his chosen course of action, then chuckled quietly. 'Twould make a fine story, if he got out of this alive. He wondered, too, if the king had sent other emissaries to Lord Cambraige.

Black Hawk grimaced. Who ever would have thought Comfrey would fall to the likes of Cambraige. The earl had been all too trusting as the years advanced on him. Now he lay buried, and his daughter was shut up in the castle with a man little known for his chivalry toward women.

"Lord, protect her. Protect Lady Laural." The rustle of grass and the snort of a horse alerted him, but it was too late to hide in the underbrush. Head up, he watched Lord Cambraige and a band of his men plunging through the wood.

At that moment the hunting party crashed into the open. No time to run. No time to hide. Praying for wisdom, the peasant smiled vacuously at the ponderous lord who sawed indiscriminately on the reins.

"Ho there, fool. Why be thee in the Comfrey woodland? 'Tis stealing a rabbit mayhap for your own stew pot?"

The peasant winced at the red flecked foam on the animal's mouth from Lord Cambraige's heavy hand on the reins. Anger flashed in his eyes, then faded. Anger only clouded his judgment. Sweeping the moth-eaten cap from his head, the peasant bowed low to the ground. "M'lord. Forgive please a poor man. Aye be an honest man, Aye be."

He stilled a groan as a lash sliced through his thin garment. Everything in him wanted to confront Lord Cambraige, but he held himself in check. The arrogant lord's time would come. He'd see to it.

"Ride him down," he heard one of the party call out.

"Let him be our prey, Cambraige. We're tired of the same sport. Give the man a head start."

Black Hawk heard the rustle of silk against silk, the readying of weapons. Next to him Lord Cambraige's horse snorted and shook his head. Barbarians all, riding down an innocent human for sport. His hand itched for his sword and his trusty destrier, but his hands were empty of weapons and his well-trained warhorse was miles away.

He had prayed for Laural's protection, but he needed the same. From long experience with difficult circumstances, the elusive legend lifted his request to the only one who could help. "Jesus, help me."

It came to him then, a story he'd once heard from the Holy Writ. How the great King David, when captured by his enemies, feigned madness. "Thank You, Lord," Black Hawk breathed as he slowly straightened.

His eyes glazed over and saliva dripped from his mouth. He heard Lord Cambraige gasp, "He is mad. The man is completely mad."

Lifting his head, Black Hawk bayed at the sky, barking and yelping. Like a rabid dog he snapped at Lord Cambraige's horse, who whinnied and nervously backed up. The group parted, letting him through their midst. No one wanted to come in contact with him or even get near him, fearing his affliction might be contagious.

Almost enjoying the havoc he created, Black Hawk snapped and feigned right and left. He knew he had but moments before Lord Cambraige would collect his senses and have him hunted down in earnest. He used those few moments to advantage.

Before Lord Cambraige knew what he was about, Black Hawk slipped into the forest and quickly disappeared into the underbrush. He knew how to hide in the underbrush, how to confuse the hounds and set them off on the wrong scent. He knew how to bide his time, only never before had the stakes been so high. Never before had his heart been involved. He almost groaned aloud at Laural's fate should he fail.

He stilled his frustration in silent prayer. *Lord, please keep me from being seen. Help me to realize that this enterprise and Laural's future is in Your hands, not mine.*

Long after the hunting party returned to the castle, Black Hawk left his hiding place and moved like a shadow through the forest. Retrieving his animal from a friendly outlying farmer, he made his way back to King Edward.

Entering the castle in an enveloping cape, the legend bathed in a large wooden tub and scraped off his beard with a sharp knife. Only then did he allow his page to assist him into his hose and slip on his shoes. Kneeling at his feet, the page fastened Black Hawk's shoes before helping him into his chaussures, then into his tunic and surcoat.

Feeling quite the thing again, the knight headed toward a private meeting with Edward. Lady Ramona found him before he reached the king.

"M'lord. You have returned." Her long diamond earrings clinked in time to her words, and her green silk gown swished as she caught his arm.

Taking her hand from his arm, the knight lifted her delicate white hand to his lips. "As lovely as ever, m'lady, but you must excuse me. His Majesty commands my immediate presence."

"Poo," she pouted, her bottom lip sticking out. "Always coming and going and no one knows where. When will you favor me with your presence?" Her eyes assessed him boldly.

"I am the king's to command," he told the overly bold woman sternly. "Lady Ramona, later."

Smiling up at him, she once more took his arm. "We make a handsome pair, do we not, m'lord? I shall walk with thee to the king's chamber. Let him see how you favor me."

The knight stilled a groan at her audacity, but decided not to argue. As he feared, Edward's countenance brightened with approval as they entered together. "I say, you are in fine looks Ramona. Belike your face blushes with the presence of a certain lord on your arm?"

The knight doubted the lady knew how to blush, but he kept his peace. As one of the king's vassals, there was little he could do to gainsay the king's command. It might well take all his ingenuity to keep the king from declaring his intentions toward the Lady Ramona. Once the king commanded him to make her his wife, he would have little choice in the matter.

He must play for time, time to deal with the situation at Comfrey and to free Lady Laural. "Your Highness, I have grave matters to discuss," he said carefully, unhanding Ramona.

Sighing, Edward nodded. "Run along, dear. We have matters to discuss."

Ramona curtsied and with a frigid smile left the room. Fury burned within her. Not one of her suitors had ever proved as elusive as this one. Jealously she wondered if another held his heart. With a toss of her haughty head, she shook off the thought. But. . .just to make certain.

Swinging about she put an ear to the partly open door. Inside the deep voices rose and fell, but she made out little of what they said. One name caught her ear—Lady Laural.

Lady Laural! Who was this woman whose name defiled the lips of the man she claimed for herself? She would not have it! Heedless of the consequences, she would have marched into the room but for the sound of footsteps in the hall. Pulling the door quietly closed, she hurried to her chamber.

Stamping her foot in agitation, Ramona paced back and forth in her room. Somehow she must discover the identity and location of this Lady Laural. If she was indeed the woman who held the heart of the noble lord, well, there were ways to deal with upstarts who aspired above their stations. Ramona was not in the king's favor for naught.

Wednesday next, Cambraige arrived at the castle. He did obeisance to the king, bowing so low it nearly toppled him. Edward eyed him with a jaundiced eye.

"What brings you, Cambraige?"

"To ask leave to hold Comfrey. The earl, God rest his soul, was murdered by his own Celtic kin. Dreadful thing that."

Ramona eyed Lord Cambraige, whose elaborate hunter green silk tunic slimmed his ponderous body and emphasized his masculinity. With effort she focused on the deadly dull proceedings, hoping for a glimpse of one particular Norman lord.

Her survey brought her back to Lord Cambraige. Pity he had but an English title. Yet something of his arrogance attracted her. Just then, the king's questions invited her attention.

"And his daughter, Lady Laural. Is she well?"

Ramona watched Cambraige cringe, then straighten, his eyes on the monarch's face. Silently Ramona cheered his courage, even while her eyes narrowed at the name of a potential rival for her lord.

Nearby a broad-shouldered man languidly observed the proceedings. "A lady? Seek you His Majesty's permission to marry the chit?"

Cambraige purpled. "Nay, m'lord. Lady Laural is a mere child, Sire." He paused, "I would not wish you to be uninformed. Your Majesty, may I speak freely?"

King Edward sighed, tired of Lord Cambraige's condescension. "Speak Cambraige. I will not hold your words amiss."

At Lord Cambraige's glance toward the lord languidly perusing him, Edward growled. "Pay Lord Strathouse no mind, Cambraige. He has little ambition in thy direction."

Cambraige cleared his throat. "Lady Laural, is. . .how might I put it delicately? She is infirm, Your Majesty, and as such, fit for no man to wife. I would hold Comfrey as the girl's guardian, not as her husband."

"Until when?" asked the Norman lord.

Stilling a shudder, Lord Cambraige ignored the lord, addressing his remarks to the king. "I shall see to her future, Sire."

"I had no notion the chit was not the thing." For a long moment in which Cambraige stood frozen in time, afraid to move or breathe, the king considered his proposal.

Lord Strathouse suggested. "Your Majesty. If the wench is infirm, marriage might not be the thing, in this case." He nodded in the direction of Lord Cambraige. "Cambraige appears to have the situation well in hand, Your Majesty."

"So it would appear." The king stared at the heavily built Cambraige whose paunch gave evidence of his lack of fighting trim. "Mayhap you shall agree to join my force against the cunning Welshmen."

Cambraige bowed, relief on his florid face. "As you wish, Your Majesty. I hold Comfrey by your leave, then."

"We shall consider your request, Cambraige, as we shall consider your allegiance to our crown."

A crafty look flashed in Lord Cambraige's eyes, then disappeared in such effusive gratitude the irritated king waved him away.

Long after the king and his retinue had retired, Lord Strathouse met with Lord Cambraige in a darkened corner. "I have come as you asked. What dost thou want?"

Lord Cambraige smiled. "I overheard you tonight, m'lord. Like you, I am tired of the Normans lording it over good Englishmen. 'Tis time we set up our own king."

Lord Strathouse leaned back against the wall. "I have Norman blood, but my mother was a lovely English rose. In some eyes that makes me less of a man. Aye, Cambraige, I shall listen, but what benefit shall I receive?"

"If all goes as I plan, mayhap Comfrey itself. Of a certain

the untried Lady Laural."

"She is a mere child, you said."

"Woman enough, m'lord."

"She is infirm, you said. Be you attempting to bribe me with damaged merchandise?"

Lord Cambraige shook his head. "She is a young innocent, m'lord, ripe for a man's arms."

"But not yours."

Again the shudder which Lord Cambraige was unable to control. "I never could cope with imperfection in a wench. 'Tis her hands actually. In face and form she is whole." Lord Cambraige could only guess at the thoughts running through the mind of the man who loitered in the shadows with him.

Slowly Lord Strathouse said, "I will listen to your proposal. Methinks a man could be content with a fief like Comfrey."

five

The Lord is thy shade upon thy right hand.
Psalm 121:5

Penned up in her austere tower chamber, Laural shook her head to clear a surge of dizziness. She bit her lip as she studied the courtyard below. Without the window to the outside world she felt she would have gone mad. A thick pallet on the floor was the only furnishings allowed her. There she stayed day and night. Cambraige permitted only the privilege of joining him at table for meals. Laural did not pretend to enjoy the command appearance and only picked at her food.

Surveying the area immediately outside the window she wondered again if there was any way to escape from her prison. Even if she did, there was still the problem of leaving the castle. Her father had built the castle all too well, but then, he never thought his own daughter might need to escape. She smoothed her palm over the stone walls which spread flat down the side with no handholds or footholds.

This morn had been no different. The guard escorted her to the great hall where the trestle tables were laid with silver for herself and Cambraige, silver which so recently had warmed to the hand of her father. Others made do with earthenware vessels and carved wooden implements.

All courtesy, Cambraige bowed her into one of the two heavily carved chairs set at table. Once she sat, Cambraige plopped down into his own sturdy ornamented chair, lifting his chalice in salute. His men quickly sat on the long wooden

44

benches on which they slept during the night and which were pulled away from the walls during mealtimes.

Lesser retainers and what was left of Comfrey's men hovered at the furthermost end of the hall with the serfs. James the Steward also sat disconsolately at a distant table, his bandaged head in his hands.

After the huge main meal, Laural tried to speak to James, only to have Cambraige block her way. "Nay, m'lady."

For a moment she glared at him. "I wish to know if James be well."

"He's alive, m'lady, for now." Cambraige's eyes glittered with menace until Laural feared for the steward.

"As you say, m'lord." Curtsying stiffly, she straightened her shoulders and lifted her chin before swishing out of the hall with the guard at her wake.

With only her maid for company, she watched Cambraige and a small hunting party, all girded in their silk tunics, race from the bailey laughing and shouting. The harness on the sleek animals jingled as they clattered across the bridge.

Mazda followed her gaze. "The whole smells of bad fish, m'lady," sniffed the servant. "Has he no fear of God nor man to go ahunting so soon after the master's death? Cambraige is not wont to be so foolish. What of the Celts? Fears he not they might come again?"

Dressed for the day in a white gown with gold thread, Laural slowly nodded. "Aye. Unless he has naught to fear."

"M'lady, be you meaning your sainted father did not meet his death as his lordship claims?"

Glancing toward the door which thankfully was fully closed against the guard's listening ears, Laural spoke more sharply than intended. "Mazda, upon your faith, make no mention of this to anyone."

"Fear not, m'lady. These ears be remarkably deaf." The

studied innocence on the face of the matronly woman brought a twinkle to Laural's eyes.

Turning back to the window, Laural murmured more to herself than to her maid, "By forest law, none can hunt but the overlord. Cambraige assumes much. He claims guardianship of my person. Will he also claim my hand?" The thought brought an anguished prayer to her lips.

"Lord, if Black Hawk is real, can You not send him to the rescue?" She let the words die on her lips. Black Hawk? Did he truly exist? Better to ask for an angel to swoop from the heavens. "Jesus, protect me. Give me your wisdom to guide me. Help me know what to do so Comfrey might be reclaimed from Lord Cambraige's petty cruelties."

With nothing to do, Laural slept away the afternoon. Awakened by the returning hunters, she stretched her aching muscles and levered herself to her feet. The pallet was a far cry from her comfortable curtained bed in her private chamber. Did someone else sleep there now?

Her stomach rumbled, for she had eaten little since the death of her father. A certain weakness pervaded her limbs, and she leaned against the cold walls until the dizziness passed.

This would not do. If the Lord provided a way of escape, she must not bungle the opportunity. "Lord, help me to trust You."

❧

Once again, Laural sat down to eat next to Lord Cambraige. After the priest gave the invocation, the servants bustled about with large platters of food. A paste of minced meat had been spread on bread. Laural forced herself to eat her fill. Straightway she felt strength return to her limbs and alertness to her mind.

Under the table she heard the dogs scrabbling for scraps. Goblets clanked, and boots thumped on the rushes growing filthy with crumbs and bones. Laughter erupted to her left and she glanced down the table toward a wiry knight hefting his goblet.

"I say the poor duffer was beside himself, drooling like some idiot."

"An idiot who slipped away from us. Made for poor sport, that," chimed in another.

Hearing the discussion, Lord Cambraige growled, "Should have ridden the fool down when we had the chance."

Laural blanched, her insides churning. What manner of men were these?

Deliberately she turned her attention to the troubadour tuning his lute. Light from the smoking torches in the wall brackets played over the face of Lord Cambraige, giving him a sinister appearance. He smiled in amusement when she shrank back from his fowl breathe on her cheek.

"M'lady be too grand for the likes of Cambraige? Take care, m'lady."

Laural shifted her eyes from his face to gaze about the hall. The benches were being pushed back, and chessboards were brought out along with backgammon.

A jester cavorted about the cleared floor space. When he was finished, Cambraige nodded toward the traveling troubadour.

In a mesmerizing tone, the gaunt balladeer began the *Chanson de Roland* which emphasized all that Cambraige was not—chivalrous and charitable:

> Roland is daring and Oliver wise,
> Both of marvelous high emprise;
> On their chargers mounted, and girt in mail,
> To the death in battle they will not quail. . . .

Verse followed verse through the battle, from Ganelon's treachery to Roland's courageous death.

Though she listened to the story, Laural's heart cried silently for another song, a song of Black Hawk. To her surprise one of Cambraige's own men suggested the tale. Once more the balladeer tuned his instrument. A smile lit his face as he began to sing:

> Ye men and women of noble birth,
> Sons and daughters of the earth,
> Hear ye the tale of a noble Lord,
> Who holds our hearts by deed not sword.
>
> Who be this shadow of the night,
> Lord or Spirit who fights for right?
> None other so brings truth to light,
> This knight who's heart is white.
>
> In armor black as the abyss,
> Slashed with a cross as white as mist,
> The dragon hides as he is stalked,
> By the legend, the great Black Hawk.

Sighing, Laural set her chin on her hands, her heart beating in time to the rhythm. Did Black Hawk truly exist or was he but an imagined creation for a populace who needed something, someone in which to believe? Her father always smiled at the question. "He is real enough, Leelah. Legend or no, Black Hawk is all that be courageous and good."

Father had stopped then and patted her head as she gazed up at him from the stool by his feet. "Black Hawk is only a man, Leelah. He is a great man to be sure, but a man—not a savior. We must keep our eyes, as he does, on our real Savior, Christ Jesus."

As the troubadour finished singing, Laural received permission to return to her room. Having completed her simple preparations for bed, Laural prayed for guidance until exhaustion claimed her. At least as long as she stayed at Comfrey, hope was not lost.

The next morning Mazda pulled her from her sleep. The servant's mouth was tight and her face grim. "M'lady, thee must needs be up and dressed."

"Mazda, what is it? What's wrong?"

"'Tis his lordship, m'lady." Even while she spoke she hurried Laural into a gown of deep blue and clasped a jeweled belt about her waist before dressing her hair. "He be leaving Comfrey."

"Praise be. There is a chance yet of release."

"Oh, m'lady. His lordship commanded me to ready you for the journey. He be returning to Cambraige castle straightway, and you are to accompany him."

"No." Rushing to the window, Laural stared down into the courtyard where pages and squires, servants and serfs hurried to do the bidding of the purple-faced Lord Cambraige. A large cart was being readied along with the horses. In the smaller carts, Laural recognized several of her father's prized possessions. "How dare they strip Comfrey of her treasures?" she cried, then gritted her teeth.

"I shall make him pay," she promised herself. "If it takes a lifetime, I shall bring him down."

In her ears rang the tale of Black Hawk, but she closed down her heart. There was no Black Hawk. He was but a legend. A disconcerting voice whispered, "Is God also just a legend?"

"No!" she cried, feeling her heart grow cold with dread. "Lord Jesus, help me," she prayed, but no help came.

Before the sun had fully ascended, Laural found herself bumping along a narrow rutted road to the most dreaded castle in the region. Once ensconced within the castle of Cambraige, there would be no escape.

Throwing back her shoulders, Laural prepared to face the future with courage. Inside her heart chilled with fear and dread.

Her first sight of the castle two days later did nothing to mitigate her terror. Built of black stone, the walls of the stronghold loomed over the countryside, blocking out the light of the sun. The surrounding trees whispered eerily to each other as they passed. No birds sang on the branches, and the one rabbit brave enough to dash across the path was brought down with an oath.

King Edward's father had once commanded the fortification to be dismantled, but Lord Cambraige's father had outfaced even the king, so the castle stood, a monument to rebellion, a monument to the tyrants who ruled with sadistic pleasure. Laural had heard stories that she had found impossible to believe. Now, as she passed under the dark gatehouse, a chill coursed down her spine.

"Lord, please. . .don't fail me now." The clank of the portcullis rang in her ears as it imprisoned her within the castle walls.

A prayer leaped to Laural's lips. She saw no escape and yet something within her refused to give up. Head high she rode into the castle courtyard. Though her back and legs ached from the long ride, she took care not to let her exhaustion show.

Lord Cambraige eyed her disdainfully. "I see you made it in fine mettle, or," he sneered, "are you planning to take to your bed now that we're here?"

"As long as it isn't yours," Laural retorted, then bit her lip.

She sensed the blow coming and moved her head in time to avoid being knocked off her palfrey. Nonetheless, she grabbed the reins of the animal which reared in fright. Too late. A moment later, Laural lay in an undignified heap on the cold packed ground.

Lord Cambraige roared in laughter and made no move to help as Laural levered herself to her feet. She gritted her teeth to keep from telling Lord Cambraige just what she thought of him. The glint in his eyes told her that he already knew. Grabbing her chin, he glared down into her face.

"You be on my fief now, wench. There is no escape." He forced her to look at the well-patrolled battlements. "I trust no one and I make certain everyone knows exactly where I stand. As for you," he released her so suddenly, she stumbled and almost fell once more, "you have the freedom of castle and bailey."

He laughed at her shocked surprise. "There is nothing outside these castle walls, m'lady. Trust me, not one of my vassals or my serfs will lift a finger to aid you. Try to escape and I'll hunt you down like a renegade bear and dispatch you with less compassion."

"You have none," she spit at him.

"Precisely. Remember that, wench."

"When the king hears how you're treating me. . ."

"From whom shall he hear? And what shall he hear? That the Celtic wench tried to warn her kin and had to be brought down." He shrugged, "Regrettable, but. . ."

Laural swallowed with difficulty. Her words rushed out too high. "If I stay?"

"We shall see." She shivered under his leer which quickly changed to disgust at the sight of her clenched hands. "Such a pity."

Inside the keep, Cambraige's maiden aunt, who had charge of the household, eyed Laural with a decided chill. "Lady Laural. I shall show thee to the lady's bower where we sleep."

Lord Cambraige forestalled her. "Nay. A private chamber if you please, Mistress Haverman."

"But Ian. . .m'lord," she added at his scowl. "The chambers are taken."

"Then throw someone out. Let them sleep in the great hall for all I care. Lady Laural will have her own chamber."

The solid, boxlike woman made as though to argue when Lord Cambraige raised a threatening hand. Though Mistress Haverman did not visibly flinch, Laural saw the hesitation in her eyes. Her heart softened toward the woman, but not for long.

"Why does the likes of this chit rank a private chamber?"

"Who knows with whom she might share it." Lord Cambraige actually winked at the huge woman, whose features were criss-crossed with a map of lines.

The woman threw Laural a sly glance. "You shall not wed this feeble wench?"

"What fustian." He shuddered. "Think you I would touch such a one?" He flung out a gloved hand. "Take her from my sight."

The woman's grip on her arm left Laural no choice, and she stumbled after the woman. Before long she found herself the possessor of an insignificant, but private chamber. From the way Mistress Haverman handled the situation, Laural had no doubt the woman kept the reins of Lord Cambraige's household well in hand. No doubt, either, that the woman held her in deep dislike.

"Lord Jesus, can anyone save me now?" For a moment Laural thought of Black Hawk, then once and for all dismissed her girlhood ideal. She was on her own.

six

*Our eyes wait upon the Lord our God,
until that he have mercy on us.* Psalm 123:2

For all the inconveniences of her situation, Laural found herself less supervised than at Comfrey. No guard dogged her every step, and she had been assigned her own private chamber—however small. 'Twas the privacy that mattered. Her bedchamber was the only place where she felt free from watching eyes, though not from the sharp ears of those passing by in the hall.

Already a week had passed. For the most part Cambraige left her alone for which she daily gave thanks. Other times he abused her with cruel jests and physical punishment for no discernible reason. He laughed when she fought him. Laughed and threw her away with the threat. "One day I'll find use for your charms, my dear. One day."

Though not entirely private, the chapel proved a place of refuge for her battered soul, if not her body. "Why, Lord, why is this happening to me? What have I done to make You hate me so?" She paused, "Jesus, will I leave here alive? Please, help my people. Save them from Cambraige even if You won't help me, please. Please. . ." The words trailed off. What good did it do to pray? And yet, something within her sparked to life in the quiet sanctuary—a spark of hope which would not die.

That hope died a few nights later. In the unremitting darkness of her small bedchamber, Laural brushed at the irritation on her cheek as she awakened slowly. Something soft

53

brushed against her face. Irritated, she made a grab for the illusive insect that tickled her. Her hand instead closed around the long shaft of a feather. At the same instant, she realized she was not alone in her tiny room hollowed out of the thick walls of the castle. A male figure stood at the partly opened door by her bed.

Frightened, the petite girl sat up, clutching the fur coverlet around her in the chill. "Who are you?" she whispered shakily into the sudden menace of the night.

"Come, Leelah," said a low rasping voice. "Meet me straightway in the south tower room."

"But that is the tower which is crumbling."

"Aye, and unused." His voice lowered even more. "'Tis Black Hawk, Leelah."

Laural gasped, "Black Hawk? Is it possible? Do you really exist?" She sputtered as hope sparked again. "Leelah. That name. Only my father called me by that name." Into the darkness, she strained her eyes, but the visage of her night visitor was hidden in shadows.

He turned away. "I shall await you." The deep voice faded into the darkness.

Black Hawk! Was it possible? Laural threw on the gown nearest at hand and clutched the dark feather that had woken her. Even as she surreptitiously made her way toward the tower, another thought hit. Was treachery planned? She hesitated but a moment. What more had she to lose?

As she swung open the massive door and stepped into the inky blackness lit only by moonlight through a slit of a window, a dark form detached from the shadows.

"Be of good heart, my dear." Then as though reading her mind, he added, "'Tis not for treachery I asked thee hither."

His words rallied Laural's usually solid practical sense. "Sir, why are you here? You must leave straightway. If they find you in the castle, they'll murder you. . .and not pleasantly."

The chuckle sounded again softly. "Faugh! I care not a jot for their petty games. I must know. . .are you the king's loyal liege woman still or has Lord Cambraige turned your pretty head?"

Anger coursed through Laural. "I'm not some vacillating traitor to be had by the likes of him. How dare you? If my father were still alive. . ." Her words trailed off into a sob. "Why doesn't the Lord hear my prayers? First my mother, then my f. . .father. And I am a prisoner of that horrid Lord Cambraige, who. . ." She dared not breathe her suspicions, not to stranger. Not even a stranger who claimed to be her childhood hero.

She heard the illusive Black Hawk suck in a breath. "Precisely why I find myself here, m'lady."

Laural rolled the soft feather in her hand. "Why here? Why now?" Her heart pounded erratically at the nearness of this legend. How often had her dear father regaled her with the heroic tales of this apparition who moved about righting wrongs under the king's standard. Though Laural half suspected her father knew more of who this phantom was than he admitted to, she could not pry the information from him. From her childhood—not so long past, she mused—she had held a not-so-childish tendre for the dashing unknown knight.

Hoping he did not hear the loud pounding of her heart, she asked a more important question. "How know you Father's name for me?" She blinked back the tears, feeling again the tearing pain of his loss.

Angrily she wiped the tears from her eyes. Black Hawk would think her but the child others so often mistook her for. She did not realize her wide innocent eyes contributed much to the assumption of her youth. But under her petite, delicate bone structure and her heart-shaped elfin face surrounded with clouds of silver-streaked hair, she was indeed a woman full grown. Why she had seen seventeen summers already! But could he see her in the thick darkness?

The rasping voice pierced her thoughts. "Your father was a good friend to me. He spoke much of you, Leelah. Better than a son to him you were. . .even after the accident." He grasped her hand in the darkness with an adeptness that took away her breath.

Or was it the touch of his warm hand on hers? She shook away the thought. She was a woman full-grown and must put away her silly childish romance of dashing white knights and maidens fair.

"I understand he had the stallion who crushed your hands destroyed. He blamed himself that the horse kicked his way out of a rotted stall, knowing, as he did, of the horse's unusual viciousness. He blamed himself that your visit home ended so disastrously." Black Hawk sensed the girl's pain and gently stroked the hands drawn up into half fists. They were the most obvious result of the accident.

"He kept me home after that." She drew a deep breath. "No one wanted an infirm maiden on their estate."

"He kept you at Comfrey because he loved you, Leelah. After the death of your sainted mother, he needed you as much as you needed him. I do too."

"Me, what fustian! I am little more than a prisoner here. Why does the great Black Hawk need me? What aid can I possible give you?"

"My dear, you sell yourself too cheaply."

"Too cheaply." In her agitation she missed his endearment. "Like Lord Cambraige needs me." She shuddered, as she pictured the solidly built man who had so precipitously become her guardian. . .and would have become more, but for her hands.

Black Hawk chuckled. "I have no desire for your father's fief. But I see Cambraige has made plain his plans." She trembled, shocked she revealed so easily her thoughts to a man she had never before met and, even now, would not recognize in the light of day.

In the dark, Laural grimaced. Instinctively she moved her hands. "Never thought I would favor these hands as they be now, but they have so far saved me from the earl's advances."

She sighed. "He holds my presence befouls his castle. He cannot bear to touch a cripple, or already I'd be wed." Sarcasm bit her words, hiding the bitterness she still felt over no longer being the whole person she once had been; hiding also her searing bitterness over her father's untimely death.

Laural bit her lip to stop her prattling. "I'm sorry," she whispered as hot tears prickled her eyes.

"My dear, do not be sorry. Leelah, there is nothing wrong in sharing thus with me. Have you had no one to confide in? Did Cambraige allow no woman to accompany you?" He felt the shake of her head. "I suppose not. For all his arrogance, he is unsure of himself."

Laural stiffened not only at the words, but also at the tenderness with which they were spoken. "I be attended by his servants," she managed to explain. "But you came not to hear my woes. Kindly favor me with your request, m'lord. Mayhap I may be of some small service."

Black Hawk smiled in the darkened chamber. He squeezed her hand. "My Leelah, I need your eyes and ears. Your father was right proud of your retentive memory. What you hear, you recall. I need that. Your king needs that."

Laural felt a large warm hand on her shoulder. The intensity of its warmth brought a gasp to her lips. "I will do anything you ask of me," she whispered.

Black Hawk cleared his throat. "I believe there be a plot afoot to harm His Majesty."

Laural gasped again. Squeezing her shoulder, Black Hawk continued, seemingly unaware of the sensations his touch created in Laural. "It troubles me to tell this, Leelah, but your father's death we believe to be more than an untimely accident."

Laural struggled with conflicting emotions.

Black Hawk's grip on her shoulder tightened. "I need to know if your father confided anything of this nature to you or if you have any information he might have wished to pass on to me."

Laural shook her head. "Father said nothing of such things to me, though I did suspect. . ."

Her words trailed off as her night visitor explained. "Belike he had something but was cut down before he could pass it on."

Laural's mind leaped back to that afternoon. "Cambraige. He was head of the hunting party. Never have I favored him. I thought him greedy for the land. You suspect more?"

"Ah, dear Leelah, you have been bestowed with as sharp a wit as any man." Laural felt a sense of pride at such praise, not lightly given.

Silently she waited, while Black Hawk tactfully tried to put his proposition to the girl. "You hear what others are not privileged to hear, for few take note of your presence. Mingle with the knights and ladies, pick up any information you feel might be useful. Even a seeming bit of nonsense might be significant. You understand."

"Aye, m'lord. I shall be most discreet in this mission, haunting Lord Cambraige most effectively."

Black Hawk tensed. "Do not submit yourself foolishly to danger, or collapse with the vapors at anything you might hear."

"Faugh! I am not some weakling to faint at the first sign of danger." She sensed Black Hawk's amusement at her obvious disgust. "They watch me constantly, but only to make sure I make no move to escape. Even so, I feel invisible to everyone for all the notice they take of me."

"My most humble apologies, m'lady," he said formally, a hint of laughter in his rasping voice. He held her hand to his cheek. "You are a brave young woman."

He paused, then added reluctantly. "I must needs depart, Leelah. I trust my visit will remain our secret."

"Of a certain, but how will I contact you? Where will you be?"

Black Hawk laughed softly. "I'll not leave you long, Leelah. I'll attend you straightway. You'll know me—"

"By the Black Hawk's feather."

"Aye."

Before Laural realized what her visitor planned to do, Black Hawk leaned over and softly kissed her innocent lips. "Do not fear, my dear." With those words, Black Hawk once more faded into the night.

Suddenly chilled, Laural hurried back to her chamber and her warm bed. For a long time, she remained awake. Shivers shot through her as Black Hawk's kiss played over and over in her mind—her first real kiss. The man, the legend, had actually kissed her!

"Lord," she breathed in awe, "You really do care!" A few moments later, Laural fell asleep with a smile on her sweet red lips.

seven

The sun shall not smite thee by day,
nor the moon by night. Psalm 121:6

❧

When a matronly servant brought Laural's breakfast to her the next morning, she found Laural already up. "Just set it on the table." Laural instructed her.

With a nod, the maid set the tray on the small high wooden table beside the bed. Laural dismissed her with a smile and sat down before picking up the mug of cider. It burned her throat as it went down, bringing tears to her eyes. More slowly she broke the hard biscuits and ate them with deliberation before finishing the drink.

Thinking of the feather, now safely hidden away, she sighed thankfully. The consequences of being found with the telltale symbol were too gruesome to contemplate.

Laural finished her breakfast just as the maid returned with a basin of water. Shivering, Laural quickly splashed herself clean in the cold water, then grabbed the rough towel to dry herself. Straightening, she stood while the servant pulled first a thin woolen shift over her head, then a white silk tunic brightly embroidered with red and blue flowers at the neck and cuffs.

After fastening the sleeves, the maid pulled a deep blue bliaut over Laural's head, and tightly laced up the sides to reveal the sweet curves of Laural's young figure.

Gathering the long skirt, Laural sat gracefully on a high oak stool as the maid brushed out her long silken strands and braided them. "Want it up, m'lady?" the woman asked.

Laural hesitated but a moment. "No thank you, Alice. Let it down. Mayhap a ribbon. . ."

The woman found a blue ribbon to match the bliaut and tied it at the end of the braid that hung down Laural's back almost to her thighs. "There ye be, m'lady. All ready for the chapel service."

"Thank you, Alice. That is all." The maid inclined her head and left her mistress's presence.

Kneeling for morning prayers in the back of the small chapel, Laural sensed the disturbing presence of her guardian; sensed his disdain for the elderly gray-haired priest intoning the blessing with uplifted arms.

Surprised at the reverence of the elderly priest, she wondered momentarily where Father Andrew, Lord Cambraige's own clergyman, had got to. But then, except for his garb, she would not suspect he was a man of God. Her lips twisted in disdain. Man of God, hardly.

Father Andrew ate without the manners of the lowest peasant, gorging himself at every meal. With pride he downed more wine than Lord Cambraige, wiping his sleeve across his mouth as he finished a long draught. So much for abstemious priests.

Despite the restrictions of the church which forbade clerics from participating in hunting, war, theater, or games of chance, Father Andrew relished life in all its forms. Any word or look of dismay from Laural brought swift retribution, sometimes in the guise of lewd comments, but more often from the back of Lord Cambraige's hand. Twas no wonder Father Andrew left the services to a cleric who had at least a nodding acquaintance with God.

In all her sheltered life, Laural could not have imagined such depravity as she found within the walls of the fearsome castle. As much as possible, she closed her eyes and ears to the infidelities, the prevarications and half-truths used to jockey for power and position with Lord Cambraige. It amused him to keep his men at each other's throats, no one trusting another.

It sickened Laural, and she felt the evil within the castle binding her like a shroud. But for that visit from Black Hawk, she might well have lost hope. Instead, she tightened her lips, more determined than ever to bring down Cambraige.

For Laural, the very presence in the sanctuary of the man she suspected in her father's death roused an anger which destroyed the peace she sought. Hastily she bowed her head and crossed herself asking forgiveness for letting these matters intrude in on this holy place.

"Lord Jesus, help me. I don't want to be so filled with hate. I see hate and evil around me every day. I see how it destroys everyone it touches, but I hate him, Lord. I hate Cambraige, and I'm not sure I want to stop hating him. What am I to do?

"I want to help Black Hawk. . ." She paused, "Jesus, sometimes I wonder if I conjured him up out of my own disordered mind. Did he truly come? Is there truly hope? Did You send him?" Gulping, she bit her lip as she clasped her hands in prayer.

"Please forgive all my questions, Lord. Just help me. Help me bring Cambraige down and discover the truth about my father. Amen."

Since she had so precipitously arrived at the fortified castle, Laural had found the chapel a sanctuary. . .a place to meditate; a place to pray; and, most of all, a place to grieve for her father.

"My God, help me," she whispered, begging for the courage to do as the great Black Hawk asked of her. "Don't let me fail him. Please don't let me fail him. Or You."

After the priest had finished and Lord Cambraige, followed by his retinue of knights, had departed, Laural's head remained bowed, her hands clasped in prayer. Slowly she recited what she had learned by rote, the power of which she had only recently discovered. "Our Father which art in Heaven, Hallowed be thy name. Thy kingdom come. Thy will be done in earth, as it is in Heaven. Give us this day our daily bread. And forgive our debts, as we forgive our debtors. And lead us not into temptation, but deliver us from evil: For thine is the kingdom, and the power, and the glory, for ever. Amen."

Forgive us as we forgive others? "Lord, does that mean I have to forgive even Lord Cambraige? Lord, help me, I can't do it alone." For a long time Laural remained in the chapel. Her knees ached. Still she stayed. Head bowed, eyes closed, the silence swelled until it seeped into her shuttered mind and heart.

'Twas only then her heart opened and she began to feel a measure of peace.

With a casualness belying her anticipation to outface Lord Cambraige, Laural made her way down the long narrow flight of stairs to the great hall.

A cold draft hit her as she lifted the curtain separating the warm stairwell from the vaulted chamber. Much of the heat generated from the two huge fireplaces situated at either end of the hall funneled up the stairs leaving the cavernous hall decidedly chilly.

This morning she had no eyes for the elegant intricate tapestries and banners hanging about the room in such profusion that the cold gray stone walls were virtually covered. Not even the colorful banners could dampen the chill in the great room.

She spared a smile for the crudely dressed servants busily cleaning the floor pallets. Once again, she was angered at Lord Cambraige, who was more concerned about the outward appearance of his castle than for the well-being of his serfs. Not that he was all too clean. The rushes on the floor were littered with bones and the remnants of many a meal.

Not only was Lord Cambraige less than mannerly or clean, he was cheese-paring as well in all matters except those which touched him personally—like his grand attire or his food.

A large-boned, buxom serving girl approached her. "What does m'lady wish?"

"Nothing, Rosy, thanks." For a moment she chatted with the maidservant, though she knew she might well incur Lord Cambraige's wrath by doing so. It disgusted her that Lord Cambraige, like so many others of her station, thought of servants as less than human and often treated them with a carelessness and brutality they would spurn using on their animals.

Her father had taught her differently, as had her own experience. Had she not spent much time in the kitchens of her father's castle, at times feeling more at home and accepted there than on the dais of the great hall? In the kitchens she became acquainted with both the joys and sorrows of her father's serfs, joys and sorrows not much different from her own.

Besides, she had long ago learned that nothing which went on among the high-born lords and ladies of the manor escaped either the eyes or the knowledge of the servants. Most of the gentry believed that servants and children were both deaf and mute (as well as witless), and spoke quite freely in front of them. Because of her elfin size and quiet demeanor, Laural was often treated with the same arrogant disdain reserved for an insignificant child, a girl-child at that.

Laural had every intention of exploiting this tendency to dismiss her with a pat on the head and a wink or, in Lord Cambraige's case, with the back of his hand. Gingerly Laural felt her jaw, still bruised from Lord Cambraige's last assault. Fury raged within. He was no better than the two debauched knights who had visited Comfrey just a year ago.

At that time, while busily embroidering a tunic in the great hall of her home, Laural overhead the two visiting English knights conversing near her at the long table.

The knight in the black and red tunic guffawed loudly. "She be a lovely piece, that village girl."

"Unwilling that she be," laughed the other knight. "And her sister. I was the first to bring her to heel. All that dark hair, wondrous fair." He grunted lustfully.

"I go to her this afternoon. Comfrey breeds them lusty. Quite the fighter."

Laural stiffened. Ducking her head to keep her expression from showing, Laural forced herself to continue sewing. Her stitches grew ragged, and she longed to close her ears to the obscenity flowing from the mouths of the two men. She ached for the two girls, good girls she knew, who had been as innocent as she herself. And what of the elder girl's fiancé? The rage he must feel!

When she was able to slip away unnoticed, Laural ran to find her father. "Father. Father." She found him in the stables and dragged him into a corner for privacy. Comfrey laughed down at his daughter's flushed face.

"What womanish folly be this?" Gently he tucked a stray lock of hair behind her ear.

"Father, I am sore troubled." Her face grave, she recounted the conversation she had overheard.

Comfrey's smile faded into rage. "Their deed is most foul. I will see to it, daughter. Rest assured, they *will* be punished!"

He had kept his word. The knights had been flogged and forced to pay damages to the family; an action they felt to be quite beneath them. But even in their anger, they had no one on whom to turn their vengeance, for they had no memory of an elfin girl sewing in the corner. Laural started at her sudden recall. The knights who swore vengeance, had they not given sword-oath to Lord Cambraige?

Closing her eyes, Laural prayed for the same anonymity now. More than ever before, she must take care not be noticed. She smiled grimly. In trying to avoid Lord Cambraige, she had already been perfecting her technique, because she feared that one day he would overcome his repulsion and marry her just to get her land—or worse, take her without benefit of ceremony or clergy. No, she must take care not to be noticed.

Demurely, Laural sat on a long bench near Sir Ranalf Wentworth, a stout, ill-smelling man who constantly wiped his fat wet hands on his stained tunic. She grimaced at the smell but stood her ground, counting on his vanity to give her important clues.

She did not wait long. For though early in the day, the stout knight was already heady with his unrelenting thirst for strong ale. Seeing the child through unfocused eyes, Wentworth raised his mug. "Let me tell you about the time. . ." He took a long swig.

"In the time of my great-great-great-grandfather, a Welsh chieftain, old William backed by his Norman forces declared himself Lord of Wales. Year of our Lord 1071, it be. 'Tis then he gave away our lands to the blasted Englishmen. Tried to pen us up like rats. Marches, he calls them. Marcher barons, he calls them. Marcher barons who cared not a fig for either king or true Welshmen.

"The king gave some of us English names, English lands

to pacify us, but there be no pacifying a true born Welshman. So we fought. Aye," he swigged mightily of his heavy pewter ale mug, "fought his hordes and won! Fought with the Griffith and got Henry to recognize Llewelyn as Prince of Wales. Rightly so for so he was. We Wentworths serve the Llewelyn," he smirked, "and his kin—"

"Aye, Ranalf," called out a visiting knight in black, "but Llewelyn never recognized King Edward as the true and rightful heir to his father Henry. Owe your allegiance to the king or the Welsh rebels?"

The question stopped Sir Wentworth with his mug halfway to his thick lips. He gulped convulsively, seeming to realize for perhaps the first time that he was not in some Welsh hideaway, but in the main hall of a man who professed sword-oath to Edward, the English King.

"I serve Lord Cambraige!" His cry echoed and re-echoed about the long hall as Lord Cambraige's knights took up the cry. Raising their ale mugs in salute, they effectively diffused Sir Wentworth's ill-spoken words. Smiling he swigged deeply and took up his tales again, but with more caution.

For the next hour Sir Wentworth regaled everyone in the large room as he roared out stories of his real or imagined heroic exploits. But Laural waited in vain for anything which could help Black Hawk. She grew bored with Wentworth's recital and sickened by his foulness. Suddenly the ale-soaked knight glanced over her head and fell silent.

The lord of the castle, resplendent in a fresh bright green tunic embroidered in black and gold at the neck and about the hem, strode into the room. His gold brown hair gleamed in the sunlight filtering from the high narrow windows into the dim hall.

Striding to the table with a calculated arrogance, Lord Cambraige turned haughty narrowed eyes toward Wentworth.

"Be still, you drunken lout." He aimed a kick at the knight, which his victim received with a muffled yelp. Sir Wentworth fell silent, his face ashen.

Laural could have sworn she saw the same disgust in Lord Cambraige's cold eyes for the drunken Sir Wentworth that he shown toward her. She was thankful he ignored her presence as he sat down in his cushioned high-back chair at the center of the long table. He motioned for the man with him to take the chair next to him.

The tall, broad-shouldered man moved with an uncommon grace and commanding assurance for such a large man. He dwarfed Lord Cambraige, who was no mean man himself. Laural surveyed the man's silver-on-black tunic. The fine material showed off his strength. *Aye, he be a fine figure of a man,* thought Laural, then blushed as her gaze raised and with a shock met the man's arresting gray eyes on her.

Lord Cambridge, following the man's gaze, nodded in Laural's direction. "Lady Laural Comfrey, my ward, Lord Strathouse."

To Laural's surprise, the man stood and moved to her side. As he took her maimed hand, Laural waited for revulsion to settle on his features, but to her amazement the man bowed and kissed her hand. She shivered at his touch, blushing furiously under his steady gaze as he continued to hold her hand.

"Lord Strathouse?"

"Lady Laural," he murmured before returning to his seat of honor beside Lord Cambraige, his eyes full of secret amusement.

With a bow, he turned his attention toward Lord Cambraige, leaving Laural, totally disconcerted, staring after him. She could not wait to leave the hall for a turn in the courtyard ward. Yet the meal had just begun.

"Laural," roared Lord Cambraige as though she were some underling. "Get you to the table. Nay," he forestalled her attempt to sit with his minions at a long refectory table, "Lord Strathouse requests that you share his trencher."

Heads turned curiously in her direction, and Laural's anger burned as she lifted her skirts to make her way to the dais. Had she mistaken the glance of surprise the lord threw Lord Cambraige? Was this another of Lord Cambraige's manipulations?

"Lord Strathouse," she acknowledged reluctantly, taking her seat on the other side of the imposing lord. From the corner of her eye, she studied his finely chiseled profile, then blushed as his penetrating gaze caught her surreptitious survey.

"Dost her ladyship find ought amiss with my face or person, mayhap? A smudge perhaps on my nose?"

The amusement in his eyes further discomfited her, and her blush deepened. "Nay, Lord Strathouse. I. . ." What could she say? That something about him drew her to him, or worse, the idea that if she kept her composure, she might be able to discover the reason for Lord Strathouse's visit to the dark castle.

His features proclaimed his French heritage. What then had a Norman lord to do with the likes of Lord Cambraige? Questions danced in her mind, but she would have to wait before she made any cautiously posed inquiries. Father Andrew chose that moment to rise to his feet. Absently she noted the absence of the elderly cleric who presided over the chapel services.

The arrogant priest intoned a shallow self-aggrandizing invocation which left Laural cold. Beside her she heard Strathouse mutter, "What sop."

Laural quelled the giggle bubbling up inside at the lord's

irreverent, but oh-so-accurate assessment. As the cleric boomed out, "Amen," Laural lifted her head at the same instant as the lord beside her. A moment of amused understanding flashed between them before Laural blushed and turned away to watch the procession in front of the table by the steward directing the household staff. The pantler followed, distributing bread and butter.

Even before the pantler had finished his task, Lord Cambraige bellowed for the butler and his assistants. "What's keeping you louts? Bring in the wine and ale." For emphasis, he thumped his mug on the table.

Laural ground her teeth in frustration at Lord Cambraige's ill manners. As though sensing her condemnation, he impaled her with a malicious glare. "Bethink you'd like to eat in the kitchen with the rest of the serving wenches?"

Laural's cheeks stained with fury at this insult. "At least the company would be more congenial," she retorted, then winced as Lord Cambraige reached around the visiting lord to slap her. His fist never connected.

Lord Strathouse deftly reflected the blow. "I say, Cambraige. Surely you could tilt at a more worthy opponent than Lady Laural."

His gaze locked with that of Lord Cambraige. To Laural's relief, 'twas her erstwhile guardian who looked away first. "As you wish, Strathouse." A wry smile touched his lips. "Mayhap you shall enjoy the spoils as I cannot."

Laural puzzled over this exchange only momentarily, for Strathouse took up the first course brought in by the kitchen assistants. He chunked the meat sliced from the huge beast that had been roasted to sizzling perfection in the maw of the fireplace and brought to the table on a spit. Laural had no option but to open her mouth for the meat stabbed on his knife, dripping in it's own juice.

Having grown used to the usually lukewarm offerings at Cambraige's table, Laural was surprised when the sizzling meat warmed her insides nicely. She giggled as Strathouse caught the juice drizzling down her chin with the edges of the large tablecloth changed with each course, wondering why his touch sizzled down her spine.

Sternly she reprimanded herself, but the damage had been done. For the first time since coming to the dark castle, Laural almost enjoyed the meal. "Come you from the king's court?" she inquired.

"That I do, m'lady."

"You have spoken to King Edward, then?"

"Numerous times, m'lady," said the lord, his lips twitching.

Despairing of his sparse answers, Laural groaned inwardly at her inability to get the Norman lord to talk of himself. How different from the effusive Lord Cambraige, who sought to proclaim his greatness at every opportunity.

"How came ye to know Lord Cambraige?" Laural tried more directly, praying Cambraige would not overhear their conversation. Strathouse caught her nervous glance over his shoulder.

"Come now, Lady Comfrey. There is no need to concern yourself with your guardian. He is well occupied."

Overhearing a particularly low comment Cambraige made to a passing serving girl, Laural's face reddened. "So I hear," she managed and witnessed that twitch of the lord's lips again.

"Well," she demanded, "am I to be your entertainment now?"

This time the twitch ripened into a smile, then a chuckle. "Lady Laural, are you offering yourself freely?"

The implications of her statement slammed the breath from

her lungs, and for a moment, Laural gasped for air. Her face bloomed rose red. Embarrassment vied with anger. "M'lord, I didn't. I never. I wouldn't. Fustian! You confuse me so." This admission left her perilously close to tears. What was the matter with her anyway?

Lord Strathouse sobered, his eyes kind. "'Twas a slip of the tongue, Lady Laural. My apologies for using such to your disadvantage." His eyes twinkled, "Am I forgiven?"

"I am, you know. I mean. . ."

Strathouse lowered his voice. "There is no shame in being a maiden."

Laural covered her cheeks, willing them to stop giving her away. "I know. I fear. . ."

Strathouse squeezed her hand under the table. "While I am here, Laural, you have nothing to fear. Now as to the king's court," he said more loudly as Lord Cambraige quirked an eye at their tête-à-tête.

He lowered his voice again. "I met Lord Cambraige there. He came to petition for Comfrey."

Laural straightened, "Did the king, did the king grant his request?"

"Not yet, little Laural, not yet."

Laural glanced over his shoulder to make certain Lord Cambraige did not listen. "Did you hear of a knight named Destrun?"

For a long moment, Lord Strathouse studied the elfin face whose eyes pleaded for an answer. Laural's eagerness to hear of the worthy knight disquieted him. In truth it angered him as well.

"He did indeed come to court." He paused, then added, "Or so I heard."

"Then you do not know of him yourself?" Disappointment filled her eyes.

"Let us say, his business was with His Majesty. I believe you can safely leave the business in their hands. Unless there be some personal attachment between the two of you."

Her infernal cheeks blossomed under the intensity of his gaze. "Destrun is a kind and dear friend, Lord Strathouse. I be concerned as to his welfare."

"He is in fine form. Does that make your heart beat faster, Lady Comfrey?" he said sharply.

"M'lord? You mistake the situation."

A delighted grin twisted the lips of the lord. "I am glad to hear it."

About to question this puzzling statement, a loud guffaw interrupted her. Despite her low conversation with Strathouse, she could not but be aware of Lord Cambraige's increasingly bawdy suggestions and ruder jests. Though all ate with their fingers and knives, Lord Cambraige appeared to take pride in his gross manners as he slobbered in his goblet and guffawed when his mouth was stuffed with food.

Lord Strathouse, in contrast, made certain his hands were clean, wiped the goblet before offering her a drink, and never spoke when his mouth was filled with food. His manners as much as his gentleness drew Laural to him.

As each course was cleared away and the next one set, Laural alternated between a desire to continue her acquaintance with the gentle lord who had shielded her from Lord Cambraige's abuse, and a certain hope for the meal—and the enforced proximity to Lord Cambraige and his equally debauched men-at-arms—to end.

With Strathouse in residence, surely she would find other opportunities to speak with him. Mayhap there was more she might learn from the Norman lord. Why was he at the castle? Why did Lord Cambraige heed his defense of her? Any other reasons to see the lord, Laural refused to consider.

With mixed feelings she made as to rise after the last course of fruits, cheese, nuts, and spiced wine.

"Where art thou going, wench?" called Lord Cambraige.

"For a breath of air, m'lord," Laural returned with as much composure as she could manage.

"You beg leave of your master?" Lord Cambraige enjoyed baiting her, enjoyed abusing her when her control slipped.

"As you wish, m'lord," managed Laural.

"Let her go, Cambraige," said Strathouse.

Laural did not miss the steel in his voice and was surprised at this his second defense.

Lord Cambraige nodded affirmation. "Get on with you then," he barked, then jeered. "'Tis not as though you can escape Castle Cambraige."

His ominous statement brought her respite crashing in, and Laural hurried from the great hall to keep herself from an unwise outburst. As she passed, Lord Strathouse caught at her arm, but she shook him off.

Once outside in the fresh air, she tried to shake free of the man's unsettling effect on her, but just as she freed herself of the shadow on her mind, Lord Cambraige strode out of the keep followed by Sir Wentworth, pages, squires, and other knights.

Standing back and thinking herself unobserved, Laural watched the men in their colorful tunics and surcoats swing onto the spirited palfreys, each held by a young squire, knights in training. Then holding the still-hooded hunting hawks, the eager young squires swung onto their own lesser mounts.

Laural gasped in dismay as a tall man in a familiar tunic rode toward her hiding place. Strathouse grinned down at her blushing face. An amused twinkle in his eyes, he bowed his head in her direction, "Wish you to attend the hunt, m'lady?"

Vigorously Laural shook her head.

Lord Strathouse chuckled. "Thou hast not seen the last of me, m'lady." He swung his palfrey toward the gate. "Good day, Laural."

As Laural watched him canter his horse away from her to join the others filing through the gate, she bemoaned her telltale face and treacherous heart. "Stuff and nonsense!" she muttered threateningly under her breath as she made her way back to the hall, not sure whether she referred to herself or to Strathouse.

As the days passed, Laural found her attempts to avoid Strathouse only succeeded in making him seek her out. She was rather startled to have Lord Cambraige relegate her to the table next to Lord Strathouse, where she was forced to share his trencher. With amusement he sliced the choicest bits of meat and held them for her to eat and sopped the softest pieces of bread for her. His constant attempts to cosset her angered and excited her, leaving her disconcerted and frustrated.

"Rise not in your stirrups," he whispered at the flash in her eyes to his latest teasing remark.

Laural closed her lips to keep a retort from leaving her lips. She had hardly been complaisant the last few days. And what of her mission to gain information for Black Hawk; Black Hawk who trusted her enough to give her this mission? Sighing, she took the morsel Strathouse held out for her. Despite this Norman lord's insufferable attentions, she would help Black Hawk. She had given her word, and woe betide anyone who got in her way.

That afternoon, Laural made her way to the chapel. There and only there would she find the peace to sort out her thoughts, her feelings about the Englishman who encroached on her day and invaded her thoughts even at night.

Only here could she excise his powerful pull on her inner being. Head bowed, she prayed silently for a return to some semblance of the composure she had fought so hard to regain. "Lord, what am I to do? I must not let feelings, any feelings for Lord Strathouse, keep me from my mission. I still don't understand why he stays. He does not appear to be under Lord Cambraige's thumb, and yet. . .there is something. Does he know something? Help me find out, Lord. And Lord Jesus, guard my heart." She must not allow her growing tendre for the handsome Strathouse to stay her from her chosen course.

Hiding away in the chapel had become such a habit, Laural reckoned not that the Norman lord would feel an attraction to the place not felt by Lord Cambraige.

His shoulder brushed hers as he knelt beside her in the wooden pew with its blue velvet-covered kneeling benches. Silently, Laural cried out. "Oh, Lord, may I not even here find peace from this man? What must I do to still his conspicuous interest?"

Her prayers were answered when the very next day, Strathouse bid her adieu. With good heart she wished him well, hoping not to see him again for many a day. Or did she? Her treacherous heart played her false as his fingers caressed her soft cheek.

"You'll not forget me, will you little Laural?"

"Nay, but you must go, m'lord."

He sighed, his eyes revealing a deep sadness. "Aye, that I must. The king is taking the queen to Caernarvon, then returning to Rhuddlan momentarily. My place be by his side," he paused, "for now." He brushed a kiss on her forehead. "I shall return Laural. Rest on it, I shall return."

Lord Cambraige jeered when he caught Laural staring after Lord Strathouse as he rode off. She retorted and felt the sting of his fist. "Keep a civil tongue in that head, wench, or I'll cut it out. Your gallant is no longer here to protect you."

Fury burst forth within her breast. With a hand to her face, Laural turned from Lord Cambraige's cruel laughter, muttering, "I shall bring you down, I shall."

Determined to outface Lord Cambraige and discover the complete truth about her father, Laural slipped around the castle like a shadow. Even so, it was a shock when she caught her guardian out.

She had not meant to eavesdrop as she walked past the small room off his first-floor bedchamber. Here, Lord Cambraige held court with his most trusted vassals. Realizing the heavy oak door was ajar, Laural trod quietly, not wishing to disturb Lord Cambraige in estate business. Suddenly she heard a name that made her stop and back quickly out of sight. Again she heard it, her father's name.

Straining to listen, she jammed her hand in her mouth. She must not make any sound that would give away her presence. Dazed, Laural listened in horror. Lord Cambraige's voice spoke up cold, and deliberate.

"We must plan most carefully. There be much at stake. Wentworth." Cambraige's voice grew deadly. "You will forswear your ale—it causes your lips to move much too freely. If you dally with me, Wentworth, you will find thyself at the far end of an accident not unlike Lord Comfrey's."

Laural bit her lip until it bled, not missing the whining oath of homage Lord Cambraige demanded of Wentworth. Then, one after another, the others too swore an oath of fealty to the traitorous lord. Lord Cambraige had admitted to her father's murder—boasted of it, in truth—but there was more.

Laural listened, her eyes growing wider. Surely she could

not have heard aright. But there, Lord Cambraige spoke again. "My cousins' deaths must needs be avenged. They must not have died in vain. Our dear King Edward must die! And with him, all English traitors to our name and blood!"

eight

The Lord shall preserve thee from all evil.
Psalm 121:7

❧

Hearing the strident voice of Mistress Haverman from down the hall, her heavy footsteps drawing ever closer, Laural swallowed the bitter gall rising in her throat, and turned back up the hallway. She must not be seen. Her face revealed far too much of the anger and pain she felt at the proof of Lord Cambraige's perfidy.

Even as she sought a refuge to examine her feelings, her face grew hard with determination. Laural sought the semi-obscurity of the formal gardens which were fragrant with the heady scent from a profusion of roses and columbines and other flowering plants. Overhead, birds chirped cheerfully in the trees. *As though,* Laural thought, *all was well.*

Laural sat down on a marble bench half hidden in the bushes and set her head on her hands. Fire burned in the eyes that usually looked out into the world with an unusual openness and innocence—an innocence that had been slowly changing in the realities of the brutal world she had been born into. No longer could she forswear her deep-rooted hatred of the man who had become her protector. No longer could she pretend all was well. No longer was her mission just an exciting adventure that touched her not. She now held information critical to the very life of her king. The thought brought sweat to her clenched palms.

"Forgive," she heard. She glanced around to find who spoke, only to realize the voice came from deep within.

"Forgive? Lord, I cannot, will not forgive that blackguard for what he has done. I do not yet know how he managed to attack my father when his men surrounded him, but I will discover the whole. Even You cannot expect me to forgive such a one."

"I forgave those who crucified Me."

A lump choked her throat. "But Jesus, Cambraige murdered my father in cold blood. He oppresses our people. If You are a God who cares, surely You do not wish Lord Cambraige to add Comfrey to his holdings. Forgive? I do not think so, Lord. . .not yet. I am not ready."

Fury burned fierce within her. Her stomach churned nauseatingly. "Black Hawk," she whispered, "I have something for you now. How may I reach you? Lord, please send him, send Black Hawk to me."

As much as she desired to see Black Hawk, he did not attend her. Her prayers begged, but Laural felt they dropped like lead to the floor. Night after night she lay stiff and still in her bedchamber listening, hoping, praying for the man to come to her. Her information burned in her, growing heavier with each day. Somehow she must warn the king of the plot against him.

For all her efforts, Laural learned nothing further as she waited for Black Hawk. Doubts filled her heart and mind. Had she run mad the night he appeared? Had her own desperate heart conjured him up to bring her the hope which day by day slowly drained from her.

Daily Laural knelt in the chapel. "Lord, even if You cannot help me, please save the king," she prayed. "Stay the hand of Lord Cambraige and his men at least until Black Hawk is able to discover the truth."

She bit her lip. Had he no confidence in her? Mayhap his mission for her was but a sop to test her loyalty. Laural clenched her fists in frustration. Indeed, she be loyal, but how to prove it? What must she do if Black Hawk did not come? "Please, Lord Jesus, make him return." Her thoughts turned to Lord Cambraige, and a cold, hard shell formed about her heart.

What if Black Hawk had been caught, tortured? The very idea chilled her. Would not she have heard?

Her head, it seemed, had scarcely touched the firm pillow when a growl from the doorway alerted her. "Leelah." Grasping her covers to her chest, she sat up.

"You're here! You're all right!" Her relief telegraphed itself to him.

"Aye, Leelah. But there are guards about. South tower," he growled and was gone.

Moments later, Laural, who had barely avoided being caught out by one of those guards, cautiously entered the dark tower. She jumped as a large hand cupped her face. A kiss brushed against her waiting lips.

"My dear," he murmured in his low rasping voice, "you missed me."

"I thought you would never come back. I was afraid. . ." Her voice trailed off at his low chuckle.

"I have a fondness for my lady's company."

Laural flushed in the darkness, but Black Hawk felt the hotness of her cheeks. "Ah, knowest thou," he said softly, "your father sought you a suitable match?"

Laural felt her face grow hot again as she acknowledged, "Aye, he pledged he would favor only a man upon whom I bestowed my favors. We had no chance to discuss the matter further because. . .because they murdered him."

Oh, Papa, if only you had listened and stayed at the castle instead of going out with Lord Cambraige that day!

Black Hawk held her close. "Lord Cambraige will seek

your hand, and your land."

"Nay, praise God. I disgust him, but he wants Comfrey."
Black Hawk heard the anxiety in her tone. "If only Papa. . .
if I wasn't as I am, mayhap Papa might have found a suitable mate."

"Aye, your father spoke of such womanish folly." He sensed
Laural's anger rise. "Don't be so easily cast down. He loved
you well, did he not?"

"He did," agreed Laural, knowing full-well most high-
born ladies had little or nothing to say in the man chosen for
them to marry. Marriages were arranged not by wont of the
compatibility of the two involved, but by the comparative
wealth and status to be gained. She stiffened at her visitor's
next words.

"Once he feared for your life, however, my Leelah." Black
Hawk paused. "He pledged your troth to keep you safe."

"No! He promised!" Laural quickly lowered her voice.

Beside her Black Hawk tensed. Laying a restraining hand
on Laural's shoulder he listened, awaiting some sign she
had been overheard. When no unusual sound disturbed the
night, he relaxed once more.

"I beg pardon," she breathed, "but I knew of no such
pledge. Who. . .who? Do you know. . .how could he? Papa
never broke a promise, and he promised I would hold my
husband in high esteem."

"Aye, Leelah." This time Laural sensed Black Hawk's
amusement. "I believe your father did not play you false."
Pausing, he growled dramatically. "Leelah, thou art pledged
to me."

Laural gasped. Black Hawk's hand quickly covered her
mouth, then released her. "How be this possible?"

Black Hawk stroked Laural's cheek. "Do you not favor me?"

"Aye, but only as a legend, a childish fantasy." She trembled under his hand.

She heard sadness in his voice. "I had hoped you would come to know me before I claimed your hand, but events have not fallen out to my satisfaction. In truth you belong to me, and in time, I will claim you as my wife."

Laural shook her head. The conversation seemed but a disordered dream, but then had not her whole existence since the death of her beloved father been so? "Thou knowest me not. Who am I to the great Black Hawk?"

"Think you so little of yourself? Or me? I know of your bravery when you told your father of the two English knights. I know of your dexterity with that dirk you always carry. Did you not once throw it at a mad dog, saving the son of one of your father's vassals? Ah, Leelah," Black Hawk's tender voice sounded near her ear, "I know much of my maiden-shy betrothed."

Laural stared at her amazing night visitor, but in the ebony darkness could see nothing of his visage. "You let my father pledge my troth, having never seen me?"

"Nay, Leelah, I have observed you many times." The gentle hand on her cheek made her shiver. "Your face is ever before me." He smiled, not adding that her innocence, bravery, and intelligence had quite disordered his mind, giving no quarter for any other woman's inviting eyes.

From the first moment he glimpsed her out riding, her hair whipping out behind her in the wind, her face aglow with excitement and the freshness of youth, his usually steady pulse had begun to pound along with the mare's hoofbeats.

Lord Comfrey, watching him through narrowed eyes, had said, "The maiden has not yet fixed her affections, so I trust you shall not dally with them. Truth to tell, I want you not to meet her. . .not yet."

The man had turned to his friend in amazement. 'Twas

unknown for a parent not to seek his favor, not to vigorously pursue his suit for an eligible daughter. Lord Comfrey's determination had intrigued him. "Might I be so bold as to inquire why?"

"There will be time later. Let me tell you of her." Only later had he understood his friend's tactics. Only when Black Hawk was surely caught did Lord Comfrey speak of his daughter's problem, but by then it did not matter. All he could see was Laural's face, her slim body leaning slightly forward over the withers of her large horse, her gown enhancing her slender figure.

Black Hawk shook his head and looked down at the young woman before him.

"Thou art Black Hawk's woman. Forget it not. Lord Cambraige shall in no wise take you from me." He paused. "But enough of this. Have you word for me?"

At his assurance, a weight fell from Laural, and unconsciously she straightened. Black Hawk sensed her relief. "You swear."

"Aye, m'lady. By the Holy Scripture, I swear."

"Thank you. Thank you." Tentatively, Laural reach out her other arm to her betrothed. He enfolded her in his long arms and held her close. She savored his kiss against her soft innocent lips, trembled in his arms. Wonderingly she closed her eyes.

Her contented sigh brought Black Hawk to his senses. She was, after all, an innocent. Gently he released her. "My dear," he said softly. "I came for another reason."

Laural pulled away and turned her head in humiliation. Black Hawk pulled her head back, his strong fingers under her chin. Brushing a kiss against her lips, he chuckled. "Turn not away, Leelah. There be time for us soon enough."

His voice shook. "Meeting is not safe, Leelah. For you

. . .or me."

"I had no right. . .I shouldn't have. . ." She stuttered out her hurt and humiliation at his rejection.

Abruptly she found herself caught in another embrace from her visitor. "I am not rejecting you, my Leelah." Black Hawk told her gently. "I must be strong for both of us, and we have many things we must discuss. Meeting you is becoming more difficult in the castle. Is there no other place to meet?"

"I am not watched as I was at Comfrey, but I fear Lord Cambraige has made certain I do not wander far." She hesitated. "I do walk in the garden. If I knew when you might come, I could contrive to be there."

"And take a chance of being overheard?"

"Possibly."

"I shall think on it, Leelah. Now, have you news for me?"

Pursing her lips, she recalled her mind to the matter at hand. With careful deliberation, she laid out for him all she had seen and heard. "There be six, mayhap seven, who are privy to Lord Cambraige's plans. The rest, I suspect, be mere pawns. I have been praying for the safety of the king." She added shyly, "Is there time to take action?"

"Cambraige is a careful man. He lays his plans with much care. Rest assured the king is safe for now. But," Black Hawk added, "I need to know the names of those who have given sword-oath to Lord Cambraige. Are there any, I wonder, who might overset the matter?"

"I heard Lord Cambraige warn Sir Wentworth against drinking too much ale, so he must have been in the room. Sir Wentworth speaks overmuch when in his cups. He might favor me with the names you need."

"Nay, Leelah, you must not put yourself in danger. Just keep those ears and lovely eyes of yours open."

She gripped his shoulders. "You're leaving then?"

Again he embraced her. "Aye, you know I must, but you are never alone."

"How can that be? I am alone." Her voice broke as her fear broke through. "Since Father, I am alone, all alone."

"No, Leelah. You are never alone. I know your father taught you differently."

"You mean Jesus is always with me."

"Quite so, Leelah."

"I. . .I don't know, Lord Black Hawk."

At his chuckle, she retorted, "What else am I to call you?"

"My beloved?"

This time she knew he teased. "Black Hawk!"

He drew her close. "Forgive me, my dear. Now, why do you doubt God's care?"

Licking her dry lips, Laural whispered, "Because I can't forgive Lord Cambraige."

She waited for his condemnation, but instead she sensed his warmth. "Ah, Leelah. Do you not know God loves you regardless. Neither of us will ever be perfect enough for His love. That's why He died on the cross. He took our hurt and our guilt and our sins."

"But He wants me to forgive." Tears choked her. "And I just can't, not yet. I hate Lord Cambraige for murdering my father."

"Of course you do, Leelah. Forgiveness, like love, is not a passing emotion. It is a daily, an hourly, a moment-by-moment choice."

"But I don't choose to forgive. I can't." Her anguished cry was cut off by Black Hawk's kiss.

"I beg pardon," she whispered, realizing how her raised voice had placed them in danger.

"Leelah. Give yourself time. Grieve for the loss of your

father, but also remember he is with the Lord. He would not want you to turn your back on your faith. God won't turn His back on you."

Laural choked back her tears. "I wish you were not going away."

"I must. Leelah, my love, I must inform the king of these things."

"You will return?"

"Aye, I'll return as soon as my way is clear." He turned at the distant scrape of metal against stone. "I have lingered too long, my love. I must go. Remember, do not put yourself in danger. You must obey me in this matter. And remember, too, God loves you. . .always."

"Aye, m'lord," sighed Laural. "I wish—"

"Ah, Leelah," Black Hawk held her hard against him, kissing her one last time. "You shall not be alone, I promise you. I'll be closer than you know."

Suddenly, he disappeared into the darkness. For a long while, Laural stared in the direction where Black Hawk had gone. She heard again the possessiveness in his voice. The great Black Hawk, her childhood hero, wanted her! And she loved him, loved him until her heart fair burst. How was it possible to love so completely, so quickly?

Her father had done right by her. A gentle smile on her lips, Laural hurried back to her chambers. Moments later she fell asleep, clutching a black feather in her hand.

≈

The next afternoon Laural sat in the great hall beside an unfinished wood table, drinking a mug of fresh warm milk. She was close enough to the great fireplace to feel its warmth. The plump matronly cook stirred the huge iron pot hung over the flames with a ladle too big for Laural to lift.

Maids and servants bustled about her. Some chopped

vegetables for the pot, others worked over a rough dough, another sliced huge portions of meat. In the corner two maids giggled. Suddenly catching the drift of the conversation, Laural strained to listen.

The taller of the girls giggled again. "Sir Adam still be makin' promises to her. Sayin' he be more than a mere knight anytime now."

"Jest talk, like as not," sneered the other girl.

"I overheard 'im meself," protested the first girl. "Said things be achangin' fer 'im. Goin' 'ave a fief of 'is own."

"How's that?"

"I know naught. Mum and all that or it bides ill for me."

At that moment the cook yelled, "To work you good-for-nothing wenches, or you'll feel the end of the whip."

Squealing, the two young girls hurried to their work, leaving Laural to muse over their words.

Thoughtfully, Laural found her way to Lord Cambraige's study, but she did not hear anything of any consequence. Discouraged, she wandered into the gardens, away from Lord Cambraige, whose temper grew more odious with each passing day, away from the tension which hung like thick fog over everyone.

Low voices drifted to her through the thick hedge. Hearing a chuckle she knew came from Lord Cambraige, Laural stopped. Lord Cambraige had not laughed in days! Listening closely, Laural identified the other man with him as Sir Wentworth, who had been oppressively correct in his behavior since Lord Cambraige's warning. Glad the hedge's thick leaves hid her from view, Laural edged nearer the bushes.

"Dear Lord, don't let them hear me," Laural prayed earnestly when she heard Lord Cambraige's next words.

"Fools! Witless fools the whole lot of them. David most of all for playing both sides. . .but unwisely."

Wentworth murmured a reply too low for Laural to hear. Afraid her harsh guardian might discover her presence, she made as to move on, her heart constricting at the very sound of his voice. Then she stopped. Was not this what Black Hawk wished of her? True, he said not to put herself in the path of danger, but if she remained motionless, who would know she was on the other side of the hedge?

Swallowing her fear, Laural kept listening. Had she not safely eavesdropped on Lord Cambraige previously? Might she not do this simple task as well? She had no more time for reflection as Lord Cambraige's words drew her undivided attention.

"Aye, Cousin David thought to once again beg the king's favor. I could not sanction his treachery. He knew far too much of my own ambitions, and it was much too soon, much too soon."

"Ah," Wentworth said as though suddenly realizing the full impact of his lord's words. "You betrayed your own cousin!"

Lord Cambraige laughed harshly, making Laural shiver. "I held little charity for my dear cousin. His punishment be just. Think what shock he must have felt to find himself surrounded by the hated English in his own country—in a bog, no less!"

"Snowdon. . ." Wentworth's words were too low for Laural to hear. But the one word reminded Laural that Llewelyn's brother, David, had been captured near Snowdon. He and his family were then hauled to Rhuddlan before David met his cruel end. Laural's heart went out to his family. She shivered at man's cruelty to man.

More than anything she wished to get away from the cold dangerous man across the hedge. Instead she closed her mouth firmly so as not to involuntarily give vent to her horror; to the bitterness that constricted her heart and mind against this monster who so casually deprived her of the one person who loved her most truly—her father.

Lord Wentworth's mumbling ceased, and Laural could hear Lord Cambraige's answer all too clearly.

"Aye, Lord Comfrey be a weak man. He had no intention of forswearing his sword-oath to the King, not even in practical matters, as do the other borderland lords. Until he came to power, rightly it was said, 'the king's writ does not run north of the Wye.'

"Comfrey, faugh! We be well rid of the likes of him. Much too honorable for my taste, or the taste of his fellow barons." He guffawed, "I take more than a fiefdom. I want the whole. I shall have either Comfrey's fief—without wedding that useless daughter of his—or the allegiance of he who holds it by my hand."

Laural covered her gasp with her hand, praying Lord Cambraige had not heard the minute sound. Was the man so sure of himself that he already was parceling out land not yet his own? Preposterous. Or was it? Had the odious lord promised her hand to one of his minions? She sickened at the thought. Trembling she pressed closer to the hedge.

"My plan is coming to fruition. Soon now the whole of the. . ." Lord Cambraige's voice trailed off as the two men moved farther away.

Straightening, Laural strained to hear more of their conversation, but to no avail. Thoughtfully, she contemplated the import of Lord Cambraige's unguarded words. She must let Black Hawk know this latest treachery. He must be told, but how? Her heart raced within her. Danger threatened her king, and once again she could but wait. Clutching her hands to keep them from trembling in frustration, Laural walked slowly back to the great hall.

nine

He shall preserve thy soul. Psalm 121:7

❧

Though she spent almost every evening in the gardens before retiring and lay awake night after night, Laural's restless nights were not disturbed by Black Hawk. Instead, to Laural's dismay, it was the enigmatic Lord Strathouse who returned to the castle.

Continually she felt his penetrating gray eyes following her, watching her. Her color rose as she disdainfully met his penetrating eyes, her defiance draining away into fear that he could somehow read her mind. She began to fear the sight of the large man with that knowing smile and discerning gaze.

Once more she found him beside her in the chapel. He walked the gardens with her at night. He escorted her on her rides. She was grudgingly grateful to the man for getting Cambraige to give her leave to leave the castle walls in his company. Riding past the guard on the delightful mare Strathouse chose for her brought a smile to her lips. 'Twas like escaping doom, albeit temporarily. Nonetheless, Lord Strathouse's penetrating questions and knowing gaze discomfited her, even as her heart betrayed her.

Pleading a headache, Laural planned on having a serving maid bring a tray to her bedchamber only to have Rosy come to her with Lord Cambraige's angry summons to appear before him in the great hall. Once again Laurel found herself tabled beside Strathouse, his eyes dancing in silent amusement. Laural clenched her teeth to keep herself from flying out at him.

"Be not wroth, m'lady," he said softly, holding out a tender chunk of deer meat dripping in thick gravy.

"Why," she whispered, "must you plague me so?"

"And I thought the lady desired the comfort of my presence."

Laural snorted. Her unladylike sound was covered by the noisy chatter about her. "*You* hold yourself too dear," she said sharply, then suddenly realized her twist on the words spoken by Black Hawk. For a moment her face softened.

The look did not escape Strathouse's sharp eyes. "So the lady has softer thoughts. A softer heart as well, mayhap?"

Laural straightened quickly, almost choking on the chunk of meat pie Strathouse stuck in her mouth at that moment. *On purpose,* thought Laural indignantly, grabbing her goblet to wash down the morsel. Glancing up, she once again witnessed a twinkle in her companion's eyes.

"You. . .you. . ." She could not go on, and while at table, there simply was no way that she could stop her companion's behavior.

After dinner, Laural turned deliberately from her companion to listen (with seemingly total absorption) to the minstrels who acted out their ballads as they strummed their lutes and sang of love. She hardly heard the words until her companion leaned toward her, a wicked smile on his lips. "So the maiden has a penchant for words of love. Has the maiden then fixed her affection?"

Laural turned to Strathouse in consternation, fearing his inquisitive eyes. How much did he know? How much did she reveal? With a gaucherie she had not shown for years, Laural nervously excused herself and hurried to her chamber.

In the dim flickering light of the single thick bedchamber

candle she carried up to her room, Laural tried not to tremble as she tore at the lacings first of her bliaut and then her gown. Throwing them onto the floor with the rage she could not show Lord Strathouse, she muttered, "He will not deceive me. I will not be gulled by his handsome face."

Laural stopped in the process of throwing her chemise onto the pile of clothes on the floor. "Handsome? Faugh!" she chided herself. "His face means nothing to me."

The next day, Lord Strathouse continued teasing Laural during meals. Angrily she sought out Lord Cambraige after the noon meal and demanded, "I thought you wanted me for yourself, so why are you throwing me to Lord Strathouse? Trust you his loyalty so much, my lord?"

The lord's cold survey of her angry person made her wish she had not approached him. What hope had she that he would favor her plight? "I will do with you as I see fit, Lady Laural. If Strathouse wishes your company, I see no reason to deny him what he, however misguidedly, wishes." He paused, then said cruelly, "You are certainly more than I can tolerate. I am in possession of your father's fief and your person. I need not your hand.

"I be sick unto death of your presence. If you wish to continue to have my favor, you will show Strathouse all the maidenly charms you may have, though I must confess, I have seen none." He added slowly, "You do understand. You will give Strathouse anything he wants."

Laural blanched, gulped. "He has spoken naught of pledging my troth," she breathed. "Or of marriage."

Lord Cambraige looked at her for a full minute before roaring a bone-chilling laugh. "Pledge your troth! You simpleton! Think you I would allow it? I will not give over your land to some greedy suitor. You are under my protection, m'lady. Never shall I allow you to marry, never! There shall be no legitimate heir to the Comfrey title, the Comfrey lands. Never! But you may ply your wares, few as they be, for his lordship."

"No!" cried Laural. "No, he wouldn't. He wouldn't!" She backed up, but Lord Cambraige jerked her face up with such force he wrenched her neck and left marks on her cheeks. "Hold your tongue, wench, or you will lose it." Lord Cambraige left her trembling, frightened, but as he walked away, her face darkened with determination. . .and hatred.

"To outface you, murderer," she hissed under her breath, "I would even lose my tongue, but woe betide the lackey who tries to bed me without priest."

Her wrath boiled, threatened to explode. Fearing she would vent her fury unwisely, Laural made for the heavy door of the great hall. She had to find a way to dissipate the fury wrenching her bitter heart. She had to find some inner peace. Mayhap in the chapel. . .

Even in the stillness of the sanctuary, Laural's heart pounded out her anger, an inner rage she was loathe to pour out before the God she had been taught to reverence with all her being. The words trembling on her lips were anything but holy. Rebellious thoughts consumed her.

"Lord God." she started again, "Our Father." Paused. "Faugh! Lord, I hate him. I hate Cambraige. He is a murderer. He is a monster most foul. How can You allow him to walk this earth when You took my good and dear father? What kind of God are You?" Her anger simmered, boiled over.

"Are you listening God? Black Hawk says You care, that You love me even if I don't forgive Lord Cambraige. But how can You even ask such a thing?"

"My Father asked it of me," came the quiet answer.

Laural stared at the cross over the altar. "How could You

forgive those dreadful people what they did to You?" she whispered.

"Because I cared for them as well. Hate is not an answer."

"You are a holy, majestic, just God. How can you permit men like Lord Cambraige to live, to murder good men— like my father, like the King!"

Silence filled the sanctuary, a silence filled with pain and questions and hurt. Finding no peace, Laural fled the chapel.

At the door of the great hall, Strathouse's mildly teasing voice sounded directly behind her. "Mayhap the lady needs company."

Taking her arm, he all but dragged her into the courtyard. Hailing a stableboy, he sent the lad off for his destrier and Laural's palfrey.

They waited without speaking, Strathouse keeping a grip on Laural's arm. Realizing it was senseless to struggle against his superior strength, Laural stood beside him, seething in anger. The boy ran back to them straightway, two fine animals dancing behind him. The boy held Strathouse's large, black horse while Strathouse helped Laural onto her more lightly built, but just as well-bred, chestnut mare.

The man's touch sent strange shivers of warmth through Laural, disconcerting her once again. His eyes told her he knew of her response and found it amusing. How she despised the man!

Furiously Laural kicked the mare into a canter and left his lordship to scramble onto his horse and thunder after her through the arched exit over the north gatehouse, over the lowered drawbridge, and down the path past the village. The guards watched their hurried exits with knowing smirks. Laural heard one whistling a bawdy tune as she passed.

Bending over the little mare, Laural let the wind whip past her bare head, tearing her hair free of its restraints. It trailed out gloriously behind her as she urged the mare forward.

As she felt the mare's body move beneath her, Laural admonished herself, *I love Black Hawk. Black Hawk needs me.* Then why, oh why, did Strathouse's presence so affect her?

When at last she slowed the mare, she found Strathouse riding along beside her. "Ah, m'lady, you ride as well as any man. 'Twas a fine gallop. Just what the black needed." He smiled down at her, the corners of his mouth turning up slightly in the teasing smile Laural so despised. "You cannot escape me, Lady Laural Comfrey," he said softly.

Laural studied her mare's tousled mane. How did he know? For some time they walked their horses side by side. Neither spoke. The air chilled slightly as the horses entered a wood. The path narrowed, but not enough to force Strathouse back as Laural had hoped. Branches slapped against her legs, but she made no complaint.

His voice startled her almost as much as his words. "You fear Lord Cambraige."

Despite her treacherous heart, Laural did not trust the man at her side. Did he wish to undermine her place in the castle? Not that it could fall much lower. "Aye," she said slowly, bitterly, "I hate him! I fear him."

"You do not trust him."

"Surely you jest! Trust him, I do not."

"Do you trust me more than you trust Lord Cambraige?"

"Aye, m'lord." She paused, then added, "For what that be worth."

"I am called Douglas, m'lady. Would you favor me with my name?"

Laural nodded. "Call me Laural." Her pet name flickered through her mind, bringing uncomfortable thoughts of Black

Hawk. For a moment, Laural studied her companion. Mayhap he would let something further of Lord Cambraige's plans slip.

"Ah," her companion said softly, watching her face closely, "that is not how your intimate friends speak to you, is it?"

Laural tensed. Color stained her pale cheeks. How much did he see in her face? How much did he discern from her actions, her words. She bit her lip in vexation. 'Twas a dangerous game she played. She must keep her mind clear. "Nay," she finally admitted, but explained nothing more.

Reaching over, Douglas lay a hand over hers as she held the reins. "Laural, whatever else you think of me, I wish you to be assured that under no circumstances will I hurt you. Can you trust me that far?"

Did she detect a hint of sincerity? Laural searched his face for the truth. "Aye, Lord Strathouse—Douglas—I trust you that far."

He smiled, giving Laural the distinct impression he knew exactly why she hesitated, why she did not trust him overmuch. His eyes bored deep into hers, making her catch her breath. Longing to go on staring into those deep gray eyes forever, she swayed toward him.

The swish of her skirts brought her to her senses. With a cry, Laural straightened. Grabbing up the reins, she urged the mare into a canter in order to free herself from Strathouse's mesmerizing presence. He was no longer that simple to dismiss, for her admission of trust had, in some strange way, put them on a more intimate basis. She chided herself soundly as she led the way back to the castle.

For the first time it seemed a haven rather than a prison, but only momentarily. Lord Cambraige striding in the bailey brought it all home again. She was a prisoner. He waited impatiently for Strathouse to hand her from her horse before addressing her.

"Lady Laural, my aunt is down with some womanish fever. You must take over for her. Women," he muttered, "such a bother."

"Will she be all right? I shall mix a potion of sorrel straightway."

"Nay, there is much for you to do. Let the other women take care of her."

Eyes flashing, Laural faced the ponderous man. "Think you so little of your aunt? Have you no compassion?" Fury built until she heeded not her tongue. "'Tis no wonder you've lost three wives."

She never saw the blow which lifted her off her feet and sent her flying. Her last coherent thought was of warm arms carrying her. She awoke with a dreadful headache, but Lord Cambraige, brooking no excuse, had her roused from her bed to attend the household duties. If only she could learn to hold her tongue around the man.

Nursing a sore head, she busied herself with the myriad of chores handled dispassionately, but efficiently by Mistress. Haverman. Laural relished overseeing the household— from making candles, to overseeing the meals and, of course, the servants. She was kept too busy to do more than give general directions to those in charge of the various areas. Had she the time before Mistress Haverman's recovery, she hoped to have the castle gone over top to bottom.

As at Comfrey, Laural eagerly awoke, or would have but for her sore head. The wound on her forehead gave mute testimony of Lord Cambraige's method of obtaining obedience.

After dressing, Laural attended morning prayers. If she had time, she grabbed a biscuit and a swallow of cider to break her fast before instructing the servants on their duties for that day. She helped plan hunting forays and other festivities—anything to brighten the gloom of the dark castle.

At Lord Cambraige's specific orders, she did not oversee the accounts or meet with the steward. Neither Lord Cambraige nor his aunt trusted her overmuch, and she often felt his eyes upon her. Strathouse, too, seemed to bide his time, leaving her to her assumed duties, though he did inquire about her health.

"Dost thou still suffer headaches?" he asked, gently running a finger across the dark puckered wound.

"I fear so. I understand 'twas you who carried me to my chambers. I. . .I thank you."

"Umm. Small thing to do, m'lady." He spoke lightly, but his eyes glinted dangerously as they glanced toward Lord Cambraige.

That look buoyed her. Surely Strathouse could not be in league with Lord Cambraige and wish him such ill. Yet while there appeared little love lost between Lord Cambraige and his aunt, Laural well knew that Mistress Haverman was completely loyal to her nephew.

Lord Strathouse drew Laural's attention once more. "Little Laural," he whispered, "I should have taken better care of you."

Her heart soared to dangerous heights. Gulping at her traitorous feelings, Laural pled work and rushed away.

Even in the darkness of her bedchamber later that night, while Laural prayed for Black Hawk to come to her, she could not put away the teasing image of Lord Strathouse, Douglas.

"Lord, help me!" she cried, staring upward into the darkness. "Help me be a true liege woman to my betrothed, to my king." She prayed and pleaded until a measure of peace stole over her.

Laural's position was quite untenable, but Black Hawk would come and would make everything right. She was certain his presence would banish the image of Strathouse from her mind. But, she wondered uncomfortably, could she banish it from her heart?

The next morning Mistress Haverman again took up the reins of the household with not a word of thanks to Laural. She showered Laural with rude jests and disparaging comments. More than once Laural turned to find herself being observed by the woman whose sharp eyes were filled with intense hatred.

That afternoon, Lord Strathouse proposed a sedate ride with Laural rather than follow Lord Cambraige's hunting party. "I shall be delighted if you would grace my ride with your presence, m'lady."

Reluctantly, Laural raised her eyes to his, then blushed at the depth of feeling she found there. Blushing more furiously she glanced away. "Lord Cambraige—"

Strathouse waved his hand in dismissal, only to drop it as Laural flinched. "I would never strike you, Laural. Never!" Slowly he raised his hand to cup her chin. "If I could but take you away from all this."

Laural's eyes widened, then dimmed as he let the though dangle. "But you won't. I understand."

"You understand nothing!" he hurled back harshly. "There are matters of which you cannot know."

"Try me," she challenged.

Something flashed in his eyes, then disappeared. Deliberately he baited her. "How shall I try thee, maid?"

He caught her hand mid air. "I wouldn't, you know. 'Twas in jest, I spoke." Turning over her hand, he kissed the palm. Sparks radiated from her hand to the vicinity of her heart.

"Lord Strathouse!" she protested, snatching back her hand.

"Don't tempt me then." His eyes flashed a warning. "And don't try that again."

"Or you'll beat me as does Lord Cambraige?" She cringed at the depth of her own bitterness.

"Do you truly believe me to be capable of such behavior?"

Silently she shook her head and watched a smile tug at the corners of his lips. "And you apologize?"

"Aye," she sighed.

The smile broadened. "Then your penance is to ride with me this afternoon. 'Twill give you the chance to be rid of a certain overbearing shadow."

Laural glanced up in surprise. "You noticed Mistress Haverman, then."

"Quite. She mislikes you mightily. I might add that, but for my own interference, Lord Cambraige's own somewhat backhanded protection could well have been withdrawn."

"Then I am in your debt, m'lord."

"Umm." His fingers felt the heat of her soft cheek. "I shall remember that, but for now, m'lady, we ride."

Strathouse led the way through the wood to a quiet spring. From what Laural had heard at the castle, Lord Cambraige was a harsh master who bled his people and his land. Even in the wood, his influence was felt by the presence of woodwards who guarded the area from peasants. The penalty for taking anything from the wood without permission was death. Even on such a fine day, Laural's thoughts of Lord Cambraige's brutality stole her peace and made her feel imprisoned.

Closing her eyes, she made a concerted effort to forget Lord Cambraige for the afternoon. It was hard to think about him when the sun caressed the earth. A gentle breeze kept the heat from being oppressive, while before them the spring bubbled invitingly.

Strathouse pulled up his destrier, swung smoothly to the ground, and left his horse bending down to tug at the tufts of sweet meadow grass. With a teasing smile, he put up his hands to span Laural's tiny waist. Reluctantly she let him help her from the saddle, hoping he did not realize the unsettling effect his touch had on her.

When he did not at once remove his hands, Laural moved from the circle of his light embrace. Chuckling, Strathouse released her, only to take her arm and guide her over the rough ground to the spring. With a sweeping gallantry which made Laural smile, Strathouse removed his cloak and spread it over the flat gray rock beside the stream. He bowed low. "For you, m'lady."

Entering into his bit of silliness, Laural curtsied. "Most gallant of you, m'lord."

Strathouse pulled her down beside him on the covered outcropping. As they sat in silence, the warm sun beamed down its warmth, making Laural drowsy. About her she heard the raucous call of a jay, the scream of a badger some ways distant, the soft swish of leaves overhead.

Gently Strathouse put his long arm around Laural and laid her head on his shoulder. His deep voice sounded pleasantly in her ear. "Laural, about Lord Cambraige."

"I don't want to think of the dark castle today," she murmured.

"The dark castle, is it? Aye, 'tis indeed the dark castle." As though debating with himself, he stared down at the soft woman on his arm. "As you wish, m'lady. For now, nothing exists but God in His heaven and us. Let me tell you then of King Edward's court."

"Please do."

Secure in the circle of his arm, she enjoyed listening as he regaled her with sad, sometimes amusing, stories. Leaning on his shoulder, she envisioned the opulence, colors, and pageantry. She could almost see the elegance of the lords and ladies who graced the court. She laughed at the human foibles and at Douglas's rueful voice as he talked of them.

"Do you not like the court?" asked Laural, glancing up at her companion's strong face. "It sounds so grand."

"I admire the king and his lovely queen," countered Strathouse, avoiding a direct answer.

"You would not betray him?"

At Douglas's hesitation, Laural's heart sank, and she sighed in disappointment. Strathouse pulled her closer. Her heartbeat quickened. Without answering her question, he began to relate a story about the king that she had not yet heard.

"Before Edward became king, he went on a crusade to the Holy Land. Our good queen, but a princess then, accompanied Edward. When Edward was poisoned by his enemies, it is said she herself cut the wound and sucked out the poison."

"Did she truly do that?" Eyes wide, Laural looked up at her companion for confirmation.

Strathouse shrugged. "Others say she wanted to, but that actually the doctors tended him. The queen refused to leave her husband's side. They had to drag her from the tent."

Laural sighed deeply. "I've heard she accompanies him wherever he travels. She loves him. . .really loves him, I mean. And does he truly care for her?"

"Aye," Douglas's arm tightened about Laural. "Edward never looks at anyone else. Even now, after all these years, they are besotted with each other."

"Truly." Laural leaned away from Douglas to examine his face. "Be he a faithful man—be the king faithful to his wife?"

"Quite." Douglas glanced down at Laural with some

amusement. "That meets with your approval, I trust."

"Of course," retorted Laural. "I had heard it told, but I could scarcely credit what I heard. . ." Her words trailed off.

Douglas laughed. "Some mates are faithful, Laural, even in court circles."

Laural observed his countenance thoughtfully. "And you?"

Douglas chuckled. "I be not wed, m'lady." Leaning over, he kissed Laural lightly.

Closing her eyes, Laural responded to his kiss. When it deepened, she abruptly pulled away. Her face flooded with humiliation and embarrassment. "Nay!" she cried her voice breaking in consternation. Her hands covered her burning cheeks.

Douglas surveyed her distraught face. "There be another." It was not a question.

Her face averted, Laural nodded. "I'm sorry," she whispered, then added, "You frighten me."

Douglas pulled her stiff body close to his side again. "Why is that, little Laural? What dost thou fear?"

"At times you seem to know what is in my mind. I fear. . ." When she did not continue Douglas spoke firmly.

"Tell me plainly, Laural, what dost thou fear from me?"

Laural tried to squirm from his hold, but he held her firmly. "Tell me, now," he commanded.

"Lord Cambraige. . ." She began so quietly that Douglas had to bend closer to hear her. "He believes you wish to. . . to dally with me, nothing more."

"And you. Believe you this?"

Laural shrugged. "I know not. But Lord Cambraige will not give me to wed, only to—"

"Fustian!" The word exploded from Douglas, his face hard with anger. "Do you think that of me? Do you?"

Laural trembled under his rage, her own rising. "What do I know of you? You came to Cambraige Castle. I be no fool—you have business with Lord Cambraige. Knowing his character, tell me, m'lord, tell me something to ease my doubts. How else may I know the complete truth? Lord Cambraige made it clear no man would want me for else."

"No one, Laural?" the question was spoken softly, but Laural heard. The image of Black Hawk flashed in her mind. He wanted her, wanted her because she could help him, wanted her because her father had pledged her to him. But did he truly want her as a wife? Did he truly love her?

The question startled her and her face paled. Her lips tightened. Whatever Black Hawk's reasons, never, never must she betray him. Twould be the same as betraying her father.

Douglas watched the emotions play across her face. "I will not hurt you, Laural," he said quietly. "I will not force your secrets, but you must take care others know not there is more to you than a childish face and a childish innocence.

He paused "Would you betray me, Laural?"

Plucking up a yellow wildflower, Laural picked at its petals. "I know not. If lives were at stake. . ." She glared down at the mashed stem in her hand.

Douglas sighed. Holding her close, he rested his chin on her head. For some time they sat together silent, contemplative. In the silence Laural felt him reach out and bind her to him. Even here, despite their resolve, evil intruded.

His possessiveness frightened as well as drew her. While she desired to stay by his side, she knew she must break away from his hold over her. After all, Douglas, Lord Strathouse, was friend to Lord Cambraige.

What she found difficult to accept was the thought that he was party to Lord Cambraige's evil schemes. But was he? Laural could not believe that of the gentle man beside her.

Yet. . .

Intentionally Laural forced herself to remember her betrothal to the legendary Black Hawk. Reaching up, Laural traced the lines of Douglas's face. It would be so much easier to care for a man she could see than to love a man who was but a phantom of the night.

Douglas gazed deep into her eyes. Afraid of what he might find revealed in their depths, Laural forced herself to look away. He must not discover Black Hawk. Whatever her treacherous heart did, she must not trust Douglas over much, must not risk the life of either Black Hawk or her king. Danger lurked here in the quiet forest as it had in her father's wood.

Had not her father given Lord Cambraige too much trust? Did he not suspect treachery from the lord whose insolent arrogance had always filled her with dread? Yet her father had trusted him enough to ride into the forest on the hunt with him. Trusted overmuch—and died for it.

Laural hardened her heart against the man beside her. She must not let him get too close, must not let him thaw the protective shell about her heart. Must not!

Yet with Douglas's arm warm about her shoulders, danger seemed so far away. If only she could trust him. Desperately she wanted to open herself up to him, to someone who cared. It had been so long since she had felt warm inside.

Several times, Laural opened her mouth to tell him what she was about, but she could not bring herself to do so. Soon enough she was glad she had not.

ten

Unto thee lift I up mine eyes,
O thou that dwellest in the heavens. Psalm 123:1

The next few days, Lord Strathouse endured ribald jests for "dallying with" a no-account child-woman rather then pursuing the ill-concealed charms of a local wench or the manly pursuits of hawking and hunting. Laural watched in silence, hating the uncouth behavior of Lord Cambraige's vassals, who found nothing better to do than guzzle ale and chase the village girls and deride Lord Strathouse.

Douglas's composure over the matter infuriated her, and she was not loath to speak her piece as they once again loitered beside the spring.

"Do you not care that they believe you're in your dotage because you favor me with your attentions? Most of Lord Cambraige's men ignore me as a child or shrink away in disgust like their lord. Then there is Mistress Haverman." Laural shook her head.

"She spies on you and reports everything you do to his lordship."

"Aye," Laural ground out. "I feel as though her eyes are daggers aimed at my back. She thinks you are mad to favor me." Turning, Laural searched Douglas's face, her eyes following the line from his strong jaw to the twinkle in his eyes.

Douglas smiled down into Laural's flashing eyes. "Look you to my defense, m'lady?"

"You don't defend yourself." Laural frowned as an unexpected

107

thought assailed her. "Unless," she continued slowly, "it matters not they besmirched not only your manhood, but also my virtue."

The amusement on Strathouse's face faded into such a cold wrath, Laural shivered and pulled away. "Surely you've heard them." She did not hold back the bitterness. "Lord Cambraige thinks to use me as a pawn in his schemes. You know he holds my fief and my person. I have every intention of freeing Comfrey from his heavy hand."

Pulling back his long flowing sleeves, Strathouse surveyed her thoughtfully. "Womanish folly. Leave such things to your guardian."

"Womanish folly, is it!" She shrugged away from Strathouse's arm. "A woman should be no less concerned for the rights of her people than a man. Think you I be some half-wit, an unreasoning mongrel able only to fawn on whoever throws a bone?"

"I did not say so."

"I thought you to be different, Lord Strathouse. "'Tis a surprise you favor me then, unless you have your eye on Comfrey."

The silence gave her the answer she sought. "For Comfrey," she whispered, "you would allow your manhood to be called into question and my virtue cast in doubt."

Eyes narrowing ominously, Lord Strathouse wrapped his long arm tightly about Laural's tense shoulders and pulled her against him. "Speak plainly. Who has spoken so far amiss in your hearing?"

Laural trembled at his anger, not knowing at whom it was directed, but fearing it was aimed at her.

His grip tightened painfully. "You must tell me. Who dared speak thus to you?"

"I. . .I overheard Sir Wentworth and Sir Adam argue about

us. They lay odds as to when you will. . ." She stuttered. "As to your true intentions."

Strathouse understood. "I see. 'Twas that all?"

Silence grew as Laural tried to frame the words. "They believe Lord Cambraige has bartered me for your loyalty."

"Do you think I would so easily be gulled?"

Afraid to voice her fear, Laural shrugged. What exactly did he mean? Did he think she worth so little? Or his loyalty so great?

Douglas broke the uneasy silence. "What troubles you, Laural?"

Stubbornly Laural shook her head, but he forced her answer. "You have been most attentive, m'lord. I know my humble person may mean little to you, but—"

"What fustian! Humble? Have you run mad? After alternately defending then raging at me, now thou art humble?"

Laural blinked her eyes to keep the tears at bay. What a green goose she must seem. "Leave me alone."

"Why?"

"You confuse me. You infuriate me. Oh, I don't know."

Hearing her hesitation, he cupped her chin and forced her face to him. The breeze sifted through her hair, leaving his hand tingling where it brushed against her skin. The hurt in her eyes pained him.

"Nothing wrong? Then why the tears?" With his thumb he wiped the single tear making its way down her cheek. "What foolishness be this?" Beholding the stark misery on the young woman's face, Douglas hastily reviewed his statements. What had he said to effect such misery?

"You misunderstand, Laural," he said softly, caressing her arm. "I would never barter with Lord Cambraige for you. I am with you now because 'tis what I wish. You are in my thoughts day. . .and night."

Laural gasped. Her mind flew to the night visits of Black Hawk, but he had not visited her chambers for many a night. Nor had he found her in the dark of the gardens. In truth, his visits seemed some far-off dream. Though she knew differently, at times she wondered if her own longing for love had conjured up her childhood fantasy. When Douglas leaned down and covered her lips with his own, she did not resist.

For an eternity she drowned in his embrace. Her arms stole about his neck. The warmth of his arms began to thaw the hard shell about her heart. Mayhap Douglas cared for her, for herself. She had nothing else to offer him. Nothing but Comfrey. And only that by Lord Cambraige's leave.

Abruptly Black Hawk's claim on her sounded so loudly in her mind that it startled her with its clarity. *You belong to me.*

With a cry, Laural pushed away from Douglas with such force she would have tumbled backward into the spring had he not caught her. "Laural, what is it? What have I done?"

His very words conjured up Black Hawk's rasping voice speaking tenderly. Tears started in Laural's eyes as she stared up in anguish at Douglas. "I can't," she said brokenly. "I just can't." Then she broke into sobs.

How could she be so faithless to the man her father had chosen for her; the man who declared her as his own? Had her father himself not betrothed her to the legend?

And what of Douglas? Who was he? Was he the king's loyal liege man? Surely he was not like Lord Cambraige!

Black Hawk. Oh, Black Hawk how can you desert me when I need you so much? But it was not Black Hawk who held her as she cried. She did not witness the tender frown on the face of the man who soothed her.

❧

Later that evening, Laural rubbed every trace of tears from her face in the cool water brought up for her by the young serving girl. Even as she did, her thoughts returned to the tenderness Lord Strathouse had shown her. How different he was from the rest of those in the castle.

Once she had collected herself, he had dipped his linen square into the stream which meandered by and wiped her cheeks so gently that tears started in her eyes again.

His gentle teasing dried them speedily, and his light tone helped her regain her composure. 'Twas not until he returned her to the castle that she recalled he had never fully satisfied her doubts about his motives.

He was kind and caring. Did the rest matter? Aye, it mattered a great deal, Laural decided. Pressing her lips firmly together, she determined to quell her growing affection for Douglas. Two could play his game. That is, if one knew the rules.

Laural moved to the window and stared out over the wide courtyard. Below a horse stomped his feet and flicked his tail at the flies buzzing about. Overhead, clouds obscured the sun, and a distinct chill felt like the herald of danger.

With a self-deprecating laugh, Laural left the window. Stepping out of her afternoon gown, she dressed carefully for the evening meal in a scarlet gown over a white silk chemise. Scarlet ribbons bound her hair.

She smiled as she looked down at herself. A change of gown did wonders for her spirits. Straightening her shoulders, Laural made her way down the narrow circular stairs to the great hall where Lord Strathouse waited.

Pausing just inside the door, she breathed, "Help me, Lord. Help me from making a fool of myself over the man."

She found Mistress Haverman's eyes upon her. The woman hunched slightly forward as though waiting to catch Laural

in some misdeed. Her look gave Laural pause, and for a
moment panic vied for place within her.

Did the woman knew about Black Hawk? Did Lord
Cambraige? Were they waiting for her to make a mistake?
Was Lord Strathouse's role to discover the depth of her will-
ingness to betray Lord Cambraige?

Her mouth dry, Laural ruthlessly quelled her nagging
doubts. Lifting her skirts, she stepped toward the dais where
Lord Strathouse waited. Unfortunately before she sat down,
her leg twisted and she fell heavily against Lord Cambraige.

Cursing, he grabbed her hair and snapped back her head.
Her back arched so far, Laural was certain it would break,
and she struggled for balance. Lord Cambraige's foul breath
as he cursed her mightily wafted in her face, making her
faint. Instinctively she lifted her hands to ward him off.

"Thou wilt pay for touching my person, wench." With a
vile oath, he flung her away from him toward Strathouse.
"Earn your fiefdom. Take the wench, if you are man enough."

Laural wanted to run away from the raucous laughter that
followed this exchange. Fury fired inside her even as a part
of her curled away in hurt. Another layer formed about her
heart.

Strathouse held her fast, his arm guiding her to her seat
on the side away from Lord Cambraige. "Dost thou doubt
my manhood?" His eyes narrowed in challenge. "Lord
Strathouse is a name not unknown on the lists, if anyone
should wish to challenge me."

"Nay," barked Lord Cambraige. "'Tis not the time, or the
place. M'lord," he acknowledged with a curt bow, "there
are more pressing matters."

Beside her, Laural felt Lord Strathouse relax. "As you
say, Cambraige. We shall settle this another time. Mean-
while," his voice was dangerously quiet, "keep your hands

off Lady Laural."

The two men glared at each other for an eternity before Lord Cambraige reddened, then glanced away. "As you wish. For now."

The evening meal dragged on interminably. Tension between the two men crackled like the huge hearth fires. Before the men left the table, Laural excused herself to the garden.

"Lord, send Black Hawk to me. Please send him."

Looking up into the night sky, Laural marveled at the beauty of the stars twinkling against the palpable soft blackness. The half moon caught the hedge in its silvery beams and edged the flowers in silver. Breathing deeply, Laural detect the sweet scent of flowers among the odor of greasy food and the stench of stalls that needed to be mucked out.

Sauntering toward the far end of the garden, Laural stopped. Had she heard footsteps? Was Black Hawk going to meet her after all?

When she stopped, all sounds behind her stopped abruptly. A moment later, she heard the twittering of a bird and the scratching of some small animal in the hedge. Shaking her head, Laural cautiously started forward. Again she heard the surreptitious footfalls from somewhere behind her. Again she stopped. Again silence.

Her spine prickled with fear. Slowly she turned, but she faced only darkness. If only she dared call out his name, but surely Black Hawk would not jest so.

Picking up her skirts, Laural hurried around the end of a hedge and doubled back. Stopping she waited, hidden by an overhanging tree. She had not long to wait. Moonbeams turned Mistress Haverman's face into a nightmare of menacing crags.

Sucking in an icy breath, Laural tried to still her trembling.

There was something deadly about the woman. Something about her frightened Laural as Lord Cambraige never had. Closing her eyes, Laural prayed the woman would not discover her, but that prayer, too, was denied.

"Do you think you can hide your secrets from me?" The woman's hold on her arm made Laural wince.

"Secrets?" Laural tried to sound amused. "A mere stroll in the garden. How fanciful you are." Snatching back her arm, she brushed by the woman, quelling the impulse to cringe at the very touch of the woman's robe.

Hurrying back to the great hall, Laural was disappointed to find that Lord Strathouse and Lord Cambraige had already left. She was appalled to discern the depth of her feelings for Douglas. For a time, she idled in an alcove of the great hall awaiting his return. Settling into the cushioned seat on the left of the table with its marble top, she idly fingered the cool marble of the chess playing pieces.

A young knight, whose face still held more than a hint of boyishness, challenged her. "You play?"

Laural smiled, "Do you wish to challenge me to a game?"

The young knight colored slightly, "You are but a. . ." He hesitated as though he did not trust the truth of his words. "A maiden."

"Aye," Laural affirmed firmly, another cold layer against Lord Cambraige shelling her heart. "Fear you to game with a maiden?"

Color rose in the young man's cheeks, but this time it heralded from anger. He bowed hishead sharply. "Be not wroth then, m'lady, when I check your king, for you gall me into the challenge." With that he sat down on the bench opposite her and commenced the play. Laural played with a slight smile, the light of determination in her eyes. The young knight grew sullen as she outmaneuvered him again and again, finally taking his king in a brilliant move.

Acknowledging his defeat with a nod, the young knight pushed himself to his feet. "Remind me not to gamble with you, m'lady." he said.

"Don't concern yourself," she told him. "I only play games of skill."

Walking away stiffly, he yelled for his squire. Laural watched him go, her tongue solidly in her cheek to keep from giggling at his deflated ego. That indeed would not be seemly.

As no one else wished to challenge her, Laural idly moved the pieces about the heavy board. Gradually the noisy chatter of the hall died down. Lords and ladies took themselves off to their chambers. Others shoved the long benches against the walls and rolled up in their pallets on the benches or on the floor at the far side of the large chamber.

Yawning, Laural thought drowsily about going to her own bedchamber, but her legs moved woodenly. She leaned back against the bench. *I'll move in a little while. Surely, Douglas will return by then.* She yawned and closed her eyes. Laural slept, her head pillowed softly against the side of the alcove.

Sometime later she awoke with a start. Shadows played over the large hall from the banked fire in the hearth and from the few smoking torches guttering in their holders on the far wall. Only a few voices sounded quietly against the silence of the night. Reluctantly she stretched out her legs beneath the table, wondering ruefully how long she had slept.

As Laural moved to slide out of the darkened alcove, Lord Cambraige's raised voice made her hesitate. Dare she leave now? She had no desire to incur her self-proclaimed guardian's ire. Stilling a sigh, Laural scooted far back into the alcove, praying Lord Cambraige would tire straightway and get himself off to bed.

His next words grabbed her attention, chilled her. She strained forward to listen as Lord Cambraige spoke. "The queen has been delivered of a son at the castle at Caernarvon."

"Son!" Sir Adam exclaimed, dismayed.

"Aye," said another voice that Laural identified as belonging to Sir Wentworth. "A healthy son. Not like Prince Alfonso, who there is little likelihood will attain manhood. Despite all the treatments he undergoes, he is getting weaker, but they say the new babe is healthy. He could soon be the crown prince."

"The crown prince and heir to the throne of England and Wales." Lord Cambraige's tongue then let loose such a string of foul obscenities, Laural's ears burned. She trembled at his bitter hatred.

The oaths cut off abruptly as Lord Cambraige turned to another member of his select group. "Where be the king now?"

The calm sound of Douglas's voice brought a smile to Laural's lips. "At Rhuddlan. It be said he knighted the Welshman who brought him the news. He is even now preparing to depart for the castle at Caernarvon to see the queen and his newborn son."

Lord Cambraige's voice rose triumphantly. "The time be now! We go to Caernarvon."

Several men spoke up simultaneously. Laural discerned little sense in the prevailing confusion. "Enough, gentlemen!" Douglas's command spoken low but firmly silenced the voices.

Laural choked back a chuckle at how easily he handled the other men. Her smile froze as Lord Cambraige spoke. "We will gain entrance into the castle easily enough. As a small advance party coming to celebrate the new prince, you will not be suspected of foul play. Once in the great hall where all will be congregated, you will take the king."

Wishing she could see whom Lord Cambraige addressed, Laural waited tensely.

"With the assistance of the king's knights already in my pay, the resulting confusion will assure our victory," continued Lord Cambraige. "After dispatching his royal highness, you will take the good queen hostage. Later both she and the young whelp will die," Lord Cambraige finished in a savage snarl.

Laural shivered at the sheer malice of his words, but the next speaker shook her to the core of her being. Instinctively she stuffed her fist into her mouth to keep from crying out.

The speaker was her gentle Douglas, but there was naught but hardness in his cold, practical words. "I gave sword-oath to Edward, and he believes me to be his man, his lackey. 'Twould be folly for any but myself to lead the advance force. I stand in the presence of the king. I am the only one who can walk right up to him—a quick stab and the deed will be done.

"As for the queen, she is beloved of the people. Better to curry her favor than to murder her outright. Mayhap wed her. Thankfully you have no wife, Cambraige."

"Didst thou think I would take your unfortunate wench, Strathouse? Not when I have more important objectives. Keep her for thyself, as long as you do not wed her."

For a heartbeat, Laural heard only silence. Then a low chuckle chilled her. "Comfrey is not yours by the King's leave yet, Cambraige."

"Aye, Strathouse. Not yet." His cold hard laugh made Laural tremble.

As though conversing about the weather, Lord Strathouse

continued, "As to the matter at hand. . ."

"Ah, the loyal queen. What of her?"

"Threaten her," said Strathouse flatly. "Threaten her not only with the death of the new prince, which, of course, must be done, but also the deaths of all her other children."

Swallowing, Laural tried to dislodge the lump that grew in her throat, threatening to choke her. She must not reveal her presence. If Lord Cambraige realized she knew of his diabolical plans he would surely kill her. Would Douglas stop him? What good was she to Black Hawk? What did it matter when Douglas's betrayal tore at her?

Tears prickled Laural's burning eyes. With dismaying suddenness she perceived that somehow her well-defined defenses had cracked, had begun to crumble under Douglas's gentle onslaught.

Dear God! How could I have been so mistaken about him? Laural closed her eyes against the pain shredding the warmth that had so recently begun to melt the cold shell about her heart. When did she come to love him so much? Did she not love her betrothed? *Why did you fail me, Jesus? How could You have let this happen? Make them go away, Lord. Make them all go away.*

Laural wished the voices would be silent, the men would leave, so she might slip upstairs. For Black Hawk's sake, she listened. Hardening her heart against Strathouse's perfidy, her eyes flashed. She lifted her chin in determination. So he would toy with her, would he?

Black Hawk. Did Black Hawk truly care for her? Did it matter when the kingdom was at stake? What did matter was that she trusted Black Hawk as he trusted her. The phantom figure held her heart. Laural bit down on her lower lip painfully. Aye, she loved her tender nighttime visitor.

Lord Cambraige's henchmen finally broke ranks and, with

ale-soaked laughter, left the table. Their voices grew fainter as they climbed the stairs to their bedchambers. Now was her chance to escape to her own chamber, but before she could move, Douglas stood beside the alcove, his face twisted in anger. Grasping her arm, he yanked her to her feet, causing Laural to turn frightened eyes to this horrifying stranger.

Pulling her from the alcove, Douglas hustled her up the stairs to the door of her narrow bedchamber. "Lovest thou death so much?" he murmured angrily as they stood in the darkened hallway. "Even I could not prevail on Cambraige to spare your life should he learn of your presence tonight!"

Anger and something else she could not identify rippled his tone. Surely it wasn't fear. . .for her?

"I have no intention of sending a maid to you this night," Douglas continued. "You must manage on your own. Until the morrow then."

Her temper rose. "Think you I would allow a traitor to touch me!"

The muscle on Douglas's face twitched. He grabbed her shoulders. "Think you this is some game I play? Take care Laural, for this is much larger than you know." Even as he spoke, he released her, the fury in his eyes warming to a certain tenderness.

She struggled against the warmth spreading through her, turning her treacherous legs to water. Strathouse's arms held her up. When he released her, she stared up at him in confusion. "What do you want from me?"

Strathouse chuckled softly. "You are mine. Do not forget. You are mine!" Nodding curtly, he left Laural staring after him in the light of the single candle guttering in the wall sconce some maid had lit earlier.

eleven

Have mercy upon us, O Lord, have mercy upon us:
for we are exceedingly filled with contempt.
Psalm 123:3

❧

"Lord," Laural cried, "Where is Black Hawk? I need him."
Tears streaming down her face, Laural hurried from her
chamber to the privacy of the south tower where she could
weep without being overheard. Never had she felt so hu-
miliated. Never had she felt so shamed. Pacing back and
forth, Laural hugged her arms to herself against the night
chill as she cried, "Is he ever returning, Lord?"

Then, when she least expected him, he materialized. Instinctively, Laural reached out for Black Hawk. In silence
he crushed her slender form to his chest while she quietly
wept against him.

After a time, she struggled to explain, struggled to let
him know all she had overheard, struggled to tell him about
Strathouse. "How could he?" she moaned softly, knowing
she must not make much noise.

"Have you affection for him then, Leelah?" Black Hawk
spoke in his low rasping voice. She wondered at his strange
tone.

Gulping back her tears, Laural choked out. "I. . .I thought
so. But I love you as well. How can this be?" she said in
anguish. "Am I so faithless? Why didn't God protect me
from him?"

"Protect thine heart?"

"Aye," Laural said sadly. "I tried not to let him in, truly I

120

did. I waited for you in the garden, night after night."

"I would have come, but you are being watched."

"Mistress Haverman."

"Lord Cambraige could not ask for better. Had I a choice, I would not attend you here."

"Why?" asked Laural in all innocence. "Be it because of Strathouse? Dost thou not trust me?"

Black Hawk's hold on her tightened imperceptibly. "My love, you are anything but faithless." Tilting back her chin, he lowered gentle lips to hers. Laural melted in the arms of her betrothed. At his touch, Laural closed her eyes, drowning in the sensations he invoked in her. She wanted his love, wanted to be loved for herself alone. As his kisses deepened, Laural's arms encircled his neck, her fingers combing through his long thick hair.

To her bewilderment, Black Hawk gently pushed her from him, his hands warm on her shoulders. "Leelah, my love. I am but a man. Do not tempt me beyond measure."

"Nay. . .Aye." Laural flushed at hearing her nebulous feelings put into words. "I want you to hold me," she whispered desperately.

"Dearest Leelah." Black Hawk held her close again, his voice breaking tenderly. "You are pledged to me, my love. I would be most faithless if I trifled with your innocence. I shall not betray either your own or your father's trust in me. 'Tis against all we believe. Our lives are not our own, Leelah. We belong to the Lord. He is here with us even now.

"Oh, Leelah, I sense you believe not, but Jesus does love you. He does have a plan for us, and we must look to the future. My sword is bespoken, but our time will come. There is so much I cannot yet explain."

"You don't want me," Laural's muffled words sounded her dismay against the silk of Black Hawk's tunic.

"Ah, my Leelah. I do want you. My arms ache to hold you. But this is not right in God's eyes. True love is more than a momentary greed for self-fulfillment. Love—God's love, my love—is a lasting thing. Love means being faithful and trustworthy. It is doing what is best for the other even when your whole being cries, nay!"

Laural blushed under the cover of darkness. The depth of Black Hawk's love shamed her. "I am not worthy of your love," she whispered.

"Hush, little love." Black Hawk held her close and then released her. His thumb caught the tear at the corner of her eye. "Ah, Leelah, my heart is yours, but I want you when I know you belong completely to me, when your heart is no longer torn in two. Soon, all this will be past and done. God willing, there will come a time I can explain the whole. Then we both will be free to love one another as the Holy One intended. Until then, my love." Holding her to him in an almost desperate hug, Black Hawk kissed her until Laural melted weakly in his arms.

"Black Hawk, please. Can you not tell me anything?"

Black Hawk pulled her against his chest. "You have done well, Leelah. Your father would be most proud of his daughter. The time has come to act. I will not risk your safety further. Expect me not again until this beastly business is at an end." He paused. "Though I be not always at your side, Jesus is. I leave you in His care. Pray for me as I pray for you, Leelah."

"I shall. I shall," Laural vowed.

"May you know His peace." With a feather light kiss against her lips, Black Hawk melted into the darkness. To her chest Laural clasped the long feather he had dropped in her hand. Once again tears coursed unchecked down her cheeks.

Back in her private chamber, she wept for the confusion

in her divided heart. She wept, angry at herself at the tears she could no more control than her heart.

Why did love always bring her hurt? Was it worth the price? Her heart ached, tears choked her. Firmly, desperately, she pulled the shreds of her shell about her heart. Did Black Hawk want her for herself? And what of Douglas? What a mistake she had almost made in trusting him.

Confused, angry, and ashamed, Laural cried herself to sleep, wondering at Black Hawk's remarks. Though they meant little when she had the comfort of his presence, they haunted her in the lonely darkness. What did they mean? Did he suspect only one of the two men she cared about would survive the clash that was certain to come? Her heart ached, but was it more for Douglas or Black Hawk? Could Jesus truly give her peace? Did He truly care?

Despite Douglas's betrayal, Laural could not wish him dead. Despite his betrayal, her heart yearned for him. Yet how could this be?

Deliberately Laural blanked her mind. She must trust Black Hawk. He had said all would be well. He also had said Jesus watched out for her. Did he speak truth?

"Oh, Lord," she cried silently in the dark, "help him. Help me. Forgive me for not being what I ought."

"Forgive Lord Cambraige," sounded the voice in the quiet of her heart.

"Not yet, Lord. Not yet. I cannot."

❧

The next day Laural sought to soothe her wounded soul by going to the chapel. Her heart, far from being an impenetrable shell, was writhing in agony.

She longed for Douglas while bound by vows to Black Hawk as well as to her king. She wanted so to speak to the priest, but Black Hawk's warning stayed her. "Tell no one."

The elderly priest, she knew, was dependent upon Lord Cambraige for his living. While he was a far cry from the rapacious Father Andrew, even the kindly old cleric was not to be trusted.

"Lord God, what am I to do?" Clenching her hands to keep them from trembling, Laural's bitterness surfaced. Lord Cambraige. 'Twas all his doing! How she hated him. Her hatred clung about her heart, constricting it as her shell of coldness never had, leaving no room for Strathouse's honeyed words. Hatred drove her from the sanctuary, a bitter, torn, angry young woman.

Laural studiously avoided Lord Strathouse. Mistress Haverman watched her ever more closely, so Laural gave up her nightly stroll in the gardens. Black Hawk was gone. He would not come again until. . .until what? How would she know?

Exhaustion dogged her steps, because her nights, filled with nightmares, kept her from rest. In her dreams, Black Hawk warred with Strathouse, and always, always, both died, leaving her in the clutches of Lord Cambraige and his mad aunt who clawed at her with grasping talons. Her face grew taut with tension. How she needed to be held in Douglas's strong arms. Her weakness horrified her. The man planned to murder his own liege lord! How could she still hold feelings for him?

She knew Lord Strathouse watched her with solemn eyes from that inscrutable face. She tried to tell herself she was glad he kept his distance, but she had to admit to herself that she desperately missed his company. In those moments she forced her hatred of Lord Cambraige to surface protectively.

Fleeing from the great hall, Laural made her way to the kitchens. The cooking chamber reeked of sour milk and the overpowering odor of spoiled meat being boiled with herbs to make it presentable in the great hall.

Added to the smell of food was the stench of unwashed bodies dripping with sweat in the overheated chamber. The clang of pots and utensils was interspersed with shouted commands and laughter. As Laural slipped into the room, all sounds died but the steady chop-chop of vegetables for the stew bubbling in the huge pot over the blazing fire in the hearth.

Laughter died on the lips of the kitchen maids whose eyes widened at her entrance. Laural bit back a grin at their trance. She doubted Mistress Haverman lowered herself to enter the servants' domain.

Reaching over, she wiped grime from the table. Fat congealed on unwashed platters. With a grimace, Laural watched a scullion slosh grayish water from one goblet to another. Another lowly scullion wiped out the moisture with a towel not much less gray than the water.

Unable to stand the filth, Laural motioned for the cook, who proved to be a heavy woman with a motherly face. "Mistress Haverman never comes here," the cook complained.

"That is no excuse for this." Laural motioned toward the congealing food products left out where flies buzzed and dived. "Dost thou care so little for the well-being of your little ones?"

This caught the cook's attention. "What dost thou know of the children?"

"Enough to know that everything here needs to be washed. You need to wash all the platters and goblets and utensils in fresh hot water and dry them with clean towels. Filth detracts from the general well-being as well as from the taste of the food and its life-giving properties."

Dubiously the cook shook her head. "Will that keep our

young ones well?"

"It will certainly be a start. I found at Comfrey that uncovered food or food put in unwashed or unclean pots brought sickness."

The cook glanced despairingly around the foul-smelling chamber. "'Twould take days to clean."

"Be not the health, the lives of your own children worth the time? Even now it may be too late."

Laural shuddered at the thought of what she had been eating, shuddered at the conditions of Lord Cambraige's servants. Hatred for the man continued to boil like the stew in the pot.

Though her foray into the kitchens made a friend of the cook and gave her the satisfaction that things would change to some extent, Laural found that she could not escape her problems even there.

As they got used to her presence, the serving maids once more began their work, ignoring Laural except for a glance now and again in her direction. To her dismay she overheard whispered comments about her estrangement from the handsome Lord Strathouse. The giggling of young Rosy with another young maid in the corner drove Laural from the kitchens, her face burning at their revealing conversation.

"She be not seen in 'is company anymore."

"Aye, Sir Adam told me her ladyship no longer looks with favor on 'is lordship. Bodes ill for 'er. Lord Cambraige is in a fine rage over 'er. 'E will be adealin' with 'er straightway, Sir Adam be atellin' me."

Rosy shook her head. Glancing soberly at Laural, she muttered, "Why cannot he leave 'er be? I thought better of Lord Strathouse. He seemed so. . .well, so besotted with 'er and all."

The other maid shrugged. "He be like all the other lords. They be awantin' only one thing."

Tears stinging her eyes, Laural stumbled out into the court-yard. Angrily she wiped them from her face. If Black Hawk knew what a watering pot she had become, he would be disappointed in her. Pulling herself up sharply, Laural straightened her shoulders. Her lips in a hard thin line, she walked firmly ahead with no idea where she headed. "Lord God, is there no respite?"

Stumbling, she heard her own words repeating over in her mind, *Filth detracts from the general well being.*

"Hatred is filth, too," said the quiet voice she knew to be more than her own heart.

She felt as filthy inside as she found the kitchen. Hatred entwined her heart leaving her cold and unable to think clearly. "Haven't I the right to hate Lord Cambraige, Lord? What about Lord Strathouse?" As though her prayer summoned him, she heard his voice.

"Laural, stop!"

Quelling the impulse to walk away, she waited as he cantered up beside her.

"Douglas." Laural coughed at the dust raised by the hooves of his destrier.

"Laural, look at me," he commanded with deceptive soft-ness. When she refused, he swung down off his horse.

Laural tried to move away from his overwhelming pres-ence, but he grabbed her arm and pulled her against his hard chest, forcing up her chin as he did so. "I'm sorry about the other night. I was sick with worry that Lord Cambraige might find you out."

"Nay!" Laural answered, anger hardening her face. "Do you think you can appease me for your. . .your behavior?" She tried to hide the tears that to her mortification sprang to her eyes.

"Oh, my Laural. When you put yourself in danger, I become angry with you because I am afraid for you. Do you not know you belong to me?"

"You heard him. Lord Cambraige will not let me be wed to anyone," confessed Laural.

Douglas looked deep in Laural's eyes. "Don't you know that if I desire to wed you, I shall do so?"

Without waiting for her to reply, Strathouse held her to him, his lips finding hers. For a moment Laural fought his hold, then her knees became water and she leaned into Douglas as lightening streaked down her back. In his arms, Laural's hatred evaporated like fog in the warmth of sunlight.

When Douglas straightened up, he held Laural until she could get her wobbly legs under her. Her glazed eyes gazed up at him, her breath puffed out in little gasps.

"My Laural, wish me well."

"Well," she repeated uncomprehendingly.

Douglas smiled down at her, amusement lighting his eyes. "I am going away, Laural."

"Going away!" she wailed. "Now! Why?"

Douglas stroked her soft cheek. "I must."

"Then why. . .?" Laural's words trailed off miserably. Why had he made up to her?

"I promised not to cause you hurt, Laural. After your warm good-bye, which I can be certain will be reported to your guardian, I can leave assured that Lord Cambraige will not trouble you soon. I fear your avoidance of me has made him quite wroth with thee." He chucked her irritatingly under her chin. "I told him we'd merely quarreled."

"You deceived me!" stormed Laural, her face reddening in anger. "I be thrice the fool. Begone then. You are not the king's man, but Lord Cambraige's serf."

Tensing, he murmured with dangerous undertones. "Thou art bothered, m'lady, or I would take offense at your words."

"Murderer," Laural hissed.

"Umm." His lips covered hers, choking back her accusation. Releasing her lips, he muttered, "Stay thy tongue, Lady Laural. You might keep your head on your shoulders longer."

"If you think I'll submit tamely—"

"Never," Douglas chuckled, holding her squirming body close to his. Leaning close he whispered. "If you will not be still, I shall kiss you again."

Shocked, Laural stopped fighting.

"There, that's better. Now, my dear, you will convincingly kiss me adieu."

Laural pecked his check, but Douglas moved his head and caught her lips, again leaving her breathless. Releasing her, he swung onto his impatient horse, his sword clanking at his side. With a wave of his hand, Strathouse led a party of men from the castle courtyard.

Laural stared after him, her mind refusing to function. He rode away. He rode away with a party of men. Even in her daze, Laural heard the clanking of swords, the jingle of spurs, the clinking of metal against metal. Her eyes grew wide. He rode out armed with a party of men. "Lord God, this cannot be true!"

Neither Sir Adam nor Sir Wentworth rode with Strathouse's party. With shocking suddenness she remembered Douglas asking to lead the men, lead the men who went to dispatch the king at Caernarvon. Laural squeezed her eyes tight, hardly breathing. She stilled the scream that tore at her throat.

"Oh, Lord," she breathed. "Has Black Hawk had time to warn the King? I must go. Nay, I must trust Black Hawk. Nothing can save Douglas now." Her hands clenched, Laural turned and slowly made her way back to the keep.

In the great hall, Lord Cambraige sat on the dais with Sir Adam, Wentworth, and other men-at-arms, laughing and toasting each other. Time and again their goblets clinked. Their laughter grew more and more pronounced until Lord Cambraige quieted them with a sharp command.

Laural slipped silently, unnoticed into the alcove that had hidden her so effectively before. Smoke from the fireplaces at each end of the large chamber hung in the dim room. Out of habit, she strained to hear what Lord Cambraige had to say. It would not do much good, for Black Hawk was gone. *Gone to protect the king,* she groaned to herself, *from Douglas and his party.*

"The dupes suspect not a thing. Did the fools think I be so addle-brained as to send another to take my rightful place beside the king?" Lord Cambraige laughed, sending chills dancing along Laural's spine.

"The king's untimely death at the hands of those villeins will serve only to strengthen my position as I lead my own men against them. My attendance on the king will be most timely, for I shall ride in on their very heels. Forsooth, I shall greatly mourn the king's death and comfort the good queen at the death of her husband and newborn whelp. That at least was a clever thought on Strathouse's part."

Laural tensed at his words. Had not Douglas gone at Lord Cambraige's command? Of what then, pray tell, spoke Lord Cambraige? Wentworth spoke up unsteadily as he raised high the goblet from which he had been imbibing too frequently. "We be the king's liege men as always."

Sir Adam laughed and clanked his goblet to Wentworth's. "Hail, our Lord Cambraige. *Le roi est mort, vive le roi!*"

Without thinking, Laural translated his words: *The king is dead, long live the king!* Her face froze as his words crystallized in her mind, clarifying in one terrifying instant the whole diabolical plot not only against her sovereign King Edward, but also against her beloved Douglas. . .her Douglas?

Fearful and dazed, Laural slipped from her alcove and made her way from the great hall into the courtyard near the stables. She stopped by the place Douglas had so recently held her. She thought of his body lifeless and bleeding, a traitor to the king, and for naught. He would lose his life to Lord Cambraige.

If only she knew how to reach Black Hawk, but he was gone. Gone to protect the king against Douglas. And Douglas, he must be told of Lord Cambraige's duplicity, but how? *Oh, Black Hawk, I need you now.*

He trusted her, yet in the end she had failed him; failed to uncover this most devious plot; failed him as she had failed her father. The thought startled her. Did she truly believe she was at fault for her father's death?

Laural looked at her hands, wet with sweat. "Nay!" she said aloud straightening her shoulders. "I must not fail, again. I do love him. I must not fail. I must do something. I will do something! But what?"

A look of mulish stubbornness set on Laural's usually sweet face. Tucking her bliaut into her wide belt, Laural ran toward the stables, yelling for a stableboy to saddle her horse.

"Stay, m'lady." Mistress Haverman grabbed her arm and held her firmly. The woman's face held deadly intent.

"Unhand me, ma'am," Laural commanded. She had no time for this foolishness.

The woman's grip tightened, and she began dragging Laural toward the castle. "You will come with me to Lord Cambraige. Let him see the innocent who overhears his secrets."

Laural's swallowed her shock. "Secrets? Be thou crazed?"

"Crazed like a hawk. I know my prey."

"You prey on me then." Though panic licked at Laural, in desperation she faced the woman with forced equanimity. "Why do you hate me so? Let me go."

Unsuccessfully she tried to wrench away. Mistress Haverman shook her head. "I told Lord Cambraige you would be trouble. Now he'll believe me. When I bring him the evidence of your perfidy, he'll hold me in esteem."

Laural scoffed, "He cares for no man—or woman either—other than himself. Lord Cambraige is a murdering monster. He murdered my father."

Too late, Laural saw her mistake and sucked in a deep breath at the calculating smile on the woman's craggy features. "So you know about that as well. To whom do you ride to betray his lordship? I'll not allow it, you know."

"Do you wish to hang with him?"

Mistress Haverman laughed then, a cackle that froze the blood in Laural's veins. The woman indeed ran mad.

"Lord Cambraige, now, the blood of kings flows in his veins." She jerked Laural forward. "Do not try to deny that you have been a Judas to my nephew. You shall pay."

With every moment Douglas rode farther away and the chances of catching him grew slimmer. Casting about for some way to distract the woman, Laural almost despaired until they passed a tree. Yanking back, Laural at last freed herself. Plucking up a fallen limb, she swung it toward the larger woman. She cringed as the branch connected with the woman's skull. Eyes open with astonishment, Mistress Haverman slowly crumpled to the ground. Blood gushed from her forehead.

Dropping the branch as though it scorched her hands, Laural cried, "Oh, Lord, I've killed her!" Falling to her knees, she gingerly felt the woman's pulse and found it beating steadily. Close up, the wound did not appear deep. Ripping a swath of her skirt, Laural bound up the wound.

Taking a chance, she hailed a passed lackey. "Mistress Haverman has had an accident. See that she is carried to her bedchambers and cared for."

"Lord," she breathed getting to her feet. "Don't let her death be on my hands, but don't let her wake up until I am long gone."

Picking up her somewhat bloodied skirts, Laural hurried to the stables.

twelve

*In my distress I cried unto the Lord,
and he heard me.* Psalm 120:1

෨

Glancing back furtively at the keep, Laural leaped aboard the chestnut mare and swung her about toward the gatehouse and barbican, silently giving thanks that Lord Cambraige usually had the drawbridge lowered and the gates open wide during daylight hours. Plastering a patently false smile on her face, Laural rode by the guards fearful each second a command would order her to return to the security of the castle.

"Mistress Haverman has been injured," she called out as though in explanation of her unescorted ride.

To her relief, the guards merely waved her on. If she had but known 'twas this simple to get away—but no, these guards were new. Most of Lord Cambraige's men were either with Douglas or preparing for the second assault on the king's castle. Hopefully these guards would not report her to Lord Cambraige when she did not return in good time.

Looking behind her, Laural scanned the castle for any sign of pursuit before kicking the mare into a gallop. After her fortunate escape, trembling seized her limbs. The chestnut mare's ears flicked back, and she faltered in stride as she sensed something amiss with her mistress.

"Nay!" cried Laural shaking off her fear. Leaning forward she urged the sensitive mare into a full-out gallop. Clenching her teeth, Laural focused on the rutted road in front of her, focused on Douglas somewhere ahead of her.

She prayed as she had never prayed before, all her anger toward Douglas momentarily forgotten.

How long ago had he departed? Though the mare was a swift horse with a light burden, Laural feared she was no match for Douglas's destrier. The mare rarely went at more than a sedate pace, while Douglas's warhorse, no doubt, was a stayer who would plunge on and on at a steady pace all day if necessary. Thanks to Mistress Haverman's interference, he had a good lead on her. Would it prove too much?

"Lord Jesus, You must help me reach Douglas. Please. Help me convince him to stay his course and not go through with Lord Cambraige's dastardly plans." Laural continued to pour out her heart as she rode.

Reaching a wood, Laural pulled up thoughtfully. Ahead, the road curved around the large dense forest. Hesitating but a moment, Laural turned the reluctant mare into a narrow woodland trail. One thin trail crossed another, frequently running out completely. Biting her lip in frustration, Laural tried to keep her bearings in the shadowed wood. Often she peered up at the sun, peeking out now and again over the tall trees. In this very wood, she had came to know the gentle side of Lord Strathouse.

The stream where they had sat bubbled merrily as though nothing could possibly be wrong. Hesitating but a moment, Laural sent the mare through the stream and up the other bank. For a moment, she lost her balance, then regained it again. The sun beamed down, warming her shoulders.

"Thank You, Lord," she cried aloud, thankful not only because the sun lit her way, but also for the warmth it provided.

The mare moved along willingly enough, then shied as branches slapped her shiny hide and tried to entangle themselves in her long silky mane. The tangle of trails and false trails caused Laural concern. Had she made a mistake which would not only get her hopelessly lost, but also cost Douglas his life?

Despite the unfamiliarity of the paths, Laural urged the mare on to a faster clip desperately muttering a plea for Douglas's safety. After what seemed an eternity, the leaves thinned, the branches grew less dense, and suddenly Laural found herself on the far side of the wood. Was she in time? Urgently she leaned down close to the mare's withers and let the mare run full out, urging her on merely by the sound of her voice and the slackened reins.

Unexpectedly, Laural heard ahead the thundering sound of hooves on hard-packed earth. No lone rider this. Laughter floated back on the breeze, convincing her that Douglas and his men rode on ahead. She was catching up with them! A smile of triumph crossed her face.

The first rush of exhilaration had hardly registered when the chestnut mare stumbled badly, almost throwing her. Even as Laural gathered the reins more firmly, the mare faltered and limped to a halt. The sound of the riders ahead grew fainter. Frantically Laural screamed. "Douglas! Douglas! Douglas!"

Stopping to catch her breath, she listened. Silence. Either the riders were now out of range of her hearing or they had stopped. She had to chance that he could still hear her. She screamed out her desperation and fear. "Douglas!"

The sound of hoofbeats coming in her direction never sounded so sweet to Laural's ears. Relieved, she waited as Douglas detached himself from the others and sidled his destrier next to the mare, but her relief turned to fear when she saw the dark wrath evident in his gray eyes.

"Laural, by the King's name, do you know what you do? Get back to the castle straightway."

"Douglas, you must listen! Lord Cambraige is planning to double-cross you. After you. . .after you. . ." Laural gulped, finding it difficult to put his treachery into speech. Swallowing, she forced herself to continue, her face showing her anguish. "After you. . .murder King Edward, Lord Cambraige will arrive with his vassals and claim both the queen and the country in the king's name—for himself. He plans to kill you. Everyone will think you are the traitor and he is the king's man. You must not go on. You must not!"

In her plea, Laural reached over and grasped Douglas's arm. He covered her trembling hand with his own. "Care you so much for me then, Laural?"

Glancing into Douglas's face, Laural was set back by the tenderness evident in his eyes. "I do not want you dead. Please do not do this! I cannot bear losing you!" In her anguish, the words slipped out before she could hold them back.

Strathouse squeezed her hand before setting it back onto her lap. "You must return to the castle, Laural, before they know you are gone," he said quietly. At her dismay, he smiled slightly as though to reassure her. "I cannot imagine how you slipped out without Mistress Haverman knowing."

"She caught me."

He bit back his displeasure. "Now everyone will know you are gone."

"Nay. Mistress Haverman will not be telling anyone." Douglas studied her with a disquiet that made Laural explain. "I hit her. She is unconscious, but I believe she'll be all right. I bound up her head and got her help before I left."

A half-smile twisted Douglas's lips. "Ah, my gentle Laural."

"Nay. I hate Lord Cambraige for murdering my father and for getting you to do this dreadful thing. You must not continue."

"Laural, you must return to the castle before Mistress Haverman comes to. You must leave this to me."

"Even if I wanted to, I cannot return, Douglas." As the frown returned to his face, she hurried to explain. "The mare has gone lame." She urged the mare forward a couple of halting steps. "See."

Douglas's eyebrow lowered thoughtfully. Sidling his horse next to her, he reached over and pulled Laural onto the front of his saddle. His movements were hurried and impatient. "You must ride with me, then, my Laural." His tone brooked no refusal. His arm anchored her to the saddle in front of him as he reached across her to hold the reins.

"To the castle, then?" Laural asked, not quite sure if she was relieved or not. How would Lord Cambraige respond when he discovered his carefully laid plans had been set aside by a slip of a girl he already detested? Laural shivered at the thought of his wrath.

Douglas seemed to understand and held her to him more closely. "We ride to the castle, aye, m'lady, to castle Caernarvon. Your mare will just have to find her own way back."

"But you're not going to—"

Douglas hushed her urgently as they approached the rest of the party.

"Must we ride with her?" grumbled a knight in disgust.

"Ah, Sir John, be of good heart. The lady's presence bodes well for a kindly welcome. Who will suspect foul play from the daughter of Comfrey? The Celtic wench shall gain us unsuspecting entrance." Kissing her to keep her from retorting, Douglas laughed with the others as they set off once again.

In Douglas's arms, Laural tried to remain stiff, not touching the body of the man who planned to use her in a scheme to murder her own king. Tears stung her eyes, and she brushed them away angrily.

Lord, what am I to do now? I thought You would help me stop Douglas. I don't understand, Lord. Every time I try to help, I make things worse. How can he use me to hurt my king? Jesus, help me. I don't know what to do. Why had she been so mutton-headed as to warn the man? *Lord, I can't do anything more. Please make things right. Please!*

For the first time since the death of her father, Laural realized she had stopped trying to work things out herself. She found a measure of relief in knowing there was nothing she could do, at least for the moment.

With misgivings, Laural watched the sun slip over the horizon, bathing the king's newly completed residence at Caernarvon in a kaleidoscope of rose, golds, and blues. Breathing in the beauty of the castle, Laural mourned that all too soon the only color she would see would be the color of red. . .blood red. She shivered.

"Be you chilled, Laural?" asked Douglas, gently rubbing her arm.

She shook her head, unable to speak. It had been an exhausting ride. They had stopped but once to rest and to partake of a light meal of dried meat and grain. Laughter marked the early ride, but now the men fell silent. Did the coming betrayal of their vows weigh on them? Did it weigh on Douglas?

In spite of her resolve to stay alert, Laural drifted off to sleep. As she relaxed in his arms, Douglas gathered her more securely into his arms and pushed her head against his shoulder.

Floating along, she kept hearing his deep chuckle. In the grip of her nightmare his chuckle echoed mockingly as she stared ahead into darkness. Two men held out their arms to her. She must go to one, for only one could protect her.

Only one would keep her safe, but in her dream she swung round and round unable to decide. The cry she heard tore from her own lips, and she woke with a start to find Douglas's hand covering her mouth. Her eyes wide, she stared up at him. Seeing she was now fully in control of her senses, he released her.

"Bedeviled with nightmares, dearest Laural?" He gazed down into her face steadily. "Trust me, my dear," he said softly. "Trust me."

"How can I?" she murmured. "I heard your plans." Another thought stilled her.

"Is Destrun attending the king?" she asked.

"He is a quiet man," answered Douglas slowly. "He might well be at court, then again, the king often has private affairs for him."

Laural straightened as hope lit her eyes. Was it possible? Could the tranquil Destrun, her friend, be the legendary Black Hawk? 'Twould explain his mysterious comings and goings. 'Twould explain why he rode not with her father that fatal day. Destrun—Black Hawk? It bore consideration. Mayhap there was hope. Destrun was a good man. Her heart cried, "But can you care for him as you do for Douglas?" Destrun was an honorable man. She could safely trust him, could she not? Douglas also begged her trust, but that was not possible.

Laural looked ahead despairingly at the castle with the king's standard fluttering above in the breeze. Trust Douglas? Trust the man who boasted of his ability to kill the king efficiently because of his close ties to the king?

Inside she heard the quiet voice, "Trust Me, Laural, trust Me."

"Lord, I want to, truly I do, but—"

"Laural."

"It is so difficult to hear."

"Forgive, Laural, and you will hear Me clearly."

"But Lord—"

Only silence met her continued stubbornness, a silence that frightened her. Had God left her to her own devices because of her hard heart? Biting her lip, Laural lifted her shoulders. One way or another, she must see this thing through. Destrun. He would help. After all, Black Hawk had promised to stay close. Somehow with his help, she must save the king.

Her homage, as had her father's, belonged to King Edward. Aye, she admitted she loved the large man who held her so tenderly, but she must forswear that love if it be possible to warn His Majesty. Her chest tightened until she thought the pain would kill her. But there was no time for more planning; the castle gates were upon them.

"Open the gates," commanded Strathouse loudly, the horses' hooves clattering impatiently on the drawbridge not yet drawn up for the night.

"Who goes there?" challenged the guards at the gatehouse.

"Lady Laural, daughter of the late Lord Comfrey, and Lord Strathouse and vassals."

Laural noted that he did not say whose vassals they were, though the guards would assume they belonged to Douglas. The guards called down again. "Why rides the lady with you, m'lord? Where be the lady's palfrey?" There was a hint of suspicion in the question, and Laural opened her mouth to speak the truth of the matter.

She never had the chance. Douglas's hand clamped across her mouth, stifling her as he answered. "Aye, the lady's mare pulled up lame. We had to leave the beast behind."

Laughing in sympathy, the guards slowly opened the complicated sequence of gates and portcullises between one drawbridge and the next.

Without help from inside, thought Laural dismally, *the castle is inviolate.* She gulped, an unwitting traitor to her king. *Oh Father, what can I do. What might I do? Even God has left me? Will Black Hawk be near?*

As the men rode into the courtyard, Douglas whispered softly in Laural's ear. "Make one wrong move, my love, and we all be dead. . .your king included."

Before she could reply, stableboys ran up to take the men's mounts. Wrapping his long arm about her waist, Douglas lowered Laural to the ground before swinging down from his destrier beside her. Taking her by the arm in a grip that brought tears to her eyes, he pulled Laural along with him as he led his elite group of warriors up the stairs into the great hall.

Any protest Laural wished to make died in her throat as she took in the cold mask of Douglas's face. This was a stranger she did not know, the stranger who had plotted with Lord Cambraige against the king, the stranger who right now might murder her should she prove a hindrance to his plans. But what were his plans? Did he still plan to follow through, knowing Lord Cambraige followed on his heels? There did seem to be a suppressed edginess in his efficient movements, a tightness to his lips.

Entering the newly finished castle, Laural stared about at the profusion of banners and bright ornaments not only hanging from the fresh new walls, but on the colorful court of the king as well. The tall man with graying hair drew her eyes. He lounged easily with his courtiers, laughing freely but not boisterously at the antics of the garishly dressed jester flipping about on the floor. Close by, a traveling balladeer plucked his lute and sang tenderly of love. Frantically she scanned the chamber for Destrun, but he was not to be found.

The chair next to the king was empty. Had Black Hawk recently left the king's side to raise a defense? Laural glanced around for the queen but saw her not. Somehow it was a relief, but as Douglas moved forward, his arm about her waist, the queen walked gracefully into the crowded room. Smiling, she spotted them. "Douglas, please join us." Her look included Laural, who shrank back.

Bowing, Douglas tightened his hold and forced her forward with him toward the dais. To Laural's surprise, the king held out his ringed hands to Douglas. "Ah, you have returned to the fold." He smiled, a smile that surveyed her pale face with a look so penetrating Laural hoped he actually could read her mind. Silently she sent him a message of warning.

"Be Destrun at court?" she managed. Leaning down, she whispered, "Black Hawk." Strathouse jerked her upright, scowling at her. His hand kept her from the dirk at her waist.

The king's smile widened. With a nod, he turned and permitted Douglas to kiss him before motioning for him to stay beside him.

"And who is your lovely companion?" the king questioned.

"Lord Comfrey's daughter, Your Highness," Douglas said a bit too sharply.

Laural stared at Douglas uneasily. Hastily remembering her manners, she curtsied. "Your Highness." Her stomach turned sickeningly at what Douglas planned. At the caution in his grip, she lowered her eyes, unable to witness the light go from those eyes alight with kindness, humor, and intelligence.

"Speak again, and this may well come down worse than even you imagine, m'lady." Douglas's whispered words quelled the warning in her throat.

As the king waved for a servant to bring them food and

drink, Laural noted the rest of the party had positioned themselves strategically throughout the hall. Still Black Hawk did not appear.

The queen joined her husband at the dais. At her nod, two high ranking noblemen moved down the table, leaving room for Laural and Strathouse to sit near the king. Strathouse must indeed be trusted by King Edward. What, then, had the king done to so turn Douglas from his sword-oath?

Finally across the room Laural caught Destrun staring at her in consternation. She tried to warn him with her look from her escort to the tall monarch. She never truly saw exactly what happened. In one smooth movement, Douglas leaned down to whisper in the king's ear, pulling his dagger from its scabbard at the same instant.

"Destrun. Black Hawk," cried Laural, watching as though in slow motion the blur of Strathouse's hand.

For an instant the king stared out over the hall before slowly crumpling onto the floor. The queen screamed. Laural stood stiff, too horrified to move. Her eyes riveted to the stain spreading across the king's rich blue tunic.

In her nightmare, Laural watched Douglas hold the queen from her husband, his bloody knife raised over his head. "Who gives homage to Lord Cambraige? Give voice now, or you shall feel the sword of those sworn to him. Look well to your neighbor. Where lies his fealty?"

In the ensuing confusion of knights swearing forth their loyalties, Laural watched with a detached shock as Destrun leaped into action. He took down three knights before being subdued himself. What did it matter now? She had betrayed her king, and in doing so, had failed both her father and Black Hawk, her king as well as the Lord of all the universe. Unheeded her tears coursed down her cheeks and splashed at the feet of her fallen king.

thirteen

Deliver my soul, O Lord, from lying lips,
and from a deceitful tongue. Psalm 120:2

⨝

The confusion throughout the hall faded into the background of Laural's nightmare as she stared fixedly at her king crumpled on the ground. Red spattered down the front of his tunic. Unexpectedly, the face frozen in death shifted.

Shaking her head, Laural blinked. Leaning down for a closer look, Laural hesitantly peered at the body of her king. To her bewilderment, the king opened a piercing eye, smiled crookedly at her, then closed his eye in a slow wink.

An instant later he leaped to his feet. "Take the traitors!" he roared. "Take anyone selling his soul in allegiance to the scoundrel Cambraige!"

To the sudden horror of the conspirators, the king's knights, who had been in confusion at the death of their overlord, turned on them with a bloodthirsty vengeance. In moments the halls ran red with the blood of the men of both loyalties, but the king's men not only outnumbered Lord Cambraige's men, but also fought with good heart. Soon the traitors either lay dead or were being led away.

Turning from the ghastly scene before her, Laural glanced toward Douglas. She gasped as Destrun put sword to his throat hissing, "Traitor."

The queen wrenched herself away from Douglas to see to her husband, her face lined with anxiety. The king waved away her administrations. "Dearest, I be whole. Desist Destrun. You are misinformed."

145

Confusion on the knight's face mirrored Laural's own. This uncertain Destrun could not be the bold Black Hawk who visited her in the dark of night. And Destrun's presence did nothing to her heart. She felt nothing more than affection for a lifelong friend. Her heart beat for Douglas.

As the king surveyed Douglas, Laural clenched her hands, waiting for the king's judgment. Suddenly the king's face softened and he exploded with laughter. Laural swayed. The hall grew hazy, and she fought the darkness.

Hearing Douglas chuckle, she stared up at his face and found him grinning down at her. Dazedly Laural glanced from him to the queen, who beheld her with a benign smile.

"Douglas," Laural choked out, "I don't understand." Her legs wobbled, gave way, and Douglas wrapped his arm around her waist to hold her up.

The king chuckled. "Douglas, you have done exceptionally well." His eyes hardened. "All I need now is to drag Lord Cambraige in here. His end shall be not pleasant."

"'Tis not at end as yet. His lordship plans to ride into Caernarvon, dispatch the 'traitor' who murdered you, and take over as regent in your name. Later he shall declare himself king. What we did not know is that Lord Cambraige is cousin to Llewelyn and believes himself heir to the throne of England as well as Wales."

"We shall see about that," said King Edward darkly. "We shall be ready when he arrives. Destrun—" After barking a few terse orders, the king turned back to Douglas. "The whole plot could have come undone had you not discovered Lord Cambraige's duplicity. Now we shall be prepared for his next move."

Douglas looked down at Laural. Giving her a hug, he said to the king, "My lady uncovered Cambraige's plot, not I. She rode out to warn me against him."

"Ah, then I owe you my life, as I owed it to your father. . . and to Lord Strathouse."

Laural's mouth dropped opened. "I knew it not," she managed. "But I. . .how can this be? I saw him strike you down."

Edward laughed. "A bladder of pig's blood," he revealed with a wink.

Laural slumped against Douglas in relief, her lingering doubts of him vanishing. "Oh, Douglas."

"So the maiden did not know." The king sobered.

"Nay, Sire," said Douglas smiling tenderly at Laural. "She tried to the end to warn you, to enlist the aid of Black Hawk with whom she seems well acquainted." His lips twitched. "I had to keep a tight grip on her or she would have foiled our own plans to discover how far Lord Cambraige had gotten in his encouragement of disloyalty among your vassals."

"Do you hold this man in high affection?" asked the king of Laural.

Blushing, Laural lowered her eyes. "Aye, Your Highness."

"Yet you would have betrayed him to save your king."

Tears swam in Laural's eyes as she looked into the king's face. "I swore my allegiance as did my father, Sire. I keep my promises."

"Come here, child," commanded the king, his face soft with compassion.

Laural stumbled forward, almost tripped, then blushed furiously as King Edward caught and steadied her. "My most humble apologies," she stuttered, angry that things seemed to be going from bad to worse. Her father would have hid his head in shame at her bumbling behavior before her king. "I'm sorry," she said again. Still a small voice inside her rang joyously, *You did not fail! You did not fail.*

King Edward chuckled. "You are a brave young woman.

Should all my vassals be as loyal and brave, I would have few concerns. Now, m'lady, what favor might I bestow on thee?"

Laural's eyes widened in surprise. "Why, I ask nothing of thee, my king. I but did my sworn duty."

The king nodded, a look of satisfaction in his eyes. Comfrey had been well served by his daughter. She would hold his lands for him in lieu of a son. He would find a match worthy of her courage.

Lord Strathouse cleared his throat. As the king glanced up at him, Douglas stepped forward. "I would succor the king's favor." Laural glanced up at him in amazement as he took her hand in his.

"What may I grant you, Douglas? You have served me well."

"And will continue to do so, Sire," said Douglas. "But I petition the king for the hand of Lady Laural in marriage—this night if the king favors my suit." He bowed.

Laural shook her head, unable to take in Douglas's request. Could it be, could it possibly be he truly wished to marry her? The nightmare began to take on the qualities of a fantasy, a fantasy like those she had dreamed of in the far-off days of childhood—before the death of her mother, before her accident, before Cambraige plotted the death of her father.

The king and queen smiled at Laural and Douglas. Suddenly a young and obviously angry woman pushed her way next to Strathouse. "Your Majesty, might I remind you that he belongs to me?"

Frowning, Edward turned the whole of his royal disapproval on his ward. "Lady Ramona, may I remind you I rule England? You wear not his seal ring upon your finger."

"Your Majesty, I understood."

Laural felt Douglas tense, then relax as the king waved away Lady Ramona's petition. "We shall find you a man worthy of you, Ramona. Strathouse has made a request, and

I shall grant it straightway."

With a strangled cry of rage, Ramona glared at Laural before swinging about and marching from the room.

"Thank you, Sire," said Douglas.

Edward's eyes narrowed. "I mislike what I did. I see now that woman needs a man to handle her. I must see to it soon."

A smile once more lit his face. "For my life, I grant your request, Strathouse. You shall have Comfrey's daughter and his land holdings as her dower. There be no one I trust half so much with his fief." Lifting a regal arm, he commanded the priest be brought straightway.

"Sire," spoke up the queen. "Let me first see to Lady Comfrey's attire and send orders to prepare a bridal chamber."

At the king's nod, the good queen whisked Laural away to her own bedchamber. There Queen Eleanor directed the preparations for a wedding chamber. She ordered the search through her own wardrobe and the wardrobes of the other ladies for a gown to fit Laural's slender body. Pointing at her own middle with a soft smile, the queen said, "I fear my own robes would be much too large."

"Thy son, Your Grace. My felicitations."

"He is a robust lad. You shall see him in time." Queen Eleanor perused the gowns paraded before her.

"We have not much choice, my dear, you are so petite," she laughed pleasantly. "In London, and you will have to attend me there, we are much more civilized. Ah, but here." The queen delightedly held up a white silk gown.

Queen Eleanor motioned for her own women to disrobe Laural. Just in time, Laural rescued her dirk. No one appeared surprised at her insistence on keeping it on her person. A second maid brushed out Laural's hair and rebraided it in plaits about her ears. A lady in waiting slipped a soft blue chemise over her head. Another slipped over it a loose-sleeved, white silk bliaut with delicately embroidered edges. Slit up the sides, it revealed the chemise enticingly. Laural stood still while a servant laced the bliaut tightly to her body and added one of the queen's jewel-studded belts.

Laural fingered the delicate embroidery about the neck and sleeves. It indeed was a lovely garment. Would that Douglas might think so.

At the sight of the elegant queen and her entourage, the sounds of the room hushed. Waiting. Expectant. Only the king in a fresh tunic of rose and gold silk, Douglas in a tunic of black and silver, and the brown-robed cleric stood on the dais. Laural smiled faintly as she followed the queen. At his nod, Laural stepped timidly to Douglas's side. The admiration in his eyes repaid her effort at dressing many times over.

Sensing her shyness and discomfort at this intimate moment, Douglas took her trembling hand in his. The slightly hunch-shouldered priest reverently opened the Scripture he held in his hands. Laural visibly relaxed under his kindly gaze. His voice boomed throughout the quiet room.

Solemnly, sincerely, Laural repeated her vows while Douglas repeated his in a low but tender voice that twisted Laural's heart. She loved this man, she loved him! How could she ever have thought him evil? Why did she not trust him when he asked?

Even as Strathouse placed a seal ring on her finger and the priest firmly pronounced them husband and wife, a stir at the door caused everyone to turn. With a look, Douglas stilled Laural's cry of alarm at the solid form of Lord Cambraige moving boldly through the throng to the dais, followed by his retinue that included both Sir Wentworth and Sir Adam.

Bitter anger licked inside Laural. Was Lord Cambraige again to snatch away her chance at happiness? Where was Black Hawk now? Disappointment in him flared and died. She did not understand. Could she not trust him? Black Hawk? Her betrothed. Her eyes widened as her ring sparkled in the candle light. What had she done?

Just below the dais, Lord Cambraige stared from Strathouse to the commanding and very much alive figure of King Edward. "What treachery be this, Strathouse?" he muttered to Douglas, his face suffused with rage. His men-at-arms hesitated uncertainly at the sight of the king, obviously alive and well.

As Lord Cambraige climbed onto the dais his eyes narrowed. "Laural, how came you hither?"

"His Highness has consented to our marriage." Douglas spoke mildly, though Laural felt him tense beside her. Strathouse raised her hand for Lord Cambraige to inspect the seal ring. "Lady Laural be my lawful wife, Cambraige."

"What folly be this? I be the girl's guardian," Lord Cambraige roared in fury, moving ever closer to the king.

"Stand, Cambraige! Your plot be known. Your head will join those of your cousins on the tower of London." The king's voice grated harshly, angrily. Laural shivered at the sheer dispassion of the king as he spoke Lord Cambraige's death sentence.

When the king raised his hand, Lord Cambraige and his men swung into action, an action born of desperation. With a movement too quick for Laural to follow, Strathouse deprived Lord Cambraige of his sword. Stepping back, Lord Cambraige pulled a stiletto from his sleeve. Raising his arm he began to launch it straight into the chest of the king.

Perceiving his intent, Laural cried out and flung herself against Cambraige. "Nay!" Quickly Lord Cambraige grabbed her, pulled her against his hard chest, and thrust his knife against her throat. Gulping, Laural felt its sharp edge hard against the smoothness of her white neck.

"The interfering wench dies should anyone follow me. You, my king," he sneered in Edward's face, "will command safe passage from the castle for myself and all who ride with me."

Slowly Lord Cambraige backed away, dragging Laural with him, his arm wrenching her body painfully. She grimaced as the knife edged a scratch along her neck and drew a thin line of blood which trailed down onto her gown.

"Laural!" The anguish in Douglas's eyes cleared her mind as nothing else could. Douglas edged to one side, but Laural would not wait. Her face hardening with determination, she forced herself to go limp against Lord Cambraige.

At Laural's unexpected move, Lord Cambraige stumbled slightly but recovered quickly, growling at his hostage as he shifted her dead weight on his arm. Focusing all her hatred, Laural slipped her ever-present dagger from her sleeve and slashed back into the soft, unshielded side of her antagonist. Again she slashed, her dagger lashing out her pain. Cambraige grunted, his breath leaving him in a whoosh.

His hold did not loosen, and Laural felt his knife dig into her neck, making her swallow convulsively. She stabbed again at the man behind her, venting in that thrust all her pent-up bitterness and anger. Revenge burst the cold shell about her heart into white hot heat. Her eyes flashed as, at last, her dagger found its mark.

Lord Cambraige cried out. Stumbling back, he released Laural, but not before the knife sliding down her neck left a long shallow slice from her chin to her shoulder. Blood flowed down her arm.

Hearing the wild, angry howls of a pack of wolves finish-

ing off their victim, Laural swayed, sickened at the sound.
Suddenly Douglas's arms pulled her close, and she heard
his murmured endearments as he held her tightly against
him. Caring not that her blood stained his fresh tunic, he
clutched her to him, not wanting her to see the slaughter
taking place in the hall.

At last there was silence. Laural struggled in Douglas's
arms until he reluctantly released her. "Don't look!" he ordered her. His command came too late.

Stepping back, Laural almost tripped over the fallen Lord
Cambraige. His lifeless eyes stared up at her in dazed surprise. Nearby, the king gazed down in cold fury at the traitor on the floor. In his hand he held a bloody sword. Laural
gulped, shuddered.

Bile filled her throat at the part she had played in the
violent downfall and death of her enemy. Had her hatred
kept her from seeing another way to bring him down? The
thought horrified her.

Oh, Lord Jesus, what have I done? her anguished soul
cried out. *Why didn't I let you help me forgive him sooner,
Lord!*

Evil as he was, he was but a man. Was his poisonous
hatred of the English worse than the hatred which had so
filled her with bitterness that it had kept her from reaching
out to those around her—from reaching out for love—had
kept her locked up in her own private fear? Was it not fear
that had caused her to hold Douglas at arm's length? Suddenly, Laural realized it was not Lord Cambraige's presence in the chapel that had disrupted her peace, but her own
bitter hatred.

Oh, Lord, she cried out silently, *Forgive me. Make me
clean and whole inside. Lord, help me. Please forgive me.*
Suddenly, peace settled over her like a balm. As though on

signal, her body slumped as much from blood loss as fatigue.

Leaning down, Douglas picked Laural up in his strong arms. "Where is our chamber?" he asked the queen. "We go. . .alone." Without comment, she told him. Douglas carried his love from the carnage of the hall, up the stairs, to the quiet of the bridal chamber.

Douglas tried to lay his bride on the bed piled with brightly colored covers and pillows covered in embroidered silk. Light from the sconces set high on the stone walls flickered over Laural's pale face. She turned her head toward the heat emanating from the large fireplace that took up most of the wall opposite the four-poster bed.

Her arms held Douglas close. "Don't leave me. Please don't leave me. Please don't let them touch me. Don't let them come in here." Sobs of shock and exhaustion shook her voice.

"My darling," Douglas murmured to his wife. Gently he loosened her gown, slipping it down over her injured shoulder. Whipping off his sash, he pressed it against the wound, stopping the last of the blood.

"Hold it there," he ordered, pressing Laural's hand to the makeshift bandage. Getting up, he dampened a towel from the water in the basin on the washstand. Returning, he carefully cleaned the wound. At his gentle touch, Laural's heart warmed, easing the ache about her heart. As he finished, Douglas found a clean strip of linen in a trunk by the door and tenderly bound up her shoulder.

"Oh, Douglas. I didn't trust you. I didn't trust God, either. How foolish I have been." Her face tightened. "Will they come here? Will Lady Ramona gape at your bride? Douglas, I can't. I can't."

Smiling down at Laural with heart-stopping tenderness, Douglas lay down beside her, clasping her shaking body close to his chest. "My darling," he spoke gently, "there shall be no bedding ceremony. You have been through much this day already."

"Oh, Douglas. Those women are all so beautiful. I could not bear to have them disrobe me." She shuddered at the thought of the ladies and gentlemen standing around the bed, staring down at her and Douglas in their marriage bed.

Once when she had questioned her father about this tradition, the muscle in his left cheek twitched, and she thought he stilled a smile, "'Tis but tradition, Laural. Nothing to rise up in your stirrups over."

"But, Father, why is it done?" she had insisted.

Her father frowned at her, clearly discomfited. "Enough, girl. It is not for you to question such things."

Now she looked into the face of her husband. "Thank you, Douglas, but tell me, why is such a thing done? The very thought makes me ill."

Douglas smiled at his modest little wife. Somehow inside he felt a warm glow that he, and he alone would see his wife. "'Tis done to assure all that neither man nor woman hath some deformity which would make the union null and void. It leaves no room for annulment. But Laural," he said softly, "you may be certain the ladies will return in the morning to rip the sheets from the bed." He held Laural more tightly as she shivered in his arms.

"Ah, Laural. You be much too sheltered, but," he hushed her protestation, "that is one of your endearing qualities. I love you, my dear. I know you are pure. I care not what the crones feel they must do in the morning."

Laural smiled. "Crones! Oh Douglas, they be far from crones. However could you have chosen me over them?"

"I love you, Laural," he said simply, his lips finding hers.

fourteen

*Our soul is exceedingly filled with the scorning
of those that are at ease, and with the contempt
of the proud.* Psalm 123:4

ð

In the privacy of their wedding bedchamber, Douglas's kisses grew more ardent. Breathless, Laural drowned in her husband's embrace.

A sharp knock at the door brought a growl to Douglas's throat as he reluctantly answered the imperious summons. Even more reluctantly, Laural followed him, her heart pounding. Had something gone awry? Surely the rebellion had been quelled with the death of Lord Cambraige.

Laural missed the exact words, but not the demanding tone in which they were spoken. She heard Douglas's sharp retort, the slam of the heavy door, and the snap of the bolt shooting home.

Frightened by the angry scowl on his face, Laural stepped back toward the hearth. Seeing her look, Douglas made an effort to calm himself. Holding out his arms, he gathered her to him. "Ah, my dear. 'Twas but some of the knights come to perform the bedding ceremony. I bid them begone. Tonight you belong to me, to me alone."

Belong to me alone! Remembering Black Hawk's promise, Laural stiffened at her new husband's gentle words and stepped back from the circle of his warm arms. "No, not to you alone."

With a chuckle Douglas tried to pull her back into his embrace. When she resisted, he glanced down at her in puzzlement. "What is wrong, Laural?"

Laural shook her head. Turning, she stared into the flickering fire. She felt him, tall and warm, behind her. "Douglas," she said quietly, "I love you."

Chuckling, Douglas turned her about and smiled down into her tormented face. With a long finger, he smoothed the furrows of her brows. "I love you, too, my dear L. . . Laural."

Miserably she studied the tender face smiling down at her. "Oh, Douglas, I do love you, but. . .but. . ." She could not look at that loving face any longer. "I hold affection for another as well. I belong to him, too. I have betrayed him in wedding you, and betrayed my father who betrothed me to him. In this, I have failed them both," she wailed. The peace that had so recently been restored to her fled.

She tried to pull away, expecting Douglas to turn once again into the cold angry stranger who she knew existed within this gentle man. His hold on her tightened. "Just who be this paragon who so holds your heart, Laural?" His voice was low and calm.

"Black Hawk," whispered Laural. "He said he would not let me go, Douglas. He said when Lord Cambraige's plot was revealed I would know but one love." Laural regarded Douglas's beloved face through tears. "Why do I feel cut in two? I thought I loved Black Hawk, and I do, but when I realized he was Destrun I knew I held only brotherly affection for him. Be that what he meant about having only one love? I cannot love you both?"

She gulped, hating to hurt her husband but knowing she must tell him the truth. "How can I be a proper wife to you when I failed my father by marrying you instead of Black Hawk? Oh, Douglas, last time I saw him I. . .I didn't want him to leave me. I had to tell you. I am so ashamed, so sorry. . ." Her words trailed off as she sank weakly onto the thick hearth rug. "I. . .I didn't know then that he was Destrun."

Regarding his bride with compassion, Douglas dropped down beside Laural and pulled her unresisting body into his long arms. "Oh, my dearest love," he whispered.

Putting a finger under her chin, wet with her tears, he gazed into her tearful eyes before kissing her with a longing that left Laural weak with love for this large, tender man.

"Oh, Douglas. However can you still love me?" she cried when finally she was able to get her breath.

"You belong to me."

"But. . .but what about Black Hawk?"

The amusement in Douglas's eyes confused and angered her. She turned away when he stroked her cheek. "Black Hawk must have what he wants, my Laural. . .even you."

Laural stiffened and swung to face her husband, shock in her eyes. "Douglas!"

Something tickled the back of her neck, her cheek. Reaching up, Laural grabbed the irritant. She stared at the feather clutched in her hand. . .a black hawk feather! "What? How?" She stared at her husband questioningly.

Smiling, Douglas said, "Come here. . .Leelah."

Tears started in Laural's eyes. "Be it possible? Please tell me plainly." Laural's anguished, hopeful face tore at his heart. "Destrun?"

"Be simply the king's man, not the legendary Black Hawk whose place I have filled for the past ten years since the death of the first Black Hawk—my father." Tenderly he gathered her more closely into his arms, resting his chin on her head. "Aye, my dear. I meant not to tease you thus. Black Hawk had need of you, yet I wished to court you as well. Forgive me, my love, for the pain I have unwittingly caused you."

"Oh, Douglas. God was answering my prayers all along. I just wasn't ready to listen. Douglas—Black Hawk—I love you. I love you whoever you are." She raised her lips to his willingly. The last shreds of the cold, hard shell surrounding her heart melted away, leaving her dizzy with untrammeled joy. Love flowed from her heart like water from a spring, a spring of love, God's everlasting forgiving love. Never again need she be afraid to give—or to receive—love.

"Leelah," said Douglas seriously, releasing her lips after a long while, "you must never reveal Black Hawk's secret. The king has enemies and has need of Black Hawk."

"I swear," she said solemnly, "by all I hold sacred, I shall never breathe the truth to anyone."

Without another word, Douglas carried her back to their bed. Holding her close, he murmured, "Thank God, He kept you safe for me."

"Oh, Douglas. . .Black Hawk." Laural said. "I love you." Covering her yawn, she murmured, "I love. . .I'm so tired . . .I'm sorry." Her words trailed off as she fell asleep in her husband's arms.

Tenderly her new husband held her until he, too, slept.

Laural and Douglas awoke the next morning to a stream of bright sunlight streaming in the narrow window, but they did not open the door until both were dressed for the day, sometime close to noon.

"Do you think we might send for my clothes?" Laural asked as Douglas pulled the fasteners on the side of her gown more tightly before tying them.

"I'll send a messenger straightway," he said, "though I must confess I have a definite partiality for this particular gown."

Laural hugged her husband. "Aye, my love. But 'tis the only gown I have. My only other gown, regrettably," she flinched, "is spotted a very unbecoming red, and this gown is stained from travel." She tried to keep her voice light. Douglas enfolded her in his arms.

"It is over and done. And now you are part of Queen Eleanor's court. We shall see if we cannot have the seamstress sew up some new gowns for you. How would you like that, my love?"

"Oh, Douglas. If truth be told, I have need of gowns. Most of my others are quite threadbare. At least I can show my face in this lovely, if stained, gown."

Douglas had scarce unlatched the door when a party of richly gowned, giggling young women burst in to inspect the sheets. Frowning in irritation, Douglas formally introduced the tall young woman who headed the group as Lady Ramona, the king's ward. To Laural's shock, the woman batted her large green eyes at Douglas invitingly. Never had Laural seen such an overt display of charms.

"Ramona, must you do thus?" remonstrated Douglas, taking Laural's arm.

"If you must have your Celtic bride, then I shall have my own entertainment." Ramona smiled from beneath her lowered lashes. "Come ladies," she said haughtily. "We must strip the sheets."

Douglas fumed as the women went about their work. As soon as the sheets were gathered, he said, "You have what you came for, now leave." Grabbing Lady Ramona's arm, he firmly escorted her and her ladies from the room.

"The nerve of that woman," he fumed, leading his bride downstairs to the great hall.

≈

If Laural thought her time at Caernarvon would be an idyllic honeymoon, she soon found she had been much mistaken. Her newfound faith and her vow not to let hatred build again within her were tried again and again.

In the court, she found herself stifled by the men who made it clear a woman was not to speak unless bidden by her male protector. More than one woman bold enough to speak up was hushed with a harsh, "Hold your tongue, woman."

But it was the women themselves who caused Laural the most grief. She could not begin to compete with the court women in their elegant gowns and sparkling jewels. Though Douglas procured a diamond tiara and pendant for her, neither her gowns nor her jewels impressed the ladies of the court.

Douglas apologized. "The rest of my family jewels, I fear, lie safely at my estate near Windsor Castle. These we shall retrieve when the king returns with his entourage to London."

Laural smiled at his chagrin and murmured, "'Tis no matter." And in truth, much more than jewels or clothes set her apart from the other ladies.

Encouraged by Lady Ramona, the other ladies of the court looked down their long noses at "that Celtic wench." They shook their lovely heads over her small size and recoiled from her hands. Dismissing her out of hand, they gushed over Douglas—the hero of the hour.

"'Tis true," Laural overheard Ramona say with a sneer, "he but married her for her father's vast holdings."

Another slender, dark-haired woman giggled. "And what of you Ramona? You have lost him, and I hear tell the king seeks another for you."

"Nay. I may never bear his seal ring, but I'll wager a new gown he'll be mine by the end of the month."

Laural turned away. The infidelity and licentiousness of the court sickened her. She had expected something different in Edward's court. She hated watching the lustful eyes of the noblemen surveying her petite form while making crude remarks to her husband. Only at night could she relax with her husband. Only in Douglas's arms was she content. He, too, seemed content, but for how long? Her prayers grew desperate.

"Lord Jesus, I love him, yet I have little to offer but Comfrey. I miss home so much. Can we not go home to Comfrey? Be there hope for us?"

How long before he tired of her thin body and sought the obvious charms offered by Ramona or one of the other women? Laural blushed hotly, thinking of how she had offered herself to Black Hawk. It must have greatly amused him when he had so many other comely ladies willing to volunteer.

Her respect and admiration for her king and queen expanded with her intimate knowledge of court life. Despite all the available women, King Edward had eyes only for his queen, and she for him.

Over and over Laural asked herself, *Does Douglas, like the king, truly want his wife alone?* As days and weeks passed, Laural grew tired of being pushed aside while other women hung about her husband.

Because they were newly wed, perhaps the king would release Douglas. They could go to his estate—anywhere away from the king's court! In her discontent, Laural took action—she prayed.

This time she also listened. "Will Douglas leave court for me?"

"Do you trust your husband, Laural?" asked the voice.

"I want to."

Again that dreadful stillness. "I do. I do. I will trust him. I trust You, Lord. I trust You."

"Then talk to your husband."

Gulping back her fear that Douglas would dismiss her request out of hand, Laural waited for her opportunity.

fifteen

The Lord shall preserve thy going out,
and thy coming in from this time forth,
and even for evermore. Psalm 121:8

❧

"I do not wish to offend, Douglas," said Laural, confronting her husband in the privacy of their bedchamber one evening several days later, "but I doubt I can tolerate this place one day more."

Douglas reached out to enfold her in his long arms, but Laural stepped back. "Leelah, what disorders you this eve?" The amusement in his eyes faded into bewilderment.

"See you not! The women are all so beautiful. They want you. Ramona. . ." Laural choked, remembering Ramona's boast. "Ramona boasts you want her." She surveyed her husband's rugged, handsome face.

"Edward needs to see that woman settled and soon," grumbled Douglas.

Biting her lip, Laural asked, "Why ever did you choose me? Ramona claims you sought Papa's fief." She glanced away, trembling at the burst of anger that flashed in her husband's eyes.

He gripped her shoulders and held her eyes with his. "Faugh! Be this what you believe, Leelah? Tell me plainly. Is it? Do you think me unfaithful?"

A sob shook Laural. At once, Douglas's visage softened and he pulled her to him. "My love. Leelah. I love you. Trust not Ramona's tattle overmuch." He spoke softly, but commandingly.

"Douglas, she said you would lose interest in me by the end of the month." At her words, she felt him stiffen. "Oh, Douglas, can you not get leave from the king for us to go away from here? To Comfrey, mayhap."

He heard the hesitant plea. "Be you homesick, my love?"

Frustrated at his dullness, Laural pushed away. Did he not wish to understand? "Douglas. I must get away from here before I go completely mad. Do you not even notice? These ladies do not recognize our marriage. They think you care not for me. They flatter you, but at best, they ignore me. At worst. . .at worst. . ." Laural sighed. "They treat me with more contempt than Lord Cambraige ever did."

"Are you certain?" Douglas stared down at her in surprise. "This is Edward's court."

"Nay, Douglas, I lied! Everyone dotes on me, especially dear Ramona." Laural wrenched from him angrily.

She waited for him to come to her, to calm her. When he did not follow her, her heart sank. "My dear, look at me." Douglas commanded.

"Why, to tell me to hold my tongue?" she retorted, too enraged to take care with her words. "Am I naught but a woman, and my pain but womanish folly?"

"Laural. Look at me, now!" She sensed his closeness.

Slowly, Laural glanced up at her husband, frightened at what she might find revealed in his eyes. Did he despise her? Had she misunderstood God's direction?

"Laural. . .Leelah," he said carefully, touching her cheek with aching gentleness. "I realized not what was happening. I beg you accept my most abject apologies. My mind has been on the king's business, and I assumed all was well with you."

At Laural's shocked stare, he chuckled. "Close your mouth, woman. Are my words so much a surprise—for a man completely charmed not only by his wife's mien, but by her mind and courage, as well as her faith?"

"Oh, Douglas, my faith is so weak. But I do love you so very much," whispered Laural as her tears flowed unchecked.

Holding her tightly, Douglas said regretfully, "My dear, you please me well, and I would like nothing better than to take you to Comfrey, but. . ." He sighed. "I must attend the king until he speaks to the noblemen who are gathering to demand a Welsh successor. Then. . .then, my darling, I shall take you away. We will set Comfrey to rights as it was when your father was alive. You have my oath on it."

Smiling down into her soft, half-closed eyes, he stroked her cheek. "'Tis time those hoydens learned to acknowledge my wife." Thoughtfully he ran his long fingers through her hair. "Ah, my love, leave it to me. All will soon know just how important my wife is to me."

The next morning as Laural's maid dressed her hair, Douglas handed the young woman a familiar feather. Staring at it, the maid trembled. Laural glanced up, afraid of what her husband might be revealing. "Douglas!"

He silenced her with a kiss before addressing the startled maid. "This must adorn my lady's hair this morning."

"Aye, m'lord." said the maid to her jauntily departing master.

What purpose might the feather serve? Laural wondered. Surely he was not going to reveal himself for her sake. Nay, that made no sense. The feather would be recognized, that Laural knew. Her first hint of Douglas's plan came with the maid's hesitant question as she set the Black Hawk feather among the bright blue ribbons holding up her braided hair. "Do you know him, m'lady? Know you Black Hawk?" She spoke the name with awe.

"Aye, I know him right well." Laural smiled at the instant

respect she saw in the eyes of the young maid.

The court women reacted no less quickly. As Laural appeared for the long noonday meal, they stared at the feather with a mixture of curiosity and disdain. Head high, Ramona approached her and said with condescension, "I understand your father was a friend of the great Black Hawk. The feather came from him. . .your father, did it not?"

"Nay. I received this from Black Hawk himself," Laural said firmly, watching the older woman's eyes narrow. A slight noise made her catch the eyes of King Edward, who was just seating himself at the table on the dais. His lips twitching with a repressed grin, the king of England closed his languid eye in a slow wink.

Ramona also noticed and reddened with anger. She misliked having the Celtic wench replace her in the king's favor. "That is not possible." With a sneer, Ramona addressed the women gathered about them. "Do you believe this? The Welsh maid is so crazed she actually believes she knows the great Black Hawk!" Then she laughed while the others giggled.

"Enough Ramona," commanded the scowling king. "She indeed knows the man, and quite well. 'Tis high time I find you a mate."

At that moment, Douglas approached Laural. Bending over her, he ardently kissed her hand. Amusement danced in his gray eyes. "I see my lady wears the standard of my rival."

"Rival!" Ramona screeched in a half laugh. "Her? Your Celtic bride favored by the great Black Hawk? Douglas, are you touched?"

"Douglas, please," pleaded Laural, afraid of what he might next say.

In feigned surprise, Douglas glanced from the giggling

women to Ramona's unbelieving countenance. "This explains your insulting behavior toward my wife. Knew you not she was Black Hawk's chosen woman? She is all a man could find: innocence and a deep abiding faith in Jesus Christ."

As one, the women gasped. Ramona tensed, her eyes jealously surveying the petite young woman by Douglas's side. "She be your wife now," she challenged.

"Aye, m'lady," agreed Douglas. "And I plan to keep her . . .and make her content with me. I find that most difficult when you lovely ladies refuse to acknowledge her as my wife . . .as my one and only love." He viewed Ramona through cold narrowed eyes. "And that she shall be, now and ever."

Gasping, Ramona stepped back at his forthrightness. Ignoring her response, Douglas continued firmly, "My lady is a very special lady. Know you not she spied for Black Hawk? She was betrothed to him."

As he paused to gaze tenderly down at her, Laural saw the dawning of reluctant respect for her in the eyes of the court women. A young women with pearls looped through her luxurious raven hair asked, "Why did she not wed Black Hawk? Perhaps he threw her over."

Giving a deadly cold smile, Douglas tilted Laural's chin toward him. Leaning down he savored her lips in a long kiss. Sensing Laural tremble, he held her to him to keep her from falling. When he released her, she leaned against him weakly. Douglas chuckled huskily.

"Black Hawk's woman chose me. She loves me, but she said it was not an easy choice. So you must understand. If I do not please her, she could always return to Black Hawk —or could were it not for her desire to please the Lord God as well as her husband." He paused again, solely for dramatic effect.

"I know she may go to Black Hawk at any time she

desires. But she is my wedded wife, and I shall do naught to hurt her. Do you now understand? You will acknowledge my wife. She shall have your respect." It was a command. He tightened his arms about Laural and again kissed her until the room spun and she wanted nothing more than to be forever in his arms.

For her ears alone he whispered, "Oh, Leelah, if I were but free at this moment. . . ."

With reluctance, he released her. Their embrace caused a stir, and not a few jests were made by the males present. Such comments might have continued throughout the meal had not Douglas's cold countenance turned on each offender and quickly squelched the more audible comments. Later when Douglas left with the king, and the queen left to be with her son, Laural found herself surrounded by expectant court ladies. Expecting more of their harsh jests, she tensed.

"Be it true what Doug—Lord Strathouse said?" asked one woman. "Do you know Black Hawk?"

Laural faced her. "Aye." The woman sighed.

Laural watched Ramona fight her dislike and jealousy. In the end, she swallowed her pride to inquire, "Might you acquaint us with Black Hawk?" Laural noted her slight breathlessness.

Shaking her head, Laural laughed softly and relaxed. "Nay, m'lady." She held up her hand to forestall Ramona's protestations. "Black Hawk remains, as always, a very private man. To reveal his identity would not only betray his love, but might endanger his future usefulness, his very life, for he is not only the king's man, but God's as well.

"I care deeply for Black Hawk. I keep always his secret." *And mine,* she added to herself. Aloud she added, "My husband, Douglas, would not wish me to foolishly endanger a man who has done so much for the king, and I love my husband very, very much." Under her breath she murmured, "Thank You, Lord, for the words to say."

Ramona's eyes flashed confusion. "Do you love God so much?"

"Aye. He has proven Himself trustworthy, and I will follow Him. 'Tis He who brought me my husband."

Ramona's face blanched. "Then I never had a chance. If God is on your side. . ."

Sensing the woman's inner struggle, Laural lowered her defenses. "I finally obeyed Him," she said. "He loves everyone, m'lady."

Ramona merely shook her head.

From the looks on the faces around her, Laural knew she finally had their respect. Though Douglas's words might not completely end their attempts to gain his notice, at least the women would take care not to provoke either Laural's or Douglas's ire.

Laural sighed. Mayhap she could tolerate court life for a time, but only for a time.

❧

Not many days later, Laural stood proudly by the side of her husband, who stood next to his monarch. King Edward, true to his word to present his Welsh subjects with a Welsh ruler, brought forth his newborn son. Even in his grief for Prince Alfonso's resent untimely death, the king understood the possibilities now available to this son who had become, on the death of Prince Alfonso, the crown prince and heir to the English throne.

Tenderly he held up his son before the delegation of Welsh noblemen. "Here is your crown prince. He has been born in your country—a Welshman—and I give my oath his first words will be Welsh. I declare him the Prince of Wales."

After the first shock, the Welsh nobles began to cheer.

"Fiat! Fiat! Vie le Roi!" "Hurrah! Hurrah! Long live the king!"

Proudly Laural smiled up at her tall husband. The last heaviness on her heart, the last doubt about her husband's love for her melted away under his tender gaze.

Douglas's arm stole about her waist as he smiled down at her, his eyes misting at the undimmed love and pride in her eyes.

She nodded and leaned against him, finally at peace with herself, with her love, and with her faith.

Thank You, Lord, she breathed in heartfelt gratitude, looking forward to a life of loving, unfettered by fear, anger, or bitterness. Douglas's smile widened in understanding as she quietly squeezed his hand.

Tenderly he mouthed, "Tomorrow, Leelah. Tomorrow we go home to Comfrey."

A Letter To Our Readers

Dear Reader:

In order that we might better contribute to your reading enjoyment, we would appreciate your taking a few minutes to respond to the following questions. When completed, please return to the following:

Rebecca Germany, Managing Editor
Heartsong Presents
P.O. Box 719
Uhrichsville, Ohio 44683

1. Did you enjoy reading *Black Hawk's Feather*?
   ❑ Very much. I would like to see more books
     by this author!
   ❑ Moderately
     I would have enjoyed it more if _____

     _____

2. Are you a member of **Heartsong Presents**? ❑Yes ❑No
   If no, where did you purchase this book?_____

   _____

3. What influenced your decision to purchase this
   book? (Check those that apply.)

   ❑ Cover   ❑ Back cover copy

   ❑ Title   ❑ Friends

   ❑ Publicity   ❑ Other_____

4. How would you rate, on a scale from 1 (poor) to 5
   (superior), the cover design?_____

5. On a scale from 1 (poor) to 10 (superior), please rate the following elements.

    ___Heroine   ___Plot

    ___ Hero   ___Inspirational theme

    ___ Setting   ___Secondary characters

6. What settings would you like to see covered in **Heartsong Presents** books?_____

_____

_____

7. What are some inspirational themes you would like to see treated in future books?_____

_____

_____

8. Would you be interested in reading other **Heartsong Presents** titles?   ❑ Yes   ❑ No

9. Please check your age range:
   ❑ Under 18   ❑ 18-24   ❑ 25-34
   ❑ 35-45   ❑ 46-55   ❑ Over 55

10. How many hours per week do you read? _____

Name _____

Occupation _____

Address _____

City_____ State_____ Zip _____

Heartsong Presents Classics!

We have put together a collection of some of the most popular **Heartsong Presents** titles in two value-priced volumes. Favorite titles from our first year of publication, no longer published in single volumes, are now available in our new *Inspirational Romance Readers*.

Historical Collection #2 includes:
- ❤ *When Comes the Dawn* by Brenda Bancroft
- ❤ *The Sure Promise* by JoAnn A. Grote
- ❤ *Dream Spinner* by Sally Laity
- ❤ *Shores of Promise* by Kate Blackwell

Contemporary Collection #2 includes:
- ❤ *Design for Love* by Janet Gortsema
- ❤ *Fields of Sweet Content* by Norma Jean Lutz
- ❤ *From the Heart* by Sara Mitchell
- ❤ *Llama Lady* by VeraLee Wiggins

Each collection is $4.97 plus $1.00 for shipping and handling. Buy both collections for $8.99 plus $1.00 for shipping and handling.

Available through **Heartsong Presents**
toll-free 1-800-847-8270
or send orders to:
Heartsong Presents
P.O. Box 719
Uhrichsville, Ohio 44683
http://www.barbourbooks.com

Prices subject to change without notice.

Heart♥ong

HEARTSONG PRESENTS TITLES AVAILABLE NOW:

_HP 28 DAKOTA DAWN, *Lauraine Snelling*

_HP 40 PERFECT LOVE, *Janelle Jamison*

_HP 44 DAKOTA DREAM, *Lauraine Snelling*

_HP 51 THE UNFOLDING HEART, *JoAnn A. Grote*

_HP 63 THE WILLING HEART, *Janelle Jamison*

_HP 64 CROWS'-NESTS AND MIRRORS, *Colleen L. Reece*

_HP 67 DAKOTA DUSK, *Lauraine Snelling*

_HP 71 DESTINY'S ROAD, *Janelle Jamison*

_HP 72 SONG OF CAPTIVITY, *Linda Herring*

_HP 76 HEARTBREAK TRAIL, *VeraLee Wiggins*

_HP 91 SIGN OF THE EAGLE, *Kay Cornelius*

_HP 95 SIGN OF THE DOVE, *Kay Cornelius*

_HP 96 FLOWER OF SEATTLE, *Colleen L. Reece*

_HP103 LOVE'S SHINING HOPE, *JoAnn A. Grote*

_HP104 HAVEN OF PEACE, *Carol Mason Parker*

_HP111 A KINGDOM DIVIDED, *Tracie J. Peterson*

_HP112 CAPTIVES OF THE CANYON, *Colleen L. Reece*

_HP115 SISTERS IN THE SUN, *Shirley Rhode*

_HP120 AN HONEST LOVE, *JoAnn A. Grote*

_HP124 HIS NAME ON HER HEART, *Mary LaPietra*

_HP127 FOREVER YOURS, *Tracie J. Peterson*

_HP128 MISPLACED ANGEL, *VeraLee Wiggins*

_HP131 LOVE IN THE PRAIRIE WILDS, *Robin Chandler*

_HP132 LOST CREEK MISSION, *Cheryl Tenbrook*

_HP135 SIGN OF THE SPIRIT, *Kay Cornelius*

_HP136 REKINDLED FLAME, *JoAnn A. Grote*

_HP140 ANGEL'S CAUSE, *Tracie J. Peterson*

_HP143 MORNING MOUNTAIN, *Peggy Darty*

_HP144 FLOWER OF THE WEST, *Colleen L. Reece*

_HP147 DREWRY'S BLUFF, *Cara McCormack*

_HP148 DREAMS OF THE PIONEERS, *Linda Herring*

_HP155 TULSA TEMPEST, *Norma Jean Lutz*

_HP163 DREAMS OF GLORY, *Linda Herring*

_HP164 ALAS MY LOVE, *Tracie J. Peterson*

(If ordering from this page, please remember to include it with the order form.)

···········Presents·······

Great Inspirational Romance at a Great Price!

Heartsong Presents
Love Stories Are Rated G!

That's for godly, gratifying, and of course, great! If you love a thrilling love story, but don't appreciate the sordidness of some popular paperback romances, **Heartsong Presents** is for you. In fact, **Heartsong Presents** is the *only inspirational romance book club*, the only one featuring love stories where Christian faith is the primary ingredient in a marriage relationship.

Sign up today to receive your first set of four, never before published Christian romances. Send no money now; you will receive a bill with the first shipment. You may cancel at any time without obligation, and if you aren't completely satisfied with any selection, you may return the books for an immediate refund!

Imagine. . .four new romances every four weeks—two historical, two contemporary—with men and women like you who long to meet the one God has chosen as the love of their lives. . .all for the low price of $9.97 postpaid.

To join, simply complete the coupon below and mail to the address provided. **Heartsong Presents** romances are rated G for another reason: They'll arrive *Godspeed!*

YES! Sign me up for Heartsong!

NEW MEMBERSHIPS WILL BE SHIPPED IMMEDIATELY!

Send no money now. We'll bill you only $9.97 post-paid with your first shipment of four books. Or for faster action, call toll free 1-800-847-8270.

NAME _____

ADDRESS _____

CITY _____ STATE _____ ZIP _____

MAIL TO: HEARTSONG PRESENTS, P.O. Box 719, Uhrichsville, Ohio 44683

YES10-96

"That prim and proper exterior
doesn't fool me for
one minute," James said.

"I know underneath there's a latent passion so explosive that it frightens the hell out of you. You can't
hide or run from life forever, Skye."

All the color drained from her face.

"Don't you see?" he continued. "Can't you understand? I've been trying every way I know to break
through your damned defenses."

"Why?" she whispered.

"Because I want you," he replied. "Very badly—and
my patience has about run out."

Burying his head deep in her sweetly scented hair, he
kissed the hollow of her neck, traveling slowly up her
neck to her face, her mouth...

Dear Reader:

After more than one year of publication, SECOND CHANCE AT LOVE has a lot to celebrate. Not only has it become firmly established as a major line of paperback romances, but response from our readers also continues to be warm and enthusiastic. Your letters keep pouring in—and we love receiving them. We're getting to know you—your likes and dislikes— and want to assure you that your contribution does make a difference.

As we work hard to offer you better and better SECOND CHANCE AT LOVE romances, we're especially gratified to hear that you, the reader, are rating us higher and higher. After all, our success depends on *you*. We're pleased that you enjoy our books and that you appreciate the extra effort our writers and staff put into them. Thanks for spreading the good word about SECOND CHANCE AT LOVE and for giving us your loyal support. Please keep your suggestions and comments coming!

With warm wishes,

Ellen Edwards

Ellen Edwards
SECOND CHANCE AT LOVE
The Berkley/Jove Publishing Group
200 Madison Avenue
New York, NY 10016

Second Chance at Love

SATIN AND STEELE
JAELYN CONLEE

SECOND CHANCE AT LOVE
BOOK

Second Chance at Love books are published by
The Berkley/Jove Publishing Group
200 Madison Avenue, New York, NY 10016

To Terry and Larry
With love and gratitude

SATIN AND STEELE

Chapter One

AT TWO O'CLOCK in the morning, Skye Anderson was driving very carefully along the rain-slick streets of Dallas, making her way toward the airport.

Driving, even at this early hour of the morning, did not normally make her nervous, nor did rainstorms make her uneasy, but there was a definite feeling of tension deep within her. This was a luxury Skye didn't allow herself anymore, and she really didn't know why she felt that way.

Dallas had had one of its violent spring rainstorms that night, but, characteristically, as quickly as it had come, it was now nearly gone, leaving behind only a light mist and extremely hazardous driving conditions to cope with for the slim young woman behind the wheel.

1

A slight frown creased her forehead as she concentrated on making the final turn into the airport, heading, not for the main terminal, but for the lesser-known area of the airport where only the private aircraft landed.

Slowly she negotiated her blue Mercedes between the buildings and thought of what she would do once inside the lounge that was reserved for the passengers and pilots of the private aircraft that were constantly coming in and out of Dallas at all hours of the day and night.

What had occurred tonight shouldn't have happened, especially at this critical time. It had been a senseless, stupid mix-up, but since she had been wide awake when the airport had called, she had said immediately that she would come. As usual, it wasn't so much the storm or what was going on around her that had kept her awake, but what was going on inside her head. From several years of experience, Skye knew that only activity would clear her head of its disturbing thoughts, if only temporarily.

Skye pulled her car skillfully to the curb in front of the private terminal. The Mercedes belonged to the company for which she worked and was a precaution she was sure that Jonathan Hayes had taken in order to ensure that she have a dependable, well-kept car.

She shrugged into her heavy shearling jacket and stepped out into the cool, damp air, breathing deeply, trying to clear her mind, but not really knowing why.

Walking swiftly, she stepped through the swinging door into the brilliantly lit building. Her sky-blue eyes—eyes as blue as the Texas skies under which she had been born—quickly adjusted to the light.

Now the usually clear eyes were frowning. Where in the world was everyone? This was really too much! At such an important time, why did everyone have to suddenly become so incompetent.

Slowly she climbed the stairway that took her to the observation lounge overlooking the tarmac. The lights on this level were dim and restful and a lovely melody drifted over the P. A. system. The music was as beautiful and haunting as the woman who walked quietly across the soft indoor-outdoor carpeting.

An unnatural stillness hovered in the air as she looked out of the huge windows toward the sleek, silvery bird of a jet that stood there—waiting.

Damn! she thought as she turned to view the lounge where functional but comfortable sofas and chairs had been placed strategically for easy conversation, some completely hidden from view by screens, columns, and plants for those weary travelers who wanted a short rest. But the room was empty! Completely empty! Or was it? What was it that made her feel she was not alone?

Sighing, she chided herself for being so fanciful and, taking off her jacket, she walked over to the courtesy phone placed on one of the tables to dial the airport customs office. John Weaver, the assistant officer, answered, and Skye was immediately grateful to hear the voice of another human being. It must be this strange night, she thought.

Hanging up after having obtained Mr. Weaver's promise to come right over, she stood in the center of the lounge, wondering what in the world had come over her, what was causing her to feel so strange.

A slightly taller than average young woman, she

was delicately boned, but had the softly curving figure of a mature woman. When the airport had called, she had hastily pulled on a pair of old, well-fitting wheat-colored Levis and a black turtleneck sweater which emphasized the paleness of her creamy complexion and the gorgeous mane of indescribable color that spilled loosely halfway down her back.

She flung her hair over her shoulder as she moved restlessly back to the windows to look out at the jet. No lights in the cabin. They must have decided to try to sleep while this mess was cleared. She had no idea why the men on that jet should be causing her such sudden anxiety. She had known they were coming, and she had already met most of them. It just didn't make sense!

Except—the thought seemed to come from no-where—James Steele, the legendary owner of the Steele Corporation, head of the giant conglomerate that was to take the Hayes Corporation into its family. As yet, no one here had met him. His name had dominated first the sports pages and later the business sections of every newspaper in America. The man had moves both on and off the football field that no one had seen before or since.

The last she had heard, he was in the Mideast, and it wasn't certain whether he would be able to be in Dallas for the completion of the takeover. Still, she had made sure that the necessary accommodations would be ready for him just the same.

James Steele, she mused thoughtfully. From all accounts the man was just like his name—hard, cold steel. Skye put her finger to the window and traced a raindrop's path until it joined with another and became indistinguishable from the rest.

"Mrs. Anderson!" John Weaver was coming up the stairs two at a time with a clipboard in his hand. His face was perplexed. "I wasn't in the office when the plane landed, and I was just contacted. I'm really sorry, but I'm afraid I had forgotten they were expected. The paperwork seems to have gotten lost in the shuffle.

"I can't imagine how this happened," he continued quickly, almost as if he were afraid of letting her get in a word. "We're always on duty at the main terminal, but usually when we know ahead of time the day and approximate hour a private plane will be arriving from out of the country, we make certain that there is a customs officer here to clear the passengers." He shook his head. "What can I say? To have gotten you out of bed was really unforgivable."

Calm now that there was some positive action she could take, Skye looked at the man, her blue eyes clear and sharp. "Mr. Weaver, forget the inconvenience to me. I'm rarely asleep at this time of night anyway," her beautiful, low voice drawled with barely suppressed anger as it drifted across the quiet lounge. "It's those men on that plane that you should be worried about." She gestured toward the window. "That plane happens to be carrying the future executives and just possibly the new owner of the Hayes Corporation." Not once did she raise her voice, but the man before her was quelled visibly.

"A week ago, I personally contacted your office and told them that these men would be flying in tonight, probably from the Mideast. I was assured that there would be someone here who could expedite their clearance. Flying all night into one of our infamous spring storms couldn't have been much fun, and then to be told that they couldn't be cleared until a customs official was found has got to appear the height of stupidity to them. Now, those men are tired, possibly hungry, and probably very angry. I want them cleared immediately!"

The man in front of Skye seemed to shrink before the well-controlled, soft-spoken young woman. "Certainly"—he was already backing down the stairs— "absolutely. I'll get things under way."

As he was turning, Skye said, "Mr. Weaver, you'll have Mr. Quincey call me first thing in the morning, won't you?" She spoke quietly, but she might as well have hit him with a hammer. John Weaver walked away, dreading the coming morning when he would have to face his stern boss.

Watching him walk away, Skye sighed and rubbed her temple in a slow, circular motion. What was wrong with her? she wondered. She rarely got this angry. Walking over to the phone, she dialed the number of the hotel where she had reserved accommodations for the men. The Hayes Corporation always used this particular hotel because it had easy access to their building.

"Night manager, please." Her voice was pleasant now. "Mr. Raggers, this is Skye Anderson. How are you?...I'm fine, thank you. I called because the party of men from the Steele Corporation will be arriving there in about thirty minutes, and I just wanted to make sure everything is ready...Wonderful! Also, please have the kitchen stand by in case they're hungry. I'll count on you to handle it from that end and thank you very much, Mr. Raggers. I know Mr. Hayes will be very pleased. Good night."

Picking up her jacket, Skye turned to go, but suddenly stopped. Slowly turning, she walked a few steps toward the window, and once again she was aware of the haunting melody that was being played. All at once, as if needing support, she leaned against a column. *What was it!* she thought, rubbing her temple.

The sky had cleared, revealing a full moon. The powerful jet was mirrored in the rain-drenched tarmac. With no activity around or in it, it looked beautiful and somehow mysterious.

Straightening, Skye turned and let her eyes roam slowly over the lounge, taking in the varying shades of darkness and light that were tinting the room.

And then she saw him. There, sitting in a shadowed corner not too many feet away was a man—a man who could have seen and heard her every move without her knowledge.

There was an electricity in his stillness, like a bolt of lightning that had been streaking from heaven to earth and was suspended momentarily in time.

Because of the dimness, Skye couldn't really make out his features. Only that he was big and lean and had the most extraordinary eyes. They were luminous in the darkness, like a cat's, searing her with their intensity.

It never occurred to Skye to try to speak to the man. Oddly enough, she felt no alarm or fear about the strange man's presence. He seemed to be just part and parcel of this eerie night, almost as if he wasn't

real, as if his look of total and concentrated determination hadn't touched her. Yet.

Mentally shaking herself, she straightened and put
her jacket on, lifting her heavy hair free from the
confines of the collar. Then, determinedly, she walked
across the lounge, down the stairs and out into the
night.

Chapter Two

THE FOLLOWING MORNING, Skye was already at her desk by 8:30, going through the morning mail and sipping her second cup of coffee. Today would be busy and she wanted to get a few things organized before "the brass," as Beth Ann called them, arrived. "The brass" were the same men who had been on the plane last night.

For some reason, she simply couldn't concentrate yet. Lack of sleep, maybe, she thought, but deep down she knew that wasn't the case. It was because today would mark the beginning of the end of a busy, if not contented, segment of her life and the start of a new, unknown period. For as soon as the new executives took over officially, she was going to resign, to rest a while, perhaps travel and to decide what to do next with her life. Thanks to Jonathan's careful investment of the insurance money, she had more than enough to tide her over.

Skye swung her swivel chair away from the desk so that she sat facing the window. She loved the look of Dallas after a rain—all freshly washed and brand-new, as if God had decided to give the human race another chance. However, she wasn't seeing the view of busy downtown Dallas, or the bright Texas sun drying all traces of last night's rain, or the modern skyscrapers of glass and concrete seemingly trying to outdo one another in an effort to reach up into the blue, blue sky overhead.

Sipping her coffee, she was looking back five years in her mind to the time when, at nineteen years of age, only six months after marrying her high-school sweetheart, she had lost her husband and the baby she had been carrying. She had been in the car, too, barely escaping with her life, but the surgeon was forced to remove the baby growing inside her, together with her womb, in order to save her life. Two days later, she awakened to an empty feeling that she had never been able to shake.

Her life had been spared, but her world had been destroyed. At the time, she couldn't understand why she should have to face a world without the warmth of her gentle, considerate husband or the feeling of movement in her stomach which told of the new life growing there.

But day had followed day relentlessly, and, to her surprise, the world continued unchanged. She pulled herself together and enrolled in a secretarial refresher course that led eventually to her present position as personal secretary to Jonathan Hayes, the president of the Hayes Corporation.

Skye hadn't wanted to do any of it. All she really wanted to do was spend her days in bed with the covers pulled over her head. But some tiny spark of self-preservation she didn't know she possessed made her climb out of bed every morning, and somehow, she had managed to get through the last five years a day at a time.

She had learned to numb her emotions, and as time passed, living became easier—largely, she felt, because of Jonathan Hayes, who, immediately upon looking into those pain-filled blue eyes, took her under his wing and became the father figure she had lost when she was fourteen years old. Her mother had followed her father a few years later.

Jonathan, carrying alone the ever-increasing weight of his business despite weariness and ill health that come with age, nevertheless had taken the beautiful young widow as one of his many responsibilities. He not only furnished her with a lovely apartment in one of his company's apartment buildings, but also gave her a luxurious, but dependable car—a company car, he called it—in order to lift some of the financial burden from her shoulders and at the same time ensure that she was well and safely cared for.

In return for Jonathan's kindness, Skye had taken it upon herself to reorganize her employer's schedule, his office, and even, to a certain extent, his company. Not in any business sense, certainly, but along the more human lines of the personal approach in everything that touched his life while at the office. Her instincts told her that here was a man who was working much too hard, and the impersonal world of business was imposing far too much of a strain on him.

So she had humanized his business life. To her way of thinking, it was nothing, and it had given her a purpose. But to Jonathan Hayes, it was something special, because she had brought beauty and graciousness into his impersonal business world and had taken some of the routine workload from his shoulders. To him she was a phenomenon, and he had given her carte blanche in the redecorating and reorganizing she had undertaken that first few months. The arrangement had evolved so that each received mutual benefit and a measure of protection.

Skye was a coward about life, she freely admitted to herself. She felt she would be stupid not to be, because, in a split-second—with tires squealing, metal crunching, and glass breaking—fate had taken all that she held dear away. Life seemed fickle to Skye, and she had learned not to count on anything. She had consciously and deliberately built a wall around herself, and she was determined never again to let herself feel or care to the extent that she could be hurt with such devastation.

But, at the same time, Skye felt she had stayed under the protection of Jonathan and his company long enough. Places couldn't hurt, she reasoned with herself, and she wanted a change. She had decided to travel, to wander without any goal or destination in mind and without any shackles to bind or to cause pain.

A cheery "Mornin'" interrupted her reverie. Skye turned and smiled fondly as Beth Ann plopped—for

there was really no other word for it—onto Skye's
desk. She had been training Beth Ann to take over
as personal secretary to the new president of the Hayes
Corporation and Skye knew she would do just fine,
but Beth Ann wasn't as sure of herself yet.

"Are the brass in yet?" Beth Ann's anxious brown
eyes scanned the beautifully serene face in front of
her. Then, not giving her a chance to answer, she
continued, "You look gorgeous! As usual, I might
add. How *do* you manage it so early in the morning?"

Skye smiled at Beth Ann's completely ingenuous
questions. The young girl's brown hair was permed
into short curls that fell in chic disorder around her
face. "The answer to your first question is 'No,' and
to your second, 'I really don't know.'" Especially,
she added to herself, since I've had just a few hour's
sleep.

Beth Ann looked thoughtfully at Skye for a moment. This morning Skye's hair was swept back into
a severe French twist, showing the delicate bone structure of her classically oval face. Her hair seemed to
be shot through with about five different colors, rang-
ing from wheat, to gold, to amber, to red, with a few
strands of gray making the combination all the more
interesting.

Beth Ann thought ruefully of what she wouldn't
give for one-tenth of Skye's beauty and grace. But
Skye was totally unaware of her appearance and her
affect on other people. She took all compliments with
a simple shrug and a demure "thank you." Consequently, no one who knew Skye could possibly be
jealous—only unobtrusively protective of her frag-

ility. Unobtrusive, because Skye rarely talked to anyone about her past tragedy and she would let no one get too close in case she would have to reveal too much of herself.

Beth Ann continued to stare at Skye with loving exasperation. "My mama always told me that a girl had to suffer to be beautiful. Well, I've suffered!" she stated dramatically. "I've had my hair tortured into curls and pulled, with great pain"—she emphasized the last three words—"through tiny little holes of a plastic cap so that strands could be frosted a different color. My body has been exercised to the point of exhaustion, my stomach starved, my lashes dyed . . ." She paused for breath and frowned at Skye, who looked amused. "And I could never achieve your effect if I lived to be a hundred!"

"That's because you are you, and your individuality is very attractive," Skye returned kindly. "Beauty is a gift of God—nothing a person should feel smug about at all—and it's sometimes more of a liability than an asset." She had fended off too many unwanted passes not to know the truth of what she was saying, but Skye also wanted to give Beth Ann confidence. "All the individual features that serve to make up Beth Ann Cunningham make you a very unique person, and you should never try to copy another—least of all me."

Beth Ann shook her head and smiled. "I know you really mean what you're saying, and I appreciate the nice words, but sometimes those thoughts aren't too comforting—especially when I'm in the same room as you."

Skye smiled, but her eyes showed concern. She knew the young girl would obtain more self-assurance with time. Beth Ann was very attractive, and more men noticed her than she realized.

"Did the great James Steele come in last night?" Beth Ann continued, switching the conversation back to her original question.

Skye looked up from the letter she had started to read with a slight frown. "I really don't know. We're not sure when he'll arrive. There's no real necessity for him to be here until the final papers are ready to sign, you know. Paul Garth is to be the president and the one most concerned with the running of the company, even if Mr. Steele will be the owner."

"Still," Beth Ann persisted, "you'd think he would be interested enough to look over a company of this size before he buys it. We haven't laid eyes on him, and I, for one, can hardly wait." Beth Ann hopped off Skye's desk and wandered over to the window. "Just think of it. He can't be more than thirty-eight. He was a national hero on the football field, and there are records he made while playing collegiate and professional football that still stand and may never be broken. I know because I have four brothers," Beth Ann dimpled, "and they have promised to kill me if I don't get his autograph for them."

Skye knew the truth of what Beth Ann was saying. She had seen James Steele play football on television a couple of times, and he had been something to behold. He was a flawless, confident quarterback, a natural leader, coolest under pressure, and able to throw any pass and defeat any team. Then, quitting the game suddenly at the peak of his career, he had built an empire which reached far and wide and was still expanding.

"Since that time," Beth Ann continued, unaware of Skye's thoughts, "he has become a multimillionaire in business, where he's reputed to be just as tough and ruthless as he was on the football field. And he's still single!"

Skye was not impressed by the last statement, and Beth Ann's worshipful attitude was beginning to get on her nerves. "I'm sure he has every confidence in Paul Garth's ability, or he wouldn't be putting such a young man in charge of this large a company. Not to mention the barrage of lawyers and accountants that have been flying in and out of here for the last few months. Everything is just about settled."

Beth Ann walked back to the front of the desk, "Skye! Do you have to be so calm and reasonable all the time? It's not everyday a mere working girl gets to meet a gorgeous hunk of man like the famous James Steele. Why, I can't count the number of glamorous women he's been involved with." Beth Ann's dimples came into view again.

"Right," Skye returned. She had not really been concentrating on what Beth Ann was saying, but she glanced up and saw the look on Beth Ann's face. "Therefore, since he's not likely to be interested in us other than the competent secretaries we are"—this last was stressed—"let's stick to business. Here's some morning mail I want you to take care of, and there's a list I left on your desk last night." Beth Ann took the mail and returned to her desk outside Skye's office where for the time being she worked as Skye's assistant.

A buzzer sounded, and Skye picked up her note-book. Her office was connected by another door to Jonathan Hayes's office. His office was located at the end of the building and had floor-to-ceiling glass on two walls that gave a breathtaking view of Dallas. The third wall, about forty-five feet away, was an enclosed area that contained a kitchen. Here, Skye and George, Jonathan's long-time chauffeur, cook and personal servant, prepared and served Jonathan and his business associates anything from coffee and rolls to a light lunch, or, with the help of the restaurant upstairs, a full dinner. Skye had decided at the outset that it would be more personal to serve business as-sociates in the office-lounge she had created than make them go to a restaurant.

Now, walking into her employer's office, she glanced to the left of Jonathan's desk to see the small circular conference table with phones and chairs in place ready for use. To the right was a chocolate-brown suede sofa and chairs which had been arranged in a semicircular grouping, composing a conversation area. In the middle of the semicircle was a large rec-tangular pecan cocktail table, and on the floor around the table were several large throw pillows in shades of apricot and gold. It was from here that Skye usually dispensed coffee with such casualness and friendliness that the men sometimes forgot they were gathered there to discuss business. Her glance continued farther down the room where an oval pecan dining room table was located. In a pinch, the table could be stretched to seat twelve. Behind that was the door to the small but efficient kitchen—or galley, as George called it.

Her eyes went back to the center of the room, where Jonathan sat behind his enormous desk. He was sixty-five years old and looking younger all the time, Skye thought ruefully, now that the weight of his business was about to be lifted from his shoulders. He was a widower, but his children and grandchildren made up his life.

She walked across the expanse of thick cream-shag carpeting to his desk to have her third cup of coffee for the morning. This was just one of the rituals they had established together over the last four years.

"Good morning, my dear," his brown eyes looked at Skye fondly. "Did you sleep well last night?"

"Yes, Jonathan, thank you," she smiled back. She didn't want to worry him about her sleepless night or the middle-of-the-night trip to the airport. She knew he would be horrified at the thought of her driving alone so late at night. "Let's let some of this beautiful day in, shall we?" She walked to the corner of his desk, pushed one of the several buttons there, and the beige floor-to-ceiling curtains swept back automatically to reveal the brilliance of the new day.

Surely nothing bad could happen on a beautiful day like today, she thought, trying to forget the apprehension she had felt the night before.

Being on the thirty-fifth floor, the glass walls gave the people in the office the feeling of sitting in the sky, with only the tops of other skyscrapers to mar the view of the plains that surrounded Dallas. She poured their coffee and sat down in a chair almost adjacent to his own. He liked her to work closely with him, and the corner of the desk was an ideal place for her notebook and papers. It also gave ready access to his phone.

She gazed at Jonathan lovingly and on impulse asked, "Are you sure this is what you really want to do, Jonathan? After all, you're not *that* old, and you may get bored with retirement."

"I know, but I want to sell before it's too late. There's a lot of living I've been putting off, a lot of things I've always meant to do but just never had the time, and now I will. Quite a few of my contemporaries waited too long and either lost their good health or their life. I'm determined it's not going to happen to me. Besides," he grinned, "I wasn't always around when my children were growing up, but I want to be there for my grandchildren."

Skye sighed and nodded. She had known the answer. I'm really in a strange mood, she reflected silently.

"How 'bout your decision? You know, it's not too late for me to stipulate that the apartment and car remain yours." He paused and looked at Skye for a moment. "Or even to tear up your resignation," he added as if he had just thought of it.

Skye shook her head. "Thanks, but no thanks. I don't know what I would have done without you these past four years, but it's time I stood on my own."

"Well, you know I worry about you, and you also know my thoughts on the matter, but you've still got a few days to change your mind." He smiled, then changed the subject. "Did our young men arrive last night?"

"I believe there was a slight mix-up about clearance, but yes, they did arrive." Skye hid a smile because Jonathan called them "young men." It was true, though, that most of James Steele's key men were in their thirties. Paul Garth was only thirty-two—pretty young to be taking over a company of this size.

For the next half-hour, they dealt with some of the things that Skye felt they should cover before Paul Garth and the rest arrived. They were just finishing when Gloria, their vivacious receptionist, buzzed through to let Skye know that "the brass" had arrived.

Jonathan looked at Skye and said cheerfully, "This is it!" His mind was made up, and he was anxious for the takeover to be completed. His only doubts were about Skye herself.

Chapter Three

As SKYE WALKED down the long corridor that led from the executive suite to the main reception area, she took several deep breaths. That strange nervousness she had experienced at the airport just a few hours before was returning. What in the world did she imagine was about to happen? She was being fanciful again, and it wasn't like her.

This morning she had dressed sleepily in a golden-yellow silk jersey dress, with a perfectly fitted bodice, long, graceful sleeves and a V-neck that left her creamy throat bare with no jewelry to clutter her appearance. She opened the two big leather-covered doors that led to the reception area. Her skirts flared out from her legs as she turned to shut the doors behind her, then turned again, to pause at the top of the four steps that would take her down into the large reception area.

She spotted Paul Garth and several of the men with him and smiled. She and Paul had gotten on well when he had been here on previous visits. As she moved down the few steps, her light, subtle perfume drifting behind her, it appeared as if all the available sunlight in the room had suddenly found its way to her, surrounding her, and giving the impression that Skye was bringing the golden light with her as she walked.

Nodding briefly to Gloria as she went by, Skye held out her two hands, which were taken eagerly, "Paul, how very nice to see you again. Mr. Rutherford, Mr. Jenson, Mr. Tyler," she smiled sincerely to the Steele Corporation lawyers. "I hope your flight wasn't too trying and you managed to get some rest." The three men nodded affirmatively, each smiling in varying degrees at the beautiful young woman standing before them.

Skye's voice was soft and musical, and her slow Texas drawl was easy on the ears. She looked again at Paul. "I must truly apologize for our inhospitable Texas weather last night. That's no way to welcome people to our great state."

Paul, still holding Skye's hand and looking at her as if he couldn't quite believe she was real, drew her a few steps to his left. "Don't worry about it. Your charming welcome has more than made up for it. Skye," he continued, "I'd like you to meet Jim Steele, our lord and master. Jimmy, Mrs. Skye Anderson."

The man to whom Paul was introducing her stepped

from behind a huge latticed screen, where she supposed he had been looking at an unusual painting that Jonathan had picked up in Mexico a few years back.

Skye found her own small, suddenly cold hand enveloped in a huge warm hand, and her sky-blue eyes looking into the most incredibly deep-black eyes she had ever seen. All at once she knew!

This was the man who had been watching her last night. She had not thought consciously about him since she had left the airport because, in a sense, he hadn't seemed real. But she had been very wrong about that—and wrong, too, about not connecting him with the apprehension she had been feeling.

Nothing she had ever read about the man, or pictures she had seen of him, had prepared her for the sheer physical impact of James Steele. Tall, wide-shouldered, skin dark, almost the color of old copper, and hair as blue-black as the sky at night with wisps of silver drifting through it. The light beige silk suit, with a slightly darker beige shirt, accentuated his darkness and emphasized his athletic muscular frame. Ever since he had burst into national attention as a young collegiate football player, there had been speculation about him, some concerning his heritage. Spanish-American, Indian, no one could quite agree. And he never bothered setting them straight.

"Skye, how nice to meet you at last." Was it her overworked imagination, or had her name come out as a caress? His eyes seemed to hold some secret amusement. "Paul has been singing your praises since his first visit to your beautiful city."

Ignoring his compliments from habit, she tried to

recover from the shock and the fact that he still held her hand. "Mr. Steele..."

"Jim, please," the interruption came from a low, husky voice that sounded like honey flowing over gravel.

Skye continued hurriedly before she panicked altogether. "We had no idea you would be able to come today. I hope the accommodations were satisfactory."

Paul broke in, giving Skye a chance to rescue her hand, "Jimmy was able to wrap up his Mideast deal sooner than expected and join us. Wasn't that lucky?"

Jimmy? Skye thought incredulously. How could anyone casually call such a powerful, self-assured man, "Jimmy"?

"Lucky," agreed Skye automatically. Looking up at him between her double-thick lashes, she found he was still looking at her with a puzzling amusement— almost as if, in the first few minutes of meeting her, he had been able to see straight through her defenses and read her like the proverbial book.

Impossible! Pulling herself together, she said, "Mr. Hayes will be so pleased," with what she hoped sounded like sincerity and led the way back through the double doors to Jonathan's office.

And, of course, Jonathan *was* pleased. He soon had James Steele and his entourage seated in the conversational area, while Skye attended to the refreshments.

Skye always made it a point to remember how everyone took their coffee, but after serving Jonathan, she had to brave a look at the man whose glittering eyes she'd been avoiding. "Mr. Steele, how do you take your coffee?"

He gave her a slow, lazy smile. "Black, please, and the name is Jim—or Jimmy."

She didn't answer, but poured his coffee and very carefully handed it to him in case her strangely shaking hands should spill a drop.

"I understand you had trouble with clearance last night, Jim," Jonathan said. "I hope it didn't cause you any problems. Skye informed me this morning that someone from our office took care of it. I trust the inconvenience was short-lived."

"Don't give it another thought, Jonathan." They had quickly gotten on a first-name basis. "These things happen."

James Steele's deep, cultured voice seemed to hammer into Skye's head, and she had the distinct impression he was looking straight at her as he spoke. But she didn't look at him. Instead she directed a smile at one of the lawyers as she handed him his coffee, not noticing the effect her sudden smile had on the dazzled man.

Soon business replaced pleasantries, and Skye was able to retreat behind her pose as a coolly efficient secretary, although somehow she had the feeling that she wasn't fooling one member of the group.

As the conversation swirled around her, Skye tried to analyze what was happening to her. She was very much aware of him, and to her dismay, she realized she was conscious of him sexually, as a man. That was something she hadn't felt for a long time. She was not sure she had ever felt it, at least not to this extent.

James Steele possessed that rare quality known as presence, and beneath it there was something else—

a barely contained violence. Under the civilized guise, and the sophisticated poise, and the athletic bearing, there was something very tough and dangerous, and Skye had no intention of getting anywhere near him.

That afternoon, Skye, Paul, and Beth Ann were huddled around the conference table in the corner of Jonathan's large office, which was arranged in such a way that different groups could work without over-hearing or disturbing the other.

Since Paul would be running the day-to-day busi-ness, it was really more important that he familiarize himself with that end of the business rather than take part in the legal technicalities which had Jonathan, James Steele, and various lawyers and accountants busy around the big desk.

Skye wanted Paul and Beth Ann to work together as much as possible since Beth Ann would be Paul's secretary when she and Jonathan left. She had taught the young girl well, and if Paul and Beth Ann were left together, they would more quickly form that par-ticular intimate relationship which was so important between an executive and his personal secretary. The kind of relationship where the secretary would antic-ipate her boss's wishes before he spoke them. Un-fortunately, Beth Ann didn't have that kind of self-confidence yet. She was shy with these powerful, self-assured young men from the Steele organization, and Skye couldn't blame her.

Skye sank back in her chair, for a moment out of the line of conversation.

When Paul had first realized that Skye would be

leaving the corporation, he had done everything to dissuade her. He was not one of James Steele's top men for nothing. He knew an asset when he saw one. But when Paul realized that Skye could not be swayed from her decision, he accepted it good-naturedly.

Listening to the exchanges between Paul and Beth Ann, she decided they would deal very well together.

It was the end of the first day of the visit from the high-powered executives of the Steele Corporation, and if it was anything to go by, Skye didn't know how she was going to get through the rest of the time they would be here. She was keyed up and on edge and incredibly aware of one outrageously dark man.

Her eyes strayed to Jonathan's desk and the intense discussion that seemed to be going on at the moment. Her glance rested on each man in turn, and against her will, her eyes seemed to stay on James Steele the longest. He had cut a wide swathe of disturbance through the office this morning as he had been taken on a tour through the executive suite of offices and then downstairs to where the girls in the typing pool and the eager young men on the rise shared a huge room.

It was no wonder the man caused excitement wherever he ventured, Skye reflected, with his perfectly controlled body, his unbelievably omniscient eyes, and his ruggedly handsome face with its high cheekbones, a nose that looked as if it had been broken several times, and a firm, determined jaw with a two-inch-long scar on it. James Steele was all male, completely in control of his life and his surroundings and anyone who happened to fall under the gaze of his eyes or the spell of his charm.

Regardless of who they were or how much attention and time he gave them, Skye had noticed with strange annoyance that everyone, without exception, had fallen into the web woven by his incredible charisma.

Now, as though aware of her considering stare, he raised his penetrating eyes to her and slowly smiled. The effect was a shock that raced straight through Skye. She felt as if she had actually been physically assaulted by his smile and touched bodily by his eyes which seemed to be taking in everything about her with lightning speed. She was rendered breathless, as if someone had forced the air out of her. If she were the type of woman who blushed, she certainly would have. Instead, Paul unknowingly saved her by turning to her and demanding her somewhat disconcerted attention to what seemed to be a slight difference of opinion between Beth Ann and himself.

"It's just that my old Mustang has broken down again," Beth Ann explained, "and I was telling Paul I'm going to take the bus home."

"That's ridiculous! We've leased a number of cars for the duration, and I'll be glad to take her home. But she seems to prefer the discomfort and inconvenience of a bus to my offer." Paul was plainly intrigued over Beth Ann's shyness around him. Skye smiled to herself. This proved the point she had been trying to make earlier. With Beth Ann's youth and brightness, she had no cause to worry or to compare herself unfavorably with others.

"Paul, please understand. It's just that Janey has to get home, too, and I have to stop at the garage to pick up my car."

"Who is Janey and where is your car?" Paul demanded imperiously.

"Janey is my roommate. She works in the typing pool," Beth Ann explained patiently, "and my car is in the garage around the corner from my apartment building."

Paul shook his head in mock dismay. "It seems I'm to have a liberated female for a secretary."

Skye smiled. "You sound as if that is a fate worse than death, Paul. You wouldn't just happen to be a wee bit chauvinistic now, would you?"

Responding to Skye's smile, Paul shrugged and laughed. "Possibly, probably, and quite definitely, I'm afraid." Then switching the conversation to her, "You live alone, Skye. Aren't you ever frightened not only of living alone, but also driving at night by yourself? What if your car broke down in the middle of nowhere?"

Skye's smile subsided as she stared thoughtfully at a point somewhere over Paul's shoulder. "Life is filled with a lot of 'what if's,' Paul, and to say I'm never frightened or scared of being alone would be foolish. But, unfortunately, being alone happens to be a very basic fact of my life, and I can't afford to think about it too much."

"That's quite an admission for a lady who looks as if a tornado couldn't ruffle her calm," broke in a deep, husky voice.

Three pairs of eyes turned upon the man, but his inscrutable eyes were fixed upon Skye's lovely upturned face. He looked completely relaxed and at home, Skye thought indignantly. He had taken off his jacket, and his vest and shirt plainly molded the rippling muscles of his powerful chest and arms.

"Fear is a very human emotion, Mr. Steele."
Skye's blue eyes had deepened to a darker blue.
"Haven't you ever felt fear of anything or anyone?"
she asked with what she hoped sounded more like
curiosity than bad manners.

James Steele bent over the table and placed the
sheaf of papers he carried in front of her. While he
was still leaning over the table, he reached out a large
finger and ran it down her smooth cheek. Very softly,
so that only Skye could really hear, he murmured,
"You, beautiful lady. You scare the hell out of me!
And"—he tapped her chin lightly—"the name is
Jim." Then, just as confidently, he straightened and
walked back to Jonathan.

Silence reigned at the table as the three occupants
watched him leave. Skye wasn't quite sure what to
think, but his touch and the tone of his voice had
disturbed her more than she cared to admit.

Skye turned to look at Beth Ann and saw absolute
awe written on the young girl's face. Paul, on the
other hand, was frowning. This worried Skye, because
he knew James Steele better than any of them.

By six-thirty that evening, things seemed to be
winding down for the day. Skye was in her office
clearing her desk in preparation for leaving. The disturbing restlessness which had started last night was
still with her, and she was exhausted. She had no idea
what she was going to eat once she got home, since
the last time she had checked, her refrigerator was
bare. It didn't really matter, though, because she
wasn't hungry. All she could think about was a hot,

relaxing bath and then, if she was lucky, a few hours sleep.

Skye picked up her shorthand notebook to glance at the notes she had taken earlier in the day. She knew if she could read over the abbreviations while the dictation was still fresh in her mind, the shorthand would be easier to transcribe in the morning. As if some sixth sense had warned her, she looked up from her notes and found James Steele standing patiently in front of her, as though he had been there for quite some time.

"Can I help you?" she inquired courteously. "I was just about to leave for the day." She hoped fervently that the last statement would discourage his coming up with more work for her. Not that he had been overdemanding. Quite the contrary. But anything he had asked her politely to do during the day made it necessary for her to be in close proximity to him— thus causing an indefinable tension in Skye that she didn't know how to deal with.

"I wanted to thank you for the work you did for me today."

"You're welcome."

"All the same," he continued, "I appreciated it since my secretary isn't with me this trip."

"I was glad to help." Skye shrugged. She wished he'd just go. She didn't want to have a conversation with someone she had been trying to avoid all day.

He sat down casually on the corner of her desk, thwarting her wish and pushing a small plant out of harm's way. "Come have dinner with me," he said, making the invitation sound like a command.

'No, thank you." Skye tried to hide her surprise

by pushing back her chair and standing up. Maybe if she continued with her preparations for leaving, he would take the hint and go.

"I see. You have other plans then?" He was looking at her with an unnerving thoughtfulness. She had seen enough of him to know that whatever or whomever he decided to focus his whole attention and potent charm on usually succumbed—he was too forceful a personality to resist for long.

Sitting on her desk, he was still slightly taller than she, but at least she was looking into his eyes instead of up at his chin. Skye knew instinctively that she needed all the advantages she could get when it came to Mr. James Steele.

"No, not really," she replied from under her desk as she bent to get her purse out of the bottom drawer. Why didn't he just take "no" for an answer. All the other men she knew did.

She straightened and ventured a quick glance at him. He was entirely too overpowering. His nearness was causing a disturbing excitement within her—a sort of basic, elemental pressure in the pit of her stomach—and she didn't like the feeling.

Skye had fought long and hard to pull herself out of the depths of her tragic sorrow. Consequently, her plan for the future didn't include becoming ensnared in the fascinating and—she was sure—sensually gratifying brand of entrapment that James Steele was noted for. His movements around the world could be followed by the trail of broken hearts which were documented faithfully by the international wire services.

He smiled gently. "Did anyone ever tell you that

monosyllabic answers make conversation rather difficult?"

Skye watched him warily. *What did he want from her?*

"Isn't an almost-employer allowed to take an almost-employee to dinner?" he persevered when she didn't answer.

"That's not the way it is," she replied looking down at her purse, pulling its strap nervously this way and that.

"That's not the way *what* is?"

He was looking at her, as if she were a complicated game plan he had just been presented five minutes before he was to play in the Super Bowl. He reached out and put a big hand over her purse, effectively stopping her fidgeting.

"I'm not an almost-employee," Skye stated a little more sharply. Why didn't he just go away and leave her alone?

"Did I fire you?" he asked with interest, as if that might be a genuine possibility and he had just forgotten.

"I *quit!*" Sky-blue eyes sparked angrily. "Now, if you'll excuse me, I'm going home."

Skye turned and walked to the door, but he was there in front of her. She had to forcibly stop herself from looking back at the desk where he had been sitting. She had to hand it to him. The man could move with the quiet speed and grace of a jungle animal. She felt as if she knew exactly how his opponents used to feel when they complained that they never knew exactly where he was going to be on the football field. How could you tackle the wind?

"Why?" he questioned, soft-voiced.

Skye couldn't tell whether he was genuinely puzzled or not. His mysterious black eyes gave away nothing.

"I think I have a right to know. When I take over, all Hayes employees will be guaranteed their present jobs."

"That's not it." She sighed, rubbing her temple lightly with her fingers. How could she explain to this incredibly self-assured man the things she had to do in her life in order just to survive. Why should she? It was not in her even to try. "It's just time for me to move on."

"Where?" One simple question, but she couldn't answer it for the life of her.

Suddenly she had had enough. She had tried to be polite, but she was tired and her head was beginning to ache. "You have no rights where I'm concerned. My resignation will be effective before you take over officially." Why she should explain this much to him she didn't know and she didn't want to stop and think about it. "Beth Ann will be the new president's secretary. Now, if you'll excuse me," she said pointedly looking at the door.

He stepped aside and opened the door, but as she passed, he put his hand on her arm and pulled her gently against him. "Do whatever adjusting you have to do in that beautiful head of yours, Skye, because I *will* win in the end."

With this startling pronouncement, he lowered his head and touched his lips softly to hers. The kiss was a light, soothing one, and he didn't seem to mind that she was too astonished to react one way or the other.

His lips were sensitive and gentle and warm—and just as suddenly as the kiss had begun, it stopped.

He ran the tips of his fingers down her cheek with a shockingly tender touch and drawled, "For a lady with such a hard shell around her, you sure are soft. Get a good night's rest. I'll see you tomorrow."

Skye was out of the building and in her car driving to her apartment before her mind started working again, and she remembered his strange words and the sensations that had surged through her at the touch of his mouth upon hers.

Chapter Four

By seven o'clock the next morning, Skye was busy in the galley preparing for an eight o'clock breakfast meeting, but her mind wasn't on what she was doing. Instead, she was thinking of the enigmatic James Steele. Surprisingly, she had slept well the night before, but with the new day, her tensions had returned and his words came rushing back to her.

That he was interested in Skye was evident, but a lot of men had been interested in her these last few years. They always backed off, however, when they realized that she wasn't like most women who liked to go out and party, and they respected her system of self-defense when they realized it was nothing personal.

But this man was different from all the rest and she knew it instinctively, deep in the marrow of her bones, much as a jungle animal senses danger. She felt threatened, and somehow she was certain he had the ability to upset her life. But Skye knew that it was absolutely essential to her future well-being that this be avoided at all costs.

She moved quickly and efficiently around the small kitchen. As usual, the breakfast was going to be catered by the restaurant that was housed several floors above them, but the men always enjoyed her hot homemade biscuits and gravy, and she was absorbed in gathering the ingredients.

What in the world was keeping George so long, she wondered. He was usually here before her for these early-morning breakfast conferences. They needed to be early because most Texas businessmen were up and out with the sun.

"Damn!" The flour must be on the top shelf, and there was no way she could reach it. She glanced out the door at the swivel dining-room chairs. That will have to do, she thought.

"Morning, Princess." Jeffrey Blake put his head around the door a few minutes later only to see the object of his greeting standing precariously on a swivel chair that refused to be still, trying to reach the upper portions of the cabinet.

"Good grief, Skye! There must be an easier way!" He stepped forward to steady her by placing his hands firmly around her slender waist.

Skye glanced down briefly, then returned to her hunt for the elusive flour. Surely they weren't out! "It might not be the easiest way, but it happens to be the quickest way, and with about a dozen hungry men to feed, time is important. I have no desire to have y'all stampede my kitchen, demanding food."

"Oh, come on now, would we do that?" Jeff asked, feigning innocence.

"The mind boggles," Skye returned dryly.

Skye liked Jeff. He was Jonathan's right-hand man and would soon be promoted to vice-president after the takeover. His tiny wife had just had a new baby, and Skye was about to ask him about them when she spied the flour. Standing on her tiptoes, she just managed to grasp the flour as the chair swiveled. Jeff steadied her immediately, preventing her fall. The arm that wasn't holding the flour came down around Jeff's neck.

"Is this a private conference, or is the public cordially invited?" came a deep, sardonic voice.

Jeff laughed. "Good morning, Jim. This young lady is constantly making the mistake of thinking she can do more than she's physically capable of. It's a good thing I happened along when I did, or she and the flour would have been in one big, inglorious heap."

One black eyebrow rose. "So I see!"

Skye looked down at the infuriatingly elegant man leaning casually against the doorjamb. "Is there anything I can do for you, Mr. Steele? Anything at all?"

A slow smile appeared on his lips. Sensual, she thought unwillingly, as the soft word came wafting back to her. "Jim."

This had been a frequent request of his yesterday and one she couldn't quite bring herself to do, although he had immediately started calling her "Skye," as if he couldn't quite bring himself to say "Mrs. Anderson."

She stared at him. She couldn't seem to help herself. The man was too damn fascinating for his or anyone's good. But she didn't acknowledge his request and, sensing Jeff's puzzled look at her unusual rudeness, she turned back to the cabinet to get the baking powder, salt, and shortening.

Jeff looked from one to the other. "Well, Princess, if you don't need my not-so-valuable help anymore, I'd better go collect my papers for the conference. Save an extra biscuit for me," he begged as if he would starve without it, "and lots of gravy."

Forgetting for a minute the intimidatingly dark presence, her blue eyes smiled at Jeff. "Anything for my gallant rescuer. Maybe even two biscuits."

Jeff made a mock bow. "Your devoted servant." And with a nod to James Steele, he left.

Skye started transferring the items to the counter, and, in her hurry, she lost her balance. Suddenly she found hands with a grip of iron around her waist, steadying her.

"Thank you," she said, intent only on getting down. But the hands didn't move.

"Damn it! Can't this company afford a step-stool for you? Do you have to risk life and limb for a batch of damn biscuits?" he asked gruffly.

"Please, Mr. Steele, I'm okay," she almost pleaded. "Just let me down." She felt short of breath, and she was aware of her heart's increased pounding. Skye knew she needed to get away from him immediately!

His hands caressed her waist slightly, doing strange things to her nerves. The warmth from his hands seeped right through her clothes. She had to force herself not to melt against him.

"Please, Mr. Steele," he mimicked. His hands suddenly tightened and he smiled like a wily coyote. His large hands nearly met around her small waist and he looked down at them encircling her.

"I'll be glad to let you down, Skye." His thumbs moved back and forth under her breasts, and the fingers on her back spread down to her hips, causing the warmth to turn to heat. "Just call me by my first name," he commanded.

Skye could feel herself panicking and tried to control her trembling. This man's long, tapering fingers were making her feel things she knew she had never experienced before. She couldn't seem to think straight, and she felt as if she were gradually dissolving into liquid heat. She looked down into the glittering black eyes that she thought surely must look like the Devil's and said unsteadily, "J . . . James."

"James," he repeated softly, bringing her body forward to lean on him, her breasts nearly even with his face. "The beautiful lady calls me James." She could feel his warm breath heating her breasts through the fabric of her dress as he spoke.

Effortlessly, he lifted her off the chair by her waist and held her against his body for a moment. Her hands reached for his shoulders, although she didn't need to steady herself, such was his complete control of her body.

Slowly, gently, he began to lower her to the floor, hypnotizing her with his steady, seductive gaze. Her legs, her breasts and her stomach, slid down his muscle-toughened physique, causing white-hot streams to course through her body. Her descent was excruciatingly slow, and she couldn't tear her eyes away from his. They were black and deep, and fathomless. Although they were separated by layers of clothing, she felt that she was coming in contact with every part of his powerful body. Her softness against his hardness was creating a fire that she was beginning to wish would never go out. It seemed that the imprint of his body would be forever seared into hers.

When her toes finally touched the floor, Skye knew that she would have fallen if he hadn't still held her so closely to him. As she watched with fascination and complete helplessness, his mouth lowered and touched hers. This kiss had no resemblance to his previous, light kiss. There was nothing soothing about it.

More fire seemed to ignite within her as the pressure of his mouth increased and his arms gathered her closer and closer. Her hands, still on his shoulders, quite naturally crept around his neck until she was holding on desperately, returning his kiss, forgetting her surroundings, knowing only that if she let go she would be lost. The kiss seemed to go on forever, his technique perfect, his mastery of her body's sensations perceptive.

"I'm sorry Miss Skye." She heard George's apologetic voice through a haze. "My alarm didn't go off . . . excuse me . . . I'll just go check on the table settings."

The sense of where she was and what she was doing returned to her gradually. More than that, she realized with embarrassment with whom she was doing it! James had relaxed his hold on her and was looking down at her with a curiously intent expression, as if he were gauging her reactions.

One dark hand came up and gently stroked through her thick, silky hair, combing it with his fingers. "Can I help?"

"Help?" she asked stupidly, realizing that her hair must have come loose at some point. She turned to look for the burnt orange scarf that matched the simple sheath she was wearing and, until just a few moments ago, had held back her hair.

"Biscuits," he reminded her softly, as he picked up the scarf and competently tied back her hair as if she were a little girl. "Tell me, do you always do the cooking for these meetings?" His dark eyebrows came together in a frown.

Skye turned away and tried to make her mind focus on the mundane process of making biscuits. "Well, not always, but Jonathan especially asked for biscuits and gravy this morning, and I couldn't refuse," she replied absently. She had to be dreaming this! How could she have let it happen?

"Can I help in any way?" he repeated with husky amusement.

A little dazedly, she looked at him and tried to picture this huge man moving about in a kitchen. The thought was ludicrous. Not that he would be clumsy, she thought, for he had an almost unimaginable pantherlike grace that seemed more suitable to a jungle than a kitchen or, for that matter, a boardroom. One movement flowed fluidly into the next, a bold purity of motion.

Remembering she hadn't answered, she turned away confusedly—but then turned back, as if her body had been cold too long and couldn't stand to be parted from its source of heat. "No, really, it isn't necessary. If you would like coffee, I'll be glad to have George bring you a cup in the lounge." She just wanted James out of the kitchen. It was too small an area, and his nearness was affecting her far too much.

Smoothly he took a step toward her until he was almost, but not quite, touching her. She could feel her traitorous body reacting to his nearness, yearning to be taken in his arms again. "Always the polite and gracious hostess, aren't you? Even in times of passion and stress. I've heard of and experienced Texas hospitality before, but lady, you have it down to a fine art."

His voice got softer now, obviously changing his tactics. "Come spend the evening with me. Dinner, dancing, whatever." He shrugged. A huge brown hand came out and, before she knew what he was going to do, gently stroked some straggling hair from her forehead, causing a now-familiar scorching sensation to rush through her body and make her shiver.

"No!" Skye's nerves made her feel as if she were going to shatter into a million tiny pieces. She had to get hold of herself. She paused and drew a couple of deep breaths. "I mean, no, thank you."

This time she did have an excuse, she thought with relief. "I'm already committed for this evening. There's going to be a baby shower for Jeff's wife, Annette, and I really shouldn't miss it." She had been looking somewhere around the middle of his tie, but glanced up in time to see his eyes narrowing. "Their baby daughter is just home from the hospital"—she realized she was babbling and should stop—"and this shower has been planned for quite some time," she finished lamely. How could this man reduce her to a gibbering idiot in just a few minutes?

His hand slid from her hair, down the back of her ear, and on to her throat with a disturbing familiarity. A shudder she couldn't seem to control raced through her body. With his thumb, he forced her to look up at him.

"I'm warning you now, Skye," he said in an incredible whisper. He didn't have to shout; he had all of her attention. "I'm not going to let you keep retreating from me forever. I'm going to continue to dig till I get under that gorgeous satiny skin of yours, and I can see what's there. And then I'm going to dig some more, until I'm all the way under it, and you have nothing to hide from me. I've known since the first minute I saw you that beneath the cool, elegant exterior you so carefully hide behind there breathes a real flesh-and-hot-blooded woman."

He smiled gently into her wide, frightened eyes. "So you can say no and run all you want to, beautiful lady, but it's not going to do you one damn bit of good. You'll surrender in the end. You'll have to, because I'll be so deep inside you that I'll know everything there is to know about you and just exactly what makes you feel, think, and breathe."

"No!" Skye cried as she desperately tried to unclasp his hand from around her neck. But he tightened his grasp slightly.

"Oh, yes!" His voice was menacingly quiet. "What's the matter? Did I actually manage to hit a nerve?"

"Mr. Steele..." Skye tried to summon indignation, but all that came out was the panic and the terror her eyes clearly showed.

"James," came the soft reminder. His one hand was more than capable of choking her, but it wasn't. Rather, as extraordinary as it seemed, his big, strong hand was actually caressing her—and, in some indefinable way, possessing her.

"J...James, I don't have any idea what you're talking about, and what's more, I don't want to know. Just leave me alone!"

His fingers seemed to be discharging fire onto the surface of her skin, and she could feel the heat seeping into her stomach and down into her legs.

This will never do, she thought. He's winning. Whatever game it is that we're playing, he's winning. He wants me to lose control, and rage at him, and tell him things I have no intention of telling him.

Trying to regain her composure, she closed her eyes and took another deep breath. Turning back to the counter, she broke his hold. Or more than likely, he let her break the current between them, she thought with absolutely no amusement. "I'll have George bring your coffee in just a moment," she stated in as normal a voice as she could manage. When she turned to look at him, he had silently gone, and she was left shaking.

This was ridiculous! He was going to be in town less than two weeks, and she couldn't continue to let him unsettle her like this.

James Steele was uncannily cunning and infinitely dangerous. She had to be on her guard every minute of his stay in Dallas if she hoped to remain unscathed. Her only hope for survival would be not to let her defenses slip again. It had been easy for him this time. Too easy. But next time would be different. On this she was determined!

The rest of the day seemed to go on forever. James didn't speak to her other than on business and always with someone else present. But he didn't have to. All he had to do was look at her—look at her with those incredibly knowing eyes that seemed to follow her everywhere.

The air between them seemed to become electrically charged whenever they were in the same room, reminding her of a summer evening when a storm was imminent. She felt other people must sense this, too. How could they not?

Skye had not intended to go to Annette's shower, only to send a gift. In the past, she had purposely stayed away from such events because of the hurt she was afraid she would feel. She imagined that seeing someone else's happiness over the birth of their child would only underscore her own emptiness and loneliness.

However, she found herself going, and she wasn't really sure why. Skye told herself it wasn't because she was afraid James would check up on her, but rather because she knew Jeff and Annette wouldn't understand if she didn't.

Whatever her reason for attending, to her surprise, once at the party, the pain she had expected to feel simply wasn't there. Oh, she felt a slight tightening in her throat when she saw their tiny baby, but she didn't dwell on it. She couldn't. Her mind was too filled with James Steele. There was no room for anything else, and she was acutely conscious that she had never been more frightened in her life.

There was a kind of magnificence about him—a raw power and absolute grace that made her own efforts to resist him seem futile. Succumbing to him would probably be the easiest thing she had ever done in her life. But when the touch of his hands on her skin ceased, the heartache just might be unbearable.

Skye's appointment for her quarterly physical examination was the next day. Because her injuries from the accident had been so serious, it had left her with a number of minor physical problems that only a handful of people knew about. The doctor kept a very close watch on her and, so far, there had been no real problems that couldn't be dealt with in his office.

When she had made her appointment weeks ago, she hadn't realized that it would coincide with James Steele's visit. With any luck, she decided, she would be back before anyone noticed her absence, since the appointment was to be during her lunch-hour.

Good fortune wasn't with her on this day, however, because immediately upon returning to the office, Beth Ann met Skye at her office door. "Mr. Hayes was asking for you." Her small elfin face was twisted to show concern. "I had to remind him that it was time for your usual quarterly physical."

Skye tensed. "Mr. Steele wasn't in the room, by any chance, was he?"

"Yes, as a matter of fact he was, and he asked why

you would be needing quarterly checkups."

"And?" Skye wasn't sure she really wanted to hear the rest. The fact that it wasn't any of his business wouldn't stop James Steele from asking questions.

"Well, Mr. Hayes is such a mother hen where you're concerned. I knew if he ever got started, your whole medical history would be discussed for the next hour. I headed him off, but he did manage to get out that you thought you were a lot stronger than you actually were, and someone had to keep an eye on you. Mr. Hayes insisted that I have you come in as soon as you arrived back."

Skye groaned. All she needed was for James to become even more curious about her than he already was. He seemed to be doing just fine in his assault of her without this added information.

"Great, just great," Skye muttered. Where was all her usual calm control of the situations and the people surrounding her, now, when she really needed it.

She turned and walked into her office, putting her purse in a desk drawer and picking up her notebook and some messages. Knowing she was in for her usual third-degree about the doctor's report, she could only hope that James was in the office that had been assigned to him for the duration of his visit instead of in Jonathan's.

Trying unsuccessfully to smooth her escaping curls back into the severe bun she had started out with this morning, she walked into Jonathan's office. She noticed thankfully that, even though James was in the office, he was preoccupied with a telephone call at the conference table.

In her simple blue sheath, she felt she was looking

very plain and businesslike, and this gave her the much-needed confidence to cross the office to Jonathan, who was standing by the window.

As quickly and quietly as possible, Skye tried to set Jonathan's mind at ease about her checkup. "I don't have to see the doctor again for six months. That's a definite improvement."

"I don't know, my dear." Jonathan was frowning at her. "I don't like the fact that you are still having these headaches."

Skye sighed. She loved Jonathan for being so concerned, but she wished he would just drop the subject. She put her hand on his arm and tried to reassure him quietly. "The doctor said the headaches seem to be triggered by tension and will disappear eventually. He said there's nothing to worry about."

She nearly jumped out of her skin when a deep voice behind her inquired casually, "Everything all right?" Without waiting for an answer, he continued, "Jonathan, you're wanted on the phone. I believe Beth Ann said it was that New York call you've been waiting for."

As Jonathan walked away, Skye turned, her eyes throwing out blue lights of indignation at James. Really, it wasn't any of his business! As far as she knew, only those who worked closely with her knew the facts of her past and that was how she wanted to keep it. James Steele was one man who must not learn anything about her, except what appeared on the surface. For some reason, she felt it was vital.

Now, as Skye stood in front of the window with the background of slate-blue sky emphasizing her bluer-than-blue eyes and dress, she felt that vague threatening feeling again—almost as if she were being cornered, like some wild animal.

"Do you always have to creep up on people like that?" Skye snapped, instinctively going on the offensive.

Black eyes glittered innocently. "Creep?"

"Creep!" Skye reiterated sharply. "As in slink! As in sneak! As in crawl on your belly like a snake!"

James smiled slowly, devastating Skye's already keyed-up senses. He seemed not one bit put out by her attack.

Tall, lean, and formidable, he was standing casually in front of her—just as if Skye were so important to him that he had all the time in the world to talk to her and thousands of people did not depend upon him for a living.

His hands were jammed into his pants pocket, causing the material to stretch tautly over his flat stomach and muscular thighs. He looked totally relaxed and self-assured, making Skye feel that much more intimidated.

"Can't you walk like a normal person?" Oh! She felt so frustrated! It had never been in Skye to be rude to anyone—especially someone as important to Jonathan as James Steele. She made a silent vow to do better.

"I was sure I did," James replied mildly.

"So people can hear you coming," Skye tried to explain more fully through gritted teeth. "You always seem to be appearing and disappearing . . . like some phantom ghost." Her hand waved weakly through the air demonstrating her words.

"I'll try to do better," James promised with what could have passed for sincerity if she hadn't been looking at his eyes. "What did you have in mind? I could always do my world-famous impersonation of a herd of buffalo."

Skye had to smile in spite of herself. He had disarmed her with absolutely no effort.

"Tell me," the man in front of her continued, throwing her further off guard, "just exactly what is the color of your hair?"

"My hair?" she repeated stupidly. She had been so sure he was going to bring up the subject of her doctor's appointment. He had seemed so interested a few minutes earlier.

"Your hair," he confirmed. "Right now, with the full force of sunlight on it," he reached out and absently toyed with an errant curl, "it has the quality of molten gold. But take you away from the sun and put you under office lights, it sometimes appears amber, with maybe an occasional coppery gleam running through it."

"I don't know what color my hair is." She jerked her head away. "It's not really important. I never even think about it." Skye was suddenly tense again. What was James up to?

As if she hadn't said anything, he continued thoughtfully, "Now, of course, I haven't seen your hair by moonlight. There are also sort of silvery streaks running through it that must resemble moonbeams dancing through the night."

Trying hard to fight against his smile that had probably dazzled more hardened, sophisticated women than she, Skye answered roughly, "That's just ordinary gray hair, James."

"There's nothing ordinary about it, I assure you," he corrected her gently.

Skye felt that somehow she were being closed in, that the huge room was suddenly getting smaller and that soon there would be no air left in it to breathe. What was this ridiculous conversation about anyway?

Her eyes darted around the room. No, it couldn't be getting smaller. There was the dear, familiar form of Jonathan on the phone. Nothing was wrong, everything was the same and her panic started to recede.

Trying to regain her composure, she looked up into amused coal-black eyes. "I can't think that you're really all that interested in my hair, James."

"Ah, but I'm afraid I am. You see, I've never seen such a perfect blending of colors and such an exotic effect. Quite a few women I know would gladly kill for that color." He gently reached out to touch another shining tendril that had escaped from its intended knot.

"Exotic?" Skye was really surprised. Too surprised to even react to his touch.

"Exotic," the incredibly nonchalant man repeated. It seemed he was always having to repeat his words to her. "What does your hairdresser do to get such beautiful colors?"

Skye looked at him and saw he was baiting her. Consequently, she was so determined not to fall for it that she walked right into his trap. Too quickly she said, "I don't go to a hairdresser, James. The color of my hair changed with my pregnan—" She suddenly stopped, realizing what she had nearly said.

Unconsciously putting her fingertips to her temple,

she rushed out with, "I mean the accid—" Oh, hell! What was wrong with her? She couldn't seem to think straight.

Skye took a deep breath and exhaled. Very slowly and very carefully she said, "I mean as I've gotten older. Now, if you will excuse me for breaking up this extraordinarily uninteresting conversation, I see Jonathan is off the phone and may need me."

"Beautiful lady," came the smooth voice, "nothing about you is uninteresting." And, surprising her once again, he walked away abruptly, treading as softly as a cat.

Chapter Five

By Friday afternoon, Skye was tired. Right now she didn't even want to acknowledge the extra hours she would have to put in at the office the next day. It had been a grueling week for her both mentally and physically.

It wasn't so much the work, Skye reflected, as the effort to maintain her poise in the face of the indomitable James Steele.

When they came into direct contact with each other, he would say or do the most disconcerting things. She felt that surely other people must notice. But aside from Paul's thoughtful look and Jonathan's benevolent smile whenever he saw them together, no one seemed to notice anything unusual. And Jonathan was no one's fool.

As she moved about the office this past week, she could feel James's eyes upon her, following her, studying her, waiting. *Waiting for what?* Her nerves were at an all-time shrieking point.

Skye had just finished eating a small shrimp salad and sat at the table slowly sipping a glass of white wine. Not that she had been particularly hungry, but she knew she had to keep up her strength, if only to shore her up for her confrontations with James.

The restaurant was on the top floor of her office building, and she often came here to eat instead of going home to her apartment to cook a solitary dinner.

The restaurant was designed luxuriously, with its individual tables sitting on several different levels amid huge potted plants. A piano was played softly in the background, and the lights were discreetly low, creating an intimate and relaxing ambience.

Sitting on the top level in a corner of the room, Skye turned in her chair to glance out the enormous windows towards the spectacular view of multicolored sunset over the gently rolling Texas prairie that reached to Fort Worth and beyond.

Skye loved Texas and all that it encompassed. It was at once a feeling and a reality. You could not stereotype Texas or Texans, although many people tried, especially now that Western ways and clothes were in vogue.

From the time Stephen Austin started the first colony in 1822 under a Mexican government, to the time Sam Houston crossed the Red River into Texas in 1832, to the time 183 courageous men lost their lives defending a decaying old mission known as the Alamo in 1836, to the time six weeks later when the enraged and revenge seeking Texans soundly defeated the Mexican General Santa Ana on the banks of the San Jacinto River, Texas had been filled with unique people who have a fierce pride in themselves and their state.

Texas and Texans are a law unto themselves. Not unlike James Steele, Skye thought ruefully, coming full circle in her observations. She turned back facing the table and took a sip of her wine. Why, Skye asked herself with great irritation, no matter what I'm thinking or what I'm doing, can't I seem to get away from the man?

Skye was wearing a cottony peach-colored dress whose yoke framed the translucent beauty of her face. With the fabric falling in soft folds to her knees, the dress was gathered in at her slender waist by a tie belt and had sleeves that were full and graceful. The dress might have made any other woman look overweight, but it only caused Skye to look as slender and delicate as she truly was. As usual she wore no jewelry. It wasn't that she didn't like jewelry; it was more that she never went to the trouble to adorn herself or to consciously try to make herself more attractive.

Because of her job, she had a wide assortment of simple clothes, but of good quality. She bought all of them at end-of-the season sales from the excellent clothing stores around Dallas, including Neiman-Marcus, whose first store was located about three blocks away from her office. Most people didn't realize what good buys you could get if you were a good shopper.

"May I join you?" The deep voice slashed through Skye's thoughts, startling her. Without waiting for an answer, James sat down across from her. His eyes ran over her with a thorough glance, frowning over Skye's hair which was drawn back into a chignon, leaving exposed the delicate blue veins at her temple and the fine, curling baby hairs around her forehead and neck.

"You know," he offered conversationally, "it's a crime the way you pull your hair back. Hair as glorious as yours should always be worn loose."

Recovering from this intrusion, for the management never allowed anyone to bother her, she ignored his comment on her hair. She wasn't going to let him start on *that* subject again. "Is there something I can do for you, James?" She should be getting used to his sudden appearances by now, Skye reflected with resignation.

Looking at her with eyes that danced with wicked lights, he said, "You're always asking me that and one of these days I'll tell you just exactly what it is that you can do for me."

He paused, evidently to see if she would blush, and when she didn't, he continued, not altogether disappointed it seemed. "But not yet I think. Not just yet." With a slight movement of his hand, he sent two approaching waiters who were bearing down on their table with great purpose back to their stations.

If I just ignore him, maybe he'll go away, Skye thought wearily. She turned her head to look back out at the day turning slowly to night. The sun was setting behind her, and it made a golden haze around her profile.

Her vow to try to be polite to this extraordinary man who had joined her so abruptly without an invitation was wearing very thin. He was something completely outside her sphere of experience, and she knew that she couldn't handle much more of him.

Skye felt a small shiver run down her spine and knew before she turned that her wish hadn't been granted. He was still sitting there, regarding her with a sort of odd patience, as if he were waiting for something in particular.

"I've been watching you from over there." James moved his head in the general direction of the bar. "What were you thinking of just then, before I sat down?"

"Nothing. Absolutely nothing," she whispered, almost without emotion. He wouldn't understand if she tried to tell him about her thoughts of the man that he was and of the state that was Texas, and how they had suddenly become intertwined in her mind.

The dark eyes across from her sharpened. "I've noticed you do a lot of that." Skye looked at him inquiringly. "Think of nothing," he explained.

Skye looked back at James without response. It seemed to bother him that she showed no reaction, but she was just too tired.

His voice took on a tiny edge of harshness. "You seem to deliberately block everything that is not related to work. I wonder what you'll do when you no longer work, what will occupy your mind."

I'll try not to think of you and this two-week period in my life, that's for sure, Skye thought, and then quickly said a prayer that she hadn't spoken out loud.

It was funny that James should think she had been able to block *him* out of her thoughts. Not that she hadn't tried. But the truth was that James Steele disturbed her to the point she had thought of very little else these past few days.

Skye took a sip of her wine and her delicately tapered fingers started to rub her temple in a circular motion. "Haven't you figured it out yet? I thought surely you were omniscient." He had certainly tried hard enough to reach into her psyche, she reflected with annoyance. "I'm going to travel. To see faraway places with strange-sounding names." She couldn't help it if that had sounded sarcastic. He seemed to know exactly how to goad her, and the look in his eyes reflected the satisfaction he felt that she was beginning to react to him.

"Oh, of course. The beautiful lady is going to travel." He gave her a long, contemplative look. "Run, you mean."

"I'm not running! I decided to travel long before you ever came to Dallas," she denied hotly.

"I didn't say you would be running from me. Though you'd be doing that, too," he said calmly and proceeded to take out a thin black cheroot from his coat pocket, lighting it effortlessly with a book of matches he picked up from the table. As he exhaled, turning his head slightly so that he wouldn't blow the smoke directly into her face, she realized he had the ability to make the most common actions seem elegantly virile.

He looked at her with narrowed, brooding eyes. "What in the sweet hell do you hope to find in your travels, Skye? Don't you know places don't count, only people?"

Strange, no matter how harsh his voice became, her name was always spoken as if he were trying to soothe her, gentle her. He had never raised his voice to her. In fact, now that she thought about it, he always spoke to her in tones lower and softer than he normally used for other people. Skye's fingers increased the circular pressure on her temple.

"James . . . I really don't understand your questions . . . or your interest. What do you want from me?"

She half-hoped he wouldn't answer her last question. She had a strange feeling that the answer would scare her to death. He was a man who commanded great power, and even though she was frightened of him and what she knew he could make her feel, she was determined not to bend to his authority.

"I warn you now, I have had no experience being a rich man's mistress, and I don't intend to get any." Oh, hell! Why did I say that, she wondered despairingly? She couldn't seem to control her thoughts or her tongue when she was around him.

James's face was unreadable, but there was a tensing of muscle in the side of his face that threw the scar threading along his jawline into prominence.

He spoke the next words with seductive and leisurely deliberation. "It would take a night—and a day—and maybe another night to tell you what I want from you, lady. But just for expediency, let's say that as the future owner of this corporation, I don't want to lose a valuable employee." His voice had dropped to a dangerous softness, as if he were a cat waiting for her to wander a little closer before he pounced.

Oh, damn the man! Her blue eyes darkened. Why didn't he leave her alone? What was he talking about anyway? As much as he traveled, he should talk!

Speaking sharper than he had ever heard her speak,

Skye said, "Secretaries are a dime a dozen, James. Business schools are turning them out by the hundreds all over this city," she said with a graceful wave toward the window.

"Yes," he agreed quietly, "but not all with the special ability you have to make an office run as smoothly and pleasantly as if a person were a guest in someone's home."

He reached over abruptly and grasped her wrist, causing her fingers to be pulled away from her temple. His black brows were drawn together into quite a formidable appearance. "Do you have a headache?"

"Headache?" How bewildering this man could be. But then she realized she did indeed have a headache—not full-fledged, but one that was just lurking, threatening. It often happened in this way. It wasn't enough to even cause her to notice unless for some reason her attention was drawn to it or it got worse.

James continued his relentless questioning. "Are your headaches a residual effect of the accident?"

Suddenly sky-blue eyes became riveted to the inscrutable black eyes. "What do you know about an accident?"

"Oh, come now." He still retained his grip on her and was rubbing his thumb across the veins on the underside of her wrist. "People may not talk directly to you about your past, but it's definitely not a secret. As a matter of fact, I knew about it from Paul before I ever met you. And Paul, I would guess, learned about it from Jonathan."

Skye jerked her wrist from his hold and unconsciously started rubbing her temple again—only this time, her fingers were shaking. "It is *my* past," she said with emphasis, "and *my* life, and I have a right to keep it private if I want. I've always heard men were worse gossips than women," she ended with disgust.

James drew deeply on his cheroot and studied her. He was leaning back in his chair and seemed to be shrouded in smoke. "Your friends are just trying to help, you know. They worry about you."

"Well, I'm fine, I'm just fine!" she stated flatly.

"Oh, yes, beautiful lady," he said very sardonically, "I can see that you are." He leaned forward and again pulled her fingers away from her temple. She hadn't even realized what she was doing.

Something inside of Skye snapped, like a young sapling breaking from the force of too strong a wind. She had had enough. She didn't know what James wanted, and she didn't really care.

Skye raised her eyes and James received the full effect of a pair of huge pure-blue eyes that showed pain to their very depths.

"Now listen to me very carefully, *Mr.* James Steele and listen well." Her voice was low, but she was speaking slowly and clearly, as if she wanted not only him to hear what she was saying but herself as well. "Over five years ago I had a husband who loved me, and I had a healthy child growing inside of me. We had been married just a few months and were on a vacation. There was . . . an accident." Skye faltered. Sometimes in her dreams she could still hear the sickening sounds that accompanied the crash.

Her eyes never left his intently watching ones, however, and she continued, ". . . an awful accident. When I woke up alone, in a totally strange and impersonal hospital, I was informed that not only did I not have a husband anymore, but that I was empty... completely empty inside. Do you understand?"

Her voice trembled and rose slightly. "The oh-so-kind doctor explained that they had had to kill my baby so that I could live." She shook her head from side to side, and her voice dropped to a whisper. "Wasn't that stupid of them."

Skye paused and drew a ragged breath. She saw with a strange detachment that James's jaw was clenched, and there was a whiteness around his mouth. She had the odd, fleeting thought that this was a hard thing for him to listen to—but at the same time, this was what he had been waiting to hear.

For whatever reason, and Skye couldn't even hazard a guess, James Steele wanted to hear what she had to say. Well, maybe once it was said he would leave her alone, Skye decided, and she continued. "They thought they had saved my life, but they didn't. I'm really dead... dead and empty on the inside, and I never expect to feel full again. I have nothing, do you understand, *nothing* to offer anyone. *Especially* a man like you."

Her voice stopped. She reached for her bag, but he put his hand over hers.

"I'm going to drive you home," James stated firmly. Skye opened her mouth to protest, but he cut her off. "I'll get someone to deliver your car to your apartment later tonight, but *I am* driving you home."

He crushed out the fire of his cheroot, stood up, and held out his hand for her to take. Skye didn't take his offered hand, nor did she say anything as she walked out of the restaurant, looking straight ahead.

James did not try to touch her again or speak to her, but calmly and quietly led the way to the elevator that quickly whisked them underground to the garage where he opened the door for her and eased her into a powerful, gray, low-slung car. She had read once that he had similar cars in major cities all over the world, waiting for him. It must be nice to have power and wealth and the pathways of life smoothed out before you, Skye thought cynically.

During the trip to her apartment, Skye sensed that James was keeping her under close observation, or as close as the dwindling rush-hour traffic would allow. She couldn't summon enough energy to care, though. She was exhausted and now her head was pounding in earnest.

Skye felt as if she had been stripped naked before this persistent, compelling man. For some reason, she had let her reserve down, however briefly, to tell him things she hated to think about, much less talk about.

She felt completely drained, and she just wanted to get out of the car and away from James Steele as soon as possible.

No matter how hard she had tried this past week to remain firm and to close him out, James had always been able to get to her in one way or the other—to disrupt her mind, to disturb her body, and to undermine her life.

And tonight he had gotten closer to her—to what she was really thinking and feeling—than any other person had in five, long years. She had opened up a very private part of herself to him. She hadn't been able to help it—that was the kind of power he seemed to have over her.

She would be all right again as soon as she got away from him, Skye told herself determinedly. By tomorrow her strength would have returned and all of her defenses would be back in place.

Her apartment was a fifteen-minute drive from the office building, and it never occurred to her for a minute to ask how he knew where she lived. After all, in a few days he would own it.

James stopped the car about one-half block from her apartment building beside a tree-lined park. As Skye started to open her door, his left hand shot out quickly to take hold of her forearm, his arm pressed disturbingly under her breasts.

His right arm slid along the back of the seat until his hand took possession of the nape of her neck under the heavy chignon.

The musky scent of his aftershave combined with the clean, manly smell of him seemed to fill Skye's nostrils. She felt trapped in a cage made out of the warmth and the strength of the hard body of James Steele—with nowhere to escape.

With the slight pressure by his hand on her neck, he turned her head and forced her eyes to meet his. Skye hoped her eyes would reveal the ice-blue reserve she had been so desperately seeking the last few minutes and she knew she had at least partially succeeded when she heard James stifle a sigh. His hand began to rub the back of her neck softly, feeling the knotted muscles of tension there.

"You're wrong, you know." He casually continued

the conversation where she had stopped it in the restaurant. "You are a remarkable lady, Skye. I've been a lot of places and seen a great deal of life, but I have never seen anything like you."

He was talking to Skye in the deeply gentle, totally mesmerizing voice he seemed to use exclusively for her. And she could feel her traitorous body wanting to respond to the hardness of his flesh and the softness of his words.

"You are incredibly beautiful, Skye, with skin like ivory satin and eyes so blue and deep a man might never recover if he allowed himself to wander too far into their depths.

"But you don't allow that, do you? You don't allow anyone to get close enough to touch you, deep down inside where you can feel it."

The left hand that had been holding her arm moved and now pressed lightly on her midriff, right under her breasts, as if to show her exactly where he meant. She could feel the heat of his hand right through to her skin.

His one large hand, that in the past had so competently curled around a football, now seemed to fit perfectly across her—and with a slight shift, his thumb moved until it was reaching disturbingly up between her breasts.

Skye couldn't seem to draw a breath. She felt she might suffocate in the small, confining space James had created around her.

Watching James warily, she realized he wasn't going to let her out of the car—at least, not until he was good and ready. Skye drew a deep, ragged breath and attempted to explain. "To allow myself to feel, the way you are talking about, James, is to open myself to pain. I'm simply not that brave."

"Of course you are," he insisted as though she were a small child in need of reassurance. "You have had a terrible tragedy, but you did survive. Look how far you've come."

Skye shook her head slowly from side to side. He just didn't understand.

"Skye," he continued gently, "you will never be able to start your life anew unless you allow yourself to experience more than just superficial feelings and emotions. How can you know all that life has to offer if you persist in withdrawing from it? To truly live, you have to accept both the sorrow and the joy. It's impossible to have one without the other. It's all part of being alive.

"You don't stop with the pain—you get on with your life, and you have done that, whether you can see it or not. It's always easier to give up, to surrender to the pain. But you didn't. In your own way, you fought back. You could not be functioning in the skillful capacity you do and be the support and help to Jonathan you are if that weren't true.

"Yet, you're only half-alive. There is so much more. Despite what you say, you do have the courage to live and to feel deeply again. Unfortunately, you're just not ready to see this."

Skye had been watching his eyes and saw deep concern and something else she couldn't interpret. It confused her already-tired mind and disturbed body, causing her to lash out as best she knew how. "What would you know about it, James? All of your life, things have come easily to you."

He looked at her for a minute and then said quietly, "Someday soon, when you're ready to listen, I'll tell you the story about my so-called easy life."

Skye looked away from him to the dark green park where the children from the area usually played. "James," she started slowly and carefully, "your victories on the football field are legendary; your amorous conquests off the field are equally famous. In fact, I can't really think of an area where you haven't been successful."

She was trying to sound cool and collected, but she wasn't sure she was succeeding. His words had affected her more than she cared admit to herself. Still, she persisted. Turning back to look at him, she warned, "But don't try to succeed with anything pertaining to me. I'm not a trophy to be won at the end of a game."

One hand was motionless though warm and heavy against her neck, while his other hand was back on the steering wheel. "Leave me alone, James." She couldn't tell if she were getting through to him or not, but she had to try.

"I've fought to become the person you so obviously are finding fault with. You—of all people—should know about the art of self-preservation. With you it's instinctual. With me it had to be learned the hard way.

"During your football career, if you saw a great big lineman bearing down on you, you turned and ran the other way." She thought she saw amusement flicker in his eyes, and she rushed on. "Well, that's exactly how I feel about you. I look at you and all my instincts tell me to run. I'm sorry, but I'm the way I am because it's the only way I can survive in this not-so-perfect world I awoke to five years ago.

"Dallas is a big city, Mr. Steele. Some of the most beautiful girls in the world are supposed to live and work in this town. I'm sure you can find something or someone to amuse you in the time you have left here."

He didn't try to stop her this time as she sprang from the car and hurried the short distance into her apartment building.

Just inside the door, something made her stop and look back at the dark man silhouetted against the light from the street. She saw the flare of a lighter, then the glow of a lighted cheroot, and soon heard the car starting up.

It struck Skye as she watched James drive off down the street, how much the man and his machine were alike—fiercely lean, dynamically powerful, and very dangerous with their full power unleashed.

Even though Skye had had the last word tonight, she had the dreadful feeling she hadn't been the winner in this, their latest exchange.

Chapter Six

SKYE HAD WORKED most of Saturday, and by the time she had left the office that evening at six P.M., the rain was just starting to drizzle. She hadn't worked well today. She had made a hundred stupid mistakes, and she unhesitatingly placed the blame on James Steele's presence.

After their conversation of the night before, she had not wanted to even see him. But, of course, deliberate avoidance would have been extremely rude, not to mention very hard to explain, especially to Jonathan.

That he had an unsettling affect on her was a truism she no longer bothered to think about. No one else seemed to notice, though, and that perplexed her. Skye seemed to be the only one that felt threatened

or in danger whenever James Steele was present.
Maybe she was finally cracking up, she thought bitterly.

Men and women alike gravitated to him as if he
were their center, their magnet. No wonder newspa-
pers wasted so much print describing him and his
activities. James was a complete enigma. You couldn't
place him neatly into any one category.

Obviously and certainly he was a man's man. He
had been the undisputed master and brilliant tactician
of one of the most brutal and violent games existing.
Mean, tough, gristled football players had followed
his barked orders without question, and he had earned
the respect of everyone who had played with him or
against him.

But women also adored James, Skye had observed
this past week with great hostility. They fell all over
themselves to carry out his slightest request, all of
which he seemed to accept with a casual amusement
and the boredom of a man who has seen it all before.

James had an air of unmistakable authority. Even
sitting silently in a meeting, he was in complete control. With a lift of one black eyebrow, she had seen
him change conversations in midstream. With a choice
of words she wouldn't have cared to repeat, she had
heard him quell a hot-headed young executive and
change the minds of men who had spent hours dis-
cussing a problem.

Skye was the only one who seemed to offer him
any resistance. And yet, this man who had had the
power to shame the most awesomely fierce football
players because of a missed tackle or late hit was
unerringly gentle with her. And it was his gentleness

to her that unnerved Skye the most and made him all the more lethal.

Now, at ten-thirty P.M., there was a terrific thunder and electrical storm in the works. The only light in the apartment was the flexible lamp that was adjusted down over Skye's golden head, giving excellent lighting for the needlepoint she was working on so studiously. Her stereo played softly in the background, providing undemanding company, and she should have been content.

Her apartment, in complete darkness except for the one lamp, was on three levels. The front door opened onto an entryway that joined a width of deep-piled carpet making its way around the apartment in a sort of gallery effect to the small screened-off kitchen.

The living room was two steps down and had the same carpeting so that looking into the living room, one had the impression of a smooth line continuing to the far wall made of glass and the adjoining balcony, and revealing a distant view of the lights of downtown Dallas. The third level was her bedroom and bath, reached by a gently curving staircase.

This evening, however, all Skye had been able to see were giant, jagged flashes of white fire, some seeming to reach to the ground in front of her. Lightning had never particularly bothered her, and tonight, with the rain beating in sheets against her windowpane, the weather exactly matched her mood.

She had taken a long, hot bath after reaching home, but none of the atmospheric electricity of either the weather or the office she had left behind had drained away from her. Brushing her hair to a fine sheen and leaving it loose to hang halfway down her back, she had donned a bronze silk caftan, with a deep, wide neckline and golden embroidery around the edges. The caftan had been a gift from Jonathan on returning from a Middle East business trip last year, and was a favorite of hers because it always felt soothing against her naked skin.

As she jabbed the needle in and out of the flower she was creating out of yarn and mesh, Skye wondered why she was so depressed. Depressed? Was that the right word? By the end of next week it would all be over. The takeover would have been officially completed, her job of four years finished. Wasn't that what she wanted?

There were still things that had to be done, naturally, and she would probably be busy right down to the final signing. Then there was the banquet already arranged for Saturday night for the old and new employees, a sort of social initiation into the new company and management.

Tonight Jonathan was sending someone over with the final draft of the contracts for her to type tomorrow. There had been some last-minute changes she must check he had told her over the phone. Fortunately she had a typewriter at the apartment and she estimated it wouldn't take her more than a couple of hours to complete the papers.

Sitting barefoot on the floor, with a cushion between her back and the sofa, she barely glanced up from the intricate pattern she was working to sing out in answer to her doorbell above the thunder, "Come on in, George, and just put the folder on the table." Skye lived in a full-security building, but she knew the doorman would send George up from a long-standing familiarity with her and Jonathan's routine. "There's coffee made in the kitchen."

Needlepoint took mindless concentration and kept her thoughts off other things. That's why she liked doing it, as evidenced by the dozen or so needlepoint pillows scattered around the apartment.

Thud! Skye nearly jumped out of her skin as the folder of top-priority papers representing millions of dollars was thrown unceremoniously on the cocktail table in front of her.

Alarmed, she glanced up to see James Steele stepping out of the blackness and into her living room just as another jagged piece of lightning illuminated the room, outlining the dark man in startling light. His eyes and face were hard with anger. He must have shed his raincoat in the entryway, Skye decided, as she took in the black pants and black turtleneck sweater molded around him as if his muscle and bone had been converted into liquid and poured into the outfit.

"Don't you keep your door locked, or do you let just anyone walk in? There are maniacs everywhere, and you happen to be a very beautiful woman," he asked and stated in the same breath.

Eyeing him warily as he advanced around the couch like a jungle predator stalking his prey, Skye found her voice. "Really, James, this is a security building, you know, and since I was expecting George, I left the door unlocked."

"Well," he drawled with a sardonic lift of his black brows, "as you, and undoubtedly the doorman can see, I am not George. And," he continued ominously, "the doorman didn't think twice before he let me in downstairs."

Although Skye had seen him angry with other people who offered far less provocation than she, James had never lost his temper with her. However, deciding not to take any unnecessary chances, she thought to placate the beast before she had the unpleasant experience of his turning on her.

She looked up at him through the showering rays of lamplight which beamed down upon her while the rain beat a perfect tune against the building. "There is probably no one in this state," she said firmly, "not to mention on this continent, who does not know who you are and what you are doing in Dallas. Especially someone who is a member of the Hayes Corporation, as that doorman is."

"Oh, I haven't forgotten who owns this building." The softness of his voice was more than a little frightening when it was combined with the menacing glint in his eyes. "Or rather who *will* own it in a few days, and the laxity of the security that I just observed is inexcusable."

Coming closer so that he could look straight down into her eyes, his voice grew milder as he said, "And, by the way, I think you greatly overestimate the extent of my so-called fame." Observing the skeptical look in Skye's blue eyes, he added, "I admit that during my football career I was in the limelight more often than I liked. But since those days, I try to stay away from any publicity, although," he admitted with chagrin, "not always successfully."

Skye had to acknowledge the truth of his statement.

She had already fielded a number of interview requests, since he had stated from the first, "No interviews!" But in order to obtain some peace, he had finally been forced to agree to hold one press conference, with all three networks represented by their respective local news teams.

Mentally shrugging and thinking that perhaps if she changed the subject she could save the poor doorman's job for him, Skye said, "Look, as long as you're here, would you like a cup of coffee?" She really wanted him to leave, but she felt she owed it to Jonathan to try to make sure that these last few days went without conflict.

It was definitely one of the hardest things she had ever had to do. James Steele had the power to get to her as no other man ever had—in more ways than one.

"Don't look now, Skye, but I detect your polite Texas graciousness slipping just a little," James commented wryly.

She tried to get up, but a firm hand shot out, detaining her. "Please, stay where you are. We might as well go over this work first, and you make a totally charming picture sitting there." Accurately reading the objection in her mutinous face before she had the chance to verbalize it, he added, "Shouldn't take us long, I promise."

And it wouldn't have, except that Skye's concentration kept slipping away from the papers spread before her on the table, to the man sitting slightly to the side and behind her on the sofa.

Several times, as she turned a page, she found her shoulder and arm brushing his rock-firm thigh. The powerful muscles of his upper legs were rigid even in relaxation, and she had to fight the urge to reach out and touch the enticing hardness she saw there. The intoxicatingly masculine scent of him seemed to swirl around her with his every movement.

Once, as Skye leaned forward to see what he was pointing to, her hair fell in a soft curtain around her, shielding her face, and he gently took her hair and pushed it behind her ear. She felt her nipples harden suddenly at the curiously intimate gesture, causing her to become very much aware that she had put nothing on under the beautiful caftan. When Skye looked around at him, she became bewildered and flustered by the softness she saw in his deep, black eyes and had to look hastily away.

A few minutes later, she found herself concentrating on his beautifully low, sexily husky voice instead of on what he was actually saying. He could have been reciting the telephone book for all the attention she was paying, and Skye had a terrible feeling he was totally alert to her confused torment.

Finally, as if in deep thought, James rested his large hand casually on her shoulder to make a specific point. His long fingers reached downward over her collarbone to where their tips rested on the swell of her breasts. After a few agonizing minutes in which she couldn't remember whether she had breathed or not, his sensitive fingers started to absently rub the sleek, lustrous material of the caftan lying over her skin, as though the feel of it gave him great pleasure. The friction of the smooth silk moving against her soft flesh with the light pressure of his fingers was nearly her undoing. Her breathing became labored, and she had to fight against wanting to sit still because her throbbing breasts seemed to desperately want more of the exciting, voluptuous contact.

In one graceful, swift movement, Skye rose and walked agitatedly around the room, turning on several more lights. Then, swinging around, with just a glimpse at James's amused eyes, she mumbled, "I'll get the coffee," and escaped quickly into the kitchen.

Upon returning some ten minutes later, bearing the coffee tray, she found James leaning lazily back on the couch with his eyes closed. She watched him guardedly as she knelt opposite him, this time in *front* of the cocktail table, and poured out his coffee, knowing by now that he took it black.

His absolute stillness was more frightening than anyone else's movements, she reflected, because she knew that at any moment his body could explode into action.

Suddenly James opened his eyes and leaned forward to accept the cup, ridding her of the notion that he'd been asleep. "This is a very tastefully decorated apartment—a little bare perhaps, for some people's taste, but nevertheless tasteful."

Pouring her own coffee, Skye said, "The Hayes Corporation is nothing if not tasteful. One can only hope that when it becomes part of Steele Enterprises, the good taste will not be lost."

With a slight mocking bow of his dark head and a gleam of deviltry in his eyes, James retorted, "Well, we can only try, beautiful lady, we can only try."

With a smile in her eyes, Skye remarked, "You

don't read the small print in your contracts, do you?"

"I read everything put before me with great thoroughness, believe me."

"Did you know that this apartment belongs to the company?" she asked.

"Yes, I did, but I would have thought that the apartment would have taken on some of your own personality after four years." With a significant pause, he added softly, "I know you can do better than this. I've seen what you can do with an office."

They were treading on dangerous territory but for some perverse reason Skye continued this line of conversation. "Did you also know that Jonathan wanted to stipulate in the contract that this apartment was to remain mine for as long as I desired, but I asked him not to?"

"It's just as well," he said, not really answering her question.

"Do you mean you wouldn't have agreed to that clause?" she bristled, forgetting her earlier resolve not to fight with him.

"I simply mean," James said quite gently, "that since you are planning to travel, you won't be needing it. Right?"

Skye nodded in agreement. Why did she try to spar with him? It was an uneven venture at best. She was out of her league. She continued, a little deflated, "The apartment was leased completely furnished." She flicked a heavy swathe of hair behind one shoulder. "There is nothing here that is mine," she glanced around, "except for those pillows."

"Ah, yes. I couldn't help but notice you're a rather prolific needlepointer. They're very nice, but it doesn't give a clue as to what you're all about. You're not really a part of this apartment. With most people, if you can read their homes—the things they surround themselves with—you can do a quick psychological study of them." He paused, giving her a considering stare. "What else do you do with your time?"

Shrugging her delicate shoulders beneath the bronze silk, she felt the material move caressingly over her already-highly-sensitized skin. "Other than working and reading, that's about it. It keeps me busy."

Glancing over her shoulders to the window, she saw that the lightning and thunder were just about over, and now all that could be heard was the steady beat of the rain against the glass. Maybe James would leave soon. . . .

His sarcastic voice interrupted her thoughts. "Keeps you busy? You cannot," he said with measured incredulity, "expect me to believe you find needlepointing so fascinating that you do nothing else!" His voice softened to melting warmth, sending tiny shivers along her spine. "Oh, beautiful lady, are you lucky that I came along."

Skye got up abruptly and walked over to the window. The evening was quickly becoming another instance of this strange man's watchfulness and innuendoes. He didn't seem to like anything about her or her life, but still he would not leave her alone. All at once, something exploded inside her.

"Don't call me that!" It was almost a scream as she swung around to face him, the silky golden thickness of her hair flying out around her troubled face.

Black eyebrows raised slightly. "I beg your pardon?"

Stormy blue eyes met amused black eyes. "You know very well what I mean."

His rapier-swift move took Skye totally by surprise. She hadn't seen him move. He was simply there, gripping her shoulders firmly enough so that she couldn't possibly get away, but gently enough not to bruise her delicate skin.

"So you object to my calling you 'beautiful lady,'" the voice was huskily soft again. "I wonder why. I've never met anyone who fits the description so aptly." His thumbs started to rub rhythmically the fine bones that protruded beneath her neck. "You're certainly every inch a lady from the top of your shining head to the bottom of your gracefully arched feet and painted toenails."

Skye looked up into the absorbing black eyes that were so unwaveringly fixed on her own and thought he could easily hypnotize her if she wasn't careful, so potent was his charm. But she could not let that happen! She should ask him to leave. . . .

"And as for being beautiful," he continued, breaking in on her thoughts in his erotically raspy voice which was causing her stomach to curl and tighten, "you are probably the single most exquisitely beautiful creature I have ever laid my eyes on."

He stopped speaking only long enough to lay a light kiss at the side of her neck and then a slightly harder one at the edge of her mouth. "So tell me, please, my gorgeous Skye, why any woman would mind being called a beautiful lady?"

"Stop it, please stop it!" Skye tried to wrench away from him, but he held her steady with his masterful, yet extremely sensitive strength.

As though he hadn't been interrupted, James put his thumbs under her chin and forced her to look at him. He dropped a sweet, tender kiss on her parted lips that very effectively took her breath away. "I think the whole answer is that you're scared to death of the attention I'm giving you, and you're afraid of the demands you think I might make on you. One-half of you is an unawakened child. You have been a wife and almost a mother, but you have never really allowed yourself to become a woman, with all of a woman's wants and needs and desires."

This time he allowed her to retreat a short distance away, watching her closely all the time.

"What absolute nonsense are you talking about? I had a husband whom I dearly loved and who loved me in return." She felt as if her carefully-glued-together world was about to be shattered. She didn't want to hear any of this!

"I'm well aware of the facts, Skye," James said grimly. "What I'm saying is that your young love for your husband never really touched the real you. I've watched you these last few days, surrounded by all manner of men, and none of them have even come close to affecting you in any substantial way."

Except for you, Skye amended silently. But before she could think of another response, he closed the gap between them and wrapped his hands in the luxuriant fall of her hair, halting any resistance on her part.

His voice lowered in subtle persuasion. "You're a very sexy, sensuous woman. You may not want to admit it, even to yourself. But you must confess, if you're honest, that you like the touch of this silk caftan sliding over your smooth nakedness. And, while you're at it, admit that short hair would be a lot easier to care for than this." He tugged lightly on the shimmering lengths twisted around his hand. "You may keep your hair bound tightly during the day, but at night, when you're alone, you let your guard and your hair down, because you like the feel of it flowing wild and free around you.

"That prim and proper exterior you've chosen to show to the world doesn't fool me for one minute, beautiful lady. I know underneath there's a latent passion so explosive that it frightens the hell out of you. You can't hide or run from life forever, Skye. You've got to stop, and it's going to be soon."

All the color had drained from Skye, and her eyes were enormous in her pale face.

"Don't you see?" he continued with a curious intentness. "Can't you understand? I've been trying every way I know to break through your damned defenses."

"Why?" she whispered.

"Because I want you," he replied without hesitation. "Very badly—and my patience has about run out."

Burying his head deep in her sweetly scented hair, he kissed the hollow of her neck, traveling slowly up her neck to her face, savoring every square inch of her skin as he went. At her temple, he pulled back and looked deeply into her bemused eyes. "It's not normal for a woman to mourn five long years and not even attempt to find a new life for herself. Oh, grieve for the baby you lost and grieve for the babies you will never have, but don't grieve for the real love and passion you have yet to experience."

She tried to pull away, but his hold tightened with even more gentleness. He was extraordinary, Skye thought dazedly. His sorcerous voice had woven a mesmeric web around her, and his magnetic black eyes held hers with an unseen force she could only wonder at. The words he was saying weren't penetrating her dazed mind, but she suddenly felt as if she would be lost if they stopped.

"Skye, Skye, Skye." He almost breathed her name instead of saying it. "Why do you insist on fighting me?"

I don't know, she said to herself, but aloud she whispered, "Because I think fighting you will save my life."

"You don't *have* a life to save."

Her throat felt dry and she licked her lips nervously, drawing his gaze to their full loveliness. "My life may not come up to your standards, but it's safe and it's dependable."

Softly, very softly he said, "Living is not safe and it's not dependable, beautiful lady, but it's life. That's something you haven't had for five years, but it's fixing to change right away."

"No!" She felt giving in to him would be like committing slow, though exquisite, suicide.

"Yes, Skye," he breathed her name again. "Come here."

He spread his legs apart and gently drew her into him, pressing the lower portion of their bodies together with his hand on her hips. She could feel the pulsing, hard maleness of him and moaned as an exciting longing invaded her.

She watched with unbearable anticipation as he

tilted his head to one side and lowered his mouth gradually until she felt his warm, firm lips brush hers, ever so gently at first. He moved one of his hands under her hair to the nape of her neck. The other was around her pulling her inexorably closer to him until they were almost merged into one.

She knew there was no help for her anywhere in the world when her soft lips parted involuntarily and his mouth confidently and completely took possession of hers. All logical thought fled her mind when she felt his rough tongue seek and finally mate with hers — teasing, promising, destroying.

Skye feared she might disintegrate from the raging blast of desire racing through her veins from her fingertips right down to her toes. She didn't know if the indistinct murmurs she heard faintly were coming from her lips and she didn't care. All that mattered was the sensation of his hard body pressed tightly against her own and the inexpressible flood of pleasure and desire her body was experiencing as his large hands roamed with complete freedom and expertise over her.

She trembled and clung tightly to James as his searing lips traveled down her neck until they touched the deep cleavage that disappeared into her caftan. With a simple, unhurried motion that left Skye gasping, his hand slid her caftan off one shoulder until her full, soft roundness was in the gentle strength of his large hand. She could summon no resistance as his mouth expertly found her hard pointed peak, and she shivered under the fiery heat of each kiss and touch, her mind whirling in confusion.

She was past coherent thought, and James could

have done anything he wanted, but gently and ever so slowly he pulled her away from him, careful to hold her arms firmly.

He was breathing unevenly as he looked down into her upturned face, her hair in shimmering dishevelment around slightly bewildered blue eyes, her mouth red from the thorough kissing she had just received.

Leaning down, he kissed her mouth with what was almost tender assuagement and whispered with an unusual roughness, "One of these days and before too long, you are going to be mine. God, Skye! Do you know how nearly impossible it is to leave you tonight with you so soft and delicious in my arms. But when it happens, I want all the walls down. I want everything you've got to give—the essential, innermost part of you. Don't ever doubt it, my beautiful, beautiful lady, I will have exactly what I want."

He kissed her with breathtaking forcefulness one more time. And before she could think of anything to say or do, he was gone, the door shutting and locking quietly behind him.

She didn't know how long she stood where he had left her, staring at the door, willing her mind to start working. But gradually she sank to the floor, and tears, tears that she had not shed for five long years, started to roll down her cheeks. Once started, they would not stop. Skye cried for the loss of her young husband, and the loss of her baby, but mostly she cried for herself.

She realized the love she had felt five years ago was nothing compared to what this dark, powerful man could make her feel if she let him. Because, all at once, what he had said made perfect sense to her.

And to her horror, she now knew how easy it would be to let herself fall in love—really in love—with James Steele. She couldn't allow that to happen. The situation was impossible.

This was a man who was used to playing games superbly. His jet-set life was not for her. He flew from girl to girl, company to company, country to country as fast as his customized jet would take him.

Sure, he wanted her to feel something for him. She was a challenge to him now, a game. He wasn't used to meeting resistance. But eventually he would fly away from her, too. And when he left, she could be so totally devastated that she might not recover from the loss—*this* time.

Chapter Seven

SKYE DIDN'T SLEEP very well that night and was up at dawn, pacing restlessly. She couldn't get the things that James had said to her out of her mind. His words held more truth than she wanted to acknowledge, and they kept ricocheting around her head in an effort to gain her attention.

In desperation she sat down at the typewriter and produced the revised contract in record time. With nothing else absorbing on the horizon to claim her attention, she threw on a pair of jeans and a sweater and drove to the office.

Except for the few guards she encountered, the office was empty and lonely, and she couldn't seem to stop herself from wondering what James was doing today—who he was with.

Climbing back in her car, Skye drove aimlessly through the deserted streets of the downtown area, emerging on the other side to notice the Old City Park situated just across the expressway. She had known it was there, of course, but had never taken the time to tour it.

It struck her how incongruous it was that this peaceful microcosm of Texas history was located right on the fringes of downtown, cosmopolitan Dallas.

There weren't many people at the park yet, and Skye became caught up in the rich history of the North Central Texas area that had been preserved in the charming park.

The land on which the park was situated had been first a buffalo trace, then an Indian campground. Skye found herself wondering what the early settlers would have thought of the area now—not just the physical changes, but the tremendous speed at which lives were lived today.

An elderly man dapper in a brown tweed jacket with a houndstooth hat adorned with a feather approached her. "Good morning. Would you like to buy a ticket? It would entitle you to tour all of the houses, including the largest remaining antebellum home in Dallas—Millermore. I would be delighted to show you through."

Skye's smile was genuine as she said, "No, thank you. I'd just like to continue at my own pace." She had already found several of the homes she could peer into. There were a total of twenty-two restored structures on the twelve-acre park, including a schoolhouse, a church, and a bandstand, all characterizing life as it was lived between the years 1840 and 1910.

The twinkling brown eyes and friendly smile of the man showed understanding at Skye's reluctance to have her private thoughts intruded upon. "If you change your mind, I'll be over at the train station, and if I can be of any help in answering questions, please let me know." Turning to walk away, he added, "Don't forget to browse through our general store. It sells a lot of crafts our own artisans make."

Skye knew the Old City Park was operated by the Dallas County Heritage Society and that many of the members who were retired gave their time voluntarily.

As she continued her solitary tour, Skye's thoughts turned increasingly inward. The early pioneers who had settled this region so many years before had not been cowards, or they would never have started the small community on the banks of the Trinity River. None of them had had easy lives, but they had vision and courage aplenty, and it made Skye feel very small and inadequate.

In the cool light of day, away from the heat of James's body, Skye finally made herself face a few facts with as much honesty and forthrightness as she could muster. Everything he had been saying to her these past few days had been working slowly on her consciousness, like water constantly dripping onto a rock.

James had been right about a lot of things. Five years earlier, she had withdrawn into herself in an intuitive attempt to allow a restoration period for her scarred and battered emotions and in an instinctive defense against any more pain. In the process, however, she had blocked out any chance of warmth or comfort or love.

She had gritted her teeth and forged ahead, neither looking right nor left, doing what she thought she needed to do to survive. That in itself had shown a certain amount of courage and perseverance in the aftermath of her grief. Now however, surviving no longer seemed enough. And she had James to thank— or curse—for that. One smile from James and she had realized her scars had long since healed. One look from him, and she had become aware of how cold and barren her present life was.

James had been a catalyst for her, but he wasn't her answer. Surely he would cause more problems than he would solve. Maybe travel wasn't the right solution for her either. Oh, hell! She wasn't sure of anything at this point! In a few days' time her job would be ended, and that would be time enough to decide. Right now, she had one more week of James to get through. . . . And there her thoughts came to a screeching halt.

James. What decisions could she come to about James? The answer was: she couldn't. There was absolutely nothing she could do about him.

He was much too exciting, far too terrifying. He was an unknown quantity, a rugged individualist— too dynamic to ignore, too complex to predict, too wild to tame.

And she wanted him. Inconceivable, but there it was. It was time she faced that fact, too. She didn't know how much longer she could or should come up with plausible reasons not to give in to him. Nothing she had said or done since his arrival had made the slightest bit of difference to him, anyway. He always did just exactly as he wished.

However, it stood to reason if she recognized the pitfalls, she could avoid the pit. She could try to maintain an objective distance, a sort of unemotional detachment, from the man. And just maybe—if she were lucky—she might escape relatively unharmed from James Steele's visit to Dallas.

Monday morning dawned bright and clear and much too early for Skye's liking. She had had her usual trouble sleeping during the night, and today she felt out-of-sorts and lethargic.

She had faced a few home truths the day before, but had not reached any really satisfactory conclusions. Her theories had been faultless, but theory very often collapsed in the face of reality, and she had a terrible feeling that she was kidding herself if she thought she could maintain any sort of perspective about James.

She dreaded seeing him and would much rather have stayed at home. Maybe that was why she felt so discontented and vague this morning; but, whatever the reason, nothing seemed to be coming out right.

It started when she was dressing. Deciding she couldn't manage her usual cool, sophisticated look, she settled for casual chic with a full tiered skirt, finely textured cashmere knit top and belt and boots, all in shades of brown and gold. She left her hair loose—a first in her history of employment with the Hayes Corporation—and didn't question why.

Then, somehow, she arrived at work an hour late. She wasn't sure of the reason. She had gotten up at the usual time. It just seemed that she had spent a lot of time accomplishing very little. Even making her bed had been a gigantic task.

Once at work, Skye had to fight the urge to turn around and go home again. She had always prided herself on being one step ahead of matters at the office, but things seemed to have gotten under way just fine without her—a situation that upset Skye even more.

She was sitting at her desk studying, with a disgruntled eye, the pile of mail already opened and neatly sorted when Beth Ann burst in exuberantly. "Mornin'! Isn't it a beautiful day?"

Skye wasn't even sure Beth Ann had seen her faint nod or had heard her even weaker "Well, actually..." before the young girl started chattering again. "Did you have a nice weekend? What did you do? We found the contracts you typed. Did you bring them by Sunday? How dreary!"

"Beth Ann—" Skye tried to interrupt.

"Did I sort the mail okay? You lucky girl! New York in the spring and a gorgeous man, too! Are you packed yet? I wouldn't even have come into work this morning if I had been you."

"Beth Ann!" At Skye's raised voice, the younger girl stopped, surprised.

"What in the world are you talking about?" Skye was sorry to be speaking so sharply, but Beth Ann was perfectly capable of conducting the entire conversation by herself.

"Why, your trip to New York, of course."

"My trip to New York?"

"Yes, your trip with Mr. Steele." Beth Ann was looking at her with concern. "Skye, are you okay?"

"With James! Are you out of your mind?"

Beth Ann looked at Skye doubtfully. "Well, I don't know. Paul told me Mr. Steele was leaving this afternoon for New York, and you were going with him."

"Beth Ann, there must be some mistake."

"No, Mr. Hayes confirmed it." Beth Ann was beginning to brighten up again. "It will be a trial run for me, working solo as the president's secretary."

Skye felt a little desperate. Her mind couldn't seem to grasp what was happening. Her going *anywhere* with James Steele was out of the question, much less to New York. What was going on? Maybe if she just went back home... Beth Ann broke into her thoughts again. "Do you think I can handle it? I've been doing pretty well lately and Mr. Steele said..."

James! Instantly Skye's mind became crystal clear. Of course—James! Why hadn't it occurred to her before. He was behind this. Why was she sitting here trying to make sense out of Beth Ann's ramblings when she could go straight to the original source— because Skye had absolutely no doubt that James had arranged whatever it was that Beth Ann was talking about.

"Beth Ann," Skye interrupted the soliloquy, "where is Mr. Steele now?"

The young girl's eyes narrowed at the hardness she heard in Skye's voice. "Why, in his office. He's having a meeting with—"

"Thank you," Skye jerked out, cutting short Beth Ann's statement. She was out of the door and down the hall before she had time to remember yesterday's commitment of unemotional detachment. The *nerve* of the man!

At his office door, Skye didn't even pause, but
charged right in. There he was—seated behind his
desk, damnably attractive in an expensively cut suit
of so dark a blue it looked almost black. His shirt was
startling white in comparison. The gold watch gleaming against the dark skin of his powerful wrist and the
gold pen he was holding in his long fingers provided
the only splash of color.

She heard an astonished "Skye?" from Paul, and
in her peripheral vision, she saw half a dozen men
sitting around the room. But she couldn't be bothered
with them. All of her attention was centered on James.

He was leaning back in his chair in an attitude of
relaxed readiness, and his eyes had not left Skye's
since she had first entered the room so precipitously.

She was absolutely furious! How dare he sit there
with such studied insouciance. She felt her hands ball
into fists at her side. She knew he was up to something;
but, whatever it was, he wasn't going to get his way
this time!

There was complete quiet in the room. If Skye
hadn't known better, she would have sworn that the
other men present had stopped breathing as they observed what must seem a very strange scene between
the two people in the center of the room.

Skye, her anger vibrantly apparent, her eyes sparkling with fury, her hair clouding around her flushed
face, had never been more beautiful.

James, deep and dark, his eyes studying Skye with
a quiet, hooded intensity, was overpowering in his
stillness.

Ultimately it was he who broke the deafening silence. Turning his head slightly, and without taking

his eyes off Skye, he said one soft, commanding word—"Paul."

The men, led by Paul, all moved at once, vacating the room in a matter of seconds—and then Skye and James were alone.

Skye released her pent-up breath and exploded. "Beth Ann just told me that I'm supposed to be going to New York with you this afternoon."

"That's right," James answered, level and cool.

"No, that's not right! I don't know what you think you're up to, but—"

"I have to fly to New York this afternoon on business," James cut in. His voice seemed not to be lifted above a conversational tone, but it had the clear ring of authority. "My secretary, who would usually accompany me, is sick. I'm taking you instead."

"You are not playing a game called 'Interchangeable Secretaries,' James. You can't do that. I have a job here. I have work to do. Jonathan—"

"Has fully agreed that you will be the one to go with me," he interrupted her again.

Skye had started pacing back and forth in front of his desk, her skirt and hair flying out about her every time she turned. James's unreadable eyes followed her progress, his elbows on the arm of his chair, his fingers steepled together.

"There is too much to do here. Beth Ann can't possibly handle it all."

"Skye," James stated with tightly controlled patience, "you know as well as I do that everything is just about done, and Beth Ann can handle the rest with the greatest of ease. She'll have full responsibility next week, anyway."

"Jonathan—" Skye started to say.

"Is more than happy to accommodate me in this matter," he finished for her.

Something in his tone made Skye stop pacing and turn to look at him. "What do you *do* to people?" she asked with amazement. "You've even gotten to Jonathan!" She paused to shake her head. "Well, Mr. Steele, you can't order *me* around."

"Try me, Skye. Just try me," he returned in a steel-lined, velvet tone that sent shivers up and down her spine with dismaying velocity.

Skye took one more look at the tough, implacable man and turned to flee, but she was pulled up short at the door by his haunting voice. "Oh, and Skye—don't bother to change. You look extremely beautiful."

Ten minutes later Skye was sitting at her desk holding her aching head in her hands when Beth Ann popped around the door. "Mr. Steele wanted me to tell you that he and Mr. Hayes have gone out for a while, but that he will pick you up at your apartment at one o'clock and to please be ready."

Back at her apartment, Skye flung off her clothes and threw open her closet door. "Don't change my clothes!" Skye stormed aloud to the empty apartment. "I'll show him!"

Determined to defy him in this one thing if no other, she pulled out a plain lightweight, navy wool gabardine suit with matching high heels and blouse. The only details to relieve the severity of the suit were a ruffled collar on the blouse and a slit up the side of the slim, straight skirt.

Slowing down just long enough to take a couple of aspirin, she dressed and pulled her hair back as tightly as she could manage, twisting it in a knot and jabbing the gleaming mass with pins to hold it in place.

Stuffing her suitcase with several comparably severe outfits, she was standing outside her apartment building promptly at one o'clock, suitcase at her feet, when James pulled up.

Making no comment on her appearance, he stowed her case efficiently in the back of the car. After he was seated, however, he reached over and in one, quick, dexterous movement, relieved her tortured hair of its pins, allowing the heavy length to swing free.

"From now until we get back, you will wear your hair loose," he commanded in the same steely, velvety voice she had heard earlier in the day. "You, my beautiful lady, should be beaten for the things you do to your hair."

Her first reaction was indignation at his highhandedness, but as she opened her mouth to protest, his came down in a soft, warm kiss, causing her mental processes to stop for a long moment. Then his hands came up to massage her head lightly in a consolatory action, just as if he knew she had a headache.

"Stop fighting me on any and everything, Skye," he urged in a complete change of tone. "Give it a rest. Don't be afraid to trust me." Now he was being perfectly charming, entirely soothing. "We're going to be together for the next few days. Try to relax. It won't be so bad—you have my word." And, giving her one of his devastating smiles, he started the car.

As they drove away, Skye had to admit the pain

in her head was easing. At the same time, she had to wonder at James's words. He had almost sounded as if he were talking about a seduction instead of a business trip. She must be getting paranoid!

Approaching the big silver jet, Skye couldn't help but recall her thoughts when she had first seen the plane a week ago on that early, rainy Monday morning—how beautiful and mysterious it had appeared then. She still retained those impressions as James helped her aboard with a solicitude and care that somehow didn't seem out of place.

Just inside the door of the plane, James put a possessive hand around Skye's arm. A man of medium height and build was there waiting, smiling broadly.

"Skye, I'd like you to meet one of the best pilots in the air today, Greg Somerville. Greg, this is Mrs. Anderson."

Greg seemed a very unlikely pilot to her, but he was in keeping with the energetic young men James employed. He was not wearing a uniform, but was dressed casually in tan slacks and a green shirt. Intelligent brown eyes shown out of a happy-go-lucky face. "Don't let him kid you, Mrs. Anderson. *He's* the best pilot around."

Skye looked at James in surprise, but James just shrugged in a slightly bored manner. "I don't do much of the actual flying anymore. I just don't have the time."

Greg was eyeing Skye with open admiration. "I can sure see why he doesn't want to be up in the cockpit this trip!"

"Greg," James drawled in a repressive tone, "is everything aboard?"

"Yes, sir," Greg answered, speculation evident in his voice. "The rest of the crew, food, drink . . . and no steward, just as you requested."

"Good, then let's get this baby in the air—and, Greg, hold all calls."

James had turned away and only Skye saw the look of surprise that crossed Greg's face at his employer's last request. Evidently, holding calls was not the usual procedure.

The luxury of the interior gave Skye pause. She could feel James's eyes upon her as she took in a lounge, thickly carpeted and richly furnished in masculine shades of black, brown, and gold. If she had been decorating the plane, Skye thought irrelevantly, she would have done it in softer tones. Still, the bold, dynamic decor suited its owner, and he had probably paid someone quite a bit of money to get the effect.

In addition to a couch and several comfortable-looking chairs, there was a large desk, a complete communications center, and a well-stocked bar. She supposed the passageway Greg had disappeared down led to a galley and then the cockpit. The other passageway opening off the lounge at the opposite end she could only guess at.

Affirming Skye's feeling that he had been watching her, James volunteered, "That leads to a restroom and my private bedroom and bath. Would you care to see it?"

"No . . . thank you." Her words had come out a trifle more weakly than she had intended.

"Do you know anything about planes?"

"Nothing." She smiled at him. She had decided she would try to make the best of a bad situation. After all, it was only going to be for a few days, and New York should be interesting. Besides, her head had stopped aching.

A muscle moved in the side of his face, his jaw clenching and unclenching, as James observed Skye's smile, but he said, "This is a 727 I had converted in order to be able to cover great distances without stop-overs."

"Oh? I guess that's important." Skye felt a little out of her depth with such a high-speed life-style.

"It used to be," James said cryptically.

During takeoff, James sat in a chair opposite Skye; but once the plane was in the air, and after ascertaining that Skye required nothing, he moved to the desk and soon became immersed in paperwork.

Skye wasn't sure what she expected, but being ignored by James was a new experience and one she wasn't sure she liked. Don't be a fool, she told herself sternly as she flipped rather vehemently through a magazine. This is exactly what you've been wanting!

They had been in the air for about thirty minutes when Skye began to feel uneasy for no apparent reason. She glanced over at James, but all his attention seemed to be centered on the work he had brought aboard. Somewhat reassured by his attitude of routine normalcy, Skye willed herself to relax.

She tried to get interested in the magazine, but couldn't concentrate—a faint hammering had started in her head. There was a tension growing in her, an unexplained fear.

Glancing out the window, Skye tried to decide what was bothering her, what was wrong. It wasn't just the unusual fact that James was ignoring her. He obviously had a great deal of work to do and that was why he had asked no calls be put through to him. But there was something else—something she couldn't quite put her finger on.

Endeavoring to still the tremors of uneasiness that were running along her nerves, she picked up another magazine. After a few minutes, however, she put the magazine aside as a lost cause and looked idly out the window again.

Barren brown land, dotted with an occasional clump of green, and divided by ribbons of barbed wire, was rushing past them in a blurred motion.

Not entirely comprehending what she was seeing, Skye turned to look at James—and what she saw made her blood run cold.

He had given up any pretense of working. His pen lay motionless on the desk, and he was leaning back in his chair, hands folded, watching her. His face was shadowed and impenetrable, and his black eyes told her absolutely nothing. Every muscle in his body seemed to be tensed, waiting for something.

Skye looked back out the small window and realized she should be viewing something entirely different on the route to New York—a giant patchwork-quilt tableau of lush farmlands planted in various crops and in different stages of cultivation and growth.

She looked back at James. His eyes were cold and hard. Even to her ears her voice sounded shaky. "Why are we flying over West Texas?"

"Because we're going to California."

"California!" Skye wanted to scream at him, but her voice wouldn't raise above a whisper. Her throat was too dry. She couldn't even manage to swallow. "You said we were flying to New York... on business... You told Jonathan..."

"I lied," James stated flatly and without apology.

"James—" she started, then stopped. She didn't understand any of this; she couldn't seem to think. Her head was pounding with an alarming intensity now, and she felt as if she were going to be sick.

Some of the hardness seemed to go out of his eyes—there might have even been a touch of compassion—but when James spoke, his voice was firm with resolve. "I've borrowed a friend's beach house for a few days. I want us to spend some time together, away from the pressures of the takeover, so we can get to know one another better. I don't want you to have any more excuses, no apartment to run and hide in, no work to lose yourself in." His voice softened as he added, "I want you to learn to trust me."

"Trust!" Skye jumped up and walked partway to his desk. "James! You've just *lied* to me. As a matter of fact, you've just kidnapped me! That's definitely against the law. *Even* in Texas. Even for you! You *cannot* take me forcibly to California."

"Who's going to stop me?" James replied with deadly softness.

Skye sank back down into her chair rubbing her temples. He was right, of course. Who *was* going to stop him? She certainly couldn't talk the pilot into turning back. As nice as Greg had seemed, he was no doubt a loyal Steele employee. Once they landed— and she didn't even know where that would be—she could try to enlist the help of passers-by. But James was well known, and chances were either no one would believe her fantastic story—or else they would have no wish to cross him.

For one hysterical moment she actually glanced at the airplane door, but James was apparently following her thoughts because he murmured quickly, "Don't even think it, Skye."

She looked up at him with a newfound fatalism born of painful experience and thought, what was the use? She had only known this fantastic man one week, but it was long enough to finally realize she couldn't win with him. She had made various resolutions all week long, only to break them. Her efforts to oppose and resist him had been futile—and look where it had gotten her!

He had asked her to stop fighting him. Well, apparently she really had no choice in the matter. In fact, her mental and physical health probably depended upon it.

He had also asked her to trust him. This she was not sure she could do. How could you trust a man who made up his own rules as he went along? And why did it seem so important to James for her to trust him, anyway?

"How's your head?" he asked quietly.

Skye realized she had been staring at him. "It hurts." Her voice was barely audible, but he had heard her, because the next thing she knew he was lifting her from her chair and carrying her into the bedroom.

Instinctively, Skye stiffened, but James stood her on her feet when they reached the bedroom and took her face gently between his two large hands. "Relax,

Skye, relax. It will never, ever be rape between the two of us—I promise you, and you *can* believe it." His voice was deep with compelling tenderness and, surprisingly, his tone and his words soothed her.

"I want you to try to get some rest and get rid of that headache. You've had it since this morning, right?"

Skye didn't confirm or deny this statement. Why bother? It hadn't even been a question.

"Get that damned suit off, and I'll be back in a minute."

She tried to read his face before he left the room, but all she saw, strangely enough, was concern.

Skye felt almost too weak to stand. Cautiously eyeing the king-sized bed with the black satin coverlet and matching sheets and pillows, she stripped down to her slip and panties and climbed into bed.

When her head stopped hurting, Skye promised herself, she would ask herself why she was lying in James Steele's satin-covered bed, in the middle of the sky, soaring high above misty-soft, downy-white clouds. But not now.

She opened her eyes only long enough to drink down the glass of brandy James brought to her. Then the cool, smooth luxury of his bed claimed her.

Chapter Eight

SKYE CAME SLOWLY awake to the sensation of kisses feathering over her face and neck. She felt no pain, only a heavy tranquillity diffusing her limbs, occasioned by the deep, satisfying sleep she had just experienced.

Stretching slightly, she heard an indulgently amused voice ask, "Feeling better?"

"Yes," she replied in a voice drowsy with sleep. She was surprised—the pain in her head was completely gone. Tentatively opening her eyes, she found the plane was motionless with an uncharacteristic quiet. "Where are we?"

"Los Angeles International Airport," James replied absently. He was smoothing the bare skin of her shoulders with the sweetly sure touch of his hands.

Skye found herself thinking how easy it would be to get used to the feel of his hands on her body—permanently.

"How long have we been here?" If she focused on mundane matters, she would be all right.

"A little while. I decided to let you sleep." James ran his hands under the fragile straps of her lace slip and pulled them down off her shoulders.

"Ivory satin on black satin," he murmured. "Do you have any idea how desirable you look lying against those black satin sheets?" He trailed a line of kisses across her collarbone then lowered his head to nuzzle the hollow between her breasts.

Skye shook her head helplessly. It was no use. All of her inhibitions had been allayed with sleep. She had no defenses sufficient to fight the insidious feelings his lips were creating.

His hand stopped, palm down, right above her heart, which thudded heavily against it.

It was inescapable. James lowered his head and gave Skye a slow, burning kiss, while his hard body pressed her back against the softness of the bed.

Skye responded without thought, unconsciously moving under him until James drew back slightly and released an unsteady breath. His eyes shone brightly down into hers.

"You had better get up and get dressed unless you want to spend the next few days right here in the plane. I've brought your suitcase in. Pick something a little more...comfortable to wear then that—that...suit."

Skye's heartbeat steadied somewhat. It angered and confused her that he could return to normal so quickly.

How could he think of such commonplace matters at a time when she was still burning from his touch?

"I don't have anything more . . . comfortable, James. I packed for a New York business trip. Remember?"

James appeared to be taken aback momentarily, but recovered quickly. "Don't worry. There are always plenty of leftover clothes at the house we're going to. People either forget them or deliberately leave them behind until their next visit. I'm sure you'll be able to find something to wear—not that I particularly care whether you do or not. Just so long as you don't wear that . . . suit."

Regardless of his feelings about her much-maligned navy suit, it was serviceable, and it was just about all she had. She put back on the skirt and blouse, leaving off the jacket, but neglecting to button the top three buttons of the blouse. Splashing water on her face, she felt one hundred percent better than she had a few hours before.

The plane was parked off to one side, away from any buildings, and there was no one nearby as they descended the stairway and walked to a waiting car much like the one they had left behind earlier in the day back in Dallas. It obviously paid to be a man as rich and powerful as James Steele when it came to arranging clandestine arrivals, Skye thought wryly.

After making sure her seat belt was securely fastened, James started the high-powered car and with an expert casualness Skye had to admire, headed out of the thronged airport into a maze of wildly congested streets and thoroughfares.

He had changed out of his business suit into tight-fitting black jeans and a gray, short-sleeved knit shirt.

His masculinity nearly reached out and touched her, it was such a tangible thing.

Skye stared out the window, trying to ignore her unsettling reaction to him, attempting to take an interest in her surroundings, but there was a thick haze hanging over the city that depressed her.

James glanced at Skye and laughed. "I see you're admiring the local air."

"Is it always like this?"

"More or less. The L.A. Basin seems to be a natural collector. It used to be called the *'Valle de Mil Fuegos,'* or 'Valley of the Thousand Smokes.' The term originated when the first Spaniards arrived and noticed how thick the air was with the smoke from the hundreds of thousands of Indian campfires and brush fires which frequented the area. It's worse today, of course."

"Does it ever get any better?"

"Perfectly clear days are very rare," he informed her. "It does clear up for a while when the Santa Ana winds blow. Of course, then the brush fires start. Heavy rains will also clear the air, but then you have the problem of mud slides. How do you like it so far?" he teased.

"Oh, it's charming," she assured him sarcastically, then went on to another subject that was bothering her. "Is there always this much traffic?" The amount of traffic was almost frightening, yet there was a certain order to the chaos.

"Pretty much," he responded matter-of-factly. "Actually, I'm sparing you the freeways."

"Excuse me if I'm not grateful, Mr. Steele, but I

was supposed to be three thousand miles away," Skye countered tartly.

"You'll enjoy it out here a whole lot more," James stated certainly, his black eyes sparkling with amusement.

"Where exactly are we going?" Skye took the opportunity to ask the question uppermost in her mind.

"Malibu. Some friends of mine, Mary and Arthur McFarland, have a house on a mile or so of secluded oceanfront property. The beach is completely private. There'll be no one around to bother us—especially this time of the year and in the middle of the week."

Skye looked at him in astonishment, exclaiming, "Do you really think that's a recommendation?"

James gave her one of his irresistible smiles, guaranteed to make her forget almost any objection. "Now, now. Don't get testy. It's not at all becoming."

"I'm sorry." She delivered the false apology with considerable asperity. "It's just that I've never been kidnapped before, and I'm not at all sure how to act."

At least the last part of her statement was right, Skye reflected. She really didn't know how to act. She was having a hard time reconciling her justified anger at being taken to California against her will with the almost treacherous need James was so expert in creating in her.

"It's really very simple." James reached over and picked up her hand and, drawing it to his lips, he kissed it lightly. "You just put yourself in my hands, and everything will turn out fine."

While Skye's mind was aflight with the imagery of herself in his hands, they turned north onto the

Pacific Coast Highway. The view was breathtaking, and the air was much clearer. On their left the ocean glistened lazily in the late-afternoon sun. On their right, beautiful houses hung precariously from the hillsides, some looking like castles from another time, some looking like super-modern health spas complete with pools and tennis courts.

James handled the car with superb ease, driving around the curves and through the traffic with complete self-assurance.

He must have made this trip many times before, Skye mused. I wonder with whom?—the question leaped unbidden into her mind. Had he ever kidnapped anyone else? No, probably not, she silently answered her own question with resignation. He wouldn't have to.

"You seem to know your way around very well." As soon as the words were out of her mouth, Skye cringed with embarrassment. They had come out sounding as if she were accusing him of something dire. "Do you come here often?" she tacked on lamely.

"I know Southern California quite well," he acknowledged, commenting on her first statement, amusement in his voice. "I went to school out here, you know."

"Oh, no, I didn't know." She felt like such a fool.

"See, our enforced togetherness is working already," he pointed out smoothly. "You learned something about me you didn't know before."

He grinned broadly at her, not fazed by the cool look she gave him, then continued, "And I do make frequent use of the beach house. Mary and Arthur don't use it that much when school is in session. They have three teenagers—two girls and a boy.

"Arthur is my personal lawyer," he went on to explain, "but he is also a friend of longstanding. Their beach house is the one place I know of that I can be absolutely alone without the intrusion of telephones or press or well-meaning friends and business associates."

Skye nodded silently. She had just learned something else about James. She would never have thought of him as the type of man who would need to escape from anything or anyone. He seemed to attack life, rather than retreat.

"And, no, I've never brought anyone else here before."

"I didn't ask that," Skye protested indignantly. How could he read her mind like that?

James just smiled and changed the subject. "I own some coastal property farther north, just below San Francisco. One of these days I'm going to build my own place."

"Why haven't you before now?" Skye wondered aloud.

James turned to look at her. "I've never had a reason before now."

Skye couldn't think of anything terribly bright to say to that and instead watched with interest as they made a sharp left turn onto a much smaller road.

Twisting and turning for a mile or so, they soon made another left turn and drove up to a gate nearly obscured by heavy bushes of red and white oleanders. James reached into the glove compartment and pulled out an electronic transmitter. He pressed it and miraculously the gate opened.

The gravel road snaked down to the water, revealing a neat, clean-lined, unpretentious structure beautiful in its simplicity and size. The house, perched on a small cliff overlooking a large cove, was constructed of redwood and glass and blended in with the wild beauty of its environment. It was hard to believe that such a place could exist so close to Los Angeles.

Bougainvillea cascaded down the cliffside, and everywhere Skye looked bottlebrush, oleanders and African daisies were bursting with color.

"I'm impressed," Skye said and meant it.

As James unloaded their cases and unlocked the door to the house, Skye walked around to the front and continued on to the edge of the cliff. It wasn't a high cliff, and there was a railing at the edge on which she could lean. Steps chiseled out of the cliff led down to the isolated beach, where waves foamed rhythmically into the sandy shore.

Skye sighed with pleasure. A large catamaran, flying bright orange and red sails, was making its way lazily in front of a golden sun, sinking in glorious splendor far out over the Pacific. Over her head, seagulls drifted on the soft currents, and below her, sandpipers scrounged for their evening meal.

A languid breeze caressed her face and blew through her silky hair with the gentleness of a lover. The peacefulness of the scene seemed to envelope her, to permeate through her layers of accumulated tension.

She had to accept the inevitable. It was a very definite fact that she was to spend the next few days here with James. He had seen to that. To fight it any more than she already had would be foolish.

How many people got the opportunity to stay in such a beautiful place, and get to know a man like James Steele better? Maybe it *was* possible to learn to relax with him. She was going to have to try. Perhaps she would even be able to come to terms with the undeniable attraction that sparked between James and herself. She really had no choice in the matter.

She felt James come up behind her and turned to look at him.

"What do you think?"

"I think it's beautiful," Skye answered honestly.

"I agree." He wasn't looking at the view, though; he was looking at her. "But what I want to know is, do you think you'll be able to rest and unwind here?"

"With you?" She voiced what she had been thinking.

"Am I really that terrible, Skye?" he questioned with a strangely pained expression on his dark face. "Am I really such an ogre?"

Her voice and eyes were solemn as she said, "You've been hard on me, James. You know you have."

"There's not a mark on you, baby. Most people who know me would say I have been infinitely gentle with you." His voice was a husky softness, and she had the impression it was touching her.

Skye turned and stared broodingly out at the sea. He was right, of course, but then she was right, too. They were both right, really. It was a gentle hardness he had used on her, and it had been most effective.

She turned back to him. "Why?"

He looked at her for a long moment, considering his answer carefully. "I hope you will have your answer by the time we leave here."

At her puzzled look, his mood became lighter. "Come on," he teased gently, "smile for me, and I'll gladly tell you the secrets of the universe." He reached out and ran the back of his hand down her cheek. "You're here to rest and enjoy. Remember?"

Skye did smile at him. Suddenly she was happy. When James turned on the charm, he was impossible to resist. If there were any inherent dangers in the situation—and she would have to be stupid to think that there weren't—she was going to ignore them—at least for now.

James opened the front door and allowed Skye to precede him into a crowded entryway. She almost tripped over a large basket standing just inside the door. It was overflowing with a varied assortment of beachballs, footballs, volleyballs, and Frisbees.

"Ooops! Sorry about that," James laughed. "I did mention that Mary and Arthur have three teenagers, didn't I?"

"Are you sure these are just for the kids?" Skye grinned.

"Of course! I'm too old for that sort of nonsense," he asserted with an attractive self-derision.

"Ha!" she retorted unbelievingly. Maybe the soft sea air had already started working on her brain. She felt easier, freer to tease.

James gave her a distinctly threatening look and retaliated gruffly, "Come on, lady. Let's get you settled in."

He led her through the main living area and walked

on into an adjoining room with her suitcase. But Skye lingered. She liked what she saw. Big overstuffed couches and chairs covered in flowered chintzes were arranged around a huge stone fireplace. Grass mats and cotton throw rugs were scattered across a Spanish-tiled floor. Colors of green and blue predominated, casting a cool serenity over the entire room. A high-beamed ceiling, along with the enormous front window, gave space for light to reflect to every corner of the room.

At the back, she could see a nice-sized kitchen divided from the rest of the house by a long bar, and a door which she assumed would open into another bedroom. A loft containing a desk, a couch, and overflowing bookcases looked out over the living area.

The house looked like exactly what it was—a well-used, comfortable retreat, albeit an expensive one. Malibu real estate didn't come cheaply, and the price of oceanfront property this size could probably feed a small country for a year or more.

James re-entered the room with a mock scowl on his face. "Damn it, Skye! When I lead, I expect people to follow!"

Skye laughed, a clear, golden sound, and watched with fascination as James became instantly still. A muscle in his jaw tightened, and then he moved to walk over to her, putting his hands on her shoulders.

"Do you know that is the first time I've ever heard you laugh?" he said huskily. "You smile beautifully, and sometimes it even reaches your eyes, but you've never laughed in my presence."

Skye couldn't begin to comprehend the emotion she saw on his face, but when he pulled her into his arms and held her close, rocking back and forth slightly, she didn't care. It was a gentle, strengthening embrace—no passion intended—and she accepted it with gratitude.

James pulled back and took Skye's hand. He led her into another large, airy room that was obviously the master bedroom. Done as casually and in the same colors as the rest of the house, one wall was given over to built-in drawers, a huge closet, and a full-length cheval mirror. A cushioned love seat and small table stood against the opposite wall, while the back wall held one intimidatingly large bed. It faced a wide window which, along with a sliding glass door opening onto a redwood deck, provided the same view as the room they had just passed through.

Seeing the bed, some of Skye's tenseness returned. "James, I...er...I can sleep somewhere..."

"You can sleep right here, as a matter of fact. I'll sleep in the loft. There's a couch up there that makes up into a bed, and I've slept on it many times before. There are only bunk beds in the back bedroom, and they run a little small for me." He chuckled good-naturedly.

"Feel free to look in any of the drawers or closet and help yourself to what you need. They're communal. I'll see to dinner."

"You?" She remembered his offer to help her in the office kitchen a week earlier.

James shot her an amused glance. "Did you think you were going to have to cook?"

Skye shrugged. "I really haven't given it much thought. But since you bring it up, I find it a little hard to picture you working in a kitchen; and if it comes down to uneatable food or me cooking, I would much prefer to do the cooking."

"No way! I've made a thorough study on the subject, and that is totally against everything I've ever read regarding kidnapping etiquette."

"Kidnapping etiquette!" Skye's voice raised in disbelief as James ducked out the door. The man was not to be believed! But, then again, why should she doubt him?

After a quick shower and an even quicker peek in the closet, Skye decided to put back on the same blouse and skirt. As James had promised, the closet held a wide assortment of clothes, but she couldn't yet bring herself to wear any of them.

Skye turned out the bedroom light and walked into the darkened living room. A light streamed into the room from the kitchen, and she could see James tearing lettuce for a salad.

Even though there were no lights on in the main area, the room glowed warmly. James had lit a fire in the cavernous fireplace and it cast a warm flush throughout the room. Flickering candles on a small table intimately set for two in front of the fire provided additional light.

The coziness of the scene before her very nearly sent her scurrying back to the bedroom. However, her newly acquired knowledge of James assured her that he would never let her get away with that, and, instead, she walked over to the window.

The moon had laid down a corrugated path of silver across the undulating black ocean. It looked so real, so solid...

James came up behind her and ran his hands down

the length of her arms. Yes, she acknowledged to herself, she was definitely getting used to his touch.

"What do you see with those sky-blue eyes of yours?" he questioned softly near her ear.

"That path out there."

"Path?"

"The one crossing the ocean. It looks solid enough to walk on."

"You think so?" His deep voice held no hint that he thought she was being fanciful. He seemed to take her seriously. "Are you considering trying it?"

"Oh, not me," she denied vehemently. Her voice was earnest with her conviction. "You! You could walk on water, I'm convinced of it."

His laugh was low and sensuous as he turned her around. "Skye, Skye, what shall I do with you? I think I'd better feed you before you get any more fantastic ideas. I'm just an ordinary man with very ordinary needs and desires."

"You couldn't prove it by me," Skye intoned seriously.

"You'll learn soon enough," was all he said as he seated her at the small table.

The wine he served her, along with the interesting beef-and-rice casserole, mellowed her serious mood. James was a charming, urbane host and a fascinating conversationalist. While entertaining her with his stories, he made sure she ate more than enough food and drank just the right amount of wine.

Skye pushed back her plate and sighed. "Don't tell me you cooked this. It was delicious!"

"No," he admitted, "that was one of Mary's. She

left it for us in the freezer, but I'll replace it with one of my own before we leave."

"That's a nice arrangement you've got going. Now, who does the dishes?" she asked cynically.

"Oh, ye of little faith. Do you really believe I brought you all the way to California just to slave in the kitchen?"

"Someone has to do it unless you have a team of efficient little elves in your bag of tricks," she pointed out reasonably.

"Skye, you wound me! *I'm* going to do the dishes. And—at the risk of repeating myself—*you're* going to rest and relax in front of the fire."

Which was exactly what she did. She was sitting at one end of the sofa enjoying the music he had put on when he came back in the room and sat down at the other end.

She looked at him and saw him watching her quietly. Something in the enthralling black eyes seemed to draw her into their depths. A brief thrill of anxiety ran along her nerves, but when he spoke, it had an unexpected calming effect on her.

"Come here. I want to hold you."

Skye moved to him before she even thought about it. His arm came around her and pulled her head onto his broad shoulder.

She started to say, "James—" not knowing how she would finish the sentence. But she heard a soft, gentle "Sssh..."

It was extraordinary. They must have sat that way for hours, not moving, but Skye had no impression of time, encircled as she was in his soothing strength.

Skye felt as if she had been there forever, and she felt she never wanted to leave.

The ocean roared on uninterruptedly beyond them, while the fire crackled with untiring motion in front of them. Skye felt totally at peace within the oddly safe cocoon of James's protection.

After a while the warmth from the fire and the strong arms, coupled with the steady rise and fall of his wide chest, produced a somniferous effect on Skye. She tried to stifle a yawn, but James caught her at it and sent her off to bed with a disappointedly chaste kiss on her forehead.

Chapter Nine

SKYE STRETCHED AWAKE the next morning to the alien sounds and smells of seagulls screeching and onions frying. Seagulls? Onions?

The unusual soundness of her sleep had produced a temporary disorientation upon waking. It took a minute, but then it came to her that she had spent the night in a California beach house with James Steele, and that he was obviously cooking some kind of breakfast, judging by the tantalizing smell.

The thought of James made her bound out of bed and hurry out to the kitchen. After their compatibility of the evening before, she couldn't wait to see him.

Combing her fingers through the long tangles of her hair, she walked over to the bar slightly out of breath, and then stopped dead at the sight of James in a pair of athletic jogging shorts and a T-shirt extolling the virtues of Southern California surfing across its back. The ultracasual outfit all too clearly exposed his hard-muscled upper arms and the brawny power of his well-developed legs.

As if he had sensed her presence, James turned from his work at the stove and laughed. "You look incredibly sexy this morning. That jersey never looked that good on me."

Skye covered her mouth with her hand in quick embarrassment. In her haste to get to James, she had forgotten what she had put on the night before. After bidding him goodnight, she discovered she had forgotten to pack a nightgown, so absorbed had she been in packing utilitarian clothes that she hoped would upset James. Despite her earlier reticence, she had rummaged through the drawers for something suitable to sleep in and come upon an old, faded football jersey with the name Steele printed across the back and a number James had once made famous emblazoned on the front. It was obviously one of his old jerseys, and she hadn't been able to resist putting it on. The jersey had fallen to the middle of her thighs and had felt so good and right against her skin that she had decided to leave it on and wear it to bed.

Now, for the first time, Skye became uncertain about her actions. "I hope you don't mind my wearing it. I forgot to pack something to sleep in, and I found this in one of the drawers."

James reached over the bar and took her chin in his hand. "No, I don't mind. I love the idea of you sleeping in something of mine—even if it isn't my arms."

He placed his thumb on her bottom lip and gently pulled it open. Then replacing his thumb with his lips, he gave her a deep, melting kiss. He tasted of coffee and smelled wet and tangy, as if he had just had a shower. Skye's mind spun with his closeness.

"Are you hungry?" he asked against her lips. His voice was a husky grating along her senses.

She shook her head slightly and then whispered back, "I never eat breakfast."

"You'll eat this one, I guarantee." He withdrew from her and returned his attention to the stove.

"What on earth are you making? It smells delicious."

"Oh, not much," James informed her carelessly. "Only a few potatoes, a couple of onions, a batch of sausage, and half a dozen eggs."

"Good heavens! Has the coast of California just been invaded?" Skye laughed. "What army are you expecting to feed?"

"Just you and me, my beautiful lady, just you and me."

Suddenly Skye was starving, and just as suddenly she didn't mind James calling her "beautiful lady." As long as he put "my" in front of the phrase, it seemed okay.

A short time later, Skye pushed her plate back and groaned, "That has to be *the* all-time best breakfast I have ever eaten."

James surveyed her empty plate with a smug look on his face. "Don't tell me you are actually complimenting my cooking!"

"It's got to be the sea air that made it taste so good," Skye teased. "It can't be your cooking!"

"Don't bet on it," he told her with a grin, "because you would definitely lose. Why don't you go change while I clean up in here and then we'll go down to the beach. I've got to put a chicken in the crockpot for our dinner tonight. It's frozen and will take several hours to cook."

"Are you going to spend all your time in the kitchen?" she asked wonderingly. He was finally making a believer out of her.

"The point is, *you're* not," he stated flatly. "Now, scat!"

Skye sat at the bar where they had eaten breakfast and looked at James. There should have been something absurd about this large, tough-looking man moving about the well-appointed kitchen. But there wasn't. Rather, there was a certain sureness in his movements that seemed to apply to the rest of his life as well.

"Unless you would like some help getting out of my jersey?" he asked suggestively.

That got her moving, but she left the room with the knowledge that a few days would never be enough time to get to know James Steele. A lifetime would not be long enough.

Twenty minutes later she emerged from the shower wrapped in a bathrobe she had found hanging on the back of the door and faced the problem of what to wear.

The business suits she had packed would not be appropriate, and they would most certainly be too hot. Skye's brief glimpse out the bedroom window had assured her that it was a beautiful day.

Reluctantly, she started through the drawers. She

had been tired the night before when she had looked through them; but this morning, the longer she looked, the more she found that she was having fun. There was an enjoyable quality about the idea of wearing someone else's clothes, knowing you didn't have to shop for them, and you wouldn't be wearing the clothes long enough to get tired of them.

Finally, she found a pair of cut-off jeans that, although they were a little tight, would do. Pulling them over her bikini panties, Skye saw with mixed emotions how enticingly they cupped her firmly curved bottom. The last wearer, probably one of the McFarland teenagers, had evidently split the side seams an inch or two, causing the shorts to show the length of her nicely shaped legs to their best advantage.

Next, she found a turquoise tank-top. Putting it on braless, because she hadn't packed a strapless bra, her full, supple breasts strained against the thin cotton.

Not bothering to see if any of the sandals she saw in the closet would fit her, Skye walked out to face James, barefoot and barelegged, feeling unaccountably shy. It was as if, without the armor of her sophisticated working clothes, she had no more barriers to hide behind. And, in a way, she didn't.

She stopped just inside the room and at first didn't see James. The room was still and empty, and a moment of panic assailed her until a glimpse of color in the loft attracted her attention. She turned and saw James standing by the railing, looking down at her.

He seemed to fill the space between them with his hard vitality. Skye could almost *feel* the air between them as it had suddenly become so highly charged. He was staring at her with such intensity that it flustered her. His eyes missed nothing about her, and she felt herself growing warm under his stare.

All at once, Skye recalled a question that had been nagging at her subconscious for over a week and asked, "Do you remember the night you arrived in Dallas?"

"Very well."

"Why... Why were you watching me... so quietly?"

James moved with a deceptively slow grace down the staircase to her, his eyes fastened on her with a strange need. Reaching her, he drew Skye to him and threaded his hands through her hair, grasping and holding her head with tender possession.

Right before he claimed her lips, James answered her question, muttering roughly, "Because you're so damned easy to watch!"

The kiss was long and probing and made Skye forget her brief shyness. She returned the kiss with a rising passion that astonished her because it had appeared so suddenly and out of nowhere. Her mouth was completely open to his, their tongues joining in a frantic search for an elusive fulfillment, and her breasts were crushed against the solid wall of his chest.

A quiver of longing shuddered through her as she felt James gradually break off the kiss. His mouth quirked with self-derision and he commented shakily, "I hadn't planned to do that—at least, I hadn't planned to until I saw you in that outfit."

"Then I take it you think what I have on today beats the suit I had on yesterday?" She smiled teasingly.

"By a country mile," he assured her dryly. "By the way, have you burned that suit yet?"

"James!"

"Okay, okay," he relented. "If I promise to try to control my baser instincts, would you come for a walk with me?"

Skye was wise to the gleam in his eyes, but she nodded her agreement because, at the moment, she could think of nothing she would rather do.

The sun beamed down on them, and the sand felt warm under their bare feet, as they walked hand in hand, mile after peaceful mile. Even after they rounded the point that protected the McFarland beach, they didn't see many people. A man jogged his dog past them, a young mother played with her babies in the sand, and an older man lay on a blanket, engrossed in a book. The golden day seemed to have been created especially for them.

A light, carefree attitude overtook Skye, and when she looked over and saw a football someone had abandoned on the sand, a germ of an idea began to form in her head. She broke loose from James's hand to run over and pick up the ball. Then, throwing it as hard as she could against the hard expanse of his chest, she yelled gaily, "Let's see if the old man still has it in him."

James smiled indulgently, tossing the ball up and down easily and catching it with one hand. "What did you have in mind?"

"Oh, I don't know," she returned daringly. "How bout a little touch?"

A strange glint entered the black eyes, but James

said mildly, "Great! I love touch. Here"—he threw the ball at her—"let's start out by playing catch for a few minutes so you can get used to the feel of the ball."

It was definitely not as easy as it looked, Skye soon discovered. The ball was regulation sized and seemed awfully big to her small hands. She found she almost needed to use two hands when she threw it, and she had a sneaking suspicion James found her efforts to imitate his own perfect spirals comical. However, his tone was serious as he suggested, "Maybe we better go back to the house. I wouldn't want a pro scout to come along and snap you up for his team."

"Ohhhh, you!" Skye gathered her courage and attempted to run past him, keeping the ball tucked into her side; but, unfortunately, "attempted" proved to be the operative word as the game began.

James had no difficulty "touching" Skye, tagging her at will, impeding her progress effortlessly. Skye, on the other hand, would scream with frustration whenever James ran with the ball. Even though she knew, without a doubt, that he was curtailing his considerable expertise and power, she was rarely able to tag him. And those times she did, Skye suspected it was by his design. Finally, getting tired of trying to tag James as he whizzed by her, she hurled herself bodily at him.

Saving her from hurt, James turned laughingly and caught her, falling to the sand. His large body shielded her from the force of the fall and protected her with his strength.

Laughing at her own foolishness, Skye looked down at James and something caught in her throat. Her breath came in gasps from her exertion, but James's breathing was steady and sure, his chest rising and falling evenly. She was lying on top of him, her curves fitting exactly to his hard masculine contours.

His hands slowly reached up and drew her down to his lips, causing her hair to fall in a golden veil around them. The kiss was without beginning, without end. They seemed to flow into one another as James turned her over onto the soft sand and covered her with his body. One hand slid under her top, grasping one of her breasts and teasing the nipple until it became hard and tight. Skye moaned with an undisguised longing.

James's kisses—insistent, urgent, intoxicating— were unearthing long-buried sensations and building feverish aches. She returned the kisses with all of her might, her hands running up and down the rippling muscles of his broad back. Skye wasn't thinking, she was only feeling.

There was a trembling—within, without—and abruptly, his hands stilled on her body. Skye heard a distant sound reminiscent of rumbling thunder; and then, incredibly, the ground started to shake violently under them. The vibrating lasted just a few seconds, but it was more than a little frightening and terribly unnerving. Skye realized that she had just experienced her first California earthquake.

Looking up, she saw James smiling at her. "You probably think that was an earthquake," he drawled, "but it wasn't."

"I'm almost afraid to ask," Skye grinned tolerantly, "but okay, I'll bite, what was it?"

"It was just your reaction to my kisses," he told her smoothly.

"I don't think so, James," she teased softly. "You may be good, but you're not that good."

"Are you scoffing at my proficiency?" he asked with feigned disbelief.

"Let me put it this way." Skye giggled in a manner totally unlike her usual sophisticated self. "I've heard of the earth moving during lovemaking, but *that* was ridiculous!"

"Well, let me tell you something, my beautiful lady. You haven't seen anything yet!"

Even though James laughed when he said it, it had been an emphatic statement, and Skye wasn't sure if there was a threat behind the remark. But whether there was or not, it brought back to her the struggle that her increasingly obvious need of him was creating within her, and it troubled her.

Their passionate mood broken for now, they walked back to the beach house in companionable silence, where James insisted they spend the rest of the afternoon doing nothing more strenuous than reading and listening to music.

As the afternoon wore on, James retreated to his kitchen, as Skye now thought of it, to debone the chicken that had been cooking all day.

After a time, Skye, curled up in a corner of the sofa reading, glanced out the window and noticed that a fog was moving in from offshore. It was odd that one half of the view was clear, while the other half was clogged with the creeping gray mist. She watched with interest as the mass steadily approached. By the time it was finally dark outside, the fog had completely engulfed the beach house inside its moist womb.

Skye walked to the kitchen to report this phenomenon to James and found him melting cheese in a double boiler and absorbed in chopping onions with harrowing speed.

"What on earth are you doing?" she exclaimed.

The black eyes fastened on her in surprise. "We are going to have chicken enchiladas tonight," James replied in a tone that suggested she might be just a little slow in realizing that fact.

"Wouldn't you like some help?" she entreated.

James looked at Skye and smiled gently, almost as if he knew she couldn't stand the fact that he didn't need any help.

"No, Skye, I wouldn't. Go find something overwhelmingly pretty to put on, and I'll meet you in front of the fire in an hour with a glass of wine."

Thus dismissed, Skye retreated to the bedroom and, after showering, surveyed the bulging closet once again. There were several dresses that conformed to James's description and looked as if they would fit, but one in particular caught Skye's eye.

Trying it on, Skye stepped in front of the cheval mirror and gasped at the effect reflected back at her. It was a long semitransparent cream gauze, obviously made in Mexico, which brushed her bare ankles with a full, swirling skirt. A wide lace waistband that reached up to her breasts was backed only by her own smooth skin. The neckline was a generous vee, and the sleeves fell full and loose to her delicate wrists. It was perfectly modest, Skye assured herself, trying to ignore the sensuous stretch of skin revealed through the lace.

She had washed her hair in the shower earlier, and now Skye brushed the multicolored, golden-hued strands until they shone and cascaded down her back.

This evening they ate on pillows in front of the roaring fire—the blaze providing the only light in the room. As James watched with uncommon interest, she demolished four enchiladas in record time.

Skye looked at him sheepishly. "Okay, okay," she admitted grudgingly, "they were good."

"Good?" he inquired blandly.

"They were delicious and you know it," she conceded wryly. "Where did you ever learn to cook like this?"

James rose and took their plates into the kitchen, returning to refill her wineglass. Skye looked into the fire and knew it had been a long time since she had been so at ease, so happy. She was enthroned comfortably amongst a pile of oversized pillows, with James just an arm's length away. Reaching out and touching him would be so easy, she thought, gazing at the strong face reflected by the light of the fire.

The dark, starless night and the encircling gray fog enhanced the cozy, shadowed warmth of the room. Skye felt very snug, very secure; but it had to be a false security, she reminded herself sternly. This evening could only be a memory stored up against the time when James would leave, as he surely would.

He had been gazing pensively into the fire since he had returned from the kitchen with the wine. Watching James, Skye couldn't help but wonder what went on in that brilliant mind he possessed—a mind that could single-handedly conceive and build a vast financial empire.

She knew she could never begin to understand the burdensome weight he carried alone on his broad shoulders. And yet, here he was, sitting with her in front of a fire, seemingly content, his powerful body totally relaxed.

When James finally spoke, it startled Skye, who had been so preoccupied with her thoughts about him.

"I had to learn to cook very early in life or starve," he answered her previous question in a flat, emotionless voice. "I was abandoned as a small child and reared in a succession of barren institutions and equally loveless foster homes."

"I had no idea." Skye's heart contracted at the thought of James as a lonely, uncared-for little boy.

"Not many people do." He laughed mirthlessly, hurting Skye, piercing her heart to its very core.

"Oh, don't get me wrong," he continued. "There wasn't that much conspicuous cruelty. It was just that most of the people simply didn't give a damn. I had two choices: toughen up or die. So I toughened up, and when I was fourteen, I finally ran away. I lived on my own as best I could, working at odd jobs and falsifying records so that I could attend school."

James was talking quietly in a voice that didn't ask for pity, but just stated hard facts.

"You see, I had a burning desire to learn, and I

discovered I had a natural athletic ability. Because of it, I was courted and fawned over. And if anyone suspected that things weren't exactly as they should be with me, they looked the other way, because I could always lead their teams to victory."

His tone was decidedly cynical as he went on with his story. "I don't know what would have happened to me if I hadn't run into Bob Pruitt, my high-school coach. He was a tough old man, but a genuinely good person—one of the few I had met up to that time.

"He eventually found out, of course, that I had no parents and was living on my own. And from that time on he made sure I was well taken care of. But he did more than that. He went one step further and showed me how I could use my raw abilities to earn a future for myself. Because of that, I worked twice as hard as anyone else and ran three times faster. And the rest, as they say, is history."

James turned from the fire and saw the tears standing in Skye's blue eyes. He put out a finger and caught one as it spilled over onto her cheeks.

"Don't cry for me, Skye," he begged softly as he gathered her in his arms. All of the hard cynicism was gone now. "It only matters what I am today. And the only reason I told you is because I want you to know everything there is to know about me. It's one more wall down between us."

Skye couldn't explain why she cried. It wasn't pity. James was still the most dangerous man she had ever met. There was no vulnerability in him. His strength went all the way through. But for a little while she cried for the neglected, defenseless child he had once been—and would never be again.

His story had moved her unbearably, and she knew she would never again look at James in quite the same way.

The darkness and the fog continued to eddy around them, but inside James held Skye, talking softly to her until her tears ceased and her eyes closed and she slept.

When Skye awoke the next morning, she was in the big bed wearing only James's football jersey and her lace panties. She lay still for a moment, thinking, trying to remember, but all that came to mind was her falling asleep in James's arms, as if it were the most natural thing in the world.

Rising gracefully out of bed, she walked over to the window and looked out on a beautiful day. The ocean rolled before her in shades of gray and green, and the sky was a pure blue.

On the golden sands below her, James was jogging. It stirred her blood just to look at him. He ran with all the easy, fluent motion of a natural athlete—a beauty of strength and coordination of muscle.

She walked out to the deck to watch him, and he saw her and changed directions. Bounding up the cliff, he ran to her, his body covered with a fine film of sweat.

"Good morning." He kissed her mouth softly. "Did you sleep well?"

Skye nodded. "I-I must have. I don't remember. James, did . . . did you put me to bed last night?"

He laughed down at her. "It was no trouble, I assure you." Turning, already moving away from her, he said over his shoulder, "Breakfast will be ready in about fifteen minutes."

The thought that James had undressed her last night sent Skye back to the bedroom thoroughly confused. What was she going to do about her growing desire for James, as opposed to her fear of being hurt? She supposed it all depended on whichever emotion was the stronger, the fear or the desire, as to which one won out.

The ocean had looked so inviting that Skye arbitrarily decided to go for a swim after breakfast. She was almost defeated in that purpose, however, when she searched the drawers for a bathing suit. She tried several on, but most of them were skimpy bikinis that were either a size or two too small or revealed too much.

At last, she settled on a royal blue top that was cut fuller, concealing more than the others, and closed in the front between her breasts. The matching bottoms were brief, but they would have to do. Over the suit, she put back on the cuts-offs she had worn the day before.

James's eyes flamed when he saw her walking barefoot up to the bar, her midriff bare and her hair streaming down her back, but he said nothing. He merely dished her up a Western omelet and watched silently while she ate it.

When she finished, however, James reached over the bar and removed the napkin she had been patting her lips with, replacing it with his finger as he outlined the full shape. "I'm going to make us a pot of chili for today. Why don't you finish reading the book you started yesterday?"

His subject matter was ordinary, but his tone was low and erotic. For no reason, Skye became angry.

"Do you realize that ever since we've been here you've been telling me what to do, what to eat and what to wear? I'm tired of it, James! Just stop it! Believe it or not, before you came along, I was more than capable of making my own decisions..."

James dealt with her brief rebellion by simply reaching over and kissing her quiet. It was a deep, searching kiss and Skye reciprocated totally. His hand slid inside the bikini top and rubbed her breast, fondling the nipple until it stood erect.

Skye groaned with frustration at the width of the bar between them. She wanted nothing more than to feel the hard length of James against her. His kisses and caresses were not satisfying her, and she felt oddly bereft when he eased away.

"I'm going down to the beach," Skye announced defiantly, with a tremor in her voice.

But she didn't, at least not right away. Instead, she moved restlessly around the house, straightening pillows here and there and surreptitiously watching James as he moved deftly around the kitchen.

She walked up to the loft with every intention of making his bed. But, much to her dismay, she found herself stroking the sheets where James had lain in the night, hugging his pillow to her warm body, restively wishing it were him.

What was wrong with her? Skye stood at the railing of the loft and looked broodingly out at the ocean that was as full of conflict as she was.

Maybe it was what James had said last night about there being one less wall between them now. When Skye thought about it, there were almost *no* walls between them anymore.

It was a situation fraught with danger, but one she had no control over.

She felt as if she were hurtling down a long, dark tunnel toward a bright light—and she didn't know if that light was an onrushing train or not.

Chapter Ten

THE BEACH WAS deserted, and the sky was a cloudless crystal-blue. Skye sighed with pleasure as she spread out the large beach towel and sank down onto it.

Even though the breeze was slightly cool, the sand beneath her had retained the warmth of the day. Shutting her eyes and laying perfectly still, Skye could feel her tense muscles uncoiling, the last of the knotted tension inside her subsiding.

She didn't know how long she had lain there before she felt a shadow move over her. Skye slowly opened her eyes and felt a force so strong it seemed as if she had been hit in the stomach with a sledgehammer.

Standing above her was James, the sun directly behind him outlining his powerful body. She had the sudden urge to shield her eyes, as if to look on him would do her irreparable harm. Even though she had seen him in shorts and a T-shirt before now, it had done nothing to prepare her for this.

He was a man with a rawly beautiful, superbly built body. Fine black hair crossed from his strong arms over to the muscular plane of his chest, descending down his diaphragm and disappearing briefly into his tight black swim trunks, only to reappear again to travel down the long, granitelike legs. An overall picture of tough, solid, resilient strength.

Leisurely, her eyes moved back up the length of him, drinking in all of the potent male power that was so blatantly exposed. When her eyes finally arrived back at his face, she surprised a deep, dark glow burning within the startling black eyes.

He slowly extended his hand toward her. "Come on, beautiful lady, let's see if you look as good wet as you do dry."

It had been years since she had gone swimming, and she couldn't remember ever swimming in the ocean, but she broke the hold James had on her hand and ran ahead.

She found the water cold and exactly what she needed on her overheated body. Skye wasn't a strong or a fast swimmer, but she struck out, trying to swim through the swells instead of over them—not always successfully, however.

James, who she knew could have swum circles around her with one hand tied behind his back, seemed content to keep pace beside her, never drawing ahead of her and hardly ever turning his eyes away from her.

She had been in the water about fifteen minutes

and was beginning to tire when her leg became entangled with something. It frightened her, and she let out a startled yelp. James was beside her in a split-second, holding her up while she pulled the seaweed from around her leg.

Skye had been alarmed at the unknown substance twined about her leg, but it was nothing compared to the panic that attacked her when the slickly wet, nearly naked body of James wrapped loosely around her. She knew he was just supporting her, but the thin layer of silky water that flowed between them did not lessen the impact of the pure, unadulterated maleness of the man, and she could feel very clearly the effect she was having on him, too.

She took a deep breath and swam toward the shore. Her legs were weak and trembly as she walked out of the water and collapsed on the towel, and Skye knew it wasn't soley because of the unaccustomed exercise of swimming.

Dripping wet and face-down on the towel, she took great gulps of air to try to get her breathing back to normal.

Sensing James off to one side drying himself, she decided to wait a few minutes before getting up. Maybe he would go back up to the beach house.

Skye was beginning to shiver from the coolness of the air on her wet skin when she felt James lower himself close beside her and the pressure of his large hands gently wringing the water out of her hair.

Next, she felt the excess water being softly wiped off of her shoulders and back. Running his hand slowly and deliberately down her spine to her waist, she felt his tongue touch her shoulder where his hand had previously been. A scorching sensation jolted through her as she felt the velvet roughness of his tongue slowly licking up the remaining drops of water his hand had missed. The shocking lapping of his tongue continued over what seemed to be every square inch of her back and shoulders.

He had rubbed most of the moisture from her waist and Skye gasped as she felt his hands move lower, onto her softly rounded buttocks and begin to lightly and rhythmically squeeze, while his tongue glided onto her bare waist.

Her hands slowly curled into the warm sand in an involuntary response to the fire coursing through her body, that was as much a part of her as the deep, ragged breaths she was beginning to draw through her parted lips.

As James's hands continued to work her buttocks gently, Skye felt his tongue run down her lower spine to dart across to the back of her legs. Long velvet strokes moved up and down her legs until she thought she would scream with the pleasure that was destroying her body.

The prolonged caressing of his long, wet tongue was driving her slowly out of her mind, yet it was not in her to stop him. James had not said a word since he had started his assault, and she moaned aloud as she felt his mouth softly bite the tenderness of her inner thigh, time and time again.

Skye spread her legs slightly to give him greater access, and she could feel her body grind into the sand with the sweet agony that was consuming her entire being. But there was nothing she could or wanted to do about her wanton response.

There were no bones left in her body as she felt him turn her over. Opening her passion-glazed eyes, she focused on two black flames that looked as if they could easily consume her into their dark depths.

Her moist, parted lips wanted nothing more than to be completely possessed by his, and her pleading eyes and writhing body told him so plainly. But, without releasing her gaze, James started combing through her salt-laden hair with long, sensuous movements until her hair lay fanned out about her head, dark gold, with little droplets of moisture clinging to the individual strands.

Then, lazily turning his attention to her face and neck, he started with the pulse point just behind her ear, gently drawing in any remaining wetness with his warm mouth, trailing beneath her chin with tiny licks and kisses to the point just behind her other ear where he gently bit the underside of her earlobe.

Skye couldn't stand any more of his exquisite torture. Her arms had been holding on to his broad shoulders, but now she reached up and pulled his head down to her mouth. He didn't disappoint her.

Lying almost completely on top of her, James gave her a hard, brutal, soul-destroying kiss, showing her, finally, that his need was just as great as hers.

She felt James quickly and expertly unhook the top of her bikini and the cool breeze off the ocean briefly touch her aching, tautened breasts. As his manipulating tongue and mouth took certain possession of one hard, pointed peak and his hand the other, her stomach contracted in hard, violent passion.

Skye felt as primitive man must have felt eons ago—as if she were being enveloped and made one with the natural elements of the universe: the cool air surrounding her, the warm earth supporting her, the water spraying her with a fine mist as it crashed to the shore somewhere beyond her.

And James. James, who at this moment could only symbolize fire—fire he was creating deep within the very core of her being.

Arching her hips up into his, she felt James's intense response and heard his harsh, uneven breathing. Skye thought she could easily die if her body was not given some relief soon from the fierce wanting of the man who was feasting on her breasts as if he had been starved too long.

Suddenly, however, she became aware of the tears easing out of her tightly closed eyes and running unheeded down her cheeks. But more than that, she discovered she was frightened—frightened of the raw, primitive, savage feelings of desire that were being unleashed so easily inside of her. These feelings that had unknowingly lain dormant until James Steele had come into her life—and into her heart.

Skye went motionless. *No!* It couldn't be true! But even as she was thinking it she knew. She was well and truly in love with this brilliant man with the mystical black eyes, and the knowledge hit her with all the force of a giant wave crashing down on top of her. She couldn't seem to assimilate the information fast enough. It was entirely possible she might even drown with this new knowledge.

The very thing she had been guarding against these last five years had happened—almost overnight, if she were to be honest.

Skye opened her eyes and saw that James had stopped his exploration of her body and was watching her intently. His breath was coming in harsh gasps, but he said very slowly and very clearly, "I want you, Skye. I want you more than I've ever wanted anyone or anything in my entire life. And I know you want me."

Skye's head began to shake from side to side even as she whispered, "No. Please, James, no. I'm afraid . . ."

With a strength born of fear and purpose, she rolled out from under him and ran up the steps to the house, holding her top together as she ran.

Somehow she had to clear her mind before she saw him again. Skye knew she couldn't tell James of her love for him. He had said, "I want you, Skye," not "I love you."

He might want her more than anyone he had ever known, but once he had her, he would leave her—just as he had left all the other women that had passed through his life. She was sure of it, and she didn't know if she had the strength to withstand the pain that she knew would come, as surely as low tide followed high tide.

Once in the house, she headed straight for the shower, stripping off her bikini as she walked. Skye stepped into the shower and turned on the water full force. Rapidly shampooing the salt water out of her hair, she tried to clear her passion-fogged mind by letting the hot water beat down on her with pulsating intensity.

But when Skye felt the sudden draft, her eyes flew

open to behold James standing there, his magnificent body naked, his black eyes full of the concentrated determination she had seen once before.

He stepped casually into the shower with her as if he had done it one hundred times before and shut the door with a solid click. With every sign of knowing exactly what he was doing, James picked up the soap and rubbed it between his hands to work up a lather.

The shower stall was not very big, but Skye tried to move as far away as possible. The sight of his dark body, completely naked, was bringing back the throbbing, aching need in her that had never gone far away.

Fixing her with an unwavering gaze, he said in a soft, slow voice that was at once unnervingly seductive and completely mesmerizing, "I have asked you, Skye, to trust me, to stop fighting me. Well . . . the time has come. I won't let you run from me anymore."

James reached out his large, soapy hands and stroked down her trembling body. Rubbing slowly and deliberately up her arms, across her shoulders, and down around her breasts, he continued with such a deep, sexy softness she felt herself dissolving. "Don't be afraid. Not you, my beautiful lady . . . never you. Give me your softness; let me give you my strength."

Both of his hands, cushioned by soapy wetness, were making slow, concentric circles around her breasts, working around and out on them until they reached the diamond-hard points that seemed to be straining with the anticipation of what was to come.

Once there, he gently tugged on the tips, pushing and pulling, pulling and pushing, until she shut her eyes and moaned with the pleasure and the pain of it.

Then leaving them, his hands traveled down to the flatness of her stomach. Kneeling down in front of her, his one hand moved to her lower back, gently pushing her belly into the soapy hand that was traveling around and around her navel.

Then his hands lowered to the sides of her hips and around to the inside of both her thighs. Up and down his hands traveled, until she thought she wouldn't be able to support herself, such were the violent tremors racking her body.

James stood up, and Skye sagged against him with weak longing. Tomorrow wasn't reality. James was here, now, in all of his hard, virile sensuality, and she really couldn't think about the consequences. Skye loved him with every fiber of her being, and that was all that mattered—at least for now.

Gathering her close in his arms, he pulled her into the spray of the shower. And there, with the warm water cascading down upon them, carrying the last vestiges of soap away, his mouth finally claimed hers in a long, slow, drugging kiss.

"Skye, Skye, Skye," he breathed into her mouth, "I want you too badly to let you go now."

Reaching out one large hand, he turned off the water, opened the shower door, and secured a towel around each of them. Lifting her high in his arms, James carried her into the bedroom and lowered her gently onto the bed, following her down.

Their towels fell away as their burning flesh touched, igniting their passion into a white-hot inferno that raged between them and could be assuaged only in one way that was as old as time immemorial.

The groan that came from deep in the back of James's throat held near-pain as he parted her thighs and entered Skye, thrusting smoothly and deeply and powerfully. After that, there was only feeling—pleasure unrestrained—a building, aching pressure until, in one fierce, furious, almost unbearable second, their world spun away from them and dissolved into a sweet, soft deliverance.

When next Skye woke, the room was bathed in alternate layers of moonlight and darkness. Stretching lazily, she found herself being held securely in the comfort and warmth of James's arms.

Gently easing herself away from him, she crept into the bathroom and leaned back weakly against the door. Shaking her head from side to side, she whispered to herself, "I'm not sorry. I'm not!"

Whatever had happened in the past, and whatever would happen in the future, she could not have done anything differently in the present. Their lovemaking had been inevitable from the first, as surely as spring follows winter and things that had lain dormant bloomed into life again.

Skye quickly washed and wrapped the voluminous bathrobe around her. Opening the bathroom door, she walked silently over to the sliding glass door to look up at the brightly lit night sky.

James had whirled into her life with the devastation of a Texas tornado. He had touched her deeply, to her very soul, and she would never, ever be the same again. She had found new strength and courage in her love for James. She had walked too long in the shadows. Now, for a day or two at least, she was going to walk in the sunshine—with James.

"Skye?" Her name, spoken in a raspy, whisper of a voice, wafted across the room to her.

She turned and found James lying on his side watching her. Just looking at him made her heart swell and her eyes mist over. Oh, how she loved him!

Black hair tousled, his face softened by sleep, his fine body overlaid with the scars of a thousand and one battles that had taken place over the years on the field of football, he held his arms out to her and demanded softly, "Come back to me."

So she did. After all, what else could she do?

All that day and into the next, they stayed in bed, giving and taking, eating and sleeping, making love and lying quietly, until James said gently into the quiet, "We've got to go back."

It was Friday afternoon, and they were lying in bed, watching the sun sink slowly into the waiting Pacific.

Skye couldn't bring herself to say anything. She didn't want it to end. Not yet. She had confessed to herself her love for James and had acknowledged her own newfound strength, and she would face the inevitable pain when it came. But she wasn't ready to let him go. It was too soon.

Skye turned into him and wrapped her arms and legs around him. "James?" she beguiled with a husky sweetness, and that was all that was said for quite some time.

Chapter Eleven

MUCH LATER THAT evening, on the plane flying back to Dallas, Skye was still unable to talk. But for a different reason. The terrible pain, caused by the fact that James would soon be traveling again, away from her, was slowly closing in on her. Yet, other than giving her an occasional smile and asking if she was comfortable and had everything she needed, James didn't appear to notice, immersed as he was in paperwork and several air-to-surface calls.

Skye supposed that being totally out of contact with an empire as large as the one James ruled over, even for a few days, would create great mountains of work as well as numerous problems. Still, how could he have already forgotten her when just a few hours earlier their bodies had been locked together with heated passion?

On the drive to her apartment from the airport, James seemed as preoccupied as he had been on the plane. And, as a result, Skye sat still and withdrawn in the corner of the luxurious depths of his car.

It was early in the morning by the time they reached the apartment. Slowing to a stop at her door, James turned and looked at the pale, remote facade that Skye presented.

Reaching out long fingers, he turned her face toward him and studied her with narrowed eyes for several unsettling minutes. Then he started rubbing his thumb back and forth across her bottom lip, still slightly swollen from their lovemaking.

"I have to go back to the hotel and meet with Paul and some of the others." James spoke to her in an extremely gentle voice.

And why not, she asked herself cynically? He had gotten exactly what he wanted from her, hadn't he? After all was said and done, she had ended up just another trophy for his shelves, to gather dust and be forgotten like all of the others.

Breaking in on her thoughts, he continued, "Unfortunately, I'll be tied up most of tomorrow—or rather today—but I will pick you up tonight for the party."

"That won't be necessary. I don't think I'll be going." Skye's voice was barely audible as she gave a slight shake of her head, making James's fingers slide around to the back of her neck, instead of dislodging them as she had intended.

Skye had decided that if she could say good-bye

to James now, in her own mind, it would be easier
for her than having to see him one more time before
he left. She assumed he would be taking off early
Sunday morning in his usual peripatetic style, and she
fervently wanted the parting to be over. Skye hadn't
heard where James was supposed to be going next,
and she didn't want to know. It would be easier that
way.

She had already thought of a plausible excuse she
could give Jonathan to get out of attending the party.
Jonathan wouldn't like it, but he would accept it.
Which was evidently more than James was willing to
do. "You *are* going," he stated with perfect certainty.

Looking at the forceful man beside her whom she
loved so completely, Skye pondered on the long,
lonely years stretching ahead of her in which she
wouldn't have him. It was an unbearable thought.

"If you like." Skye sighed, giving in too easily.

"Oh, I definitely like," James ground out harshly,
as he pulled Skye to him and gave her a kiss with
such strength and tenderness that, if he had asked,
she would have taken off her clothes right there in the
car and made love with him.

But James didn't ask. He whispered only, "See
you tonight."

Skye spent Saturday in a desultory fashion, doing
a little needlepoint, a little shopping, a little cooking,
and accomplishing absolutely nothing.

She had been away from James mere hours, and
already her ache for him was growing again steadily.
Two weeks ago she hadn't even met him; now he
colored her whole existence.

Skye caught herself looking at the phone for the hundredth time and chided herself. James wasn't going to call. He had said he would pick her up.

Damn it, but she dreaded that! Would she be able to hide her hurt, her love, her need? Probably not. That's why she had felt it would be better not to see him again.

Trying to escape her thoughts, she finally fled for a long walk in the park. The landscape was coming alive with the spring rains, but Skye didn't even notice the thriving vegetation of the beautiful park, or the curious and admiring looks cast her way.

Pansies bloomed alongside white and yellow crocuses, and everywhere one looked, jonquils were bursting with color amid rows of daffodils. Nevertheless, Sky wandered without purpose or joy, trying not to remember the enchanting days and the bewitching nights she had just spent with James.

Although it was nearly dark by the time Skye got back to her apartment, she didn't bother turning on any of the lights in the downstairs area. Slowly climbing the stairs to her bedroom, a plan began to form in her mind. She would get ready early and leave before James came by for her. Once at the party, he would certainly be too busy with his duties as host to pay much attention to her, and she might be able to keep a reasonable distance between them if she was careful.

After a fast shower and shampoo, Skye blew her hair dry and pulled it back on either side of her head, securing the fullness with two plain combs, letting it hang down her back in heavy, coiling curls. Next, she applied a translucent foundation and a gleaming cheek color, then swept a blue eyeshadow over her eyes and darkened already dark eyelashes with a touch of black mascara.

Pulling on a pair of sheer silk stockings, Skye stepped into a black-and-white creation and zipped it up quickly. The dress was dramatically simple. The strapless bodice was of black silk jersey, outlined and crisscrossed with narrow bands of tiny golden pavé bugle beads. The skirt fell from a high waist in a mass of white silk chiffon.

Sliding on a pair of gold-strapped heels and picking up the matching clutch purse, she turned out all the lights and walked out of the room without a backward glance at herself. Descending the steps, the long white skirt trailed iridescently up the stairs behind her.

Skye stopped on the next to the bottom step. The living room was in darkness, but there was music playing—music she hadn't turned on before she had gone upstairs—and she could smell tobacco burning. A light was suddenly turned on in a corner of the room, and she saw James.

She had known it would be him, of course, but she wasn't prepared for the sharp pain of desire she experienced when she saw him, and it angered her that her plan of leaving early for the party hadn't worked.

"How did you get in?" Skye demanded sharply.

James stubbed out the cheroot he had been smoking and walked over to the stairs, resting one foot on the bottom step. His eyebrows raised questioningly at her sharpness. "The doorman let me in when you didn't answer the doorbell. I figured you were upstairs taking a shower."

Skye watched dismally as his eyes turned to glowing coals at a private thought, and she was able to follow his mental processes without any trouble, also remembering another shower they had taken together.

"Is that the same doorman whose job it is to protect me from intruders?" she lashed out at him shrewishly. "I guess I know why you haven't fired him yet. He's obviously in your pay now."

James's eyes narrowed at her belligerent tone. "What's the matter, baby?" he questioned, soft-voiced. "What is it?"

Skye stepped down the final steps and walked around James to the window. She was annoyed with herself—not him—and her words were coming out too defensively. She should either have stuck by her decision not to go to the party or been firmer and told him not to pick her up.

"Nothing," she sighed. "Nothing."

She felt his hands on her bare shoulders as he turned her around to face him. He surveyed her from under hooded eyes for a moment, rubbing her shoulders lightly with his thumbs.

"You look very beautiful tonight."

"Thank you. So do you."

And he did. He was impeccably attired in a custom-made evening suit of unrelenting black. His immaculate white shirt with ruffles cascading down the front and on the cuffs displayed his dark masculinity to perfection.

James moved one of his hands until the heel was resting on the full swell of her breasts exposed above the strapless dress. His fingers splayed out around her throat, caressing slightly, feeling the pulse that was beating frantically at the base of her throat.

Observing her closely, James commented, apparently out of the blue, "I've never seen you wear jewelry. Why is that?"

Skye shrugged at the unexpected question. She couldn't answer him. Her throat had suddenly gone thick with the longing that his dark hands on her pale skin were engendering.

"Do you have any?" he persisted with his strange questions.

"A few odd pieces." Skye could only whisper.

James removed his hands from her and reached casually into his pocket. "Wear this tonight."

Skye gasped. Hanging from his hand was a perfect heart-shaped diamond strung on a chain of gold so fine you could barely see it. The light catching in the many facets of the diamond struck out magical sparks. It was the most beautiful thing she had ever seen.

"That must have cost a fortune!" Skye exclaimed.

"Only a small one," he assured her wryly.

"James, I can't accept that!"

He looked at her calmly, his eyes half-amused. "Why not?"

"I-I just couldn't." She realized it wasn't a very good reason, but it was really all she could come up with. The truth was that the necklace seemed too much like payment for services rendered. There had been no words of love accompanying the gift, only an order to wear it.

"You can, you know, and you will." He made one of his surprisingly sudden moves, deftly fastening the clasp of the necklace behind her neck. When he stepped back to survey her, there was a deeply satisfied look on his face.

The diamond felt cold nestled in the hollow between her breasts, and Skye shivered. "James... I—"

"Don't say another word," he warned.

Roughly pulling her to him and kissing her tender lips with a hurtful hardness, he muttered, "Come on, let's get this damn party over with."

Skye's heart split in two. Was James eager to have this night over and done with so he could leave town? And was the necklace his rather extravagant way of paying her off for the few days they had spent together?

Well, she would wear it tonight because her brief acquaintance with James had taught her how useless it was to fight him on something he was determined about. But when he left, she would give the necklace to Paul to return for her.

It was as simple and as heartbreaking as that.

The party progressed without a hitch. The meal was expertly prepared and discreetly served by the well-trained staff of an exclusive hotel in the downtown area.

The general mood of everyone attending was upbeat and optimistic. Long-time employees of the Hayes Corporation were genuinely sorry that Jonathan was retiring, but they were excited about the dynamic new leadership of the Steele management team.

James proved to be an affable, suave host, commanding the respect and the attention of everyone around him and doing an excellent job of keeping a recalcitrant Skye constantly by his side.

Jonathan and Paul both spoke after the dinner, but it was left to James to bring the evening to a sparkling climax. Stepping to the podium, he charmed the crowd with his witty and incisive comments and was utterly gracious in his remarks concerning Jonathan and captivating in his promises for a profitable future.

Watching him, Skye could only marvel. In the short time he had been in Dallas, he had infused new life and new energy into the company. As qualified and able as Paul was, she couldn't imagine the company running half as well after James left.

James leaving! Her brain never quite let go of that fact. The knowledge was constantly with her, and her pasted-on smile showed the strain of it. She had to escape from James's unwavering surveillance—and soon.

Skye got her chance quicker than she expected. After dinner, everyone began a leisurely exit toward the ballroom, where a dance orchestra had already started to play. There were quite a few people who wanted to speak with James and they seized this opportunity to jostle for position with him. As a result, with a crowd milling about them and James's attention diverted momentarily, it became easy for Skye to slip away.

However, as Skye was edging unobtrusively to one side of the room, she was spotted by Beth Ann, who hurried over. The young girl was looking exceptionally pretty and fresh in a gown of raspberry voile, and there was a special glow about her that Skye hadn't noticed before.

"Skye! I thought I would never get a chance to talk to you, the way Mr. Steele has been keeping you glued to his side this evening. Boy, he really hustled you up to the head table, didn't he? You look marvelous, by the way."

"You look quite lovely, too, Beth Ann," Skye returned the compliment, not commenting on the younger girl's other observations. She also didn't miss Beth Ann's curious look at the diamond necklace James had given her and added hastily, "Is that a new dress?" in an effort to distract her attention.

"Yes, it is . . . thank you for noticing. I wasn't sure about it when I first bought it." Beth Ann twirled around like a model to show the dress to Skye. "What do you think? Do you like it?"

The floral print of the raspberry voile captured Beth Ann's romantic femininity, the essence of which was usually hidden under her breezy manner. Consequently, Skye was able to answer honestly, "Very much. I think it's perfect on you."

Busy congratulating herself on her diversionary tactics, Beth Ann's next question caught Skye off guard. "How was your trip to New York?"

Now, how in the world did she answer that? Did she admit that they never went to New York, that, instead, James had kidnapped her to a remote beach house in California? Or did she lie and say they'd gone to New York and make up a few details to satisfy Beth Ann's curiosity?

Thankfully, Paul saved her from having to make a decision by appearing at their sides.

"Good evening, ladies. May I say how very beautiful you both look tonight?"

Skye observed with interest the way Paul's eyes lit up as he watched Beth Ann blush charmingly at his gallant compliment. There appeared to be something developing between them other than the usual secretary-employer relationship, and she wondered idly how long it had been going on.

Usually, Skye would have noticed anything new happening in Beth Ann's life because the younger girl was so refreshingly open. But the word "usual" could not be used to describe her life the last two weeks, Skye thought wryly, and evidently she had missed something.

She was listening to Beth Ann and Paul exchanging notes on the evening, when her attention became focused on the disconcerting sight of James. He was making his way through the crowd toward them with an unmistakable purpose in his eyes and a commanding grace in his body.

Why wouldn't he leave her alone? For some perverse reason, James wanted to keep her on his string a little while longer. She had succumbed totally to him, but he wasn't satisfied. He was evidently determined to drain everything he could from her before he left. *Why*, she wondered?

The man who was causing her so much anguish stopped in front of their little group, smilingly acknowledging Paul and Beth Ann, while slipping a possessive arm around Skye.

Damn it! Did he have to be so obvious?

"I'm going to steal Skye away for a dance," James stated suavely and without apology.

"I don't *feel* like dancing, James," Skye gritted obstinately.

"Nonsense," he admonished pleasantly. To an astonished Beth Ann and an amused Paul, he nodded, "Excuse us."

The orchestra was playing a slow, throbbing love song as James led her onto the dimly lit dance floor, and when his arms went around her, fitting her tightly to him, all of Skye's resistance fled. Time and place became suspended, and everything else faded away but the two of them.

They moved together in their own special rhythm with a complete naturalness, while Skye's dress floated like a soft cloud over the high sheen of the dance floor.

How could she remain unmoved? It was as if the few hours they had been apart didn't exist, and they were back at the beach house making passionate love. For that was what they were doing, their bodies melting into each other.

Skye was entranced by the hot hunger in the black eyes which held her own so captive. He looked as though he would slide right into her if he could. She could feel the hardness of his long, muscled legs through her thin skirt, and she was filled with a terrible need that quivered straight through her.

James appeared to read her thoughts, and his hold on the back of her waist tightened so that she was pulled even more snugly against his taut hips. His head came down and his mouth nibbled on her earlobe, his tongue flicking in and out of her ear.

Skye moved her hand restlessly up into the thick hair on the back of his head. She knew anyone who happened to glance their way could only be aware of their vertical lovemaking, but there was nothing she could do about it. She was helpless in her weakness for him, as his hips moved sinuously against her to the pulsating beat of the music.

He had been holding her other hand against his chest, between their two bodies, and now his long fingers reached out and rubbed her breasts through the fabric of her bodice.

Skye gasped and tried to pull away, but he only pulled her closer, his fingers moving up and inside the low top of her dress. Skye knew no one could see his movements, shielded as his hand was between them on the darkened dance floor, and it heightened her sexual excitement to almost unendurable proportions. He was pinching her nipple lightly between two fingers, and she wasn't sure she could remain upright much longer, so intense was her longing.

Skye tried desperately to hang on to the shreds of her sanity still remaining, by reminding herself how cruel James was to be doing this to her in a room full of people. He must realize how fragile her control was by now. Her nipple was being pinched with just the right amount of pressure, causing shocks of fire to pulsate through her nervous system, and she knew she would go right over the edge of pleasure, here, in the middle of this crowded dance floor, amongst all of these people, if he didn't stop soon.

Apparently the music had ceased, for gradually Skye became aware of standing still. James had released his hold on her somewhat, but she still stood within the circle of his arms.

Looking up at him, she saw that his eyes were

glazed with the same passion she was burning with, and his lips were forming her name. But Jonathan must have come up behind her at some point, because she heard him asking James if he could have the next dance with her.

James released her, and Jonathan stepped into her line of vision. Skye fastened onto Jonathan like a drowning man would to a life raft, and if he felt her shaking, he gave no sign of it.

Jonathan immediately started a light conversation, leading her in undemanding steps to the music, and Skye supposed she answered him. Her whole attention, however, was concentrated on calming down, on attempting to regain her equilibrium.

What a fool she was to be so in love with James that a mere dance could make her go weak with wanting. Of course, to be fair, she really couldn't call what they had just done together a mere dance.

But fairness hadn't entered into it, and James had known *exactly* what he was doing to her. It had been his cold-bloodedly, calculating way of getting her back in line.

James saw *too* much. He had known she was trying once more to shut herself off from him, and the dance had been his rather sadistic, if effective, method of dealing with it.

She had to get away from his overwhelming presence as soon as possible, before she gave away the fact that she loved him. Her apartment would be the obvious place he would look for her, of course, but she knew he wouldn't be able to leave the party right away, and it would give her some breathing space.

She didn't know what time his plane was leaving, but he might not even have the time to follow her; and in that way, she could avoid the additional pain of the final good-bye.

Skye suddenly realized Jonathan had stopped talking and was looking at her worriedly.

"Are you all right, my dear?"

"Yes, of course I am." She smiled too brightly at him. "You shouldn't be worried about me on a night like this. You've worked toward this for years."

"Skye," Jonathan began slowly, ignoring her words, "did something happen on your trip to New York to upset you?"

"Really, Jonathan, I'm okay. Stop worrying," she scolded gently. She felt terrible that she had somehow given him cause for concern. How could she reassure him? Better yet, how could she change the subject?

Unfortunately, Jonathan was another man who knew her too well, and he continued with a single-minded purpose. "When James asked if I would mind him taking you on this trip, I thought it would be an excellent opportunity."

"Excellent opportunity?" Skye was momentarily distracted by his choice of words.

"Skye, I couldn't love you more if you were my own daughter."

"I know that, Jonathan."

". . . and I want only the best for you." Jonathan paused and looked at her sharply. "There's no doubt about it, my dear, the best is James Steele."

Skye opened her mouth to protest, but Jonathan continued, "It was obvious from the first that you were attracted to each other, and I felt if you were given the chance to be alone...well..." His voice trailed off.

"Oh, Jonathan." Skye shook her head weakly. It wasn't often that Jonathan was at a loss for words, but she knew what he meant.

"If you don't mind my asking, what happened?"

"James is going to leave in a few hours. I think that about sums it up."

"I see," he said, but it was obvious he wasn't convinced. "Forgive me, but I couldn't help noticing your necklace." He looked at her speculatively.

"It's from James," she confirmed his unspoken question. "He probably has a suitcase full of similar baubles that he uses just for saying thanks and goodbye."

"Skye," Jonathan chided, "you're much too smart to believe that."

"You're wrong. I'm dumb...dumb, dumb, dumb!"

She couldn't keep the cynicism or pain out of her voice, and Jonathan guessed. "You love him."

"Yes," she admitted softly, "I do, but he mustn't find out. It wouldn't change anything. Nothing slows him down, you know, and in the end, it would only make it harder for me."

An idea occurred to Skye. Jonathan had some acreage north of Dallas, and she felt the need for the soothing pampering that Jonathan and his staff always bestowed on her whenever she visited. "If I may, I'd like to pack up tomorrow and come out and stay with you for a while."

"You know you're always welcome, my dear.

Nothing would make me happier, as long as it's what you really think you should do."

"Thank you." She sighed her gratitude. Trust Jonathan to come through for her. "I need time and space to rethink some of my decisions."

The music had stopped, and Skye leaned up and kissed him lightly on the cheek. "Please don't be upset with me, but I'm going to slip out of here, if I can. I need to be alone, but I'll see you some time tomorrow."

Skye had almost made it to the front door of the hotel when she heard her name being called and froze where she stood. Turning, she sighed with relief when she saw it was only Paul.

"Why are are you leaving so early?" he asked walking up to her, laughing. "You're going to miss the highlight of the entire evening."

He obviously hadn't seen her dance with James, she thought dryly, but she asked, "What's that?"

"Dancing with me, of course." Paul's eyes brimmed with merriment.

"Oh, of course, how stupid of me." She tried to joke with him, but somehow it didn't quite come off.

Paul's tone changed immediately. "What's going on, Skye? This looks suspiciously like an escape."

"That's exactly what it is," she admitted. "You won't tell anyone, will you?" She improvised rapidly, "The crowds, the noise, the smoke—they all got to me. I needed to get away."

Paul looked at her thoughtfully for a moment. "No, I won't tell anyone, but then I don't think I'll have to. You're sure to be missed," he said pointedly.

Skye laughed with false gaiety. "In a little while, no one will miss me at all."

"Skye," Paul said her name somewhat hesitantly, "I think you should be aware of something. I've known Jimmy Steele for a long time. I've seen him with all kinds of women, in different sets of circumstances and in various locations all over the world, but I've never seen him react in quite the same way as he has with you."

He paused, but when Skye remained stonily quiet, he continued, "I know you didn't go to New York. You see, I know you went to the McFarland's, and I'm also willing to bet that something quite special happened between the two of you there." Paul looked at the set expression on Skye's face and advised, "Don't run away from it. The extraordinary lengths Jim went to in order to get you alone has to tell you something."

Skye shook her head stubbornly. "All it tells me is that James just happened to come up against someone he couldn't have right away. It's the thrill of the game that intrigued him, and now it's almost over."

Skye glanced out the doors and saw a taxi pulling up in front of the hotel. "I've got to go, Paul. Why don't you go ask that pretty secretary of yours to dance. I know it would be the highlight of her evening."

"Skye, wait—"

"Thanks for your concern," she called over her shoulder on her way out the door, "but I'm going to be okay. Good night."

Chapter Twelve

MYRIAD STARS TWINKLED their unrestrained brilliance
in the clear night sky over Dallas as Skye walked over
to the ledge surrounding her balcony that same night.
She surveyed the heavens with blank eyes, totally
disregarding the beauty before her. The warm night
air breezed across the balcony, gently lifting her skirt
and blowing soft wisps of hair around her pale face,
but she felt none of it.

Playing absently with the diamond hanging between her breasts, her thoughts were centered entirely
on James Steele—just as they had been for the last
two weeks, just as they would be for the rest of her
life.

If he followed her to her apartment tonight, what
would she do, what would she say? Dear God, she

prayed he wouldn't, because she didn't know how much longer she could hide this gut-wrenching pain she was feeling.

She wanted James badly, but she couldn't bear for him to make love to her a final time. There would be too much pain amidst the ecstasy. The quicker and cleaner the separation, the better.

Skye knew that internal injuries took a long time to heal. Consequently, she was trying to leave the wound as clean as she could, without any jagged pieces left to bleed into her soul—that is, any more than were absolutely necessary.

And then, without warning, Skye knew James was there. He hadn't made a sound, but her clamoring senses revealed he was behind her. Turning slowly, she saw him standing a few feet away. She felt no surprise at his being there—only a weary resignation.

He was still in his evening clothes, the fine fabric stretching over his powerful physique. However, he'd undone the black tie and the first three buttons of his white shirt, allowing the black hairs on his chest to curl through the ruffled opening.

He held a smoldering cheroot in one hand, while the other was thrust casually in his pants pocket. The black eyes were narrowed against the drifting smoke, impaling her with their probing deliberation. The masculine sensuality he exuded reached across the small space between them, devastating her with its force.

Once again, Skye had the impression of his having all the time in the world to devote to her. She knew the party wasn't over and that, more than likely, there were several dozen people back at the hotel waiting to see him about one thing or the other. At this very minute, his private jet was probably being fueled and readied for its next flight to unknown parts of the world.

Nevertheless, here he was, standing in front of her, enigmatic until the end, and she couldn't take her eyes off him, however much it tore at her heart.

When he finally spoke, it was with a definite command, softly given, but a command all the same.

"Talk to me, Skye."

"I don't know what you want from me, James."

"Then I owe you an apology. I thought I had been very clear on that subject."

Skye felt as if he had struck her. She had never experienced such pain.

"Yes, I guess you're right," she agreed bitterly. "You've been *more* than clear. You told me right from the first you wanted me and meant to have me, and the great James Steele always gets what he wants, doesn't he?

"Usually."

"Well, you've had me, and not just once, but over and over again. Aren't you satisfied?"

"Never."

The two words James had spoken since she had commenced her angry tirade had been delivered with a softness that was almost deadly, but Skye rushed on, blind in her pain.

"Did you come by for one more session in my bed before you left Dallas, James? Does it feed your ego to hear me moan and cry out for more . . . or do you just need one more time to tide you over until you get to your next port-of-call and your next woman?"

His face went hard with anger, but he didn't move. Skye did, however. She stepped back, coming up against the ledge. She couldn't retreat any further and, in a way, it was symbolic.

"Do you want me as your mistress? Is that it?" she cried. "To be here when you fly in and out of Dallas, welcoming you into my bed and my body."

"Skye!" The burning cheroot was sent arcing out into the darkness. Gone was all his gentleness, as her name was spoken in an uncompromisingly demanding tone. It was an ultimatum, pure and simple, and she knew it. No terms or concessions would be given.

"I can't do it, James."

"Why?"

There were a lot of things she could have said, but she knew what he wanted. There was one final wall between them and he wouldn't be satisfied until it was down.

He was relentless; he was cold and hard; he was steel. She gave him what he wanted.

"Because I love you." She turned away from him. She didn't want to see the sardonic expression that was sure to be on his face. "I know there are a lot of women who would accept you with any conditions you cared to give them, but there is no way I can.

"I don't have the courage to take you or your world on as your mistress... because while you held me, I wouldn't hurt or feel empty, but every time you left... I would die a little, until the day would come when I simply wouldn't want to live." She turned back and laughed bitterly. "I won't let you do that to me. I've discovered I have that much strength, anyway."

He walked slowly up to her and framed her face with his hands, "My beautiful Skye. Don't you know how much I love you?"

"You *want* me, James," she corrected tremulously. For some diabolical reason, he wasn't ready to let her go yet, and he was willing to lie to keep her.

"Yes, I want you. Constantly. But I also love you."

"It's no use, James. All the sweet talk in the world won't convince me. I just wasn't cut out to be your mistress."

"How about my wife?" he offered calmly.

"Wife?" she blurted out with astonishment. What was he up to now?

"I won't be happy until you're wearing my ring and you are Mrs. James Steele."

Skye shook her head in disbelief. "I can't marry you." James wasn't making any sense. He wasn't serious—he couldn't be!

His black eyes bore into her for a moment. Then he pulled her hard up against him in a long, deep, passionate kiss.

At first she fought, straining away from him, but his tongue found its way into her mouth, and she was lost. It was to her shame, however, because as soon as he felt her start to respond, he released her.

Pulling back slightly, holding her by her arms, he gasped harshly, "Now tell me you can't marry me!"

Still reeling from the force of his kiss, Skye shook her head helplessly. "Aren't you leaving town in a few hours?"

"Not without you. I never intended to."

He spoke with such conviction that she should have been convinced, but at this point, she was too confused. She had to try to bring some reason into this absurd conversation. She tried again with something that had bothered her.

"James, a man like you needs children."

"Most men would like a son or a daughter," he agreed gently, but firmly, "to love and to spoil and to teach, but I don't *need* one. The only thing I absolutely need is *you,* by my side, day and night, for the rest of our lives."

"A wife would only tie you down," she pointed out weakly.

"I *want* to be tied down, you little fool. There is no one who wants a home more than someone who has never had one."

"But . . . since we've been back here, you've been so—so . . ." She didn't know what she wanted to say; her mind was in a whirl.

"I'm truly sorry if you've felt neglected, Skye, but I've been trying to cram about a month's worth of work into the last few hours so that we can have a long honeymoon. I've had a lot on my mind—I even picked out your necklace—but the one thing that kept me going was the thought of you. I couldn't wait for the party to be over so that we could be together again. I've missed you," James ended simply.

Skye looked at him, wide-eyed with disbelief. How she wanted to believe him, but it just didn't seem possible that he really loved her.

"*Listen* to me, Skye. From the first moment I saw you at the airport, I've loved you." James laughed. "After Paul's initial trip here, he came back raving about the most extraordinary young woman in Dallas.

I listened to him and was frankly intrigued because Paul isn't usually so easily impressed with women. While he has as many as he wants, he's always been too intent on his work to take any of them seriously. I thought at the time it would be interesting to see what type of woman had temporarily lifted Paul's head out of the sands of business.

"That was until I saw you. When you walked out of the rain and into the airport that early Monday morning, so sad-eyed and beautiful and obviously angry, I knew I had to have you.

"You were so self-contained and withdrawn, though, it nearly drove me crazy trying to reach you. For every step forward I took, you took two steps back. That's why I arranged the trip to California. I was desperate. I knew I had just a short time to get through your defenses and to convince you how much I needed and loved you."

"James, all of the w-women you've been linked to in the past," Skye stammered out her last fear.

"That's right—*past*. Have you seen me with anyone else since I've been here?"

"N-No."

"Skye, I want you to understand what I'm about to say, because it's important. I've had many women, I'm not going to deny it—but I've never *felt* any of them, deep inside me, the way I do when I touch you."

His voice lowered, almost pleading. "Do you understand what I'm trying to say? I love you, my beautiful lady. I need you. What more do I have to do or say to make you believe me?"

"Nothing," she whispered. He had finally convinced her. Skye went into his arms totally assured that she would never leave them.

Lifting her effortlessly, James carried her upstairs to finish the lovemaking he had started on the dance floor an hour earlier. And while the stars played in the heavens over Dallas, James put a seal on his commitment to her so exquisitely that Skye was never to forget it.

One week later Skye found herself lying naked on black satin sheets in a bed 30,000 feet in the air. Naked, that is, except for a heart-shaped diamond necklace, which perfectly matched the circle of diamonds on the third finger of her left hand. The plane was taking her and her new husband to the McFarland beach house once again, this time for their honeymoon.

James, lazily drawing patterns on her stomach with his fingers, asked softly, "In a week or so, how would you like to drive up the coast and see that land I was telling you about? I'd like us to get started building a place of our own as soon as possible."

"Ummmm, anything you say." How could she concentrate on architecture when her body was rippling with such pleasure.

James laughed, a low husky sound close to her ear. "Why couldn't you have been this amenable to start with?"

Skye's blue eyes darkened as she twisted her head to look at him. "I don't think you realize how frightening a man you really are, James. You're tough and ruthless, and you wield a great deal of power. I saw all of that in you, but when it came to me, you used only a fine, touching gentleness, and I was afraid—afraid of being hurt."

"My gentleness with you is not a disguise," he assured her murmuringly. "I can treat you no other way. I'll never hurt you, I couldn't—you're too much a part of me. And I'll use all of my ruthlessness and all of my power to make sure you're never hurt again. Do you believe me?" James asked as his mouth moved down to fasten on one swollen breast.

"Yes," Skye moaned with longing. Yes, she did. She would always believe this black-eyed, dark-skinned man with whom she was going to spend the rest of her life.

And, as the plane droned on to California, the two lovers provided their own motion, concentrating only on gratifying each other.

WATCH FOR
6 NEW TITLES EVERY MONTH!

Second Chance at Love

Second Chance at Love ™

All of the above titles are $1.75 per copy

WATCH FOR
6 NEW TITLES EVERY MONTH!

Second Chance at Love

____ 05625-1 **MOURNING BRIDE #57** Lucia Curzon
____ 06411-4 **THE GOLDEN TOUCH #58** Robin James
____ 06596-X **EMBRACED BY DESTINY #59** Simone Hadary
____ 06660-5 **TORN ASUNDER #60** Ann Cristy
____ 06573-0 **MIRAGE #61** Margie Michaels
____ 06650-8 **ON WINGS OF MAGIC #62** Susanna Collins
____ 05816-5 **DOUBLE DECEPTION #63** Amanda Troy
____ 06675-3 **APOLLO'S DREAM #64** Claire Evans
____ 06676-1 **SMOLDERING EMBERS #65** Marie Charles
____ 06677-X **STORMY PASSAGE #66** Laurel Blake
____ 06678-8 **HALFWAY THERE #67** Aimée Duvall
____ 06679-6 **SURPRISE ENDING #68** Elinor Stanton
____ 06680-X **THE ROGUE'S LADY #69** Anne Devon
____ 06681-8 **A FLAME TOO FIERCE #70** Jan Mathews
____ 06682-6 **SATIN AND STEELE #71** Jaelyn Conlee
____ 06683-4 **MIXED DOUBLES #72** Meredith Kingston
____ 06684-2 **RETURN ENGAGEMENT #73** Kay Robbins
____ 06685-0 **SULTRY NIGHTS #74** Ariel Tierney
____ 06686-9 **AN IMPROPER BETROTHMENT #75** Henrietta Houston

All of the above titles are $1.75 per copy

WHAT READERS SAY ABOUT
SECOND CHANCE AT LOVE

"SECOND CHANCE AT LOVE is fantastic."
—*J. L., Greenville, South Carolina**

"SECOND CHANCE AT LOVE has all the romance of the big novels."
—*L. W., Oak Grove, Missouri**

"You deserve a standing ovation!"
—*S. C., Birch Run, Michigan**

"Thank you for putting out this type of story. Love and passion have no time limits. I look forward to more of these good books."
—*E. G., Huntsville, Alabama**

"Thank you for your excellent series of books. Our book stores receive their monthly selections between the second and third week of every month. Please believe me when I say they have a frantic female calling them every day until they get your books in."
—*C. Y., Sacramento, California**

"I have become addicted to the SECOND CHANCE AT LOVE books...You can be very proud of these books....I look forward to them each month."
—*D. A., Floral City, Florida**

"I have enjoyed every one of your SECOND CHANCE AT LOVE books. Reading them is like eating potato chips, once you start you just can't stop."
—*L. S., Kenosha, Wisconsin**

"I consider your SECOND CHANCE AT LOVE books the best on the market."
—*D. S., Redmond, Washington**

*Names and addresses available upon request